Endorsements for

KINGMAKERS

Excerpts from a letter by author-historian T. R. Fehrenbach of San Antonio to Austin author John Knaggs regarding his book, Kingmakers:

"I'm impressed mainly by your grasp of the ambience of South Texas – time and place – in this writing. It was a colorful era and region that needs to be captured and remembered. You do this well . . .

"I don't recall any other writer showing who these people were, how they came to be, and how they operated and could operate – the positive and negative sources of their power. Ironically, the historic (George) Parr had as much or more impact on the nation as the famous machines in Jersey City, NYC, Memphis, Kansas City, or elsewhere . . .

"In sum, I find it historically accurate in all major particulars and most minor ones, and a better account of what happened than Mr. (Robert) Caro's *LBJ* supposed non-fiction rendering."

Alfredo Cardenas, author, former mayor of San Diego, the South Texas town that was the center of George Parr's power structure, wrote:

"Born into a South Texas political family, went on to serve as a news reporter at the Texas Capitol, and worked as a political campaign consultant, John Knaggs is eminently qualified to write a novel about the state's most notorious instance of political corruption.

"In *Kingmakers, A Novel of Political Ambition and Corruption*, Knaggs uniquely captures the 1948 senatorial election of Lyndon B. Johnson.

"He won by 87 questionable votes from Jim Wells County, controlled by the Duke of Duval, George B. Parr.

"Knaggs describes the politics and uniquely portrays the area's traditional and pop culture post-World War II. *Kingmakers* depicts this event in a way historians cannot and have not."

Comments below were made by former Judge John Clark of San Antonio who, as U. S. Attorney, conducted the final prosecution of the late George Parr, most powerful of South Texas political bosses.

"John Knaggs writes with confident familiarity about the high drama and the gritty realities of South Texas political campaigns in the era of notorious political bosses like the late George Parr. His places and events, and the people who move within them, ring true to the region and the time.

"Readers who know a little Texas history will recognize some Texas legends among the cast of characters as the lives of persons large and small are drawn into the struggle between a corrupt political empire and the upstart forces of reform.

"Knaggs, a South Texas native, uses his intimate knowledge of the region and his behind-the-scenes experience in countless campaigns to paint a realistic, fast-moving picture. *Kingmakers* is a story well told."

IDENTITY OF CHARACTERS

In the novel, Lyndon Johnson is portrayed as Jordan Layman; his opponent, former Governor Coke Stevenson as Holt Witherspoon; and political boss George Parr as Frank Ganner. All other characters and names of counties are fictitious or merely facets of the author's imagination, and any resemblance to real people and events is unintentional and coincidental.

A novel of vote fraud
that stunned the nation

John R. Knaggs

Author of
**The Bugles Are Silent
Two-Party Texas
Kingmakers**

PUBLISHER

Sunridge Publishing Company
4707 Sinclair Avenue
Austin Texas 78756

© 2025 John R. Knaggs
Original cover art by Don Collins

**First Edition 1992
Second Edition 2025**
All rights reserved.

No part of this book may be used or reproduced, scanned or distributed in any manner including print, electronic, or any other form without written permission from the author except in the case of brief quotations embodied in critical articles and reviews.

Printed and published in
the United States of America

ISBN 978-1-959127-40-6

Available in print on Amazon

Library of Congress Cataloging-in-Publication Data
Knaggs, John R., 1934-
Kingmakers / by John R. Knaggs.
p. cm. ISBN 1-55622-245-9
I. Title.
PS3561.N27K56 1991
813'.54-dc20 91-37453
CIP

DEDICATION

To Helen,
steadfast wife and best pal

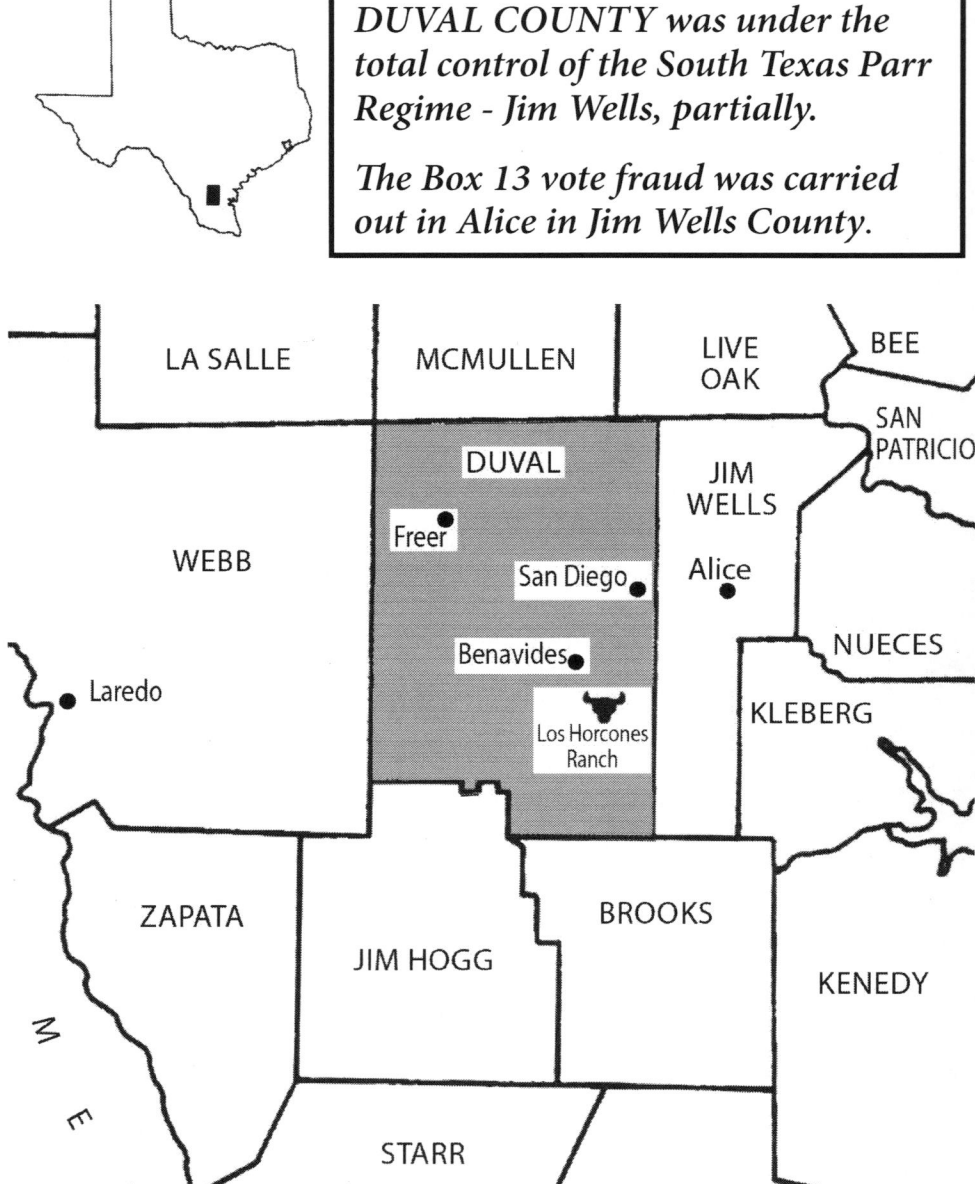

PREFACE

This is the second edition of KINGMAKERS, the historical novel portraying the flagrant vote fraud (commonly known as Box 13) that propelled Lyndon Johnson to his first election to the U.S. Senate.

A work of fiction seemed best to portray the unique, incredible nature of South Texas politics.

My writing of KINGMAKERS is based upon the realities of the time which I observed as a resident of that area.

This was an era when South Texas political machines were most powerful, controlled by politically entrenched bosses.

Soon after World War II, the Texas political arena resumed its challenge of gritty, grinding campaigns covering the vast landscape.

Several of the ranches in South and West Texas were larger than some states in the nation, containing towns and villages that somehow had to be contacted.

Back then, Texas was a one-party state. The Republican Party would field a statewide candidate but was unable to mount a competitive campaign. Therefore, the nominee of all Democratic Primaries would be elected.

Political reform was at play in the novel by a young group, also in the Democratic Primary – this one for state representative. There was also a campaign spinoff by a young Mexican-American candidate.

Johnson's high octane ambition led him to vacate his Congressional seat in order to run for the Senate. He achieved his razor-thin victory by virtue of 87 votes provided by Box 13 out of almost a million cast.

George Parr was the strongest and most manipulative of South Texas political bosses. He contended throughout that Box 13 was only a "party matter" thereby avoiding state and federal jurisdiction. Despite fierce challenges, he prevailed. How he got away with it is a story unto itself.

The map, courtesy of Eakin Press, appears in the book The Fall of the Duke of Duval (county) by former Judge John E. Clark.

As U.S. Attorney, Clark conducted the final prosecution of Parr on a tax evasion charge unrelated to Box 13 which had occurred several years previous.

Clark's book is an outstanding example of the unique culture that produced voter fraud.

Parr lived in San Diego, Texas, in Duval County which was the center of his empire. It is adjacent to Jim Wells County where the vote fraud occurred in Aice. Cotulla, the county seat of La Salle County, is my hometown.

In the novel, Lyndon Johnson is portrayed as Jordan Layman; his opponent, former Governor Coke Stevenson as Holt Witherspoon; and political boss George Parr as Frank Ganner. All other characters and names of counties are fictitious or merely facets of my imagination, and any resemblance to real people and events is unintentional and coincidental.

The first edition of KINGMAKERS was published in 1992 and received many positive reviews.

Soon after the original release, the publisher suddenly went out of business, leaving myself and several other authors with no means to proceed.

During the interim between publications, a few marginal efforts were made but were not pursued until one of my sons, Bart Knaggs, on his own initiative, thought the story is worth retelling and provided the resources.

John R. Knaggs
Austin, Texas

Chapter I

Kirk Holland finished a midmorning cup of coffee with a friend from the newspaper. The crisp February air was invigorating in downtown Austin as he walked alone from the Stephen F. Austin Hotel up Congress Avenue toward the state capitol.

When he paused to browse at a newsstand, the unmistakable raspy voice of Jordan D. Layman rang out as the gangly congressman approached with a portly, middle-aged friend. Layman was dressed smartly in a dark suit with vest and snap brim hat. His friend wore an expensive suit and a worried expression.

Holding a newspaper close to his face for cover, Kirk strained to overhear the conversation as Layman and his friend scanned newspapers dominated by the long anticipated statement of retirement from veteran U.S. Senator George M. Sledge.

"Don't push me," Layman said in a low but decisive tone. "I'm not ready to commit."

"But we've got to know. Holt is calling around the state."

"Sure, but he hasn't said he's running. He's just fishing."

"That damned old codger won't fish forever - he'll run. You've been in the House long enough. If you want to be a United States Senator, it's time to move."

"That's what you said seven years ago."

"But we've got so much more stroke now. No problem with money."

"Hell, there's always problems with money. How much would you commit?"

His friend paused. "Well, I'll match anything any of your other contributors will commit to. And I'll put it all up front, if you want."

Layman rubbed his chin, glancing at headlines from newspapers trucked in from Dallas, Fort Worth, Houston, and San Antonio. As if speaking to the rack of papers, he shrugged. "Holt has deep pockets, and I don't. I'm not about to give up this seat unless there's enough money to match him."

"We'll get it, Jordan. We'll get it."

Layman slung his left arm around his friend's shoulder as they departed the newsstand. "Well, we'll see," Layman said, turning to smile and wave his hat toward two friendly constituents crossing the street down the block.

To Kirk, Jordan Layman was a paradoxical politician. On the one hand, he represented the citizens of his district with a constant sense of dedication and immediacy. Let anyone ask for help with a passport, social security problem, or any question relating to the federal bureaucracy in Washington and Layman or his staff were on top of it. However, let a divisive issue start developing in Congress, or a big political question arise about his career, and Layman became the most cautious politician around.

Those who knew him well understood he was consumed by ambition and nurtured a smoldering desire to go all the way to the top. But without a handsome physical appearance or an effective speaking voice, Layman constantly reminded himself that he must practice all aspects of the art with as much acumen and skill as he could bring to bear.

The possibility of a heated contest between Layman, the energetic progressive in his early forties, and Holt Witherspoon, the shrewd aging conservative, intrigued activists in the Texas political arena. Layman claimed Franklin Roosevelt as his mentor, while Witherspoon had served as a steady, fairly popular governor before retiring after two terms.

The prize was a seat in the United States Senate, a strategic position in the national scheme of things since Texas politicians of that era were expected to be leaders of the states in the old Confederacy. Further, they would be expected to ward off a thread of a threat from the GOP.

In post-World War II Texas politics, Republican Dwight Eisenhower had shaken up things by carrying the state in his presidential victory of 1952, but conservative Texas Democrats, led by then-Governor Alan Shivers, were the key to that result. The Democratic Party, traditionally the South's party since the Civil War, still firmly controlled the power structure for electing statewide and most lower level offices. If Layman and Witherspoon, both Democrats of long-standing, should slug it out for a U.S. Senate seat in 1954, the winner of the Democratic Primary would get the prize.

As Layman and his friend turned off Congress Avenue, heading for the Driskill Hotel, Kirk shook his head, wondering what might happen. As a political writer, he relished the idea of that contest, but he had learned that the decisions for such candidacies could rest on a variety of factors, some of which the writers might never learn.

Though he had the day off, Kirk decided to stop by his desk in the Capitol Press Room to pick up the latest scuttlebutt about developing campaigns. He portrayed the role of cynic, but deep down the political process fascinated him and he enjoyed the endless speculation about candidates and campaigns.

There was also the Legislature to cover, a Legislature dominated by shrewd lobbyists, yet a body prone to heated and at times illuminating debate. It was composed totally of Democrats divided into liberal and conservative forces or, on many issues, rural vs. urban. Shifting alliances might provide some memorable moments of gap-shooting for position that only the most diligent reporters could follow. Kirk, though young, considered himself among the top political writers since he was unmatched at sniffing out the right sources to piece together a developing story.

After leaving the capitol, Kirk met his steady, Carrie, and they enjoyed dinner and the night together. They slept soundly. It was the morning after the first night they had slept together, but it was not the first time they had made love. That awkward but supremely passionate moment had occurred in the front seat of his car, parked near her sorority house in a tree-shrouded area one rainy night two months ago.

There had been other such times—catching a few moments alone parked somewhere or at his apartment with the constant anxiety that his studious, hang-around-the-house roommate would show up unannounced. Once the roommate had gone home for a weekend, they found leisure time. And it was different. It had proved to be captivating, inspiring deep feelings of closeness and tenderness they hadn't experienced.

Suddenly, the ringing of the telephone shattered the silence. Half asleep, he pulled the receiver to his ear. The call was from Mary Nell Stevens, an old friend from South Texas where he had been raised.

"Kirk, I'm sorry to bother you so early, but it's important. I'm calling from the ranch. We want you to meet with us this afternoon at five, at the Cadillac. Pick me up on the way, at four."

"Nellie," he said as he sighed, "for God's sake, no lead time. I'm busy, committed. Can't make it."

"You must make it. This is something your dad would have considered to be terribly important."

"Then tell me what it's all about."

"I don't want to discuss it over the phone. Be here at four. Good-bye."

"Nellie ... " But she had hung up.

Shaking his head, he turned to face Carrie, who was sitting up in the bed, a blanket pulled over her breasts. As she reached for a cigarette, anxiety consumed her lovely face, so soft and relaxed in sleep. She stroked honey blond hair from her shoulder as her eyes focused squarely upon him.

"Don't tell me you're thinking about not going with me to Houston."

Avoiding her gaze, he glanced past the tiny barren yard behind his small apartment toward the University of Texas campus. He studied nearby Waller Creek, where, due to a predawn shower, about a foot of water splashed rapidly through the jagged limestone bed, curling south toward downtown Austin.

His mind wandered from the soothing effect of the water to visualize a dinner party in Houston's exclusive River Oaks section. With only one suit of clothes, and that not so stylish, he saw himself as an unlikely, unhappy, participant. Yet, his love for her was so desperate that he often gave in to her demands, no matter how compromising.

Without responding, he donned his slacks and walked from the bedroom to the kitchen, where he took a bottle of orange juice from the refrigerator. After pouring two glasses, he returned to face her. "Oh hell." He sighed. "I've got to go."

"But why? What pull can she possibly have over you?"

"She has no pull, but I think I can guess what's going on, and I need to be there."

"I don't care what it is! You promised me you wouldn't spend any more time down there, except with your family. She and her friends are certainly not family."

"Now, hold on! You and I had a wonderful night, and were damned lucky to have had it at last... Besides, your parents aren't going to miss me at a big dinner party. So, make an excuse for me and go and have a good time."

"You're not being fair about this."

"Sometimes I just think we're playing ball in different leagues. The River Oaks blue blood and the nobody from somewhere in South Texas."

"I can't stand it when you do me this way! Should I answer I'm in awe of you because I'm only twenty and you're twenty-six? Should I say we're playing ball in different leagues because you've fought in a war and you work for a newspaper while I'm nothing but little Miss Carrie Clendon, a wide-eyed coed? Oh, Kirk, for God's sake, just try to remember I love you and let's keep our love the single most important thing in our lives."

"You know I love you very much, but this is something I can't just walk away from."

With a flourish, she tossed the blanket from her lithe body, gathered clothing from her luggage, and stomped toward the bathroom. When she returned, fresh from a shower and buttoning an ivory-colored satin blouse, he sought to hold her, but she kept her distance.

"At least let's have some breakfast," he said.

"No, thank you," she snapped. "I'm going on to Houston."

As her car pulled away, he waved from the curb but she never glanced back. He listened briefly to the familiar lilting sounds of chimes from the imposing tower on the nearby university campus, sounds of time by which he often checked his watch.

Then, he glanced to his right. "Well, we'll always have Louie's." He chuckled to himself with a sardonic smile, looking west from his Eighteenth Street apartment to the cozy little tavern nearby on San Jacinto Street. Between lovemaking sessions the night before, they had spent two leisurely hours there, sipping beer while listening to smooth jukebox records by Buddy Clark and Frank Sinatra, to whom the owner was partial.

Kirk walked inside to shave and shower. At five feet eleven inches and one hundred seventy-five pounds, he wasn't an imposing figure. But he carried himself and spoke in a confident manner. Clearly defined features, including blue eyes that were always alert and became intense during hot political discussions, dominated his face. His light brown hair was combed casually, never too neat or styled.

For the two days in South Texas, he packed a change of casual clothes, then dressed in a favorite outfit of dark brown slacks with light brown shirt, sans tie, and a tan corduroy coat. He walked three blocks in the cool, crisp air of that February morning in 1954 to arrive at the San Jacinto Cafe. It was a modest old place that gave generous servings for good prices. Slowly, he ate scrambled eggs with bacon but was unable to savor the food. The argument with Carrie was foremost in his mind. Dreading the long drive to Laredo, he toyed with a second cup of coffee while skimming the newspaper.

When he finished and walked outside, he glanced up the street to Scholz Garten. The landmark restaurant and beer garden's sprawling grounds served as host to hundreds of out-of-town football fans during that season and for hundreds of people involved in politics and government. Their ranks swelled during campaign time and during regular and special sessions of the Legislature.

To his right, the majestic state capitol dominated the view, "that dear old granite lady," as he termed it, in which he shared an office with two other correspondents. The Austin Capital-Times, the city's only daily newspaper, had hired Kirk three years ago. It was a coveted spot, but the modest salary kept him on a tight budget. He landed the job partly because, as a combat veteran of the Korean War, he related well to the crusty managing editor, Orland Gretard, who limped badly from a wound sustained in World War II.

Gretard allowed Kirk to take a course or two at the University of Texas, working toward a journalism degree. Prior to military service, Kirk enjoyed working part-time at the newspaper while attending school his first three years. But that dual line of endeavor was the main reason his grades had suffered, causing him to run out of deferments from his draft board.

Kirk made his mark rapidly. Politics was bred into him, plus he had a fair amount of writing skill and the ability to endure occasional drinking bouts. Most occurred at Louie's, Scholz Garten, and the Palomino Club, places where a political writer could learn a great deal more from politicians and lobbyists than he could in the more measured atmosphere of the capitol or the sedate Austin Club.

More than anything, Kirk Holland had wanted to become a fixture in Austin, the pleasant capital city which, counting the 15,000 enrollment at the University of Texas, had only a little more than 100,000 population. It was the sixth largest city in the state, yet it was the political and intellectual center with a challenging, invigorating atmosphere. It was a special place, one he could start missing at the mere thought of leaving.

To reach the highway to South Texas, Kirk drove south on San Jacinto Street past the rolling, tree-shrouded capitol grounds, then over to Congress Avenue, through the heart of downtown Austin. On the high bridge crossing the scenic Colorado River, in-bound traffic was heavy with the early flow of basketball fans from San Antonio for a tournament. There was little traffic in his lane as he worked through South Austin to where Congress Avenue became Highway 81, the state highway that ran north-south across Texas.

Just outside the city limits, he passed near Hattie's and Peggy's, Austin's well-known brothels, though neither could match the reputation of the Chicken Ranch about sixty miles east near La Grange. He chuckled, recalling the time last year when he had learned of a prominent legislator seen stumbling out of Peggy's, so drunk he couldn't handle the short drive into town. After slamming his car into a ditch from which he could neither drive nor walk, he was "apprehended" by police.

Instead of arresting him, they got his car out of the ditch, poured coffee down him, and made sure he made it home safely. Kirk's item on the caper never saw print because, his managing editor told him, "We're not going to second guess the police. If they didn't book him, we can't prove he was drunk."

Although the story was never published, Kirk had informed the legislator he knew all about the incident, thereby establishing another good news source.

Kirk was driving a 1952 four-door Chevrolet sedan, nothing sleek or sporty, but a good road car he had purchased from a friend in the used car business. As he headed south on Highway 81 toward San Marcos, he relaxed, enjoying the gentle rolling countryside on the eastern edge of the Hill Country.

A large billboard portraying Congressman Jordan D. Layman, who carried the political brand of "JDL," suddenly broke the serene landscape. Layman's picture covered almost half of the billboard, and his piercing brown eyes appeared to observe everything within range. With large nose and ears highlighted because of a receding dark hairline, Layman was nowhere near handsome, but he dominated that billboard just as he sought to dominate the Texas political arena.

Kirk believed the billboard had been left up on the state's most heavily traveled highway after Layman's easy reelection in 1952 to gain more name identification from that coveted spot. Layman billboards also remained up on Highway 81 north toward Dallas-Fort Worth and on the two highways from Austin east toward Houston. That was ample evidence for Kirk to conclude that a race for United States Senate was probably next on the ambitious political agenda of Jordan D. Layman.

The theme line on the billboard read, "All's Well With JDL."

Tacky and trite, yet effective. Layman was a longtime admirer of the late Franklin Roosevelt, but he wouldn't accept the label of "liberal" or "progressive." Instead, he was often accused of trying to be "all things to all people."

Layman might be conniving and devious, but he's one helluva politician.

As he drove past the billboard, Kirk was ready for a beer, but San Marcos was dry. He had to wait until he crossed into Comal County and reached New Braunfels, an old German settlement on the Guadalupe River, where he stopped at a roadside tavern.

Arriving at San Antonio, Kirk drove past the affluent, Anglo-dominated Alamo Heights neighborhood with its large houses and vast neat lawns. Then he wove his way through the crowded downtown area—always teeming with additional traffic on a Saturday from nearby ranchers and farmers—on out south through neighborhoods where Mexican-Americans lived on the threshold of poverty.

San Antonio was the tedious leg of the trip he always dreaded because it required almost an hour to cross and, due to the narrow, packed streets, a car, truck, or pedestrian might pop out unexpectedly. But he also loved the old city, the hub of South Texas.

Years ago, his family had often traveled the eighty miles north from their home in Justinville to shop and be entertained. His father always insisted on visiting the Alamo and the Gunter Hotel, where South Texas cattlemen congregated. Years later, Kirk and fellow UT students had toured the Pearl and Lone Star breweries, drinking their share of free beer before heading for Nuevo Laredo and a big night on the border.

On the far south side of San Antonio, he stopped at a little barbecue stand for a sandwich and a beer. On a small wooden table, he reviewed his file of election results for several South Texas counties, including those for a particular state representative district. Then he was back on the Laredo highway, heading south toward Justinville.

The terrain changed to flat pasture land with barbed wire fences, the certain mark of cattle country, flanking the straight highway on either side. A jackrabbit bounded haphazardly in a nearby pasture and a roadrunner darted across the highway, ducking under the bottom strand of a taut wire fence.

Kirk was relaxed, enjoying the drive, but giving some thought to what probably lay ahead, a serious meeting about a political battle that might consume much of South Texas. He turned on the radio to a popular music station.

While considering political variables, the music and the monotony of the passing landscape mesmerized him. The ubiquitous mesquite trees, whose leafless wintertime limbs hovered in grotesque configurations over thickets of black brush and patches of green prickly pear dominated the scenery. Those trees were conspirators of the pasture, denying precious moisture for the range grass, which had turned a deadened gray after a long summer of intense heat and a fall without much rain. A few sturdy live oak and willow trees, which hosted an occasional buzzard or hawk, broke the pattern along creek beds and arroyos, all long since dry and dusty. A tall, twisting whirlwind was harsh evidence of drouth as it danced across a barren field, kicking up reddish-brown dirt from the sandy loam soil.

Only a few pools of water remained in the riverbeds of the Medina, Frio, and Nueces, all south of San Antonio. They would stagnate if a hard rain did not come soon. An occasional windmill pumped water into a concrete tank where thirsty cattle gathered.

But most earthen stock ponds, dependent upon rainwater, were dry or stagnating in boggy mud. In such conditions, many ranchers could only graze one cow per twenty acres. They were caught between the high prices of commercial feed and the meager supply of nutrition available on the range.

Among the various breeds of cattle, only the rugged humpbacked Brahma seemed to sneer at the drouth. Near the highway, several gray-coated Brahmas followed a man with a piece of unusual equipment mounted on his shoulder. It was known as a "pear-burner," a modest kerosene-fired forerunner to the more powerful flame-thrower. As the man burned thorns off the prickly pear leaves, the plant, usually considered to be worthless on a pasture, suddenly provided a sustaining source of food and moisture for the cattle that ate it.

A rancher with cattle that wouldn't eat it faced the high cost of buying feed and the low price of selling in a glutted market. It was a grim situation in which none but the wealthy or the lucky would survive. Some of the lucky rode out the drouth by virtue of oil production or mineral leases, but South Texas didn't enjoy the widespread oil production like that in the eastern and western parts of the state.

Yet, for all its harshness, the vast, sparsely-populated Brush Country of South Texas could still affect Kirk with the same compelling mystique that had summoned O. Henry and produced J. Frank Dobie, who wrote about it with great passion and unique understanding. But Kirk reminded himself to use his head in the forthcoming meeting, not his heart. His future was elsewhere.

As he drove within ten miles of his hometown, Kirk spun through his mind the voting statistics he had reviewed in San Antonio, plus a few special considerations peculiar to this region. Anglos and Mexican-

Americans made it a bicultural society, but most county governments were run by Anglos and their communities were divided along ethnic lines. The major exception was Laredo where the two cultures had long been amalgamated with that community dominated by the Spanish-Mexican culture dating to the mid-1700s.

It was a land of large ranches and small communities, a land in which wealth and power were in the hands of a few, including political bosses who controlled many counties.

Foremost among the South Texas bosses was Frank Ganner of nearby Bantrell County. Ganner was known as "The Baron of Bantrell," and his control of his turf was complete. Kirk's late father, the county judge of Retama County, had maintained an arms-length relationship with Ganner, whose methods he had viewed with contempt.

For more than seventy miles since leaving San Antonio, Kirk's reflective mood had not been interrupted. He saw only an occasional car or pickup truck, and very little activity in the small towns he passed through. But the mood was shattered when a skinny coyote loped from the brush to his left across the highway as if following just another of his trails. Kirk hit the brakes, missing the animal by only a few feet.

Again, he relaxed as he drove up on a gentle hill overlooking his hometown of Justinville, some four miles distant. The water tower and courthouse dominated the view of the little town of three thousand population which served as the seat of government for Retama County. It sprang up on the Nueces River after the boundary settlement with Mexico and was located near one of the abandoned crossings used by Spanish and Mexican armies. It had grown modestly over the years after the turn of the century by virtue of being on the railroad about sixty-five miles north of Laredo and eighty miles south of San Antonio, a natural focal point for cattle trading and shipping.

He soon turned off the highway onto a narrow dirt road which led to the cemetery west of town. The midafternoon sun had yielded to clouds, cool winds, and mist brought by a weak norther. It wouldn't break the pervasive nature of the drouth, but it might settle the dust for a day or two.

When he reached the cemetery, he scanned the uncluttered five-acre grounds and was pleased to see no one there. Walking from his car, the only sounds were gentle rustling from a windbreak of dark-green salt cedar trees and the melancholy call of a mourning dove in a nearby oak tree. Irregularly placed gravestones mingled with patches of dried grass, purple sage, and a few mesquite and retama trees. From an area near the center of the cemetery, the eight-foot granite monument to his father dominated the entire grounds.

Always before he had visited the site with his mother and sister. Now, he stood alone, reviewing the wording as though he had never read it.

"Judge Kelvin Holland, 1886 - 1951" appeared in six-inch inscription near the top.

Below, in smaller lettering was an epitaph. "He was an honorable leader of men and a true follower of God. No man can say he didn't serve the people well."

And at the base, in even smaller lettering, "Erected by the grateful citizens of Retama County."

He had not been a lawyer, and he had never held a judicial office, Kirk mused, yet he was "the judge of Retama County" for thirty years. He was county judge, an administrative officer elected on a county-wide basis whose chief duty was to serve as the presiding officer of the commissioners court—composed of himself and four commissioners elected from precincts—which conducted the county's business.

Kelvin Holland ran the court with an even hand along with a sense of humor. He was held in high esteem by Anglos and Mexican-Americans, allowing him to serve all those years without building a political machine. His popularity and credibility were such that he had occasionally been called upon to settle disputes among constituents. They preferred his sound reasoning and logic—delivered after one hearing at no cost—to taking their chances in a court fight with legal fees they might not be able to afford.

All Judge Holland ever required for settling a dispute was for the participants to shake hands and promise not to speak ill of one another in public. Such "holding court" was widespread during the depression years of the 1930s when money in the little town was scarce.

During his early years in office, the judge did a little ranching on the side and acquired a modest amount of property in Justinville. The Great Depression all but wiped him out financially, but he had held onto his office and a few investments which paid enough for him and his wife to raise Kirk and his sister, three years younger.

The gentle mist continued to fall, and Kirk wiped his face. He considered leaving, but lingered, staring at the monument. He recalled times with his father, including vivid memories as a little boy when he had accompanied the judge on his political rounds where the Anglo citizens gathered—school, churches, restaurants, cattle auctions, rodeos, and athletic events.

Then, there were impromptu visits east of the railroad tracks to "Mexican town" where almost half of the community's population lived. The judge had always been welcomed there where he might drop by the school or church, or even some of the unpainted shanties of the poorest people. Late in the day, he might enjoy a cold beer and conversation in Spanish at a cantina, a place less tolerant citizens would disdain as a "beer joint."

Kirk recalled a few times his father took him deer hunting or hunting for dove and quail. And those special times they fished for big catfish with throw lines when the Nueces River was on a rise following a heavy rain upstream. They became precious memories because so much of the time his father had been tied up tending to county business or political activities.

"Why," Kirk whispered to the huge gravestone, "didn't you ever build more for yourself and Mother? You ran the county for peanuts and helped all those people and what did you ever have to show for it?"

Kirk looked down at the ground as though admonishing himself for having challenged his father. Then, he looked up, opening his arms in a gentle pleading gesture. "You didn't have to let them draft me, you know ... Well, I came back in one piece, but not in time for your funeral... Your own son, your only son, never made it to your funeral... "

Kirk sat upon the base of the monument, face in his hands, shivering from the effect of the wind driving the mist faster upon his face and neck. Wiping back tears, he arose, facing the gravestone again. "Dad," he murmured, "I know what you'd say if you were here. 'Do your duty, Son. Take him on. Fight him with everything you can muster.' I want you to know I'm not afraid of Frank Ganner, but I've got a great life going, in Austin. That's where I belong, Dad. This country was for you, not me. I've got no stake in it anymore."

From the cemetery, Kirk drove to the family home in town, a modest, three-bedroom, frame house, white with brown shutters. He wanted to tell his mother and sister he would return late that night, but finding no one at home, he left a note on the back door. He resumed his journey, leaving for the Stevens Ranch between Justinville and Laredo.

He arrived there on time, crossing the second cattle guard from the highway to view the large hacienda-style house dominating a cluster of buildings, stables, and sheds that formed the ranch headquarters for a spread in excess of forty thousand acres. Bending in the gentle breeze were thick fronds from two tall palm trees on either side of the stone walk that cut through San Augustine grass on the yard in front of the porch. Purple sage and bright red bougainvillea grew against the long porch.

As he climbed the steps, he paused to wave to the foreman and a couple of cowboys dismounting at the corral. He called to Nellie, who hollered from within the house that she was not quite ready and Kirk should help himself to beer iced down in a cooler on the porch.

Nothing on that porch had changed since he was last there for a lively party two years ago. Mounted on the wall were the heads of deer and javelinas, plus the customary gunrack holding rifles and shotguns. A long wooden table and leather-back chairs stood on the colorful floor tile, imported from Saltillo in Northern Mexico. Near the door to the kitchen hung a framed inscription, a quatrain by Edna St. Vincent Millay, an unlikely touch for a ranch porch but uniquely reflective of Nellie Stevens:

"My candle burns at both ends; It will not last the night;
But, ah, my foes, and oh, my friends - It gives a lovely light."

Kirk relaxed, taking a swig of the cold beer while smiling at the quotation. He'd been a friend and admirer of Nellie since high school days, though she was more than three years older. That was a considerable barrier to any romantic involvement in rural South Texas which frowned upon its young women dating any but older men.

But he recalled a silly summer night when he was eighteen and she almost twenty-two. Three carloads had left her ranch for a night of partying in Nuevo Laredo, and somehow he had wound up with her alone in a back seat for the ride home. She was so beautiful with the pale moonlight and shadows glancing across expressive brown eyes that matched the color of her soft wavy hair. Her vivacious personality had yielded to a languid mood as a result of several drinks, and they soon fell into intense necking that might have led to something more, had there been an opportunity to steal away from those in the front seat.

They didn't speak during the ride home, nor did either ever speak subsequently of those impromptu moments. The age difference barrier, bolstered by her wealth, was intimidating to his modest station.

That was eight years ago, Kirk recalled, before the war, before the return to college and his relationship with Carrie. Something akin to a lifetime.

Mary Nell Stevens preferred her friends to be male. They needed to be handsome, intelligent, and wealthy, or at least two of the three. She enjoyed lively conversation and fine food, and could drink with the best of them. Her large brown eyes sparkled during frequent smiles or laughter. They turned pensive or piercing during spirited political discussions, which she often instigated. At five foot six and with firm figure, she always made an impact upon a scene.

When she appeared on the porch in dark brown skirt, white blouse, and beige stole, Kirk admired her again as forbidden fruit, yet the most charming woman he'd ever known. She kissed him briskly him on the cheek and then reached for a couple of "roadies" from the beer cooler.

"Are we going to pick up Wedge?" he asked.

"No, he and the others went bass fishing. They'll change at the Hamilton where we're spending the night. Do you want a room there?"

"No, thanks. My mother will be expecting me home."

"Don't tell me she still waits up for you."

"I suspect," Kirk said with a smile as he paused at the porch door, "she always will."

"I'm sorry to be a little late," she said, sliding onto the front seat of his car, "but I wanted to ride those two big tanks with the men."

"Your dad was smart to dig those tanks large and deep enough to withstand a bad drouth."

"Yes, but they're getting boggy. We're forced to pull cattle out every day."

"Better than having to sell in San Antonio."

"For sure."

The mist had subsided, yielding to the afternoon sun that was again laying moisture-sapping rays upon the land and upon the backs of the reddish-brown Santa Gertrudis cattle. The King Ranch had developed the premier breed. She watched them munching commercial feed for a moment, then glanced across the parched pastureland of her ranch before they approached the cattle guard near the highway.

Then she turned to him. "You sounded a little addled this morning on the phone. Is there a problem?"

He winced, recalling the harsh exchange with Carrie. Then he smiled. "My only problem is trying to decide whether you remind me more of Ava Gardner or Elizabeth Taylor."

She laughed, reaching into her purse for a cigarette.

As Kirk eased back onto Highway 81 for the final thirty miles of the journey to Laredo, he cautioned himself to maintain a clear head, drinking nothing stronger than beer across the Rio Grande. "Nellie, I take it that you and your friends are after Frank Ganner, aren't you?"

"Yes, we've just received word that Ned Felder is in bad health, heart trouble. He's going to give up his seat in the Legislature, but Ganner has convinced him to keep it quiet until just before the filing deadline. Ganner wants to have his candidate lined up to go without opposition."

"Sound strategy, I'd say."

"Of course, and he'll win, unless we mount a campaign in a hurry."

Kirk had inherited a high sense of duty from his father, but without following in his footsteps, it was not always evident. Instead, from recent political experiences, he had developed a more obvious cynical side.

"So, you want to challenge the Baron of Bantrell and his veteran legions with a handful of your bored, sporty friends who have nothing better to do."

"Don't put it that way!" she snapped.

"I'm afraid that's the way I see it. And let me guess as to the members of the junta. There's you and the distinguished Wedge Crayton, your erudite longtime neighbor. From the seashore, there's Sidney Maylander, who would gladly duel Wedge for the title of resident intellectual and perhaps for your hand. From our nearby county of Harmon, there's Nelson Parker, who must have set a record for most years of attendance at UT before finally earning a degree. And from still another county, Waymon, there's Brewster "Brew" Blain, who makes no bones about just mulling his way through life. You know, I don't admire a damn one of 'em, and I don't even like any of 'em, except at least old Brew is amusing."

"It doesn't matter whether you don't like them. It's important for us to work together."

"My dear Nellie, there isn't any 'we' as far as I'm concerned."

"Would it improve your attitude to know that Raúl Ramirez will try to join us?"

"He's a good man," Kirk said, "but I suspect the pressure will be too great for him to be involved publicly."

"How can you be so negative? This is dead serious and we've got to be positive all the way. We've got to band together and check Frank Ganner while we can. He'll move into all these other counties, including ours, if we don't."

Readjusting to South Texas politics and changing his focus from Carrie to Nellie comprised an emotional quantum leap. Though he had never fallen in love with Nellie, as had several South Texas suitors with their unrequited emotional commitments, he admired her tremendously. She was grace and charm and intelligence, enhanced by an upbeat personality and striking natural beauty. She understood how to balance wealth and social prominence with appreciation for the land, cattle, people, and resources that provided them.

Oh, he mused, she probably wastes some money on her dress shop in Justinville, which gives her an excuse to travel to Dallas for shows and purchasing. And she should have finished at Radcliff, instead of UT, where she became a legislative aide and found the fast lane in Austin. That's part of her motivation for this venture. She's bored and would return to Austin if her candidate wins.

Gotta hand it to her for hanging tough, running the ranch after her father and mother were killed in that car wreck. Must have been three or four years ago. Long enough to test her mettle.

Now, she was instigating an uncertain, unwise political venture that had drawn him with great reluctance back to South Texas. Though he indeed admired her, he remained testy about acceding to her request to make the trip, particularly on such short notice.

"You know," he continued, "I just don't fit in with that crowd, and I don't think they can cut it politically. You need a mature community leader for a candidate."

"We can't think of one who'd make the race."

"Well, neither can I. It should be a very illuminating get-together."

She smashed her cigarette into the ashtray. "I'm beginning to wonder if I should have called you."

"I wish you hadn't."

They didn't speak again until he drove into the parking lot of the Cadillac Bar, a few blocks south of the international bridge between Laredo, Texas, and Nuevo Laredo, in the state of Tamaulipas, Mexico.

Kirk thought briefly of what might lie ahead. Though he envied them, he had learned years ago to be reasonably comfortable around the landed gentry of South Texas. So few people could discuss anything other than ranching that he found them to be compatible for brief periods, even though his lifestyle was far different.

They were products of large ranches with some oil and gas production and/or mineral leases which provided substantial risk-free income and financial protection from drouth and other enemies of the cattle business. They were not oil-rich in the standards of East and West

Texas production areas, but their families were wealthy enough to send them east to college and to Europe or wherever they might desire for vacations.

Dating back to Prohibition days, their parents had gathered for libations and to enjoy an extensive menu of American and Mexican dishes at the Cadillac Bar. They continued the practice, partly due to tradition, but more importantly, because mixed drinks were illegal in open bars in Texas.

Another reason for the enduring popularity of the Cadillac was that in cramped, crowded Nuevo Laredo, it was the only major establishment with a spacious parking lot. High stone walls sealed the lot from outside view, providing protection beyond that of the attendants, older men wearing weathered straw hats. They directed Kirk and Nellie along with the flow of the traffic that consisted mostly of expensive, relatively new cars. After parking, they walked through the back door of the long, one-story building that had housed the Cadillac since it opened in 1926.

Kirk paused to survey the place. It was about three-fourths filled with customers, a blend of South Texans in casual western attire, the obvious tourists with their gaudy purchases from the nearby market, and a few citizens of Nuevo Laredo who enjoyed the ambience and could afford the prices.

To his right, he took note of Pancho Villa's elaborate, silver-adorned saddle on display. To his left was the long stand-up bar behind which three veteran Mexican bartenders, dressed in starched white linen jackets and dark ties, shook chilled metal containers in order to produce the house special, Ramos Gin Fizz. Two others popped caps from bottles of favored Mexican beer, Bohemia and Carta Blanca. Waiters, similarly dressed, scurried about with trays held high, spreading tantalizing aromas of turtle soup, broiled trout, spicy Mexican dishes, and fresh-from-the-oven thick dinner rolls.

Kirk and Nellie wove their way through crowded tables covered with white linen toward a massive wooden column with an ornate metal hat rack. Stetsons of South Texas ranchers and a couple of snap brim hats belonging to salesmen from San Antonio covered it. They scanned the long room until they sighted Nellie's party seated around a large table under a ceiling fan at the far end of the building.

After exchanging greetings, a few moments of casual banter ensued during which Kirk nursed a bottle of Bohemia. Sidney Maylander of

Corpus Christi, seated at the far end of the table as though he were the presiding officer, reviewed notes on a legal pad.

Sidney was tall and trim, immaculately dressed as always, and on that day, he held forth with brown tweed coat, button down shirt, and soft brown tie. He held a law degree from the University of Texas but relied more on his studies at the Wharton School of Finance for his executive role managing most of his family's vast holdings.

He's a smooth operator, Kirk conceded, but a stuffed shirt if one ever lived.

Seated to Sidney's left were Brew Blain and Nelson Parker.

Brew is the least pretentious of the group, Kirk thought, and Parker is a tag-along.

Brew was tall and very thin, partly because he was hyperactive, but mostly because he chain-smoked cigarettes, dulling his appetite. Unless it was near freezing weather, he always wore a multicolored sport shirt, as he did that day. Parker wore a conservative suit he hadn't bothered to change since tending to business for his father that morning.

Seated across from Kirk was Wedge Crayton, whom he studied in silence as Wedge told Nelson about a forthcoming social function in San Antonio they might want to attend. Kirk perceived Wedge as a politically naïve intellectual similar to Sidney, but he had to concede that Wedge related better to people.

Wedge was confident and relaxed, dressed comfortably in navy blue blazer with light blue shirt and open collar. His dark hair was combed neatly, but he abhorred hairdressing of any kind and his was likely to become somewhat tousled outdoors in the wind. Six feet tall and of average build, Wedge was an attractive individual, though not one to spend much time before a mirror. Even at thirty, he could still appear boyish, with an inquisitive expression and searching brown eyes; or he could appear mature and intensely focused to the point of indignation when stressing something about which he had strong feelings.

Kirk wondered whether any of the agenda for the meeting might have been rehearsed. He envied the casual confidence displayed around the table.

A drouth ravages the land, he mused, but their pockets are still deep. None of these men has ever shouldered a rifle except to hunt deer, and they have no front-line experience in political campaigns. Yet, they're sitting here like veterans of all major endeavors with their queen bee named Mary Nell Stevens. They actually believe they're strong enough to defeat the most powerful political machine in South Texas.

"We all know why we're here," Sidney said, moving his glass of bourbon and water away from his legal pad and stack of notes. "I want to emphasize the importance of making decisions rapidly, but also on the basis of sound judgment. Some of you might not be aware of the pervasive political corruption that is practiced in Bantrell County, such as my family has endured in recent years. Our land is valued and taxed according to the whims of Frank Ganner.

"Because my father has openly criticized Ganner, our taxes were almost doubled last year while the land of Ganner and his cronies stayed at the same old low rate. The fact is, Ganner's control of Bantrell County is complete, total. He runs the courthouse where he presides as county judge, plus the city government and the school board. His hand-picked state district judge presides in his courthouse, the result of our generous Legislature creating a new judicial district there. All this affords him many opportunities for legal chicanery, such as I have mentioned, and for illegal kick-backs, which I'm told are handled almost entirely in cash. Ganner's influence has spread into Will Dodd County. To what extent I'm not certain, but he's working on it. If he takes this state representative seat, his influence will expand to five more counties, including those in which the rest of you reside, or in the case of Kirk, have resided."

Sidney shuffled the pages a moment, leaning slightly forward while lowering his voice. "I picked up some solid intelligence yesterday to the effect that Ganner has bribed Ned Felder, whose financial situation has deteriorated along with his heart condition. Felder will keep quiet about giving up his seat while Ganner grooms one of his cronies, Wally Hooper, to make the race. This is a clever ploy by Ganner and places us in a difficult position. If we don't champion justice and reform by mounting a campaign against him, the tyrant will eventually take over South Texas…"

He paused. "Now," Sidney said crisply as he placed his right hand upon the stack of notes, "I've worked through some election results that indicate we can defeat Ganner with the proper type of campaign. But we can't afford to let him get out front. We can't squander any time. Kirk, you're the old pro when it comes to politics. What do you think?"

Kirk stopped toying with the label on his bottle of beer. "What do I think? I think you're embarking on a frivolous search for Shangri-La. I've also reviewed election results for that district, and I believe you could run a perfect campaign, under the given circumstances, and you'd be lucky to get forty-five percent of the vote."

"But," Wedge said, "Ganner controls at most two counties, one of which is sparsely populated. There are five others, which contain the majority of voters in the district."

"Do you people," Kirk's tone turned derisive, "have any earthly idea about the true nature of this crazy, Godforsaken district? Well, I do. It runs from the Rio Grande on the south, north to near San Antonio. It runs east toward the Gulf Coast to within a half hour's drive of Corpus Christi.

"Look at it another way," he said, picking up a map that was open on the table. He drew a line from Laredo to San Antonio, then over to Corpus Christi and back to Laredo. "Inside those lines is the Bermuda Triangle of Texas politics. Nothing but unforeseen trouble erupts when you venture in too far… Ganner aside, you damn well must understand this district is comprised of seven sparsely populated counties in an area of more than eight thousand square miles, larger than many states in the union. There are no daily newspapers and only one radio station with limited coverage. You all know what it looks like. Mostly vast brush country with large ranches and small towns, but for a new candidate in a political campaign, it's a logistical and communications nightmare."

"Ah, but Kirk," Brew said as he smiled, "you're too negative about all this. Don't you like a challenge?"

"Brew," Kirk sighed as he tossed the map back on the table, "your heart may be in the right place, but your head sure as hell isn't. To win an uphill campaign, you've got to have a strong candidate, at least a semblance of a political organization to support him, and lots of money to fuel the engine. All of that doesn't fall out of the sky. And you may as well face up to the fact that Wally Hooper is a good old boy who won't project the image of Ganner corruption you want to run against. Ganner will spend whatever it takes. He'll do whatever is necessary to get the job done. On his turf, Ganner makes the Tammany Hall people look like choir boys, and his tentacles reach into other territory, far from his home base… You can't match that kind of power. It can't be developed in one campaign with an unknown candidate."

"It's our duty," Sidney snapped, "to stand up for justice and reform. We can't sit back and let that tyrant take over more and more territory. As our cause becomes understood, it will eventually compensate for his initial advantage."

"Damn right," Brew chimed in as Nelson smiled his approval and Wedge nodded.

Nellie glanced at Kirk, wondering if he were about to lose his temper. Instead, he sighed while peeling off bits of the label of his beer bottle.

Never, he mused, have I heard such pious, idealistic nonsense, most of it spoken from the perspective of Sidney, who doesn't even live in the district, nor ever has; spoken from the perspective of a mansion on Ocean Drive in Corpus Christi, whose owner also happens to own a big spread of land in Ganner's territory.

Kirk had decided to let them carry on for a few more minutes, then excuse himself for the drive back to Justinville. But Sidney startled him with a sudden announcement in a matter-of-fact tone.

"Kirk, when one considers all the factors, you're the top prospect. You've expressed some reservations, but I believe I speak for the others at the table when I say we're prepared to support you with the necessary funding to win the race. Your father bred politics into you, and his reputation will be a big asset in this race… I happen to know you continue to pay your poll tax in Justinville, so you'd be eligible, even though you've been living in Austin."

With raised eyebrows, Kirk glanced at Nellie as if asking how carefully she, Sidney, and Wedge might have planned this move. Then he shook his head.

He looked to Sidney and spoke in the same formal tone. "The question of my residency or eligibility is not a factor. I couldn't afford to run, much less win. Reporters aren't paid much, but it's a living wage, not the token paid to legislators. The fact is, seats in the Legislature generally go to members of the landed gentry who want to make sure their interests are protected; or to aspiring young lawyers who want to become DAs or judges or congressmen; or…" he added a touch of irony to his voice, "to wealthy young men who don't have anything better to do, and who come to Austin for a good time. I'm in none of those categories. No way would I be a candidate."

Sidney frowned. "That sounds like an unequivocal position."

"It is just that."

"Well…" Sidney heaved a big sigh. "I suppose that leaves the question before those of us at the table. If I were eligible, I would certainly offer to make the race," he said, glancing at Wedge, who was, in Sidney's considered opinion, the only other viable possibility present.

Brew caught the signal. "If nominations are in order," he said, "I nominate Wedge Crayton."

Wedge had been studying his glass of Scotch and soda on the rocks.

He expected the "nomination" to fall to him after Kirk turned it down. He knew his father would give him the green light, but his confidence had been shaken somewhat by Kirk's discouraging analysis of the district. "Well, I—"

"Ah, come on, Wedge," Sidney said, "this is no time to be squirming around."

Except for Kirk, who continued peeling the label from his bottle of beer, all eyes at the table focused on Wedge as his furrowed brow slowly relaxed. With a trace of a smile, he declared in a crisp tone, "Very well, I'll run."

Nellie sat forward, raising her gin fizz in a toast to their candidate, and they joined her, except for Kirk. She turned to him. "Well, we've got our quarterback; now we need the coach. You've got to manage the campaign."

Kirk frowned and started to protest, but she continued speaking. "To walk away from a showdown with Frank Ganner would be like walking away from all the good and just things we cherish about your father…"

Glancing toward Sidney, she continued, "I'm sure we can manage to pay you substantially more than you're making now."

Sidney nodded, but Kirk shook his head. "Nellie," he said, his eyes trained on the beer bottle, "there's so much more involved … "

"Darn right there's so much more involved," she said. "This is a high stakes political contest. Pivotal as far as checking the spread of Frank Ganner's brand of corruption in South Texas."

Under the table, Kirk ground his left fist into the palm of his right hand, refusing for a moment to meet the eyes of Nellie or anyone else. Thoughts of Carrie and his job crashed through his mind, and his stomach felt twisted and uneasy. An impulse came upon him to get up from the table and drive all the way back to Austin.

Another desperate thought replaced it. *I should ask for time, a couple of weeks to think it over.*

Why the hell must I make the decision now, at this very moment? Because I know that if they are right about anything this day, it was timing. If there's any hope of winning this race, the campaign needs to be launched immediately.

For a moment, he thought again of his father. Slowly, he looked up at Nellie. "All right, I'll do it, with the understanding that I have full control of the campaign, strategy, and tactics."

"What does that mean?" Wedge asked.

"It means you'll have to listen to me. I'm not going to tell you what your political convictions ought to be; that's your business. But I'm not going to preside over a campaign unless I set the target and the means by which we hit the target... It's not just your neck that's going to be on the line."

"Let me make something clear," Wedge said with a slight wince. "I want to win, but I don't want to get down into the ditch with this bloc-voting machine we're going to challenge. I want to fight hard, but fair. Is that compatible with your attitude?"

"I've never been up against Frank Ganner," Kirk said. "I don't know what it's going to take to win, but I want everyone to know, all I care about is winning. Second place isn't worth a goddamn thing in politics."

As Wedge shrugged, Brew offered a toast to Kirk and ordered another round of drinks. "You know," he said, "this is downright exciting. What's next, Kirk?"

Kirk took a long breath. "While we're here, someone at the table needs to get started as the finance chairman, contacting potential contributors. Also, be thinking about a campaign chairman, someone whose name will lend credibility to the effort. This needs to be a figurehead with a solid reputation, someone well respected in the ranching community with perhaps some banking ties or other business connections."

Brew took another sip of his gin fizz. "Well, let's just consider what my name would add to the campaign. I flunked out of Princeton, dropped out of A&M, and got kicked out of SMU. I'm happily divorced and haven't earned a nickel in three years."

For the first time during the meeting, Kirk smiled. "Somehow you don't quite fit the mold for campaign chairman, but I suspect you could cut it as finance chairman."

"I'm not afraid to ask for money." Brew smiled. "My dad will attest to the fact I've had plenty of experience at that."

"That's what it's all about." Kirk looked to Wedge and Nellie, who nodded.

"Nellie," Wedge said, "I want you to serve as treasurer. Keep these fellows under control and me out of trouble."

"One more toast," Brew said, hoisting his glass. "To our fearless Nellie. And since she'll handle the tedious part of the financial operation, I'll raise money for expenses only. No salary or fee. And now that all this has been settled ... "

His voice trailed off as State Representative Raúl Ramirez of Laredo entered alone and strode toward their table.

After greeting the group, Ramirez, a young attorney serving his second term, spoke first to Kirk, whom he knew fairly well from legislative sessions. When Kirk told him Wedge was the candidate, Ramirez offered a handshake and words of caution. "You're taking on a real tough one. Campaign hard, but be careful, ever watchful. They play hardball."

Ramirez declined Nellie's offer of a drink. "I can't stay. It's not wise for me to be seen here with you. My father is not a close friend of Frank Ganner's, but he's against any involvement by me to oppose their campaign. However, I brought something of a contribution," he said, placing an envelope on the table. "There's a key and address for a nice apartment in Laredo. You can have it for the duration. You're going to need a quiet place to gather now and then, outside the district but nearby. Give 'em hell."

As Ramirez departed, Brew broke into a wide smile. "Now that all this has been accomplished, I say it's high time to adjourn to the sportatorium; and, uh, Nellie, sorry to lean on you, but I'm a little short."

"Sportatorium" was a euphemism for the most popular brothel in Nuevo Laredo, Papagayo's. From her purse, Nellie produced a twenty dollar bill she handed to Brew, who limped away with Nelson at his side. Sidney excused himself to return to Corpus Christi, leaving Kirk, Nellie, and Wedge at the table.

They were restless, somewhat drained from the meeting and the fact that the activity and noise engulfed them. The seating area had become packed and the stand-up bar was overflowing.

"Well," Wedge said to Kirk, rising from his chair to extend his hand, "you've become my 'Old Podnah' whether you like it or not."

"Yeah," Kirk said, completing the handshake, "till Frank Ganner us do part... I need some fresh air."

Nellie smiled, standing up from her chair. "Wedge and I need to do some shopping before dinner. We'll meet you in an hour at the C.O.D."

While Wedge paid the bill, Kirk walked out the front door and stretched, feeling how glad he was to be away from them for an hour. They would be shopping in the few expensive places on Guerrero Street between the market and bridge. He walked to an old bar nearby named Alma Latina, where the clientele was opposite to that of the Cadillac, almost all citizens of Nuevo Laredo. He received a dime change from the quarter he had placed on the bar for a beer. He drank it slowly, easing the tension of the meeting from his mind.

Walking outside, Kirk sidestepped a few street vendors. He agreed to a shoeshine from a thin kid in tattered clothes, a kid whose large brown eyes still flashed of hope and anticipation, indicating he hadn't been on the street all that long. Using his limited Spanish, Kirk chatted with the boy as he worked. Kirk pretended he didn't understand the boy's request for a nickel, gave him a quarter, and ambled away.

He soon arrived at a plaza that covered a full city block near the main street, where townspeople strolled on sidewalks, engaging in conversation about the day's activities and pausing to sit awhile on the benches of concrete and colorful tile. It was early twilight, when hundreds of sparrows and other birds gathered to roost in the many trees around the plaza, their chirping and flapping always competing with the sounds of traffic and church bells.

He was alone, but not lonely, until he glanced across the street at Tony's, the dimly lit piano bar where his love for Carrie had first become evident to him. That was only a few weeks ago, but it seemed so distant at the moment.

She had never been south of San Antonio, and they made the most of their brief time in Nuevo Laredo.

Flashing across his mind were Carrie's mood changes that day, from total enrapture with the frenzied crowd at the bullfight, to laughter and light conversation with drinks and dinner at the C.O.D., to a soft romantic tone at Tony's where they had danced to sentimental American music the owner played, a sad-eyed, middle-aged Mexican with a flair for melodies suited to his soft touch at the piano. The intimacy they shared was intensified later that night by passionate lovemaking in his car, a rather daring feat accomplished on a country road north of Laredo. All was carried out in time to arrive at his mother's house in Justinville before her 2:00 A.M. curfew.

Soon thereafter they tried to recapture that memorable experience, but it was off-key from the start. They encountered Nellie and some of her cohorts at the Cadillac, where they stopped for a pre-bullfight drink, and Nellie insisted they sit together at the Plaza de Toros. The previous bullfight was a tense, fast-moving test of courage and skill, but Carrie found the subsequent one to be slow and tedious.

A high, swirling wind—an added danger all matadors fear and respect—caused numerous delays while their capes were soaked with water to prevent easy exposure of their bodies to the foreboding horns. Acutely aware of the increased danger, the matadors were somewhat tentative with their cape work, resulting in a lack of rhythm in their normally precise maneuvers.

Most of the Mexicans in attendance, on the lower-priced sunny side, were aficionados, knowledgeable bullfight fans who, though eager for action, were sympathetic to the wind problem. From the shady side, some impatient American tourists, who understood little about such dynamics and yearned for the constant dramatic action they had seen in motion pictures, shouted their disapproval, taunted the matadors, and even cheered for the bulls on occasion.

Kirk, who had first developed an appreciation for bullfighting by reading Hemingway, became disgusted and wanted to leave. So did Carrie, but Brew and Wedge prevailed upon Nellie to stay since they were having a good time drinking beer and taunting the tourists.

At dinner that night, Carrie found she didn't relate well to this older crowd of hard-drinking, individualistic South Texans with their loosely structured lifestyle. They shared her background of Greek-oriented social order at college, but not much else. She craved time alone with Kirk, whom she perceived was altering his personality in order to satisfy their whims.

After what Carrie considered to be an inordinate amount of boring dinner conversation, she asked Kirk to decline their invitation to Tony's, and they had returned to Justinville, both aware of the tension but choosing not to talk about it.

A loud backfire from a bus shattered Kirk's moment of reflection. After a last glance at Tony's, he sighed, shook his head, and walked slowly along the narrow sidewalks to the C.O.D. restaurant near the international bridge. When he arrived, Nellie and Wedge were already seated at a small table. He sat down next to Nellie, across the table from Wedge.

The C.O.D. was about half the size of the Cadillac. A small unobtrusive bar attested to the fact that it stressed food for its clientele, and on that night also provided a piano player, whose lilting dinner music Kirk welcomed.

They chatted a few moments while drinks were served, Nellie with a martini, Wedge with his third Scotch and soda on the rocks for the day, and Kirk sticking with Bohemia beer.

"You know, Old Podnah," Wedge said, reclining slightly in his chair, "I find your decision a bit paradoxical. You say we can't get more than forty-five percent of the vote, yet you signed on. You're not the kamikaze type."

Kirk shrugged, gesturing with his right hand. "I meant what I said, that under the given circumstances, that's my estimate of the maximum. You see, we're going to sign up some volunteers who will work hard, but we don't have the time or stroke to build a political organization equal to

Ganner's in his two counties, except maybe in our home county of Retama. We'll win Retama, concede his two counties, and in those other four, we'll fight for all we can get, but he's got a big advantage going in."

"If we out-organize Ganner in those four counties," Nellie said, "then why doesn't the advantage shift to our side?"

"This is a state representative race," Kirk said. "Those of us at the Cadillac a while ago, plus Frank Ganner, et al., comprise about all the people in the district who are going to lose sleep over this race, at least for quite a while. If it comes down to a low-interest contest, there simply won't be a large turnout of voters. But you see, Ganner can turn out his machine vote at midnight tonight if he so desires. You can bet your bottom dollar that he'll turn 'em all out on election day."

Wedge frowned, taking another drink of Scotch and soda. "Wouldn't a strong dose of advertising change that situation?"

"Maybe in a big city, but not in a rural district. Advertising will reinforce what you're doing in the field, but it won't generate a large voter turnout by itself."

"All right, Kirk Holland," Nellie said as she leaned toward him and smiled, "what's up your sleeve?"

"I wish I had something up my sleeve. The only way I can see for there to be favorably high voter turnout is out of our hands. If there's a hot contest for the U.S. Senate nomination between Jordan Layman and Holt Witherspoon, then we'd have those non-machine voters coming to the polls. People who would be up for grabs in our race."

"Jordan Layman," Wedge reflected aloud, "the great enigma. An uncouth wheeler-dealer out to make his mark and millions, yet also a sensible progressive who someday might break the Southern barrier and go straight to the top... opposed by old reliable, Holt Witherspoon. Solid conservative with clean skirts when he was governor. Quite a match-up. One helluva match-up."

"Who do you think would win?" Nellie asked.

Kirk shook his head. "Tough call. Witherspoon has an edge in statewide name identification from having recently served as governor; but for a congressman, Layman cuts a wide swath. As we all know, he has ties in South Texas. We'll find out how strong."

"What are the odds that this contest will develop?" Nellie asked.

"Promising. I'll be running traps in Austin next week and that will be right up top on the agenda with our race. And on that score, I'm going to need a little walking around money for a couple of weeks."

Nellie reached into her purse, producing a one hundred dollar bill. "Will this suffice?"

"That it will."

"For the life of me," Wedge said, "I can't understand how that feudal landlord Ganner has developed all this damned power. An Anglo politician with a constituency that must be seventy-five to eighty percent Mexican-American."

"Well," Kirk replied, pouring a glass of beer, "he inherited quite a bit of that power from what his late father had built. And remember, we always speak of Ganner singularly, when, in fact, he's been in cahoots with the Alfonso Hernandez family of Piedra Blanca for many years. Al Hernandez is a shrewd politician also. He and Ganner are the same age, went to school together. They feed off each other, but Ganner is the boss, the baron. Also, Ganner has spoken fluent Spanish since he was a little boy; some say he learned it before he spoke English... He may not provide the best in housing, health care, and wages, but he provides something, and those people relate to him."

The waiter interrupted their conversation by serving their entrees: broiled quail for Nellie, fried frog legs for Wedge, and for Kirk, cabrito, young goat, his favorite dish even though it was baked instead of barbecued, as he preferred. Guacamole salad, refried beans, Spanish rice, and thick dinner rolls augmented those dishes.

Nellie, sensing tension between the men on either side of her, diverted dinner conversation from politics until the meal was almost finished. As Wedge took his final delicious bite, he waved for the waiter, then placed an order for after-dinner drinks. Kirk declined, opting for coffee.

"You know, Old Podnah," Wedge said, "I suspect the sun will come up the day after the election, even if I should lose... I want to make this campaign more than a vendetta against Frank Ganner. I want to contribute something to the social consciousness of the people in the district."

"What the hell does that mean?"

"It means I'm not simply going to potshot Ganner. I'm going to address issues relevant to all the people, including the less fortunate."

"Wedge," Kirk countered, "let's forget about issues for a while. All you need to start out on are two points, your qualifications and the fact you're for reform, which means anti-Ganner."

"And so, all those oppressed Mexican-Americans in the district are to sit quietly on the sidelines while two gringos utter platitudes to other gringos."

"Take it easy," Nellie said, placing a hand on Wedge's wrist.

"No, that's all right, Nellie," Kirk said in a sharp tone. "Better to get the cards on the table now than later."

"I'm just not willing," Wedge said, "to run a totally negative campaign, which is what you're suggesting."

"Positive, negative, that's not the point. You're challenging the Frank Ganner machine. You must challenge, and that's the best line of attack."

Wedge trained his eyes on Kirk. "What about the need for better wages and working conditions for migrant workers? What about educational opportunity? And housing? What about abolition of the poll tax? I want to raise those issues. I want to pursue them vigorously!"

"Yeah," Kirk said, staring back, "and people in hell want ice water! You come out on those issues and you'll go down the chute fast. You won't carry Retama County, much less any of the others."

"I just don't see any forthright thrusts at all to your thinking."

"We gotta take this campaign in cautious steps," Kirk said, "and beyond what I've already laid out, there's another big variable over which we have no control, but we can hope it breaks our way. A new organization called PAMAT, Political Association of Mexican-Americans of Texas, has formed. They're independent minded, not part of the old patrón system. They ran some quiet poll tax drives this past fall, which didn't draw much attention since they were billed as a general effort to increase Mexican-American voter participation. They just might be able to mount a serious campaign for this seat now that the incumbent is retiring. Believe me, a Mexican-American candidacy would change the equation."

"Could he possibly win?" Nellie asked.

"I seriously doubt it," Kirk replied, "but he might well force a runoff, placing real pressure on Ganner in the process."

"Why would that place more pressure on Ganner than on us?" Wedge asked.

"Because PAMAT would raise the issues you mentioned. Their candidate would raise them forthrightly, with credibility you don't have, and he could solidify anti-Ganner sentiment in a way you couldn't."

"So, you're saying I should leave the difficult issues alone, key only on Ganner corruption, and hope for a lift from PAMAT and the U.S. Senate race?"

"If you want to put it that way."

"All right then," Wedge countered, "what about issues that would mean money for Texas and our region: pari-mutuel betting, liquor by the drink? Don't you agree it's pretty damn foolish for us to spend a lot of our leisure money in Mexico, New Mexico, and elsewhere when we could be spending it within our borders?"

Kirk sighed, furrowing his brow. "Well, it's just that we're starting out on a wing and a prayer. The opponents of those proposals would line up solidly against you immediately. We can't afford the luxury, at least not starting out."

"Hell, you're not leaving me any room to maneuver on issues that interest me."

"I suppose," Kirk said, "a man sometimes doesn't realize just how little maneuverability he has until he steps into the political arena. And bear in mind, your noble intentions are worthless unless you win the election. As a newcomer starting out, if you raise those divisive issues, you'll be dead in the water. You've got to dodge, weave, punch and counterpunch, all within the parameters of a plan that has only an outside chance of winning. You've got to be willing to take endless streams of advice from people who can't help you one damned bit. You've got to take criticism, even scorn and ridicule. Now and then, you'll get a slap on the back and maybe a little respect. But not much. And just remember, many people you'll meet know almost nothing about Ganner, issues, or anything else. They'll vote for you if they like you. Be a good listener."

"Should he try to dress for the occasion, or do you believe in all that?" Nellie asked, working on a long sip from her Brandy Alexander.

"To the knowledgeable people," Kirk said, "it doesn't make any difference, but there aren't many of them. Most of the time I'd suggest you dress in a crumpled, not-too-expensive suit with loose tie never quite pulled tight at the collar. Denims might be okay for such as barbecues and rodeos, but I'd make a crumpled suit the uniform. Some of these rural people will surprise you. They want to visualize you as working for them in that distant capitol, in a suit, rather than trying to make them feel that you're fresh off a horse. But they don't want you looking like a millionaire, either, so no blazers or fancy clothes of any kind. Keep it simple."

"Anything you suggest for getting started tomorrow?" Nellie asked.

Kirk produced a booklet from his pocket which he handed to Wedge. "Here's a newspaper directory. On Monday, call the publisher of each weekly in the district. Most of the publishers are also editors. Tell 'em you're going to run, and to expect a formal announcement next month at which time you'll want to buy an ad. That will increase the odds of receiving free publicity."

"Wouldn't a personal visit be better?" Nellie asked.

"There isn't time to visit them all and make next week's deadlines. We'll do that later. Don't worry, they'll be flattered to be informed and happy to expect some additional advertising revenue."

"How do I handle the problem of Ned Felder's health?" Wedge asked. "And should I mention Frank Ganner and his stand-in?"

"By now," Kirk replied, "they should suspect that something's wrong with Felder, but you should skirt any references to anybody else. For this initial phase, just make it a simple, positive pitch for yourself."

When neither pursued questions, Kirk pulled a notepad from his coat pocket. "Now, let's work up a biographical sketch you can mail to those newspapers on Monday. I assume you'll want to run as 'Wedge Crayton'?"

"Yes," Wedge replied with a nod, "except that since 'Wedge' is, in effect, a nickname, I'd prefer for my full name, Wedgefield Hawthorne Crayton, the Third, to appear at the top, with 'Wedge Crayton' underneath."

Kirk paused, dangling his pen casually without recording what Wedge had requested. *Christ, we're running the Little Lord Fauntleroy of the Brush Country.*

"Wedge," he sighed, "as of this moment, will you please forget you have any name other than 'Wedge Crayton'? You're not running for president of the country club."

"I suppose," Wedge snapped, "you don't want to list Harvard in my educational background?"

"That's correct. We'll list the University of Texas School of Law and for all anybody knows, you were undergraduate at UT."

"Dammit, Kirk, I'm proud of my degree from Harvard. Proud of my friends and associations. I'm not going to back away from all that."

"I didn't say hide it. I'm saying don't advertise it. For those few in this district who will appreciate it, it's fine. But for each one of those, there are twenty-five others out there who will equate that with the rare privileges of wealth, which they deeply resent."

Wedge shook his head while Kirk studied the questions, asking Wedge if his occupation should be listed as "attorney-rancher."

"All right," Wedge replied, "with the caveat that I don't want to hold myself out as an authority on ranching. Dad lists me as part owner of the ranch, but I really don't know all that much. My older brother is the rancher... I've never worked cattle."

"You've only been practicing law three years in Justinville," Kirk said. "It seems as though I'm missing a year or two. Active duty?"

"No military service, due to asthma. I spent some time in New York, a year or so, dabbling in writing and the theater. I toured Europe for a year. That's about it."

"We'll work around that." Kirk's voice revealed a touch of irony. "Any other skeletons in your closet?"

Nellie laughed, but Wedge had become nettled by the barbs. "You know," he said, "I believe you're one of those bitter, frustrated people who begrudges the wealthy. You're one who aspires to the station but deep down knows he'll never make it."

Kirk started to rise from his chair, but the firm grip of Nellie's hand upon his wrist and the sharp pain of her fingernails digging in made him stop. He settled back slowly in his chair, taking a long swig of beer. "Religious affiliation?" he asked.

"Episcopal."

Kirk rubbed his forehead, unable to recall having seen any Episcopal churches in the district. For our market of voters, Baptist or Methodist. Presbyterian okay, or Catholic if we really could develop an avenue to crack the Mexican-American vote. But Episcopalian?

"Episcopal," Kirk repeated, writing it down.

"Doesn't that wrap it up?" Wedge asked.

"One final question. Marital status?"

Wedge shook his head, assuming an incredulous expression. "Why the hell did you ask that? You know I'm not married. I've never been married."

"Well, you never know unless you ask. Also, I just wonder if you two are engaged?"

Nellie recoiled. "You have no right to ask that."

"I'm afraid, my dear, that as of tonight, I have extraordinary rights. Wedge's personal life may become an issue in the campaign, particularly since he's running against Mom and apple pie, good old Wally Hooper with a loyal wife and four loving children. If you're not engaged, you two don't need to be seen around much alone after sundown. If you are engaged, the word needs to be spread."

For the first time during the afternoon and evening of exchanging ideas and information, a silence fell. Kirk enjoyed his final sip of coffee before leaning back slightly in his chair, right hand resting on his chin, savoring the moment. He glanced at them, but they were avoiding his eyes and each other's.

At last, Nellie sighed, turning to Kirk. "We're not engaged."

As Kirk prepared to leave, Wedge ordered another round of drinks for him and Nellie. "Now that the inquisition has ended, I'd like to ask when you will be able to relocate in Justinville?"

"It'll take me two or three weeks to straighten things out in Austin. I'll mail you a budget and timetable in about a week. Meanwhile, try to secure a headquarters in Justinville. It should have three private offices, or cubicles, for us, three phones now, more later on. Room for volunteers to work, a storage area for materials, and adequate parking space. Air-conditioned if at all possible."

"We can use the warehouse behind my store," she said. "Fills the bill and will be rent-free to the campaign. I'll have two window units installed. They'll keep it cool."

"All right," Kirk said. "Now, we'll defer any decisions on headquarters in other counties until later on, after the campaign kick-off."

"Kirk, Old Podnah," Wedge said, toying with his brandy snifter, "we're covering a helluva lot of ground in a hurry."

"That's what we're going to have to do from now until election day. Especially you, Professor."

"Well, we're going to need to understand one another better. I voted for Adlai Stevenson last time and I'm proud of it. Did you vote for Stevenson or Eisenhower?"

"In my line of endeavor, it's not wise to go around talking about how you vote."

"You mean you won't tell us?" Wedge asked.

"That's right." Kirk tossed his napkin on the table as he rose to leave. "It's none of your business."

"You know," Wedge said to Nellie as Kirk walked out the door, "he can be a ruthless bastard, but he certainly has matured since I last talked to him a couple of years ago."

"In some ways," she replied.

Chapter 2

Keeping his eyes trained on the bright yellow line in the middle of the two-lane highway to help him stay awake, Kirk drove home to Justinville. He arrived at the house to find it quiet, his sister asleep in her room, and his mother stretched out on the couch in the front room, book on her lap and nearby radio playing soft, semiclassical music.

He kissed her on the forehead, pulled the blanket up to her chin, turned off the lamp and radio, and retired to his room. He tossed his clothes on a chair and crawled into bed, exhausted. Soon he fell into a deep sleep, his final thoughts having eased from the political arena to Carrie.

At midmorning the following day, his sister Estelle tapped his shoulder. "Mother's really been excited since she found your note yesterday. We're making custard for homemade ice cream. We'll make salad and baked potatoes this afternoon while you're cooking steak—"

"Hold on," Kirk said, rubbing his eyes. "I can't stay long. I need to get back to Austin."

"Kirk," Mrs. Holland said, as she entered his room, "I'm so glad you've come to visit." She hugged him, kissing him on the cheek. "And we can have a real treat today like we had on the Sundays when the judge was alive, and you and Estelle were here so much of the time. It's a beautiful day, let's enjoy it."

"Mother, I really shouldn't—"

"Since you've been traveling so much, you're excused from church, but you'd better have the fire ready to grill the steak when we return."

"And who," he asked, "is going to crank the ice cream freezer?"

"You can handle it," his sister laughed.

"Now, look, I'm just not going to be able to..." He sighed as they departed his room and left for church services at First Methodist, the only Methodist church in the county.

Kirk placed a call to Carrie's home in Houston, but got no answer. He found a favorite short breakfast awaiting him: orange juice, a piece of cinnamon toast, and freshly brewed coffee.

After breakfast, he strolled into the front room to enjoy a second cup of coffee while scanning the newspaper from San Antonio. The pleasant room was decorated in fine taste, not an easy accomplishment considering the modest budget with which his mother had worked all those years.

Built-in bookcases flanked the fieldstone fireplace. They contained a wide range of literature and a fine set of encyclopedias, plus several colorful antique vases she had been able to acquire during periodic trips to San Antonio. Ornate antique lamps, her prized items, were displayed on slender wooden tables on either side of the comfortable tan leather couch where Kirk relaxed.

Martha Holland had been firm in containing the judge's desire to display mounted heads of animals, restricting them to the wide hallway leading to the front room where guns, ammunition, and fishing gear were also kept.

Kirk finished the coffee and newspaper, and decided it was time to prepare for the chore he had mastered at age twelve and repeated for years on Sunday afternoons when the family returned from church services. The chore produced his favorite treat – homemade ice cream.

From the refrigerator, he retrieved the metal container filled with a gallon of vanilla custard. He walked outside to the porch adjoining the garage where the ice cream freezer had been placed alongside a large bag of crushed ice. He paused upon seeing his old friend, Strayboy, the weathered border collie that wandered to their home ten years ago. While searching in vain to find his owner, the judge had become fond of him, allowing him to stay and giving him that most appropriate name.

"You can be my helper." Kirk stroked his head while the dog wagged its tail vigorously. He set the metal container in the wooden freezer and poured ice around it, layering the ice with generous portions of ice cream salt to make it melt rapidly and tighten against the container. He cranked the freezer's wooden handle for several minutes, swirling the container in the sloshy freezing mixture, all the while poking a stick in a small hole near the bottom of the freezer in order to drain the salty ice water. The balancing act involved cranking the container as fast as the arm muscle could while guarding against the saline liquid cresting the top of the container where it might seep in to spoil the custard.

"Oh hell!" Kirk sighed when his right arm grew tired. "I'm really out of shape for this."

He switched to his left arm, lest the contents freeze with a lumpy texture. He cranked and drained for twenty minutes until he could barely turn the crank, indicating the contents were frozen solid. He then lifted the lid and removed the dasher. He packed the freezer with a few more cups of ice and placed an old towel over the top to let the ice cream set until time to serve. From the dasher, he enjoyed a few dripping samples of the delicious fresh ice cream.

After his mother and sister returned from church, he lit the fire. He used a bed of charcoal augmented by a handful of small mesquite limbs sprinkled with water, a combination his father had developed years ago. As the mesquite limbs flamed and smoked, he seared both sides of the thick piece of sirloin right away, then set it aside a few minutes until the fire had burned down to the point it would cook evenly.

When the steak was almost done, his sister appeared on the porch to tell him the salad and potatoes were ready. "This is fun, Kirk, you don't know how much fun. This is the first time we've had this meal since you were here last. And that's been… well, quite a while."

"Sis, how's it going? Does she get out and about much?"

"Nothing like before Daddy died. Just church on Sunday, maybe a bridge game every couple of weeks, and rarely a movie."

"Kirk, you've forgotten. This is Justinville, and I'm twenty-four. My old friends are all married or have moved away. I keep close to home because there's nothing else to do."

"Do you want to go somewhere else? Are you tired of teaching school?"

"Don't start grilling me. I'm not sure what I want. I know she needs me here. She misses Daddy; she misses him something awful."

Kirk studied her face a moment. In high school she had never been quite pretty enough to be a cheerleader nor assertive when she might have become a student leader. But she had been an outstanding student, winning a scholarship to Southwest Texas State Teachers College and graduating right before their father's death, in time to join her mother during the early critical aftermath.

Her brown hair was combed back into a tight bun and her blue eyes revealed a bit of sadness.

Always sincere and loyal, but so naive, uncertain, and vulnerable.

"You know," he said, "she still looks pretty self-sufficient to me. She'd probably be okay if you moved."

"Well, I'll admit I'd like someday to move to San Antonio. But not now."

"I'll be moving back to Justinville in two or three weeks. I'm going to be real busy with a campaign, but I'll help you some with Mother."

"Good. Will you live here, at the house?"

"I haven't decided."

Standing at the dinner table, Estelle asked her mother if Kirk might sit at the head of the table in order to carve and serve the steak from the same vantage point her father had occupied all those years.

Kirk paused, holding the tray with the large piece of meat, and wondered if he were to receive the designation.

"I don't know if that's appropriate just yet," his mother said.

Kirk sat down at his old place at the table, then carved the steak while glancing at his mother. At fifty-eight, her voice was less precise than he once knew, and her hand gestures revealed a slight tremor. Her beautiful face displayed a few more lines and wrinkles, and her soft brown hair was laced with ever-widening streaks of gray. Yet, her steady blue eyes remained alert and attentive as if they refused to accept the aging process.

She had always been a solid partner to his father, whose love for her was perhaps as pervasive as his love of the political leadership of Retama County. She had taught school in her home area of West Texas for a few years until moving to a school in Justinville where the town's most eligible bachelor won her hand. As the judge's wife, she was loyal and responsive. As a mother, she was even-handed with Kirk and Estelle, recognizing Kirk "to having always been a bit more high-spirited than his sister."

She was an effective civic leader, crusading for a new public library and for expanded library facilities in the high school, the center of activity in the town. She played the piano and organ equally well and, for years, sang a steadfast soprano in the church choir. Her appreciation for music was widely known and she had often encouraged the band director at the high school to teach his students something other than fight songs and marches.

She could speak to a person in an instructive manner without scolding, and she could be a considerate listener, as she thought all good teachers should be. Though Kirk on occasion resented her self-confidence, he had always admired her as a citadel of grace, charm, and intellect in a harsh and lonely environment.

Kirk enjoyed the delicious lunch, but the conversation troubled him somewhat. His mother always referred to his father in the abstract as "the judge," as though the public official aspect of his father's legacy was foremost in her mind.

In addition to the tasty mesquite-seared steak, he enjoyed the other standard elements of the meal: large baked potato with butter, and hearty tossed salad with dressing of vegetable oil and fresh lemon juice.

For dessert, it would be the homemade vanilla ice cream with chocolate syrup.

Once, many years before, his sister had suggested making chocolate ice cream, but his father insisted that chocolate syrup mixed into vanilla ice cream tasted better. And the judge's preference had endured as a family tradition.

When Estelle prepared to serve dessert, Kirk told his mother he would be moving back to Justinville for several months to manage Wedge Crayton's campaign for the Legislature.

"I didn't realize you had an interest in local politics."

"Well, Mother, this race is a little wider in scope than Dad's old domain of Retama County. It involves seven counties."

"Oh, yes, as I recall, the district includes a county or two controlled by Frank Ganner. The judge never admired him, but then he never was required to deal with him."

"We're going to have to deal with him unless we win this race."

"Be careful."

"I will."

"Well, fine, Kirk, it will be nice to have you here again, but what about finishing your degree?"

"I guess it will have to wait awhile."

"It's been waiting for years."

"Yes, Mother, I know, but it wasn't that easy for me to pick up where I'd left off, and—"

"You must not use military service as a crutch. I know you suffered, but your mind and body are able. It seems to me you've been more inclined to that newspaper work than to college. Must I remind you that Estelle completed her degree plan precisely on schedule, in four years?"

Estelle blushed as she scooped the ice cream. "Mother, Kirk has been under more pressure than I for years. It isn't fair to compare us in that manner, and—"

"It seems to me," Mrs. Holland snapped, "Kirk tends to create pressure if none exists at the moment."

Estelle feared Kirk might become angry, but he found that last thrust to be amusing.

"All right, ladies," he said with a chuckle, "let's not argue. One of these days I'll nail that degree, but until that historic occasion arrives, you'll just have to accept me as I am."

After finishing his meal, Kirk placed another call to Carrie's home in

Houston. Carrie's younger brother told him she had decided to return to Austin and departed an hour earlier.

While packing his clothes, the lilting sounds of the Stephen Foster classic "Beautiful Dreamer" came from the phonograph his mother loved as much as her piano. He kissed her and Estelle good-bye and returned to Highway 81 for the trip to Austin.

Hanging heavy on Kirk's mind during the return trip were how to cope with Carrie's reaction to his decision and how to approach his boss, the managing editor of The Austin Capital Times, for a leave of absence.

Upon arriving at twilight, he placed a call to Carrie but her roommate told him she had gone out to eat with friends. When the roommate hedged Kirk's question about the time she might return, he suspected the worst.

He pursued another question, prompting the roommate's response. "Look, Kirk, I'm not going to lie to you. She told me she doesn't want to talk to you. I'm sorry, and I'll tell her you called."

On the following morning, instead of reporting to work at the capitol, Kirk decided to first go to the newspaper building downtown. There he sought the managing editor, Orland Gretard, with whom he requested a private meeting.

"All right," Gretard drawled, accepting the cup of coffee Kirk brought him. "I sure don't remember you ever being so considerate before."

Gretard wore short-sleeve white shirts year-round, always with a frayed old tie, its knot hung loose a couple of inches below his collar. His barren office reeked of the pungent odor from stale smoke of cheap cigars, one of which was always in hand. Gretard was a squat, middle-aged man who enlisted in the Army early in World War II as an idealistic admirer of Franklin Roosevelt. He returned home with a bad limp, impaired vision, and a head full of miserable memories.

Widely known around the newspaper was his penchant for chewing out employees with sarcastic remarks delivered in a slow, mocking manner. Once, in the composing room, a new young employee had taken the liberty to change the makeup indicated on a page dummy sent from the editorial department.

When the employee answered Gretard's demand for an explanation with the reply, "I just thought it was the right thing to do," Gretard barked, "You're not being paid to think, and if you don't think about that, you won't be paid any more."

Many of the employees considered him to be a tyrant. But he had firmly directed the newspaper for seven years during which he never exceeded the spartan budget and always provided a handsome profit for the owners.

After Kirk gave his two weeks' notice and requested a six-month leave of absence, Gretard leaned back in his chair without comment, puffing on his cigar. At last, he shrugged, gesturing with the cigar. "I never heard of a leave of absence around here. When people leave, they're replaced."

"Well, I think my line of work is something special. Not many people are skilled in covering the political process."

"That's the core of the problem with you, Holland. You believe you're something special, a boy wonder."

Kirk bristled. "I know who I compete against over there at the capitol. I'm as good, or better, than the lot of 'em."

"As a writer, maybe. As one who understands what's really going on, probably. But I'm talking about as the individual."

"What do you mean?"

"You've got a chip on your shoulder. I hear that after two or three drinks, you're prone to start bellyaching about your valiant service in the Korean War and how nobody cares; or that nobody cares that so many of your contemporaries didn't get called. So you didn't waltz through the University of Texas on time. So you ran out of deferments and the draft board dropped it on you. Who gives a shit? You came back without bands playing and flags waving, but you came back the same as you left. I came back with a lousy wound that hurts when it gets cold, hurts when it gets hot, and some of the time in between. I'll trade you the bands and flags."

"I'm not here to talk about my personal feelings or your leg problem," Kirk said, getting up to leave.

"Sit down, I'm not through. Now, you're pretty goosey about your personal life, but what I'm telling you is for your own good. You're drinking too much, and that's not good for you, or your reputation, or the reputation of this newspaper. You're twenty-six, going on fifty. You've been gunning too hard in your work, wearing yourself thin. I've been intending to talk to you just to tell you to slow down."

"I've never," Kirk snapped, "had any brushes with the law concerning my drinking habits. I'm careful about that. Plus, I've always played by your five-dollar rule, which is the only real restraint you placed upon me when you hired me. And I want you to know for certain that there have been times when I was almost broke and sorely tempted, but no politician or lobbyist has ever picked up a food or drinking tab of mine in excess of five dollars. Nor have I accepted any of the gratuities around, such as hunting trips and women of the night.

"But you must understand, I need to run with some of those hard-drinking players in order to know how their game will unfold. Instead of nit-picking, you ought to know by now that covering the capitol and the political arena is a helluva lot different from the police beat, sports, or anything else that goes into this newspaper."

Any other young employee confronting Gretard would have received a cutting response, but he shrugged, tapping his cigar on an ashtray. "All right, Holland," he said with a wry smile, "I suppose I was a little rough on you, but I've given you a lot of latitude to develop yourself and you've just started to vindicate me. The fact of the matter is, I'm not at all pleased with what you're doing."

"I guess the best way to state it is that I feel a strong obligation."

"Maybe so, but you don't have the whole picture in mind. Over the weekend, I got calls from Jordan Layman and Holt Witherspoon. Now, when they're calling newspaper people like me, it means they've already cleared with their money people. They say they're just touching bases, asking for advice on what to do, but I'm convinced they're going to run for that U.S. Senate seat. You're never going to see a more gut-busting race than this one. And here you are, walking away from the unique opportunity of covering that high noon showdown in order to go get yourself immersed in a lousy little state representative race in South Texas."

"You've missed the point. We're going to take on Frank Ganner and—"

"Oh, come on," Gretard snapped. "You're not going to beat Ganner's guy, and even if you did, that's just one miserable hound you'd put among one hundred and fifty miserable hounds wandering around that so-called House of Representatives."

"You don't know much about South Texas. Down there, that one seat takes in seven counties and means that—"

"Look," Gretard said as he exhaled another puff of acrid cigar smoke, "I can't believe the way you're carrying on with all this provincial bullshit. You're sitting on a U.S. Senate race that is pivotal to the politics of Texas. Layman charging hard with something of a progressive platform, Witherspoon trying to hold the line with the old traditional faction."

"I suspect, in your position, you'll be inclined to want the paper to support Witherspoon," Kirk said.

"Not necessarily. You know, Jordan Layman is the most aggressive member of Congress I've ever seen. He'd be the most effective senator this state has ever had. Might someday crack the great barrier against the South and become President."

Gretard, Kirk mused, rarely spoke in a positive manner about anyone. All that really translates into is that the election of Layman would mean more federal dollars streaming into Austin. He would boost the economy of the community and, therefore, that of the newspaper.

"Beyond the Senate race," Gretard continued, "is the fact that Eisenhower carrying the state last time was no fluke. The Republicans might elect a congressman in Dallas this year. The Democrats' one-party system isn't going to last forever in Texas. When it changes, there will be twice as much politics to cover and it will be year-round, not just through the primary. All this on the horizon and you want to abandon ship to crusade for a lost cause down there on the edge of nowhere… Why don't you think it over?"

Kirk studied a piece of crumpled copy paper in the nearby wastebasket. He was no longer able to engage Gretard's eyes, which were glowering at him through incessant puffs of cigar smoke. For the first time in the conversation, Gretard had hurt him deeply by hammering home what he knew but had tried so hard to suppress. These times offered tremendous opportunity for him to advance his career as a political writer.

"It's too late," he murmured, still staring at the wastebasket. "I've made a commitment… I just don't want to lose my job."

Gretard paused, tapping his nearly-spent cigar on the ashtray. "Holland, you're the best young political correspondent in the state," he drawled, "but there's no way I can hold your spot open for you."

Kirk stood up from the chair.

Looking down at a stack of papers on his desk, Gretard retrieved a pencil. "You'll have a job here," he said, shuffling through the stack, "when you're through, if you want it, but it just might be on the rim, writing headlines every night. That's the best I can do. Now, get out of here, I've got a deadline coming up."

Kirk spent the remainder of the day working in the Capitol, taking time to make a few calls on behalf of the campaign and trying again without success to contact Carrie. Preparing to leave, he thought about the familiar places where political people gathered, but he wanted none of that. He recalled the places he had frequented in pre-Korea days at school when times had seemed easier and demands few, except for moonlighting on the Capital Times while contending with an occasional major quiz and the dreaded final examinations.

Most of those drinking places were located on "The Drag," that portion of Guadalupe Street that bordered on the western edge of the UT campus. Farther north on Guadalupe was Dirty Martin's, the longtime combination drive-in and restaurant that catered to college students.

He ate a hamburger there, then headed over to relax at The Oak Room, a congenial tavern a few blocks north of Dirty Martin's. Since the manager, B.B. Hencik, enforced assiduously the twenty-one-year-old drinking law, the clientele was composed of upper-class and graduate students at UT, plus young adults who lived in that area, most of whom worked for the university.

Hencik, a tall amiable fellow of Czech extraction, was working on a pharmacy degree while managing the place and tending bar. He had been a friend of Kirk's since their pre-Korea days as classmates at UT, sharing a few freshman and sophomore courses. When Kirk walked in, he waved him to a seat near the end of the long bar where he spent his time when not serving beer or set-ups for mixing drinks.

It was also a choice spot near Hencik's private phone, which Kirk was welcome to use. Kirk called a bookie just in time to place a small wager on a collegiate basketball game about to start on the East Coast. Kirk enjoyed talking to the sports staff at the newspaper about ratings of teams, then making a modest bet to enhance "sweating" the results of athletic contests even if he didn't catch them on TV or radio. He could relax and unwind by drinking a few beers, especially at The Oak Room's weeknight special of twenty cents per glass of tap beer, while thinking about how he would splurge with the three dollars he hoped to win on the game.

From the bar, he observed several couples dancing in the dimly lit back room, gliding to the smooth tones of a Nat King Cole recording from Hencik's jukebox, which was never permitted to play much louder than one would play a radio when listening alone. Kirk lost track of his thoughts while following their movement to the soft music as though choreographed for that montage of motion, with all the dancers dressed in costume - men in slacks and sports shirts; women in sweaters, skirts, and loafers with white socks.

He and Carrie had been dressed in that manner, he recalled, on their first date when they went next door for a melodrama presentation by The Austin Civic Theater. With an ample supply of beer and popcorn, they cheered the hero and booed the villain, enjoying every moment, until it ended and they came to The Oak Room. He remembered vividly the first moment they danced, the sensual touching of their bodies in an embrace that became increasingly intense. An hour later, in the front seat of his car, they had experienced their first powerful, captivating kiss.

Those vivid memories made his heart ache.

He turned away from the dancers to watch a small group of young men gathered around a pinball machine in the corner of the front room near the door. They cheered as one of their friends rolled up a big score, the machine lighting up repeatedly in a rapid, multicolored fashion. They hoisted their longneck beer bottles in gestures of triumph as the player proceeded to hit the highest mark attainable, winning five free games, plus a free beer from Hencik.

When Hencik cleared his pressing duties, he paused to tell Kirk how good it was to see him return to The Oak Room.

"I needed a place to brood in peace." Kirk smiled. "I've tuned out politics for tonight."

"And how's Carrie?"

"That's part of the brooding. Things aren't going so well right now."

"Here's one on the house," Hencik said with a characteristic big smile, placing a foaming glass of tasty tap beer before Kirk. "That'll pep you up."

The easy flow of The Oak Room scene relaxed Kirk, who was trying, with only limited success, to set Carrie aside from his concerns, at least for a night. "If she's set in concrete," he whispered to himself, "I've got to accept it and go on. Quit trying to call her. It'll hurt for a while, but I'll get over it… I'm sure I will… I must."

Hencik answered the phone and handed it to Kirk, who assumed the bookie was calling to tell him he'd won the small wager.

Instead, it was Carrie, who said, "I called the newspaper a while ago and someone said you're leaving. Is that true?"

"Yes."

"When?"

"In a couple of weeks."

She paused. "I want to see you. Please pick me up in ten minutes, at the sorority house."

When she sat down next to him in the front seat, she sighed, "You make me so damned mad I can't see straight or think straight. But I love you so much."

They embraced with a long, passionate kiss.

As he drove from the sorority house, he explained his commitment to the campaign and the timetable.

She shook her head. "Kirk, that really throws things off. You could take one course each this spring and summer and then graduate. You said the newspaper would allow you to do that."

"It'll just have to wait."

"Didn't you tell me that one journalism course is only offered in the spring? You're talking about losing a whole year! If I can stomach taking eighteen hours next fall, I'll graduate ahead of you."

"I don't control the election process."

She sat in silence for a moment as he drove south on Guadalupe Street. "Did it ever occur to you," she said as she sighed, "your personal life, and that of the one who loves you, should take priority?"

"This is something I have to do."

"And you know my father can be an impatient man."

His insides jolted at that remark referring to her father's casual offer to work him into the public relations department of his oil company. Kirk knew the offer was tied to marrying Carrie, though such a bargain had never been mentioned; nor had marriage, in specific terms, ever been discussed between him and Carrie.

"I never told him I was interested in that."

"But you know you could make much more money there than what you're making now."

"It's a mystery to me why a company would require me to have a journalism degree in order to write a mundane press release about another oil field having been discovered. Or an announcement that a new refinery is going to be constructed."

She shook her head. "That's one thing that's always bothered me about your newspaper job. They don't seem to care whether you get your degree."

"They're interested in people who can write. The degree doesn't make that much difference."

"After all these years, in and out of school, don't you want to finish up?"

"Yes," he said slowly, "but for an entirely different reason… I feel I owe it to my mother. I don't want her going to her grave believing one of her children didn't place a premium upon higher education."

Carrie laughed. "Well, at least you're honest about it, and there's no sense in us quarreling all night. I'll be a good girl if you'll promise to visit me this spring."

"I promise," he said, as they arrived in the driveway alongside his first floor apartment.

The bad news for them was that Kirk's roommate was in the apartment studying. The good news was that a low cloud cover had obscured the moon, darkening the driveway-garage area where they were parked so thoroughly the roommate or passersby could not see them. They fell into a passionate embrace that led immediately to intense lovemaking, an unleashing of all the emotions and sexual energy that had been building since the previous time.

As they finished, she held him tight for a long moment before whispering, "Kirk, something's wrong."

"Oh, hell." He let out a big sigh as he reached down. "It's torn."

From the beginning of their intimate relationship, she had been careful to tell him when a condom was needed.

"This wasn't the best time of the month," she said, "for that to have happened."

For the next day, Kirk had set up a breakfast meeting at the stately old Driskill, one of the city's most popular downtown hotels. Its ornate dining facilities with thick carpeting made it a comfortable, quiet place in which to conduct business, and the quality of the food was consistently high.

With the breakfast meeting upon him, Kirk felt the gnawing pressure of changing roles from political writer, independent of the lobby's power, to campaign manager urgently seeking funds and support from top power brokers of the state. He only knew them casually from social/political gatherings and from conversations in the galleries of the Legislature or the halls of the Capitol where they steered the course of major legislation that affected their clients. They knew him as a bright young political writer, a factor to be considered in the scheme of things, though not a priority.

Owen Warren and Vernon Maxfield were in the top echelon of veteran lobbyists in the capital city. Polished and powerful, they were influential among their peers and throughout the Texas Legislature whose members didn't always like what they heard from them, but who feared the consequences of going in another direction. For more than two decades, Warren had represented a consortium of major oil companies. Maxfield, an attorney who headed a large, established firm with a practice limited to lobbying and governmental affairs, represented a variety of clients with business and industrial interests. They didn't come to the meeting unprepared. Kirk had told them on the phone about the reform challenge to Frank Ganner and his role in it.

With his first sip of coffee, Kirk opened the discussion by assuring them of confidentiality, a statement which prompted welcome nods from both men.

"I invited you gentlemen," Kirk said, "because I wanted to set forth how we intend to conduct this campaign. Your support, financial and otherwise, could be crucial to success."

"Those are strong words," Warren said with a smile, "but remember, never lobby a lobbyist."

Kirk smiled, glancing at the veteran lobbyists whose dark suits must have cost three or four times what he paid for his.

"Holland," Maxfield said, "we respect you; that's why we're here. And we want you to know that regardless of the outcome of this campaign, we'll continue to respect you."

Kirk didn't like the sound of that statement. He studied Maxfield, but it was Warren who followed up.

"We've already run some traps on this race, and it just doesn't look good for your candidate."

"Well, gentlemen," Kirk countered with an openhanded gesture, "the campaigns haven't even been launched. How can you project what the candidates will do?"

"Things don't change much in South Texas," Maxfield said. "You can't move many votes away from where they appear to be headed."

Kirk realized he was already on the defensive and relying on other campaigns was weak strategy, but there seemed to be no other persuasive cards to play. Bringing up the possibility of a maverick Mexican-American candidacy would only conjure up suspicions of dealing with political elements apart from the usual power coalitions of South Texas. But the United States Senate race was a new factor that loomed large in the minds, hearts, and bank accounts of all the prominent players in the Texas political arena.

Kirk trained his eyes squarely upon those of Maxfield. "My boss tells me it's virtually certain that Jordan Layman and Holt Witherspoon are going to square off for the Senate nomination. Perhaps 'collide' would be a more apt description. That dogfight is going to generate the voter turnout we need to match Ganner's machine vote…

"And," he continued while turning his gaze to Warren, "may I inquire as to whom you plan to support in the Senate race?"

Kirk knew the lobbyists had lengthy ties to Witherspoon dating from his terms as lieutenant governor and governor. However, Layman had carried some big buckets of water in Congress for prominent elements of the business-industrial community in Texas.

They didn't take the bait. Maxfield shook his head a bit, toying with the handle of his coffee cup, while Warren leaned toward Kirk. "Perhaps you have a point about the Senate race generating higher voter turnout, but let's confine this discussion to the Legislature and matters germane to your race. Now, we don't see any important legislative issues to be developed. Probably be more of a popularity contest which means—"

"Oh, come on now," Kirk said with a sigh, ignoring the plate of scrambled eggs and bacon placed before him. "Nobody's even set forth a platform or discussed any issues. Gentlemen, if you'll just rely on human nature for a moment, you'll have to agree the majority of people in that district aren't necessarily going to line up to become political serfs for Frank Ganner, the Baron of Bantrell. That's a powerful issue unto itself."

"Well," Maxfield said, "more to the point. Your candidate is quite wealthy, which certainly helps a campaign in a drouth-stricken area where money will be hard as hell to raise. But that looks like his only big plus. Even then, you're not going to outspend Ganner… Your candidate has no civic credentials. Strike one. No political credentials. Strike two. No governmental credentials. Strike three.

"On top of that, he's a bachelor and doesn't even attend a church in his district. Talk about a candidate without a base. Then there's another matter that concerns us. With his family background, one would assume him to be fairly conservative, but we understand that when he was here in law school, he leaned toward The Texas Progressive crowd… Now, you may berate Ganner as a tyrant, but he's always been a power in that area. He appears to have a strong candidate in Wally Hooper, who has credentials up and down the line, and—"

"Credentials?" Kirk growled. "Hell, I've run some traps, too, and that guy and his family would starve if Ganner weren't propping him up. He gets a six-hundred-dollar-per-month retainer for doing practically nothing, and I'm sure that will increase if he wins. He's bought and paid for now; how do you think he'll perform in the Legislature?"

"Now, Holland," Warren said in a patronizing tone, "don't take any of this personally. It's business. We're not in the business of political reform; we're in the business of dealing with whomever gets elected. And we can deal a lot better with him if we've supported his campaign."

"Can't you just look at this as one seat," Kirk said, almost pleading, "out of one hundred fifty in the House? And take a chance on an upset?"

"You never know," Maxfield said, "when that one seat might provide the decisive vote on a big bill."

Neither lobbyist wanted to admit the case was closed on a race for an open seat before the candidates had formally announced. They continued eating breakfast for an awkward moment until Maxfield paused to look again at Kirk.

"This isn't easy to say, but I believe it would in your best interests to back away from this campaign and not get involved. It may turn out to be more than you bargained for, and your chances of winning just aren't good any way you cut it."

Kirk tossed his napkin onto the table. "I wanted to talk to you two because I considered you to be the most astute and responsible among the heavy hitters in the lobby, ones who would carry the banner among your troops. I had a misguided, idealistic notion that you'd welcome an opportunity to contain a political cancer in our state that will spread rapidly if not checked now.

"Instead, I find our reform campaign already being sacrificed upon the altar of pragmatism. Good old Wally Hooper will give you his vote when you need it, so that's it! You don't want independent-minded legislators! Well, you wanted confidentiality assured; believe me, you've got it! I'm going to walk away from this table and forget I ever heard what I heard! Otherwise, I'll be losing sleep I can't afford to lose!"

He left the table and stomped over to the cashier's stand to pay the bill.

"You know, Vernon," Warren said with a chuckle, "that sounded like a speech you made about thirty years ago, running for student body president at UT."

"Yes, and you voted for me." Maxfield smiled.

Kirk had to wait three days for a meeting with Jarvis Harrison, the Speaker of the Texas House of Representatives. Harrison suggested they meet at The Austin Club, the premier private club in the city, located in the Commodore Perry Building a few blocks south of the Capitol.

It was late afternoon after work when Kirk arrived at the quiet, comfortable club where Harrison's meals and drinks were always covered on an open tab provided by friendly lobbyists. He took a seat at the "Speaker's Table" in a far corner.

The tall, paunchy Harrison, who always made his entrances with a flourish, greeting several people in the bar, including the bartender and waiters, soon joined him. He placed his short-brim Stetson on the table as though he couldn't bear to leave that integral part of his attire out of sight. After assuring himself he had recognized all who warranted it, he summoned his favorite waiter for the drink order.

Harrison wore a rumpled gray suit, with coat unbuttoned, and a brown-and-green tie his wife believed made him appear younger than his sixty-one years. He was raised in a tiny East Texas community in a rural district that had always given him comfortable reelection margins. That kind of secure base was a requisite to seek the speakership and to be able to serve effectively, once there.

As Speaker, Harrison shared pivotal legislative power with the lieutenant governor, who presided over the Senate. To members of the lobby, he was equally powerful to his counterpart, though not nearly as well known throughout the state since his fellow House members elected their Speaker, while the lieutenant governor was elected by statewide vote, along with the governor. Through three two-year terms, Harrison had proven to be a shrewd, tough Speaker. He appeared to be a kind, courtly gentleman in public but often took on another personality behind closed doors.

He liked Kirk, though the young man needled him a few times in print after discovering some deal or another that Harrison had cut right where they were sitting now, or at the Palomino Club, or at a dining table in the Driskill Hotel.

Harrison had maintained a conservative East Texas image by often railing against "eggheaded liberals" pressing for integration, or by complaining about federal controls over business. However, he could easily find it expedient to support a social welfare program now and then, but only if he perceived it to be in his best interests or those of his "team." The team was an unofficial cadre of about twenty-five carefully groomed legislators who helped him run the House of Representatives.

With his East Texas drawl and flair for theatrics, he could choose to sound like an ignorant bumpkin fresh off a desolate farm, or he could utilize an enviable vocabulary of four- and five-syllable words, if he wanted to bedazzle some person or audience with his understanding of complex issues.

Meeting privately with the Speaker underscored again to Kirk the intense pressure caused by changing roles from an independent-minded political writer to a campaign manager in an uphill race seeking help, hat in hand. Kirk had rehearsed his presentation carefully, down to the relevant voting history of that district.

But Harrison would have none of it. "Holland, I don't have long today. I know all the figures, and I sure as hell know how the lobby feels about this race."

After taking a long swig of bourbon and water, he pointed his right forefinger at Kirk. "Now, tell me something different. Tell me how you're going to overcome the odds."

Kirk resented Harrison's cavalier approach as the stinging memory of his recent meeting with the two lobbyists at the Driskill Hotel flashed across his mind. "Tell me," he said, "if you're scared of Frank Ganner. Because if you are, I'm not interested in pursuing this conversation."

Harrison bristled. No one confronted him that way, not even the governor. With brow furrowed, he paused, glaring at Kirk, who stared back for a long tense moment. At last, Harrison rubbed his bald forehead, chuckled, and took another sip of whiskey. "All right, nothing wrong with getting cards on the table…

"Now," he spoke in a lower tone, "I'm going to tell you something about Frank Ganner, and if you quote me, I'll call you a liar."

Kirk nodded.

"That one sparsely populated county he owns down there and the one close by may not turn in enough votes each election to add up to much of a percentage in a statewide total. But if you're running statewide, just knowing you have that vote in your hip pocket, and the domino effect it can create in that general area… Those are factors beyond the comprehension of most people around here, or Dallas, or Houston, trying to figure out how to meet all the challenges involved in conducting a statewide campaign. But just think of that, if it should turn out to be a close race… The smart ones think about that."

With a sardonic smile, Kirk leaned back in his chair. "And Mister Speaker just might be ready to run a statewide campaign in a couple of years, so he sure can't afford to antagonize the great Frank Ganner."

"You better back off, son," Harrison snapped. "You have a way of twistin' too hard, too fast. I didn't say that, I didn't imply that, and it's simply not true. I know my arena, and I'm damn sure not leavin' it till I'm ready to retire. But you'd better understand that in this town, to the astute players, Ganner means a helluva lot more than a distant South Texas political boss."

"That's the bottom line with the lobby, isn't it?" Kirk said. "It isn't the fact our candidate is short on surface credentials."

Harrison shrugged, then ordered another round of drinks. "Let's get back to where I started. Tell me how you're going to upset Ganner."

Somehow, Harrison is trying to lead me toward the answer he wants to hear, something apart from standard strategy and tactics based upon voting history and the obvious variables.

"I've been giving it more thought," Kirk said, "while running traps. I understand that beneath the veneer of self-assurance, Ganner has a hair-trigger temper. He's never had to compete against the kind of well-rounded campaigns using new techniques I've observed over the past few years. Plus, his candidate is not all that fast on his feet. If I have an answer for you, it's that I plan to apply constant pressure up and down the line on Mr. Ganner, et al.; the kind of pressure that usually causes people to make mistakes."

Harrison toyed with his glass of whiskey. "You know," he drawled, "that's not bad, but I still believe you've bit off more than you can chew. Nonetheless, things may shape up in such a way that I may need to help you knock Ganner off balance.

He paused. "Holt Witherspoon is one of my oldest and dearest friends. Good friends in college and throughout our political careers. Worked closely together those years when he was in office here. Most all of that occurred before you came along, but believe me, the ties are strong."

Harrison took another sip, then paused to rub his chin. "Everybody around here is wondering who is going to win between Holt and Jordan Layman.

"Those of us in the hot spots—myself, the governor and lieutenant governor—have pledged to be neutral, in the interests of party harmony and unity, as we say. In truth, it's to protect our hides because there are going to be deep scars and wounds coming from this.

"Now, I've got a crawling hunch that skunk Ganner is going to line up with Jordan Layman. If he does, I'll help you. The more you can brush fire him with that state rep race, the less effective he'll be in the Senate contest."

"But if memory serves," Kirk said, "Ganner was tied to Witherspoon when he was governor."

"That's true, but there was a falling-out over some appointment Ganner wanted, a DA or something. Now, you better understand that when I say 'help,' don't look for much money. Any you get will be in cash, not to be reported. The deck is really stacked against you here by most of these prima donna powerbrokers who don't think you have a chance.

"And remember, they run in a pack like a bunch of hounds, hard to divert. Eventually, I might cool down their enthusiasm for Ganner's candidate, maybe shut off some money that he'd otherwise get... Keep me informed, and keep everything between us confidential, completely confidential."

Harrison initialed the drink tab, waved to the bartender, and rose to shake hands with Kirk.

This was, Kirk mused, all an act about our campaign. He showed up today only because he wants to help Holt Witherspoon.

He forced a smile. "Mr. Speaker, I understand your position, and any assistance you might provide us will be greatly appreciated."

On the following day, Kirk was gratified to have an opportunity to meet with Lonnie Hardner, editor-publisher of The Texas Progressive. Hardner had been traveling in South Texas researching a series for the magazine dealing with the problems of Mexican-Americans.

After his meeting with the Speaker in the quiet, measured atmosphere of the private Austin Club, Kirk sat down with Hardner amid numerous noisy beer drinkers under the tall elm trees at Scholz Garten.

It was a warm afternoon for February, and whenever the temperature crested seventy degrees, as it had done by a clear margin that day, the Scholz regulars insisted upon drinking outside. They enjoyed gathering around the weathered old wooden and metal tables in the vast, dusty beer garden area.

Hardner had been a crusading antiestablishment editor of the UT student newspaper while earning a Rhodes scholarship to Oxford.

Following his time in England, he worked for a liberal political journal in New York for three years before returning to Austin to found his own. In print, as well as in public and private dialogue, Hardner was militant in expressing his animosity toward "the corporate special interests that choke the life from our political process."

Over the past two years Kirk exchanged pleasantries with Hardner when their paths crossed in the Capitol, but they weren't friends or political allies. In fact, it was risky for Kirk to meet in public with Hardner, a bitter enemy of Speaker Harrison, but Kirk was running an underdog, high-risk campaign in which there would be no safe bets.

Hardner's iconoclastic magazine was the state's leading journal for liberal intellectuals and political activists. Though it had a modest circulation of only a few thousand, it had high impact in urban liberal and labor circles, and among the remnants of rural populism, the movement that had played a significant role in the state's political arena during the 1930s and 1940s.

The Progressive was always strapped for funds, but it had the ability to attract gifted writers. Hardner had burst onto the Texas scene by publishing this well-edited pulp magazine filled with hard-hitting essays, lively feature articles, and comprehensive coverage of legislative sessions and political campaigns. It was laced with poignant pictures and cartoons depicting the plight of the state's downtrodden, especially blacks and Mexican-Americans.

Targets of Hardner's fire generally tried to ignore the magazine, but when stung to the point of responding, they would denounce Hardner as a "bleeding heart liberal," "misguided egghead," "irresponsible radical," or worse.

As they sat down to share a pitcher of foamy beer, for which Hardner insisted upon paying his share, Kirk observed that Hardner was dressed casually as usual with open collar and no tie or coat.

No matter how many times Hardner might comb his brown hair or brush it back with his hand, some of the front portion always fell down over the top of his thick glasses. It was a Hardner trademark, along with the small notepad he always carried in his hip pocket.

"So, you're going to venture behind the mesquite curtain?" Hardner said.

Kirk took a long drink from his schooner. "Yes, and we need your help."

"You know, I wondered why you called me on this race. You don't have any liberal credentials."

"I'm not the candidate."

"I know, but as campaign manager, and the only major player with meaningful experience, you're going to run the race. Isn't that true?"

"Yes, except Wedge Crayton has a mind of his own and he'd be an independent thinker here in the Legislature."

"Crayton's liberal credentials are pretty thin. All I can recall is that he attended a meeting or two of the Young Progressive League when he was in law school."

"Lonnie, do you always have to run a blood test?"

"Let me make it clear. I don't do anything in the political arena unless I'm convinced it's in the best interests of the indigenous liberal movement of Texas."

"Well, Frank Ganner is the Number One indigenous oppressive patrón in the state. You know he'll expand as rapidly as we allow him to."

"Of course, I carry no brief for Ganner, but what if your candidate should win? What manner of substantive reform would he pursue?"

"Crayton would press for various reforms through legislation, but you can't campaign too hard on that and expect to win."

"That's the problem with you pragmatists—you're willing to sell out before the first major issue can be raised."

Kirk sighed. "I just wish you'd consider how this race fits into the scheme of things, the broader perspective."

"What is it you think I might do? You must know I have a meager circulation in that area."

"Yes, but staff people in the media at San Antonio, Corpus Christi, and Laredo read your magazine. If you were to key in on this race and the nature of Frank Ganner's record of corruption, it would stimulate favorable coverage that would reach into our district."

"I'll think about it," Hardner said, "but I want to hear more from your candidate than a strident anti-Ganner campaign. I want to hear of some measures to alleviate the plight of the Mexicano."

"On the Mexican-American front, I hear PAMAT may get serious about this race."

"Their leadership is in the process of considering it, and quite frankly, if they field a viable candidate, I'd probably favor that candidate ahead of yours. That is, assuming PAMAT will work, as it should, within the Democratic Party. If they wander off to form a purely ethnic movement, it's focus will be too narrow. I wouldn't favor that, even though much of their deep frustration about the political process is justified."

"Surely you don't believe a Mexican-American could win that seat?"

"What I believe about the winnability of the race isn't important. Raising significant issues is important."

Kirk reminded himself of an old line a newspaper advertising salesman had once told him, "Don't win an argument and lose a sale." He surmised that under existing circumstances, Hardner wouldn't budge on the legislative race, so he shifted to question his outlook toward the impending Senate race.

"Many people," Hardner said, "assume I will support Jordan Layman, but I'm not sure at all about that race. Layman claims to be cut from the Franklin Roosevelt cloth, but he carries more water for big business than a damned Republican would. Anytime anyone in the oil or construction industries says 'Jump!,' he says, 'How high?' I've never trusted him. He co-opts various liberal, labor, and minority elements with worthy federal programs, but come convention time, come some party showdown, and he's lined up with the fat cats."

"But you couldn't support old Witherspoon?"

"No, I couldn't. He's a reactionary, but he's a reasonably honest politician as far as I know, and I respect him for that."

"Isn't it also true," Kirk ventured, "if Layman should win and the Democrats subsequently elect a President, Layman would try to dominate federal patronage at the expense of your man, Senator Cavanaugh?"

"A point worth considering," Hardner said with furrowed brow. "Nobody knows how to seize and exercise power like Layman. Nobody. I'm sure he would undermine Cavanaugh, especially on the most important appointments, such as federal judgeships.

"Of more immediate concern, Layman would be supporting Eisenhower too much of the time. It's tragic that Stevenson lost to Eisenhower, and it's disgusting to see some of these Texas congressmen, Jordan Layman in particular, supporting Eisenhower's right wing foreign policy. They've ridden the Democratic tradition in Texas for decades, but let a popular military figure come along and they suddenly forget he's Republican. The overriding problem with Jordan Layman is that he doesn't just want to be President, it's gnawing in the pit of his stomach every day. He'll do anything at all to achieve his purpose. Anything."

"I've always believed," Kirk said, "that Jordan Layman, better than anyone in the political arena, can sniff the direction the wind will blow long before the leaves rustle."

"Perhaps," Hardner said with a note of disdain in his voice, "but I anticipate some crosscurrents will be blowing this spring. It may not be so easy for him."

Hardner downed his final drink of beer with a casual gesture. "Tell me, Holland, where do you really stand in this? Why are you giving up a good job?"

"That's my home turf. I feel strongly about it."

"But you're not playing ball with anyone in the power equation of Texas politics. Where do you go from there, win or lose?"

"Well, if you're trying to tell me this isn't the wisest career move I could make, I've already got that in mind."

Hardner rose to leave, shaking hands. "In any event, I'll have to admit that your race may develop into something interesting, perhaps significant. Keep me posted. I won't promise a thing, but I'll maintain a watch on it."

In the remaining days before returning to South Texas, Kirk worked hard at the Capitol while devoting what time he could to the campaign.

He had mailed a budget and timetable to Nellie and Wedge, calling for a total expenditure of $8,300 for the first primary, a high budget for such a race, but one he believed was necessary in order to attain their goal.

The timetable proceeded from an elaborate campaign kickoff in Justinville the third week in March, on through various spring activities and personal campaigning by Wedge, to the stretch run leading to the first primary on July 24. The final push would include an extensive advertising program in the district, bolstered by radio commercials on select stations in San Antonio, Corpus Christi, and Laredo. If a runoff became necessary, it would be held on August 28.

One way or another, Kirk and Carrie managed to see each other every night and to find a spot to make love. They didn't speak of the recent accident in Kirk's driveway, as though it hadn't occurred, but it weighed on their minds constantly as the precious time slipped by toward his departure.

On the final day, as she drove to his apartment to help him pack, a strong cold snap arrived in the form of a dry norther. Gusts of biting, twisting wind swept rapidly across Central Texas. They were alone as she helped him arrange all his belongings to fit in his car. They pursued their work with casual conversation as though it were part of a routine in a normal day.

But when they walked to his car for the final time, she burst out crying while shivering in the cold. Without speaking, he held her until she stopped sobbing. He buttoned her coat to the top and gave her a gentle kiss on the cheek, then on her lips.

He drove from the apartment and reached the Congress Avenue bridge. When he noticed in the rearview mirror that her car was approaching rapidly, his eyebrows shot up. He pulled into the parking lot of the Night Hawk restaurant. Out of breath, she raced to him and they embraced.

"I just didn't want you to remember me," she said, "in such a down mood. I'll be all right."

They went inside where they had coffee and apple pie, chatting as though they might somehow avoid the inevitable. When they returned to the parking lot, he lingered at her car.

He kissed her and held her one last, long moment. "It'll only be a month," he said, "till I'm back."

"A month. God, I'm going to miss you."

Chapter 3

Wade Keene, the veteran political writer for The San Antonio Banner-Press, arrived in Piedra Blanca about an hour before his late afternoon appointment to interview Frank Ganner.

A combat veteran of World War II, Keene had resumed his newspaper career soon after returning from Europe, where he had fought in the Battle of the Bulge, the final major episode during his long, demanding tour of duty as an enlisted man in the infantry.

He escaped physical wounds, but he came home a confirmed cynic who had lost valuable career time and the love of his sweetheart.

Thin and six feet tall, Keene stooped when walking and slumped when seated. He often appeared, as he did that day, in an old suit that needed pressing.

His dark brown eyes might seem at times to be unconcerned but were always vigilant. He spoke in a low raspy voice with a slight twisting lip motion that reminded some of Humphrey Bogart, a comparison he didn't discourage.

Keene was a heavy drinker and chain smoker who appeared to be much older than his forty years, due to his lackluster attire, debilitating personal habits, and the fact he was in the fifth year of a boring, meaningless marriage with no children.

In covering political activity, Keene had no favorites among politicians. He didn't believe political philosophy motivated them; therefore, the terms "liberal" and "conservative" meant little to him.

No matter what the façade, he believed all successful politicians were egocentric and self-serving, promoted by strategies they designed to meet the personal challenges they perceived to be confronting them. The pursuit of power motivated them all, he concluded, and the more conniving ones sought wealth along with it. Frank Ganner possessed too much of both.

Ordinarily, Keene covered San Antonio and Bexar County politics on a day-to-day basis, branching out only for traveling with statewide candidates and presidential candidates touring Texas.

He had suggested the assignment in Piedra Blanca to interview the controversial Ganner, who seldom strayed from his domain but whose political power was becoming legendary throughout the state. Keene had more in mind than a simple profile article.

It was Keene's first trip to Piedra Blanca, the county seat of Bantrell County, a dusty little town of four thousand, about eighty percent of which was Mexican-American.

Piedra Blanca, or White Rock, took its name from a map drawn in 1813 by a young Spanish officer whose detachment had come upon an abandoned Indian campsite.

Near a narrow creek bed, the officer had found a huge jagged rock that the Indians had plastered with a heavy mixture of caliche, abundant to that area, and water, forming a layer of crude sodium nitrate, which is solid white. Though it would be decades before a town was settled there, the name stayed with the location on the Spanish map.

Keene wanted to observe all he could, taking notes and pictures, before interviewing Ganner. He wasn't surprised to find that the few people who would talk to him were quick with their bland answers about the obvious, but would not answer pointed questions relating to Ganner. Most of the people lived in modest housing but some, perhaps thirty percent, lived in wooden shanties patched with tar paper and crinkled old license plates. Those wretched dwellings were built along streets of chalky caliche whose powdery white dust was kicked up by vehicles during the long days of the drouth.

As he toured the residential area near the courthouse, Keene observed some fine homes owned by Ganner's political cronies. He was struck by the magnitude of power at play when he pulled up across the street from the Ganner mansion.

The two-story Spanish style structure, with ten bedrooms, dominated a compound that covered a city block. Two huge archways were used for vehicles to enter and leave the vast area behind the house, which contained a six-car garage, servants' quarters, an arbor with a fountain, and a large swimming pool.

To his right, across the street from the compound, Keene scanned Ganner's private racetrack with stables where trainers attended to a few expensive horses.

A variety of trees—including the dominating palm, plus huisache, mesquite, and oleander—abounded on the Ganner estate, and a colorful mosaic of shrubs, flowers, and grass, notably the expansive bougainvilleas with their twisting branches of bright red and purple, appeared to be flourishing and well kept.

Two big sleek hunting dogs meandered quietly near the archways, the type of dogs that could chase down a scared coyote or tree an angry mountain lion.

I'll bet, he thought, they would corner a stranger in a hurry if he ventured into their territory unannounced by Ganner or his designated few.

From the mansion, Keene drove to the Corral Cafe, a small, one-story frame building across the street from the courthouse. Inside, he ordered coffee, placed his snap-brim felt hat on the counter, loosened his tie, and lit a cigarette. When a young waitress brought his coffee, he said, "You've almost got a full house. Doesn't look like the drouth is hurting business at all."

"There's mostly 'doodlebuggers' in here now. You know, seismograph people. The ones who hunt for oil. Their truck broke down today, but the drouth don't bother 'em."

"Tell me, why is it there are no hotels or motels in this town?"

The waitress giggled. "I guess it's 'cause if you're not staying over with Frank or one of his friends, you're not welcome to stay over."

Keene stirred his coffee. "Does everyone around here refer to him as 'Frank'?"

"Sure. He's a nice, polite man. He doesn't have the big head. He likes for everybody to call him 'Frank.'"

Keene, the cynic who seldom smiled, chuckled while removing some old clippings from a file he had retrieved at the newspaper morgue.

Hell, he thought, I'm glad I don't have to write about his old man's record. Nobody would believe some of that stuff these days.

The faded articles detailed how the late Ernie Ganner had built the economic and political foundation his son inherited. The elder Ganner started as a low-paid cowhand, but he learned fast about ranching and ranchers, whose wealth controlled the politics of the region.

Ernie was more perceptive than most of his Anglo friends involved in politics. He spoke fluent Spanish and easily befriended Mexican-Americans, both the wealthy few and the numerous poor.

When issues arose along purely ethnic lines, Ernie was the only Anglo leader always aligned with his Spanish-speaking friends. Such bold posturing built strong bonds of loyalty which formed the matrix of the enduring Ganner political machine.

As Ernie's power increased to the point that he took control of the Bantrell County Courthouse, controversy shadowed him. But he seemed to live a charmed political life.

Taxpayers were constantly sniping at him, questioning why funds were allegedly kicked back or otherwise misused, but Ernie was always an elusive target.

When an opposing faction finally constructed a strong legal case requiring an audit of county records, the original courthouse mysteriously burned down, destroying all the evidence.

Ernie, who became a state senator, once decided to double his power and influence by starting the process of creating a new county in which he could decide who would be elected to the courthouse offices. But at the last moment an obscure but concise provision in the Texas Constitution derailed his scheme that even his friendly district judge couldn't construe in Ernie's favor.

Ernie also learned how to play regional politics, often in league with a neighboring political boss, Will Dodd, and with the Maldonado family, who controlled two nearby counties, closer to the Gulf Coast.

Old Ernie was a rough cowhand who achieved tremendous power. He wanted to pass on the reins of his hard-won empire as soon as practicable to his precocious young son, Frank, but Ernie also came to appreciate the value of education.

He sent Frank to the University of Texas at Austin, where he studied law. Not long thereafter, the changing of the guard was underway when Ernie installed Frank as county judge at age twenty-five, with full confidence in his ability. From that spot, he was able to control all aspects of the county government as he presided over the Commissioners Court, which was comprised of four representatives known as Commissioners, each serving his or her own portion of the county.

Twenty-six years later, long after Ernie's death, Frank Ganner was firmly in control of the empire, constantly seeking more wealth and political power.

Keene strolled to his car to leave the file and get another pack of cigarettes. He looked over to the Bantrell County Courthouse where he was to meet Ganner. As Keene scanned the sturdy building of faded buff brick, it appeared more like a modest four-story schoolhouse than the bastion of Frank Ganner's immense power. Twelve steps led to the front entrance which was flanked by towering flagpoles displaying the American and Texas flags. Grass was dry and sparse on the grounds, but a few large palm trees and numerous oleanders appeared to be in good condition.

Few people, Keene mused, would ever believe this simple structure is the citadel of the vast wealth and power amassed by the Ganner family, the headquarters which taxes wealthy absentee landowners of the county, much of whose tax money goes as Ganner chooses to route it.

The courthouse was also the nucleus of the political machine which controlled the awarding of various jobs and contracts and accounted for every poll tax issued to a prospective voter, including stacks of poll taxes for voters controlled by Ganner himself. These "friends" of Ganner provided him insurance since they were sure to vote as he wished, helping him provide margins of eighty or ninety percent for candidates he supported: local, state, and national.

Keene ambled across the street to Ganner's office in the courthouse where Ganner presided as judge over the commissioners court. The four commissioners had departed a few moments earlier so Ganner wouldn't keep Keene waiting for his appointment. In keeping with the decor of the courthouse, the office was clean and comfortable, but not expensively adorned. Ganner also maintained private offices across the street and a large study-office in his nearby palatial home.

Never having met Ganner, Keene had conjured up a picture of a big South Texas political boss in western garb, probably wearing a Stetson indoors. Instead, after clearance by a secretary and bodyguard, a well-groomed, middle-aged man in double-breasted suit and fashionable tie, wearing contemporary thin-framed glasses greeted Keene.

Ganner's only concession to western dress that day was his pair of fine boots, a major element of his standard attire, and whose elevation helped him stand five feet ten inches. A broad smile and penetrating blue eyes dominated his slightly wrinkled face, with a neatly combed receding hairline, prompting Keene to think Ganner appeared more like a prosperous sales manager than a hard-nosed South Texas patrón.

But as they shook hands and sat down, Keene sensed a hint of arrogance behind the façade of pleasant confidence, the kind of arrogance Keene loved to attack.

On the wall behind Ganner's desk hung large pictures of Franklin Roosevelt and Harry Truman, with photos of various Texas politicians, including autographed ones of Jordan Layman and Holt Witherspoon flanking them.

Keene figured Ganner knew he would be in for some tough questioning, but agreed to this interview because he didn't want the largest circulation daily newspaper in South Texas to claim he had refused the meeting. The mere knowledge that a Banner-Press reporter was in Piedra Blanca that day had set the town buzzing, to which Ganner referred as he settled into his swivel chair behind his large wooden desk.

"You should have told me you wanted a tour of the town."

"I generally prefer working alone on such as that," Keene said, snapping a candid shot of Ganner behind his desk.

"Well," Ganner said with the smile still intact, "rest assured I'll be happy to show you around anytime. I have nothing to hide."

"Good, then I'd like to ask a few, ah… pointed questions," Keene said, laying aside his camera to retrieve a notepad. He proceeded to spar around with several mundane questions about Ganner's admiration for his father, the pervasive nature of the drouth, and how fortunate Piedra Blanca was to be located on the railroad between Corpus Christi and Laredo.

Then, he moved into high gear. "You've been described variously as 'The Baron of Bantrell,' 'a benevolent Brush Country dictator,' and 'the all-time most powerful political boss of South Texas'… Tell me, how do you perceive yourself?"

Ganner chuckled, taking a drink of the iced strawberry soda his secretary had served him while bringing coffee for Keene. "I don't care anything about titles. The truth is, I don't really have a lot of power. I have a lot of friends."

Keene glanced at his notepad. "I've calculated that with your influence in this county and over into Will Dodd County, you control about fifteen thousand votes. That's a lot of friends."

"I've arranged jobs for a lot of people. I've paid all sorts of bills for them—birth, death, and in-between. Many of these people can't afford hospital bills. They come to me, and I help. They've become loyal friends."

"What about poll taxes? Do you actually buy poll taxes for people and tell them how to vote?"

Ganner leaned back in his chair, gesturing casually with his right hand. "What's a dollar and fifty cents to you and me? Not much. To many of these people, it's real money. It's pay for three hours of working and sweating in that sweltering sun. What do they do with it?

"For the mother of a family, that's a sack of groceries—potatoes, beans, flour, salt, and maybe something special like eggs or candy. For the man, a buck and a half will buy six bottles of cold beer at his favorite cantina with money left over for the jukebox and to play pool.

"You think that's not something he's gonna dream about all day long toward the end of the week when he gets paid. They're not gonna give up that or the sack of groceries for a little piece of paper about which they understand practically nothing. Sure, I help some of 'em now and then. It's democratic."

"What about complaints that most, if not all, county funds to be deposited wind up in the Piedra Blanca State Bank, which you own?"

"Well, I'm going to keep the money in Bantrell County, where our citizens will benefit from it. What's wrong with that?"

"The fact that it's the only bank in town doesn't bother you? Isn't that a conflict of interest?"

Ganner chuckled. "If somebody else wants to put a bank in Piedra Blanca, he's welcome to try."

"There have been some strong complaints about how property is evaluated and taxed. I tried to call the tax assessor-collector two or three times, but he never returned my call."

"I speak for the county," Ganner snapped, "and no legal actions are pending against the county at this time. There's nothing to discuss."

Undaunted, Keene continued. "Well, I've been talking to some of the big landowners of your county who live elsewhere. Seems as though they aren't too pleased with what might be termed, 'high taxation without representation.' They contend their land is assessed and taxed at much higher rates than the land owned by you and your compadres."

"If they're so unhappy," Ganner said as he smiled, "they ought to move here and vote. Or they ought to sell their land. I'll buy any of it at fair market price. For sure, I intend to acquire more land."

"More than fifty thousand acres? Why?"

"More land, more cattle to run. Also, for my family and friends, more land to hunt deer, wild turkey, dove and quail. They gather around what we call a 'tank' and you call a 'stock pond.' Tanks are filled with bass and catfish. And we have to contend with coyotes and rattlesnakes.

"Keene, you live in the city – San Antonio. You know little about rural counties other than they provide the steak you like now and then, or cows that squirt the milk kids like to drink. Goat milk tastes better and makes better candy."

Keene had to pause, a bit caught off guard. He lit another cigarette, but returned to his cynical probe.

"What about recent actions against the school district for misappropriation of funds?"

"I'm not an official of the school district."

"But it's run by your, as you term them, 'loyal friends.'"

"It doesn't matter. I'm not speaking for the school district. Those officials happen to be in Mexico on a fishing trip."

"When they're in town, is some of their leisure time spent at illegal cockfights?"

Ganner half-smiled. "Now, we don't go around snooping in every barn and corral in the county. If some of that goes on, it's just a little valuable recreation for hard-working citizens, the way I see it. Besides, roosters like to fight."

Keene rubbed his forehead, pausing to glance at a note, reminding himself not to give Ganner the satisfaction of creating a cloud of frustration. "I also," he continued, "tried to reach the sheriff to inquire about allegations that some gambling and prostitution have been going on in this county. He never returned my calls."

Without changing his expression, Ganner leaned back in his chair. "You know, if I spent much time worrying about gossip and rumors, I wouldn't get a whole helluva lot accomplished."

"It so happens I interviewed a man who claims to have been to a place in this county, unmarked and unlighted from the outside, where he said gambling was in progress and women were available for a price."

"You tell that man, whoever he is, to come see me, or the sheriff, and make a complaint about this 'place,' if indeed it exists."

"Well, I'll have to admit you have a reputation for keeping the peace in this county, but often at a price. I understand there's something of a pistolero syndrome among your law enforcement people. They're likely to apply a little justice on the spot."

Ganner chuckled. "You know, every now and then a young Anglo buck or a 'pachuco' will puff too much marijuana, or drink too much beer, and get smart alecky with our officers of the law.

"If a little force is used to subdue these people, it's no different than the value of a teacher disciplining a disrespectful student right there on the spot. People in a beer joint or cantina are like kids in a classroom. If they see what happens for misbehavior, they tend to behave better."

"So much for due process."

"It's perfectly legal," Ganner said in a casual tone. "Every complaint of alleged brutality has been set aside by the state district judge who presides here in this courthouse."

If it weren't so flagrant and serious, Keene thought, it would be laughable.

The judge of a state district court was an elective office and the presiding judge in Ganner's courthouse was there because Ganner had applied influence in the Legislature for the creation of a new state judicial district for his bailiwick.

Of course, the judge became one of his most trusted cronies, along with the district attorney. All public officeholders in Bantrell County were directly dependent upon Frank Ganner.

"I understand you have a way of charging an unofficial franchise tax on local businessmen."

"Mr. Keene, because of my success as a political figure, I've picked up my share of enemies. They spread lies and rumors about me all the time. I've never seen any evidence presented about such as you imply."

"Is that because you're dealing mostly in cash?"

Ganner's eyes grew cold as he trained them upon Keene. He resisted the temptation to curse him as he clasped his hands upon his desk, leaning forward slightly. "You know better than to ask a question like that. If that's what you have in mind, then this interview is over."

Keene paused, lighting a cigarette. "Well then, all right, what are your sources of income? You didn't build that mansion and racetrack on hopes and dreams."

"Most of my income is derived from my ranch, inherited from my father. It's fifty thousand acres and blessed with some oil and gas production."

"Some people have said you thrive on controversy. There was a lot of publicity about your confrontation with a Texas Ranger right here in this courthouse. Looking back on it, don't you think it would have been better to have tried to keep things calm, rather than threaten a law enforcement officer?"

"Bantrell County," Ganner snapped, "is a political subdivision of the State of Texas. I'm the county judge and I run the county. Unless I receive directions from the governor or the attorney general, I'm going to run things as I see fit. That damned Ranger had no business meddling in our affairs and I so informed him."

"And he informed you he did have authority. Why risk going to jail over something like that?"

"Some of the press blew up a minor incident involving a few 'mojados,' wetbacks. It was something I could have handled without interference."

"I understand you have a lot of illegal aliens working on your ranch for such princely sums as a dollar a day."

"My foreman keeps the records," Ganner growled.

"Are you saying you don't know what they're paid?"

"Well, wage scale is one thing. I provide housing, food, and medical care. I only monitor the overall costs, which are considerable."

Keene flipped his notepad, furrowed his brow, and, after taking another drag from his cigarette, pursued his questioning into the political arena. "Who will you support if a contest develops between Holt Witherspoon and Jordan Layman for the Senate?"

"I never answer hypothetical questions."

"But won't this be an opportunity for you to extend your influence to a U.S. Senator, which you haven't quite been able to manage in the past?"

"My answer doesn't change."

"After Eisenhower, the Democrats might well elect one of theirs. Then that U.S. Senator would figure into some important patronage, choosing federal judges at the top of the list. Now, doesn't such a proposition sound rather enticing to a controversial political figure who winds up under legal scrutiny now and then?"

"You ought to be a courtroom lawyer, Mr. Keene. You're good at badgering and hounding. But if you really think you're going to get me to commit publicly on a U.S. Senate race that isn't even a race yet, then you've been hitting some bad tequila."

Keene's habit was never to ease the pace of his questioning. "All right, but what about state representative? I've encountered the same problem about returning calls with Ned Felder, the incumbent, as I did with your sheriff and tax assessor-collector."

"Apparently, Felder has a health problem."

"Sure, we all know that, but is it of the nature to prevent him from seeking reelection?"

"You'll have to ask him."

"Well, if he can't or won't run, who would you support?"

"There's another one of those 'iffy' questions. I'm not concerned about it now. I'm sure that whoever represents the district next session will be a responsible member of the Legislature."

"You know, a lot of people outside your domain in this state rep district won't appreciate it one bit if you handpick their new representative before the election."

Ganner pursed his lips. "Handpick? It's an open primary. Anyone who can pay the filing fee can run. I understand a young fellow from Justinville wants to run."

"So I hear, along with perhaps a candidate from the upstart Mexican-American outfit, a candidate who would present you with quite a challenge. Now let's quit beating around the bush. I'd bet my car title that Felder's not going to run, and I hear you're going to run one of your cronies, Wally Hooper."

"You'll have—"

"To ask him. Well, I called your man Hooper and believe it or not, he did return the call. A man of independence and integrity. But I'll concede you'd have been proud of him, because all he would say about his potential candidacy was, 'No comment.' You may need to coach him though. To four or five questions, he stayed with 'No comment,' but the tone of his voice sounded like he's running."

Unaccustomed to such an abrupt interruption and to the persistent needling, Ganner had to take a long breath in an effort to hold his temper. As he exhaled, he trained his eyes upon Keene and pointed his right forefinger toward the reporter, whose implacable expression hadn't changed during the course of the interview.

"Now," Ganner said in a sharp tone, "I'm going off the record to tell you something! You and your goddamn newspaper can go straight to hell as far as I'm concerned! I can't believe you drove all the way down here to pry into my personal business and badger me about a state representative race that isn't even a race. I want to wrap up this so-called interview. I've got better things to do."

Keene shrugged, again without changing expression. "Well, let's stay off the record and I'll give you a little advice. This state representative race is of particular interest to my newspaper because we so rarely see a meaningful political contest in this part of the state. I sense something developing that's significant, newsworthy. For your own standing as a political leader, you'd be better off cooperating with the news media instead of trying to hoodwink us by playing all your little shell games. Aren't you the least bit concerned about adverse publicity?"

Regaining his composure, Ganner said in a crisp tone, "If I were afraid of bad publicity, I'd have gotten out of politics a long time ago."

"What are you afraid of, Mr. Ganner?" Keene said, closing his notepad.

"Not much of anything."

After Keene departed, Ganner ran through a stack of county documents while taking a few phone calls. When two of his political associates dropped by for a brief meeting, he closed his day's business at the courthouse by dismissing his secretary and bodyguard.

He drove a few blocks to a small two-story brick building which contained the administrative offices for the school district. From the secretary-treasurer, he picked up ten checks, including the largest for himself in the amount of $1,500. These were for "consulting fees," listed on the record as a series of meetings, but in reality, he had called only one two-hour session with the school board to discuss renovation of the gymnasium.

Ganner always insisted upon handing out the other checks to his cronies in person as a means of always reminding them that he, not the school board, was the true source that provided them with this windfall income, vast overpayment for minor services rendered. Each year, Ganner managed to siphon from school district funds at least $40,000 for himself and his pals.

As he departed the school district office, a longtime assistant foreman at his ranch who had retired several years ago and moved to town, Erasmo Cantu, approached him on the sidewalk.

Visibly shaken, Cantu stammered in broken English.

"Dígame en español, compadre," Ganner said, placing his hand upon the elderly man's shoulder.

"Díos mio, mi esposa está muy enferma," Cantu said with a grave expression, "y ya viene el doctor. ¿Puede ayudarme?"

Ganner motioned for Cantu to get in his car and drove to the small frame home where he found the town's only physician, old Dr. Haines, at the bedside of Mrs. Cantu in a cramped, dimly lit bedroom. Ganner asked the doctor to step outside to the porch. "Can you save her?"

"I think so, but it's pneumonia, advanced. She needs to be in the hospital in Corpus Christi. Now."

"What will it cost?"

"At least two hundred dollars."

Ganner, who always carried about five hundred dollars in cash, summoned Cantu to the porch, and then he pulled two one hundred dollar bills and a fifty from his wallet and handed them to him.

"If it takes more," Ganner said to the doctor, "let me know."

Ganner drove to his private office across the street from the courthouse, located in a one-story building near the cafe. There he was scheduled to meet with his unofficial junior partner, Alfonso (Al) Hernandez.

But first, Ganner walked into his own spacious paneled office, flung his coat onto a rack, and loosened his tie. He settled into his soft leather chair behind a huge mahogany desk with new telephone, silver-plated pen and pencil set, adding machine, calendar, and wooden in-and-out basket. He had just finished thumbing through a stack of mail when Al Hernandez appeared with a couple of cold beers.

Al Hernandez had grown up with Frank Ganner, almost as a brother. He was a descendent of a prominent ranching family in Northern Mexico that fled to South Texas in the late 1800s to escape the chronic political instability of their native land.

The Hernandez family did well at ranching and began building on that good fortune by aligning with Ernie Ganner at the outset of his political career.

The transition to Frank Ganner was natural and complete. There were no written or verbal agreements between Frank Ganner and Al Hernandez. It was simply understood that, ultimately, Ganner called the shots.

However, Hernandez was far from a passive ally. He never hesitated to challenge Ganner when he grew uneasy about some questionable deal, nor did he shy away from offering initiatives and alternatives to Ganner's ideas.

As one of the four county commissioners, he was privy to all relevant information in the courthouse. He took an active role in dispensing jobs, including those for his family members and friends who hadn't been able to make a living in business endeavors or ranching.

Hernandez understood the policies, threads, and nuances involved in maintaining the vast power that Ganner exercised, and since they had operated like compatible brothers over the years, the other participants within the machine and the public saw nothing but a united front.

Some Anglo South Texans, living outside Ganner's domain, sniped about Hernandez as being "a pawn of the Anglos," but in his role on Ganner's turf, he had it going both ways. The Anglos accepted him as close to the throne while the Mexican-Americans feared and respected him because he possessed wealth and power.

In Piedra Blanca, where there was no middle class, Hernandez wore a flashy diamond ring, worth more than most of the workers earned in a decade, one strong symbol of dominance to all with whom he came in contact.

Like Ganner, he drove a big late model, air-conditioned Oldsmobile, also well beyond the dreams of most workers, and he lived in the second largest house in town. He was aristocratic, but not arrogant. He was a brown-eyed, dark-skinned "Mexicano" of the indigenous Northern Mexico-South Texas variety, who, with Ganner, mingled well among the people at the weddings, funerals, church functions, athletic events, rodeos, and other activities that drew a crowd. He was a key link in Ganner's tight chain of power.

Hernandez was of about equal height to Ganner, but he appeared younger, with a full head of black hair and few wrinkles on his face. His deep brown eyes were always alert, but he was prone to be less engaging than Ganner and more reflective, though not shy.

Behind the desk in his large office adjoining Ganner's hung his undergraduate and law degrees from St. Mary's University in San Antonio, illustrating his family's commitment to the Catholic tradition.

Hernandez recalled that when the time for decisions about college were to be made, he was frustrated by his family's choice because Ganner was being sent to the University of Texas at Austin where exposure to various cultures and ideas was greater.

But after returning to Piedra Blanca, Hernandez said to Ganner, "You know, we're both caught in a provincial web woven by our fathers. I wish I hadn't even bothered to attend college."

Ganner said, "Yeah, but we'll live a lot better than if we hadn't. We're going to make a lot of money and maybe a little history, and enjoy every bit of it."

Hernandez felt a sharp pang of guilt the first time he witnessed a shady act Ganner committed. As county judge, he steered a large road and bridge construction contract to a contractor from Houston who had promised a "campaign contribution" to Ganner of $20,000 in cash. Ganner had no opponent and wouldn't have any, so the money would be pocketed with a slice allocated to each commissioner.

Stung by the flagrant nature of the act, Hernandez confronted Ganner. "You had no right to do that. You've given him a cost-plus contract. It should have been put out for bids."

"Right? Bids?" Ganner shrugged. "What do you think our fathers sacrificed for? We take risks and carry a lot of responsibility just as they did, and we deserve appropriate compensation. Now, there's nothing wrong about something like this, so long as we can handle it… There's three thousand each for you and the other commissioners. Tax-free. I'm only taking eight. That's a damn good deal, don't you think?"

Hernandez understood that if he went along that first time, he would be hooked. He thought again of his late father's prolonged, close association with Frank's father, and of the many obligations to his immediate family, with wife and two children and another on the way.

He thought of his uncles, brothers, and cousins in need of what could be generated from the courthouse. The idea of picking up three thousand dollars for nothing was indeed tempting, but also sobering.

That was all the take-home pay his younger sister had received for teaching the entire past school year. But his only alternative was to practice law in Piedra Blanca, where his and his wife's taproots were embedded, a poor alternative without the blessing of Frank Ganner.

He accepted the three thousand dollars.

Thereafter, Ganner formed his own construction company, making it easier and less risky to manipulate county and school district funds in order for him and his cadre to realize maximum benefit.

For years, Ganner had been wheeling and dealing with practically no restraints, taking care of his cronies and constituents, enjoying ever-increasing sources of income and extending his political influence all the way into the White House.

As he maneuvered and manipulated, Ganner's cavalier attitude toward authority at last caught up with him. He had become too careless, collecting tremendous unreported sums that the Internal Revenue Service began to trace, resulting in a conviction and prison term for income tax evasion. After serving only one year of an eight-year sentence, Ganner returned to Piedra Blanca, ever defiant of authority other than that held by him and his "friends."

Soon, his civil rights were restored, including the right to hold public office, by virtue of a presidential pardon. When the term of his stand-in as county judge ended, Ganner was easily reelected. He had resumed full command, operating in much the same manner as before except for more carefully avoiding "paper trails" as much as possible, dealing mostly in cash.

On that balmy winter day in Piedra Blanca, Hernandez watched from his office window as Wade Keene departed for San Antonio. His mind wandered briefly over the past twenty-six hard-driving years with Frank Ganner.

Not so much regretting the experience, but becoming more circumspect about his life as one is prone to do after recently cresting fifty and recognizing that there isn't much more remaining to accomplish or change.

Yet, he mused, he must stay alert constantly because Ganner arose each day with an insatiable desire to protect and expand his empire, still willing, almost anxious, to take risks every step of the way.

Ganner was reading the Corpus Christi newspaper at his desk when Hernandez gave him a beer and inquired about the interview with Keene.

Before responding, Ganner handed a school district check to Hernandez in the amount of $500, compensation to the legal counsel for sitting in on the meeting Ganner had called to discuss renovation of the gymnasium. It would be listed on the records as "extensive consultation regarding important improvements for the school system."

Tossing the newspaper aside, Ganner said of Keene, "He's a smart aleck sonofabitch and nothing good will come of that interview."

"Drive you into any corners?"

"Nah, but he's on to Weedman's operation. Tell him to close it down until further notice."

"He's got quite a little investment out there. What if he balks?"

"I'll have him thrown in jail! Look, that damned reporter is going to write something about gambling and prostitution in Bantrell County. Just tell Weedman to shut down a while. It'll blow over soon if there's no evidence. Besides, that's no great moneymaker. What are we taking from it?"

"Six hundred a month, always in cash. No trail at all."

"Yeah, sure, I remember. Well, it doesn't matter that much. May be better off without it. I don't care what you do, but close it down for a while."

Hernandez knew Ganner had become bored with the subject. Assuring him the operation would be closed until further notice, he shifted in his chair, glancing at figures on his legal pad relating to various business interests.

He reported that cash flow—and it was indeed mostly in cash—was steady from the several businesses that paid Ganner for the privilege of doing business in his county. It was a large sum, almost equal to Ganner's income from oil and gas production on his ranch.

It was sufficient to maintain his millionaire status, insulated as much as possible from the Internal Revenue Service and the effects of prolonged drouth.

In fact, from such a strong financial position, Ganner had found the drouth presented him with splendid opportunities to buy cattle and land from the less fortunate, holding the cattle until the day the drouth ended and the market soared.

Hernandez' mood was upbeat while discussing business. Yet Ganner detected the voice of his friend turning cautious.

"I received a couple of calls today from our people, wondering what's going to happen in the Senate race and where we will stand."

"Hell, tell 'em to quit sitting around wondering and work harder. We don't stand anywhere until there's a race; and even then, I'm not so sure we want to commit early on."

"I agree. This is one where every bit of leverage may be important."

"You know, over the weekend I got calls from Jordan Layman and Holt Witherspoon. They both want my support, but they want it quietly, on election day, with no prior public endorsement. Man, you talk about a couple of coyotes. Some old politician once said, 'Stay out of the kitchen if you can't stand the heat.' Those guys want the roast beef, potatoes, and peach cobbler without paying the cook."

"So, you're going to temporize?"

"Yeah, it looks like it's going to be a close race, and I need to think it through carefully. Then, I want a strong commitment before I take sides. A clear understanding about what I will expect. I'm sick of some of those damned Republican president's people still masquerading as Democrats, naming the federal judges. That's for starters in this race because the real Democrats will elect the next President and we want our say about who gets the judgeships in South Texas. That's critical."

"How do you see the race shaping up?"

Ganner studied the wall a moment as though some new information might be forthcoming from the mahogany panels. "The major indicators point to Witherspoon," he said with a sigh, "but I've got a hunch Jordan Layman will be riding hard in this one. He's hungry, and this might be his last shot since he has to give up his seat in Congress."

Hernandez flipped a sheet on his legal pad. "I also received a call today from a newspaper editor in the state rep district. He said that Wedge Crayton of Justinville is going to run."

"Yeah, I got calls to that effect from Austin and in the district. What do you know about this kid?"

"A guy who became county judge at twenty-five," Hernandez said with a smirk, "shouldn't call Crayton 'a kid.' He's thirty, and he's bright, handsome, and wealthy. But no civic background and no political experience whatsoever, and none in his family."

"That's sorta the picture I got. He's a lightweight, but I don't like the idea of his getting in there now. I thought Felder could keep others from getting in until near the filing deadline."

"Well, we did all we could. I suspect they found out about Felder's health or maybe this is just a very ambitious young man."

"My contact in Austin said Judge Holland's son is involved. Probably manage the campaign. I'm damn glad." Ganner smiled. "That Judge Holland is dead and gone. He'd be nothing but trouble in this race."

"What makes you think his son won't be?"

"He hasn't lived in the district for years. Whatever experience and contacts he has will apply only to Retama County, same place his candidate lives."

"I'm not that concerned about Crayton against our candidate in a two-man race," Hernandez said, "but I hear that PAMAT may field a candidate. That, I wouldn't like at all."

"Why the hell would they do a stupid thing like that?"

"They're mostly young bucks in that organization. They're not nearly as grateful for what's been accomplished."

"Don't tell me you think any of our people would break ranks for some Mexicano kid from a new organization?"

"Not in Bantrell or Will Dodd, but in the other five counties, who knows? Things are changing. Younger people are more demanding, Anglo and Mexicano."

Ganner stared at Hernandez. "Do everything you can," he said in a stern tone resembling a command, "to keep those PAMAT firebrands on the shelf, or get 'em on our side."

Hernandez sighed, rubbing his chin. "Sure."

Ganner and Hernandez adjourned for dinner at Ganner's mansion where they were to be joined by Wally Hooper, Ganner's handpicked candidate in the state representative race soon to unfold. After arriving, they were soon enjoying ice-cold beer when Hooper joined them.

Portly and patronizing, Hooper was a middle-aged lawyer who had distinguished himself only by his loyalty to Ganner during stints as school board member, county attorney, and president of the Chamber of Commerce. To Ganner's few detractors, Hooper was known as "the palace hack," unimaginative but fairly effective in serving the monarch, and enough of a shrewd country lawyer to keep his skirts relatively clean.

Though Ganner rewarded Hooper's loyalty, he was not personally close to Hooper, who often nettled him by telling corny jokes or dull stories while constantly wiping sweat from his brow, even in wintertime.

The balding, squat Hooper spoke only limited Spanish with an Anglo accent, but as a political candidate in the Ganner scheme of things, he could count on almost total support among the voters of Bantrell and Will Dodd counties.

Ganner motioned to the cooler where Pearl and Lone Star longnecks were iced down. Hooper opened a bottle of Pearl, sat down, and gestured toward Ganner with his open left hand. "I guess you all have heard that there's a young man named Wedge Crayton from Justinville getting into the race."

"Yeah," Ganner said, "so we'll move our timetable up a little. Now, you need to get this straight, Wally, and I mean real straight. When you are asked about my involvement, here's the way I want you to handle it: 'Sure, I know Frank Ganner, but I don't expect him to take an active role in this race. Matson Pace is chairman of my campaign committee, and all inquiries, and so forth, should be directed to me or him.' Don't stray off that line. Understand?"

"I'm glad you brought it up, Frank. They'll probably try to make you the issue."

"Sure they will, but if my tracks aren't in your campaign, it will be hard for 'em to make it stick. Now, I worked out a deal today with Matson, gave him five thousand in cash. If and when you need more, it'll be there, but it will all go through Matson and he'll work up the reports so I'll never be implicated."

"That sounds fine," Hooper said, wiping his brow. "Any more word on what Jordan Layman and Holt Witherspoon are likely to do?"

"Yeah," Ganner said, "they're both running, as far as I can tell. That'll raise the voter turnout some, but I'm not worried about it."

"It won't help me," Hooper said, "not in those other counties."

"Look," Ganner snapped, "that kid ought to win his home county, Retama. You can win all the others. Most of the people who vote for Layman or Witherspoon will vote for you if you run a smart campaign. Remember, whatever I do in the Senate race shouldn't hurt your campaign."

"Well, I certainly hope you're right... I, uh, also hear this new Mexicano group might try to field a candidate. That would sure split things up."

"It's too early to tell," Hernandez said. "I'll be working on that situation."

"Frank," Hooper said in a defensive tone, "I surely hate to keep bringing up problems, but what do you think that reporter from the

Banner-Press is going to do?"

Ganner shook his head. "Shit, Wally, why worry about something like that? Let's see what the sonofabitch writes before you start wringing your hands."

Hooper brushed his forehead again. "Sure, okay, I just hope, I mean I want to get the campaign off on a positive note."

"Listen," Ganner barked, "you need to start getting your law business schedule subordinated to a campaign schedule and make plans to tour the district, the other counties, four or five times between now and the primary. You're a good trial lawyer. Stick to the same little speech, God and South Texas. Shake enough hands, spread enough money and promises around, and you'll do just fine. Pick up checks in restaurants, especially those for businessmen and ranchers. Tell all of 'em you'll never vote to raise their taxes."

He raised his forefinger as if to poke Wally's chest. "You gotta tell teachers you'll work to get all the state money you can for their schools. Buy rounds in the beer joints and cantinas. You won't get many votes there, but if you don't show up and spread money in those places, they'll brand you as a snob. Absent a Mexicano candidate, we ought to win this race with fifty-seven to sixty percent of the vote. Just don't let this young buck Crayton draw you into any embarrassing situations. Don't make joint appearances. Steer clear of him. The only way he would win is for you to beat yourself."

"But," Hooper said in a self-confident tone, "I know more about county and state government than this young fellow will ever know. I'd like the opportunity to prove that before the people of the district by debating him."

Ganner again shook his head. "Look, you've got political and civic credentials this kid doesn't have. Use 'em, but just remember, you've never been in a tough campaign, a real contest. You're talking like a lawyer who's going to outpoint his opposition in a courtroom. Out there on the campaign trail, people look at a lot more—or I should say less—than finely tuned arguments."

Hernandez, who had been listening carefully, decided to weigh in on Hooper's side. "Frank, your observation about people looking at other than issues is well taken," he said, gesturing lightly with his left hand toward Ganner, "but that prompts me to believe our opponent, unchallenged, might have an advantage among undecided voters. They'll see a handsome, intelligent young man dedicated to making an effective voice in the legislature. If Wally doesn't expose Crayton's lack of knowledge, who will?"

Ganner chuckled. "You two sound like high school students in a civics class. If we put Wally up there on display with young Crayton, the contest becomes Porky Pig versus Clark Gable."

Hernandez smiled while Hooper winced.

"I'm telling you," Ganner continued, "the way I read the voting records of those counties, we'll win a two-man race by a decisive margin if you don't wander off track."

Ganner's stunning young wife, Alicia, interrupted them. She invited them to the cavernous dining hall where Ganner sat at the head of the long mahogany table, flanked by Hernandez and Hooper. She usually sat at the other end, but with only four dining at the table which seated twenty comfortably, she indicated she would sit next to Hernandez, following a quick trip to the kitchen to summon servants.

The men settled at the table beneath an intricate antique chandelier, acquired in New Orleans, that had once burned whale oil. Soft light from the various small bulbs made the shadows from the men and chairs meld with folds in rich red drapes and along lines in the dark floor tile under brick walls connected by heavy exposed beams. No mounted animal heads, paintings, nor adornments of any kind hung on the walls. It had all been designed to create an aura of subdued opulence, made possible by unlimited resources having been spent with the goal of reflecting Ganner's unique place in his community.

As she glided toward the kitchen, Hernandez again marveled at Alicia's stoic demeanor and lithe body. She wore no makeup except for dark red lipstick, and her black dress was simple, but in good taste, clinging softly to her firm body. Her hair was swept back into a bun, highlighting the sharply defined hairline close to the eyes, so prevalent among Hispanic women. Her large brown eyes were warm, yet alert, conveying a sense of understanding and control for the vast household over which she was the director, with the unquestioned support of Ganner. She was only twenty-four, twenty-seven years younger than Ganner, but there appeared to be profound love between them.

It was, Hernandez reflected, quite a change from the long days leading up to the divorce between Ganner and his first wife, an Anglo woman who had borne him a daughter. But Ganner took care of them well, providing generous financing and some property.

During the three years of their marriage, Alicia had proven to be calm and steadfast, able to cope with those few occasions when Ganner lost his temper at home over some matter she might consider trivial. She was a native of Piedra Blanca and somehow sensed how to deal with the legend with whom she lived, yet she understood little about the nature of his financial dealings or maneuvering in the political arena.

"What the hell makes Frank work sixteen hours a day after all these years?" Hernandez recalled an old friend of theirs asking recently. He was visiting from the West Coast after a long absence.

To which he had said, "Frank has wealth, power, and a beautiful, understanding woman. He's always protecting them. Wouldn't you?"

As Alicia returned from the kitchen, Hernandez seated her and they relaxed, awaiting a dinner of indigenous South Texas food. Two servants, who spoke only Spanish, soon appeared with dishes containing carne guisada, small chunks of beef broiled in a tasty sauce; cheese enchiladas with onion cooked in them and sprinkled lightly on top; and homemade tamales in slightly greasy corn shucks, the only way Ganner and Hernandez would eat them.

In addition, bowls were served containing guacamole, made with fresh avocados cut only moments before serving; boiled frijoles, known among Anglos as pinto beans; gently steamed rice; and salsa picante, from both red and green peppers. Stacks of steaming tortillas, flour and corn, were served in small straw baskets covered by cloth to keep them warm. Ordinarily, butter was not served with tortillas, but it was on the table in deference to their Anglo guest.

She knew the men would probably prefer beer, which was available, but she also gave them a choice of iced tea.

Hernandez glanced at Hooper, wondering if he would choose iced tea as a gesture toward shaping up for the campaign. But Hooper drank two more bottles of beer during the sumptuous meal, washing down six tamales, four enchiladas, and hearty servings of everything else at the table.

Maybe, just maybe, Hernandez thought, he'll eat corn tortillas, instead of the heavier flour tortillas, which are more fattening.

But Hooper slapped generous portions of butter on flour tortillas during pauses for deciding what additional servings he would choose from among the various dishes on the table.

Ganner paid scant attention to Hooper or the light, mundane dinner conversation. His thoughts were in the political arena where he continued to ponder the difficult decision he faced between supporting Jordan Layman or Holt Witherspoon.

Ganner wanted to support Layman, but he knew Witherspoon had the advantage at the outset. Whenever he approached a difficult political decision, he reminded himself of the advice given by his father, a tough old cowhand who couldn't afford many mistakes starting out on his political career. "Son, never let sentiment overload your wallet."

As to the state representative race, Ganner was more concerned than he had let on about the possibility of a Mexican-American candidate. That could change the voting pattern in a way Ganner could not yet envision. Such uncertainty developing in a political situation he had assumed would be under control nettled him.

Had such a threat been foreseen earlier, he probably would have chosen one of his Mexicano compadres rather than Wally Hooper. But that was water under the bridge. He had made a commitment to Hooper and he would honor it.

Ganner firmly believed his long-standing machine had provided for Mexican-Americans better than they could provide for themselves through some maverick political movement. An upstart candidacy would be a direct challenge to him. If it should succeed, it might be viewed as a repudiation, which he couldn't tolerate.

Chapter 4

Once relocated in Justinville, Kirk Holland hit the ground running in his role as campaign manager for Wedge Crayton. His first major objective was to nail down Retama County as a strong political base.

To that end, he leaned on many of his father's friends and political associates. The first major event was to be an official campaign kickoff barbecue and dance on the front lawn of the courthouse and adjacent public park.

Kirk had campaign signs, brochures, and hand-out cards prepared for distribution throughout the district, with priority on Retama County. All material carried the theme line in bold type: QUALIFIED and INDEPENDENT.

He put campaign materials in every gathering place in the Justinville area that allowed them. That included the lone barber shop, three restaurants, five "filling stations" where local customers often lingered to chat with owners after their cars were serviced.

It also included the few taverns in which working men might talk politics but where the highly visible material would remind them of Wedge's candidacy.

Kirk and Wedge made personal calls on most targeted locations, traveling together as part of Wedge's political orientation. With each call, Wedge became more at ease, learning to shake hands, offer a campaign card, then await a response before proceeding with his pitch.

Most of the people they approached were friendly and receptive. Wedge wasn't a local hero, but he was a hometown boy and they liked the fact that "the judge's son" was running the campaign. However, at the American Legion Hall on the eastern outskirts of Justinville, they encountered unexpected resistance.

It was midafternoon and only one customer, a weathered middle-aged man, sat at the bar when they approached. Hank, the swarthy bartender, glowered at them from in front of a large color picture of Audie Murphy, the Texan who had become America's most decorated hero of World War II.

Smaller but no less imposing pictures of Generals Eisenhower and MacArthur flanked that picture. Near the MacArthur picture, a big poster was mounted advertising a forthcoming dance featuring Adolph Hofner and the Pearl Wranglers.

"We ain't," Hank growled, "gonna help nobody who ain't never served his country."

"The draft board wouldn't take me," Wedge said. "Asthma."

"You look healthy to me," Hank said. "I bet they didn't take you 'cause you're from a rich family."

"That's not true. My brother served in Korea. Flew twenty missions as a fighter pilot."

"He don't ever come 'round here. Guess he's too good for us."

"Look, Hank," Kirk said, "I'll vouch for this man. He would have served if he could. Now, I remember how much my dad always counted on you and your friends, and—"

"Keep your dad out of this! He was special. This guy's just a rich kid lookin' for somethin' to do."

Flushed, Wedge turned to leave, but Kirk detained him, while pointing his right hand in a mild gesture toward the customer, Elroy Griven, a small excavating contractor whose two bulldozers were idle that day.

"Elroy," Kirk said, "you fought in Europe, earned a medal for bravery in battle. Hank, you were in the middle of MacArthur's campaign to retake all those islands in the Pacific. I fought in Korea where I almost froze my butt off when I wasn't dodging enemy fire… All that's over. We need somebody to stand up to Frank Ganner. We need somebody to fight for us in Austin. Wedge here is the best bet."

Griven paused, toying with his glass that was almost empty. He pulled a dollar bill from his pocket and eased it onto the counter. "Here's for a beer for the four of us… Hank, we gotta listen to young Holland. He's damn near as smart as the judge… least smart as the judge was when he was that young."

After serving the beer, Hank took a long swig from his mug and rolled up his sleeves past elaborate tattoos on both arms, as he prepared to clean some dishes. "All right," he muttered, "I'll take two signs and a stack of them cards."

As they drove from the American Legion Hall toward the campaign headquarters, Wedge lit a cigarette, took only one puff, then threw it out the window. "I don't like this a damn bit," he said. "You're always fronting for me. You ought to be the candidate."

Kirk held the steering wheel with his left hand while making a note on the pad he always carried with him. "You lean on me. I lean on Dad. Lots of leaning… You're gonna do all right, but don't ever back away from a challenge like that… That is, unless you're convinced he's gonna knock your head off."

Kirk directed the campaign from his sparsely furnished office in the headquarters, a revamped storage room behind Nellie Stevens' dress shop on the main street, only a block from the Retama County Courthouse.

Maps of the seven counties of the district, with supplementary city maps of the county seat towns, covered his walls. Precincts were color-coded to represent degrees of potential support for Wedge.

In addition, he had posted charts and timetables for major activities, including Wedge's daily schedule and reports of organizational build-up. Recognizing the sensitivity involved with fundraising in small towns, he always kept those charts and records locked in his desk.

Wedge and Nellie occupied small offices flanking his. At one far corner of the long room, Mrs. Willis Fogel, Nellie's elderly bookkeeper, sat at a desk from which she provided secretarial help when not working on Nellie's business records.

She was the only person in the headquarters who could operate the mimeograph machine, invaluable for producing copies of memos and other material for distribution.

Because of his irregular hours, Kirk decided against living at home with his mother and sister, opting for a garage apartment an old friend rented him at a give-away price. From there, he wrote Carrie each night. He found expressing his love for her in writing wasn't easy.

But he was able to communicate to her that she was always in his thoughts, when the demands of the day were behind, and that he looked forward to her letters.

She, too, wrote each day, describing her school activities and her need to see him soon. Only once since he departed Austin had she mentioned the possibility of being pregnant. She reported her period was running late, but she had once skipped a period, so she would wait a little longer before consulting a doctor.

After receiving that recent letter, he lay awake, spinning through variables that might come into consideration, from marriage to abortion, neither of which they had confronted.

Surely, she's thinking of these, too. Maybe she just doesn't want to pressure me unless it's certain she's pregnant.

He rolled over on his back. Her parents will go on the warpath if she wanted to quit school to get married and have a baby. Lord knows I love her, but I'm not in much shape to offer her a stable life.

Kirk heaved a great long sigh. The timing's so bad. She doesn't want to get married until she graduates, and she wants me to graduate. She sure as hell doesn't want to live around here… Abortion? I don't know much about, other than barracks talk in the Army. I sure wouldn't want her risking her health with some quack… Guess it comes down to the fact she's avoiding the issue of our baby.

Kirk's personal relationship with Wedge had improved somewhat, but friction still existed over his insistence upon calling the shots about which Wedge often disagreed. If a spat appeared to be brewing, Nellie called them together with her for a meeting to air differences.

Such was the case on that day in early March, following the American Legion Hall visit, when they sat down at the headquarters to meet with Brew Blain, the finance chairman for the campaign.

"It's just a lot tougher than I anticipated," Brew said. "It's the damned drouth, and the fact Wedge just isn't known well outside our circle. I'm way below target for now. I can't raise enough to cover kickoff expenses."

"Then," Wedge said, "we'll just have to cut back. Can't we combine the courthouse rally with the one in Mexican town?"

"No," Kirk said. "The Anglos and Mexican-Americans won't mix. Maybe someday, but not now."

"Two bands," Wedge said, "instead of one. All of that moving things around. I can't understand why we couldn't get everybody to the courthouse area."

"We've got to trust Kirk on these decisions," Nellie said. "Brew, how much more is needed to get us past the kickoff?"

"Five hundred will do it."

Nellie proceeded to write a check in that amount.

Wedge opened his mouth to protest, then sighed, and turned to Kirk. "All right, but I don't know how you justify these high volume purchases of barbecue and beer, in addition to what appears to be an awful lot of campaign paraphernalia."

Kirk shrugged. "We've got to go first class on this event. It must put you on the map as a credible candidate. That means we can't run short of food or beer or soft drinks or balloons or bumper stickers. I guarantee you,

Frank Ganner will have at least one of his people at the shindig. And we'd better look damned good.

"More important, I expect some news media people from outside the district, including the one and only Wade Keene. What they report will set a tone for the campaign."

"Wade Keene's article on Frank Ganner was devastating," Nellie said. "That set a good tone for us."

"It hit Ganner a hard lick," Kirk said, "but it didn't promote Wedge Crayton. That's what we've got to do with this event."

Wedge stopped frowning. "Since Jordan Layman and Holt Witherspoon have announced for the Senate, is there any chance we could get them to appear at our event, maybe swell the crowd?"

"I've already sent them invitations over your signature," Kirk said, "that is, signed by Nellie, who is the official forger when you're not around. I doubt either of 'em would attend, but they might send well-wisher telegrams that we could read from the podium."

"Should we seek endorsement from either?" Nellie said.

"No." Kirk shook his head. "We want to be neutral in that shootout, and I doubt that either of them will want to align publicly with us or with Frank Ganner's candidate. Unless Ganner makes a public move in the Senate race, our position should remain neutral."

"Ganner's too smart for that," Wedge said. "He'll lie behind a log publicly, but he'll help old Witherspoon behind the scenes. I'd bet money on it."

"Maybe," Kirk said. "Maybe not. But that's one of the big variables out there that might have an impact on this campaign. I want you to pledge you won't make any endorsement without consulting me. I have the means to monitor that Senate situation."

"Goddammit, quit treating me like a high school kid," Wedge said, smashing his half-finished cigarette in a cluttered ashtray. "I've followed your directions this far, but don't overstate the obvious."

Kirk sighed, easing back in his chair as Nellie grasped Wedge's hand.

"Look," she said, "we're all a little edgy over putting this event together. Let's head down to Laredo for a little fun and relaxation this evening."

"No thanks," Kirk said, as all rose from the table. "I've got some work that has to be done. See you tomorrow."

Though Kirk had done well in lining up people for the campaign, he found the detail work to be far more demanding than he imagined. In addition, his scheduled work got disrupted now and then when unexpected important items cropped up. That was the case when Wade Keene's article on Frank Ganner appeared that day in The San Antonio Banner-Press.

Kirk glanced again over the article which appeared under a large bold headline reading, "The Baron Wants to be King of South Texas." The article began, "A monolithic power structure of long-standing seeks to control a substantial portion of South Texas in a high-handed manner that would make the Pendergast and Tammany Hall operatives look over their shoulders.

"Despite his sunny smile and professed modesty, the conniving and greedy Frank Ganner of Piedra Blanca is intensifying his means of directing the economic and political fortunes of the citizens of Bantrell County.

"His insatiable desire for power and wealth extends into Will Dodd County and he's aiming for higher stakes, five more counties in a state representative district. If he's successful in this venture, he'll be after the real power in those counties, the courthouse offices, in the election two years down the road.

"For the state representative race, the Baron of Bantrell is putting up one of his cronies, Wally Hooper, a Piedra Blanca attorney."

Keene's article went on to detail Ganner's operation, the groundwork laid by his late father, mentioned the Crayton campaign, and speculated on a Mexican-American candidacy. The article ended with an editor's note to the effect that this was the first in a series, with updates to appear as the campaign unfolded.

Kirk believed it was just the break he needed to help persuade House Speaker Jarvis Harrison and Lonnie Hardner, editor of The Texas Progressive, that anti-Ganner sentiment, essential to the credibility and development of the Crayton campaign, was being solidified with the help of the newspaper with the highest circulation in South Texas.

It was also a setback for Ganner's strategy of avoiding close association with Hooper's campaign. In addition to Harrison and Hardner, Kirk wanted to distribute the article to key people around the district. When the copies were ready, Mrs. Fogel had already gone home, so Kirk addressed the envelopes, then stuffed and stamped the mailing, with each letter containing a handwritten note from him, covering points he knew the recipients would find of interest.

He continued working that day alone at his desk until well past sundown. As he prepared to leave, he received a call from Carrie.

In an excited voice, she blurted out, "I'm not pregnant. I've started my period."

Stunned, Kirk paused, unable to respond.

"Quite a surprise!" She laughed. "I was beginning to wonder. Now, in the future, we're going to be a little more careful. Right?"

"Sure."

"I can't wait to see you."

"Carrie," he sighed, "I'm sorry, real sorry, to tell you I can't come to Austin as planned. There are too many loose ends hanging that lead up to our campaign kickoff. I've got to stay with it day-in-day-out."

"But… but that's much longer than you promised."

"I know, but I just didn't anticipate all that's involved. I'm used to writing about campaigns, not getting involved where all the work's going on."

She paused. "What if I hadn't started? What if I'd called you from a doctor's office to inform you I'm pregnant?"

"That's not fair. You know I love you very much. But you have to understand I'm in the middle of all this… Look, why don't you make a weekend visit down here? You can stay at the house and get to know Mom and Sis better."

Again, she paused. "I don't think so. I don't feel at home there because I know your friends set the schedule and I don't think they like me."

"That's not true. It's simply an age difference there, but you can overcome that by spending more time with them."

"We've been through this before. I don't feel comfortable with them. Drinking bouts in Nuevo Laredo won't change that."

Kirk paused. The conversation had reached an impasse, but he felt desperate to avoid a harsh ending. "Well, I'll make every effort to come to Austin just as soon as the kickoff event is over."

"You will 'make every effort.' It wasn't long ago that you promised to return. Sounds a little weaker, Kirk. Sounds as though you've been hanging around those politicians so long, you always leave yourself an out. Why not just let go and say, 'Carrie, my dear, I do care for you, when it's convenient, but this campaign means more to me than you.' How long do you expect me to wait around while you're off chasing rainbows?"

Kirk searched for a rejoinder that wasn't quite there. "I'm sorry you feel that way. I'll try to make it up to you."

"Good night, Kirk."

He wasn't a good whiskey drinker, but with a trembling hand, he poured a drink of straight bourbon and sat alone at his desk. The sudden relief from prolonged tension brought by Carrie's announcement of nonpregnancy had been replaced by a deep sense of uncertainty about where he now stood with her. He was struck with an impulse to get on the highway and head for Austin. But he looked around him, at the charts and materials, as though he needed to be reminded the campaign would collapse without him.

Oh God, he thought, I should be happy she isn't pregnant, but I'm not.

From the headquarters, he drove to the family home where he had a quiet dinner with his mother and sister. He was able to eat only one piece of fried chicken and small servings of vegetables.

Soon after dinner, he went to his apartment, turned on the radio, retrieved a bottle of beer from the refrigerator, and wrote a short, but warm, letter to Carrie. He started to undress but realized he wouldn't be able to sleep for a while. He was too stressed out to read or otherwise relax at his apartment, and he'd already seen the movie at the lone "picture show."

He decided on the only form of diversion he could think of that might alleviate the gnawing tension that was consuming him. He drove past the Nueces River bridge and turned down a winding dirt road that led to Barney's, the largest and oldest tavern in the Justinville area.

It was a long, one-story wooden structure located near a narrow slough off the main channel of the river, elevated three feet above the ground for protection against unusually bad flooding. One of its attractions was that was located behind a stand of tall, thick willow trees which prevented curious passersby from knowing who was there.

Barney Yates, the owner, was a big, jovial, middle-aged man with a large beer belly. He enjoyed smiling and saluting people in the bank when he deposited sacks of cash and overheard their snickers about "that beer joint down by the river." Rumors about gambling there had circulated for years, but a serious raid had never been undertaken.

The truth was, Barney permitted gambling with cash and only when he knew all the customers present. But he wouldn't wager himself unless he was playing, and even then, money was required to change hands behind the building.

The sheriff had long since decided it was impossible to catch anyone in the act with evidence, so he tacitly permitted the practice as long as Barney didn't allow brawling or drunkenness, which Barney usually caught before it got out of hand.

When Kirk entered Barney's, which was almost full, he noticed that nothing had changed, including the old jukebox in the center from which a twangy rendition of "I Don't Care" by Webb Pierce was blaring away.

At the far wall, in the middle of the room, were three tables for cards and dominoes. To the right of those were two pool tables, and to his left, against the near wall by the entrance, was a "long board."

It was a shuffleboard-type game designated as "long" because it was considerably longer, at sixteen feet, than the "short board" shuffleboard which was a mechanical game located at the front of the building along with two pinball machines.

His mother never knew it, but Kirk had been an occasional customer at Barney's for years. During the past two years, he had been in Barney's only four or five times, but those were memorable for shuffleboard fans, about twenty-five of whom were there that night.

Most were blue collar workers from construction and seismograph crews, the few oil rigs in the area, and the highway department. In addition, a handful of the dwindling breed of cowhands who lived and worked on the large ranches of Retama County drove to town in their weathered pickup trucks, each with a rifle mounted on a rack visible through the rear windshield.

All men were dressed in blue jeans or khaki work clothes. Some wore cowboy boots and hats while others appeared in heavy duty boots and baseball-style caps. Most were beer drinkers, who wanted their Pearl and Lone Star in longneck bottles, iced down in containers, rather than refrigerated. For the few whiskey drinkers, who came with bourbon in brown paper bags, "set-ups," or mixers, were available at a reasonable price.

The only meat items listed on the one-page menu included hamburgers, cheeseburgers, tacos, and the favored chicken fried steak, which was smothered in cream gravy on a long platter with large greasy French fries, a salad consisting only of lettuce and tomato with a squirt of French dressing, plus a couple of big thick biscuits. Fried catfish was offered when Barney's trot lines nearby yielded a few catfish large enough to fillet.

Barney's opened at 4:00 P.M. and "closed" at midnight. The law stated alcoholic beverages couldn't be served after midnight, but if a hot game was in progress at closing time, Barney simply locked the doors until the game was finished. Law enforcement officers paid him a visit now and then after midnight, but by the time the door was unlocked, no evidence in sight.

Kirk walked to the front of the building, past booths and tables in which a few women in western attire were drinking with their dates. At the bar, Betsy Lou, Barney's wife greeted him. She was an attractive, hard-working woman with a pleasant personality, though less outgoing than her husband. But she had a sense of humor and served his Pearl from in front of her favorite bar signs she had hung on the wall:

"Have another drink - it'll make you see double and feel single."

"Sure feel better now that I've given up hope"

"How can I soar with eagles when I live with a turkey?"

"Where's Barney?" he said.

"Be here in a few minutes."

"Has Gus Batey been around?" Kirk wondered about his onetime boss for a summer of work on a seismograph crew.

"No," she said. "He don't have a good way of looking at things no more. Don't hang out with his old friends 'round here like he used to. You might find him over in 'Mexkin' town. I hear he goes to some cantina over there."

"What's the problem?"

"I dunno. Barney says Gus just stayed 'round Justinville too long. With no family or nothin', he shoulda moved on somewhere's else."

"Maybe so. Well, I brought your Crayton signs," he said, handing her two posters while placing a stack of hand-out cards on the counter.

"You know," she said, "we only took these 'cause you called. None of them rich Craytons has ever set foot in this place."

"I understand, Betsy Lou, and I really appreciate the support. Believe me, it's important."

A few customers stopped by to greet Kirk, whom they were glad to see again, but mostly they wanted to watch him tangle with Barney on the long board. Several regulars could hold their own with Barney at the pool table or in games of cards and dominoes, but only Kirk could match him on the long board.

Kirk was glad Barney wasn't there just yet because he needed at least two beers before he could reach the blend of relaxation with concentration required to match wits and maneuvers with Barney. He gave Betsy Lou money to play songs of her choice and soon heard "Lovesick Blues" by Hank Williams and "Movin' On" by Hank Snow. He wasn't crazy about country western music, but it came with the territory.

When Barney ambled in, cigar in hand, he waved to his customers at the far end of the building and shook hands with those nearby. Like his customers, Barney never wore a suit or tie, but he displayed a flashy diamond ring that let everybody know he wasn't hurting. In his element, Barney Yates was a high roller.

"Well, I guess it's time for some action," Barney said, downing the final third of his bottle of Lone Star with one long swallow and a flourish. On the way to the long board, he stopped to turn down the volume on the jukebox, a sure signal that a serious match was forthcoming.

The board was mounted about three feet from the floor, a distance that made it comfortable for most people to lean on while making practice movements back-and-forth before releasing a shot. The game was played with two sets of four smoothly rounded metal pucks about the size of someone's palm. The speed and direction of a shot were determined not only by the effort one put in the hand motion upon release, but by how much powder the puck might encounter as it moved across the two-foot-wide board from the shooter's end toward the scoring zones at the other end.

At Barney's, the long board was considered to be the most challenging game in the building.

From years of experience, Barney had developed a steady game of sure-handed shooting, but Kirk understood Barney's added edge and knew one must meet that challenge in order to have any chance of winning. The floor under which the board was mounted was slightly warped, causing a barely perceptible drift to the shooter's left when shooting from the right corner of the table's end near the entrance.

Barney had perfected a highly sensitive diagonal shot, with the exact amount of force plus just a twist of spin, which caused the puck to curl gently to a strategic spot on the far left corner. Barney's left-corner shots often produced three points, or if hanging over the far edge, a maximum four-pointer score. It was a difficult spot for most players to reach, and if one didn't knock off Barney's corner placement with the immediate follow shot, Barney lagged a puck about a foot behind his first, providing protection.

Further, to contend with Barney, Kirk knew he must assess constantly the precise amount of powder on the board in those lanes where he planned to aim his shots. Powder affected velocity and, if a little thick in spots, even direction.

Barney and Kirk agreed to a five-dollar wager for a "World Series match," requiring the winning of four games. Kirk was on more than an evening of relaxation.

He was out to prove he could be an effective competitor by defeating the owner of the big beer joint who was considered the top shuffleboard player in the county. By defeating Barney, he would establish an image he wanted for the campaign, that of a bold, take-charge guy out to beat the odds.

And he would again become a fixture at Barney's, one of the most important gathering places in the county for politics, a place where Wedge could never become a fixture.

While most of the customers followed each move closely, they split the first six games. The seventh game went down to the wire before Kirk pulled it out, sending his last puck on a long diagonal shot that barely nudged Barney's would-be winning puck off the board, then spun to a gentle halt near the edge.

Amid shouting and backslapping, Barney put his arm around Kirk and led him to the bar where he ordered a beer for them. Clearing a path through the crowd, they strolled onto the deck outside where Barney gave Kirk the five dollars he had won.

"You know, Kirk, that's the best match we ever played. You little rascal, where the hell did you get that last shot?"

"Just then," Kirk said with a chuckle. "I couldn't make that one again in ten years."

"Well…" Barney smiled, "…I guess you ain't scared of playin' long shots. I admire that in a man, and that's what you're doing in this political campaign, ain't it?"

"I guess you could say that."

"Looks like a real long shot to me. Old Frank Ganner will whip his people in line like a goatherder."

"That he will, but we're going to work our side as hard as we can."

"Shit, I don't know why you do it. All the political speeches I ever heard never made no more sense than those goddamn bullfrogs croaking out there."

"Sure," Kirk said with a laugh, "but they make the laws we have to live by."

"Yeah," Barney snorted, "taxes and regulations… Oh well, good luck. What can I do to help besides display them signs and give out cards?"

Kirk smiled and turned to leave. "Keep the beer cold, and not too much powder on the long board."

Chapter 5

Throughout long, work-filled days, Kirk wove important stitches into the fabric of the campaign, leading toward the formal kickoff event.

Jeff Watson, editor-publisher of the local newspaper, helped out by writing a pre-event article and waiving the cost of an ad.

With the help of a growing group of volunteers, he had posters and hand-out sheets promoting the event spread throughout Justinville and neighboring communities, reaching out to those in the other four targeted counties.

Local campaign leaders were urged to organize at least one busload of people from each community, even if it would be half or more young people under voting age.

Kirk steered clear of Frank Ganner's home base of Bantrell County and decided against trying to work Ganner's satellite, Will Dodd County, for the time being. He and Wedge traveled together until they secured campaign chairmen for the four other targeted counties.

Among community leaders, they found sentiment divided between support for their reform issue and a resignation that Ganner's machine was too strong to be headed off. Among the general public, they found widespread apathy.

As Wedge became more secure in his personal campaigning, Kirk turned to working almost full time in Justinville, directing the campaign headquarters with assistance from Nellie and Brew Blain, whose fund-raising efforts continued to lag behind schedule.

A major breakthrough occurred when Nellie and Wedge secured Gordon Hempstead, a longtime successful rancher in Retama County, as chairman of the campaign. He was chairman of the board of the Justinville State Bank and a respected businessman in San Antonio and Laredo where he had bank holdings and other investments.

Quiet and soft-spoken but firm of mind and spirit, Hempstead was the ideal prestigious figurehead Kirk wanted as the final major element of the campaign structure.

Hempstead accepted partly because of the appeal of helping the underdog hometown candidate, but more on a pragmatic business basis, since Wedge's family and Nellie held large amounts of funds and stock in the local bank. He understood his role as a figurehead who shouldn't dabble in day-to-day activities, but he never lent his name to any major endeavor without understanding its scope and operations. He requested a comprehensive meeting with Kirk, Nellie, and Wedge at the earliest time possible, which would be three days before the kickoff.

Kirk sent a note to Carrie, advising her he would be in Austin the third day following the kickoff, a Tuesday, and would stay through the weekend. He would update his political contacts there, but make certain nights were free for her.

Her answer was a brief note, acknowledging the schedule. "I'll look forward to seeing you. Love, Carrie."

When they gathered for their final tune-up meeting the day prior to the Saturday kickoff, the headquarters resembled an army command post. Telephones were in constant use, and many people came and went, preparing for a crowd Kirk hoped would reach six hundred. Large detailed maps covered the walls, including a map of the courthouse-park area about which Wedge poked fun when they sat down.

"Don't you think we know our way around our own town?" he said.

"Sure, Professor," Kirk said with a nod, "but this shindig isn't going to be all that simple. I've divided this area into three zones. Courthouse lawn for the podium with dignitaries, plus the band and choir off to the left.

"Down here," he said, using a pointer to designate the street between the courthouse and the park, "will be the street for dancing. This other street, north of the park, will be for the fun cakewalk and other entertainment, including a play area for little children. The east and south streets around the park will be for parking only. The park grounds will be used for serving barbecue, and beverages, plus dispensing our campaign material from these three scattered booths. We're moving in fifty long tables with benches and this sound system works throughout the entire area."

He turned around to face Wedge. "At the podium it will be Gordon Hempstead as master of ceremonies. The invocation will be given by Forrest Ogden, who—"

"Ogden's the Baptist preacher," Nellie said. "How did you get him in on something where beer will be served? Did you warn him?"

"Sure. The Baptists don't drink or dance, but they want to support the hometown boy against the bad guy. I assured him that this corridor,"

Kirk said, pointing to the street on the northern edge of the park, "will be restricted insofar as dancing and drinking are concerned.

"With that assurance, and with a pledge that no hard liquor will be permitted on the premises, he agreed to give the 'invocation,' so long as it is described in his introduction as simply an opening prayer... And Brother Denson of First Methodist will end the program with—"

"You go to incredible lengths on some of these things," Wedge said. "How could religious ties be so important?"

Kirk shook his head. "Every time I think you're developing a little political acumen, you bring me back to reality in a hurry. Haven't you ever bothered to understand that the combined Baptist and Methodist congregations in this town represent the economic and political power of the community?"

"But why appeal to them through their pastors?"

"What better way?" Kirk turned a page on his legal pad. "And later we'll go after the Catholics in the plaza with Father Rodriguez."

Kirk detailed how the courthouse program would unfold, naming those to sit on the podium, with Hempstead and Wedge representing the campaign and Wedge's parents to flank him. On the other side of the microphone would be the mayor, the county judge, and the two ministers.

He paused, avoiding Nellie's eyes, but she looked at him and said, "You needn't apologize to me for not seating me at the podium, Kirk. I didn't expect to be there."

Kirk winced, then moved on to other details, ending with a contingency plan of moving the function to the high school gymnasium in the unlikely event of bad weather.

"I suspect," Wedge said, "rain would be the best thing that could happen tomorrow."

Kirk grinned. "Sure. You could take credit for breaking the drouth."

Campaign kickoff day dawned clear and bright. Plans were implemented on schedule for the Saturday afternoon of politicking and festivities.

For a quick lunch, Kirk, Nellie, and Wedge consumed a sandwich and soft drink in the headquarters while waiting for the final hour to grind by. Nellie looked stunning in a new spring outfit, a stylish blue dress with straw hat and blue hatband, and medium high heels that seemed to enhance the contours of her shapely legs.

Wedge held to Kirk's advice and dressed in one of his crumpled suits with tie slightly loose. With the temperature easing toward seventy-five, Kirk shunned a coat and wore a short-sleeve white shirt, and loose tie, and carried a clipboard with two pages of checklists.

Busloads, carloads, and pickup trucks crammed with family members rolled into the courthouse area by midafternoon when the program was scheduled to begin. Young Crayton volunteers scurried about the parking areas, asking the drivers of every arriving vehicle if a bumper sticker could be applied on the spot, and most agreed to let one be placed on the rear bumper.

Nellie departed the headquarters prior to the arrival of the "dignitaries," the designation Hempstead preferred to "VIPs." She didn't want to be confronted by questions about why she wasn't seated with them on the podium. When they arrived, they were divided and rode to the courthouse in cars driven by Kirk and Wedge.

With the dignitaries in place, Kirk scanned the crowd, which he was pleased to estimate in excess of five hundred and growing. A few men, businessmen and lawyers, wore suits, but most were dressed in western attire with open collars and sleeves rolled up twice to a position midway between their wrists and elbows.

Most women wore simple cotton dresses. None wore high heels which would have made dancing on the asphalt street virtually impossible.

Children ran about the park playing hide-and-seek in and around the booths for campaign material distribution and the barbecue stands. Parents admonished a few for tossing pebbles into the fish pond or for throwing a baseball too near an area where some older people had gathered to relax in peace.

The high school choir was moving into place on the courthouse lawn, led by its portly director, Iris Listor, a protegé of Kirk's mother. After marking items on one of his clipboard sheets, Kirk walked to the far end from the podium where the country western band, Jesse Webster and his Cowboys, unloaded its equipment and instruments, including an old piano, steel guitar, two standard guitars, and Webster's weathered violin that he called his "fancy fiddle."

Kirk approached Webster, who sported an elaborate western outfit with a large, wide-brimmed felt hat and a red bandana around his neck. "How about some patriotic music for your opening set?"

"We play mostly western swing, Bob Wills-type stuff. We don't sound so good playing the national anthem. But we could open with the state song. We play 'The Eyes of Texas' real well."

"That's not the state song," Kirk said. "That's the school song of the University of Texas, and I don't intend to antagonize all the Aggies in attendance."

"I'll be damned," Webster said. "Then what is the state song?"

"It's 'Texas, Our Texas.'"

"Sorry, I don't know it."

"Okay, don't worry about it. The choir will sing 'Beautiful Texas' and that'll do since hardly anybody knows the state song anyway. You can play 'The Yellow Rose of Texas,' can't you?"

"Sure. After that, I'll play something to liven things up, then slow it down with smooth tunes for some easy dancing."

Kirk walked to the podium to confer one last time with Wedge. "Remember," he whispered, "no matter how bland and dry it may sound to you, most of these people have come to hear you for the first time... and they don't know much about politics."

"I suspect," Wedge said as he surveyed the barbecue caterers setting up their stands, "the free barbecue and beverages, including beer, are more important than the lofty pronouncements of Wedge Crayton."

"Maybe so, but if you don't impress another soul today, try to convince Wade Keene you're a viable candidate. What that old warhorse writes in The Banner-Press could make a difference."

Wedge smiled, glancing in the direction of Keene, who had stationed himself laterally to the podium beyond the choir, a position where he could observe the speakers and the crowd.

Kirk walked across the street to the park where he joined Nellie under a retama tree. "Is he getting nervous?" she said.

"If anything, he's too loose."

Gordon Hempstead, master of ceremonies, stepped to the microphone to open the program with the Pledge of Allegiance. His presence as a father figure of the community added stature to his new role as campaign chairman for Wedge Crayton.

He was dressed in a conservative business suit with simple, but expensive handmade boots and a fine Stetson hat, which he placed upon his chair as he prepared to speak.

At sixty, he was balding but still as trim as the young cowhand he once was while learning the ranching business from his father, one of the most successful ranchers in Retama County for decades.

Hempstead took obvious pleasure in introducing his longtime friend, Forrest Ogden, pastor of the First Baptist Church of Justinville. Ogden was a big, imposing man with a strong voice.

As any veteran preacher would, he eyed the large crowd with relish. "Before we pray, permit me to say how proud I am to be here with all of you. Other than for a big football game, this is the largest crowd I've ever seen assembled in Retama County. I venture to say that despite this lingering drouth, and all the hardship involved, we have a community of people of good will, who have come together in common purpose, prepared to assist in what might well be termed a political crusade against a tyrant. For this, we should all be proud and thankful."

Holding up both arms, he bowed his head. "Let us pray. Oh Lord, we thank Thee for Thy blessings, including the very blessing of life, and the liberty for which our nation stands. We beseech Thee to guide this young man on his call to public duty; that he may respect Thee first and foremost, and then us, Thy servants. Grant him a sturdy body and sound mind, that he may acquire wisdom as well as experience along the challenging path he has chosen. Give him strength, and grant him hope for victory, for his victory will be our victory, and a victory for what is just and righteous and worthy. In Jesus' name we pray, amen."

As a wave of "amens" murmured through the crowd, Hempstead prepared to introduce the choir, dressed in dark brown robes with gold trim, representing the colors of Justinville High School. The director rose to stand beneath the flagpole which bore the Lone Star banner waving gently in the southeasterly breeze. What the eighteen-member choir lacked in volume it made up with enthusiasm as the youngsters sang "Beautiful Texas," the upbeat song written by W. Lee O'Daniel, a former governor:

> "In beautiful, beautiful Texas
> Where the beautiful bluebonnets grow;
> We're proud of our forefathers
> Who fought at the Alamo..."

Behind the façade of combat veteran and cynical newsman, Kirk Holland had always been soft on his first love, Texas. As he listened to the choir, tears welled in his eyes, though Nellie was unaware since he was wearing sunglasses. She, too, was touched as were most of the people in the crowd and on the podium, except for Wedge, who appeared to be preoccupied with other concerns.

After brief welcoming remarks, Hempstead, a longtime supporter of Holt Witherspoon, pulled an envelope from an inside suit pocket. "Our campaign is neutral in the contest for the United States Senate, but we invited both announced candidates to join us and to speak briefly. Neither candidate accepted our invitation, but Governor Witherspoon was kind enough to send us a short telegram, which I will now read: 'Fellow Texans, previous commitments in my heavy campaign schedule prevent me from being with you today in Justinville. I take no sides in the contest for the Legislature, but I want you to know how honored I am to have been invited. Please accept my best wishes for an enjoyable and meaningful gathering. I will look forward to seeing you soon in South Texas. Your friend, Holt Witherspoon.'"

Polite applause ensued, spiced by a few whoops for "Good old Holt!"

Wedge was nettled by his chairman's remarks coming across as a slap at Layman, whom he admired, and something of a plug for Witherspoon, whom he continued to describe in private as "that old political Neanderthal."

Next up to the microphone were the incumbent officeholders on the podium, Mayor J. H. Thomas followed by County Judge Julius Walls, Jr. Kirk had convinced them to give only five minutes each of welcoming remarks and endorsement comments about Wedge.

Before the featured speech by Wedge, Hempstead introduced Wedge's parents to polite applause. The Craytons were not among the most popular families in the area, and Kirk was pleased there were no boos or catcalls. To moderate applause, Wedge stepped forward for his speech, appearing confident and relaxed.

Nellie didn't share his mood. She crossed the fingers of her left hand and squeezed her right hand into Kirk's left. He placed his clipboard on a table and cupped his right hand over hers.

Wedge placed his notes on the lectern while taking a careful look at the crowd, highlighted by banners, balloons, and posters. He took a deep breath. "I want to thank you all for coming," he said before turning slightly in the direction of his parents, "and I want to thank especially my mother and father for the support they've always given me, including today, which just might be the most important day of my life… I can't say enough about my campaign chairman, Gordon Hempstead, one of our community's most outstanding citizens, who is providing invaluable leadership… I certainly want to recognize the support from our distinguished mayor and county judge and thank them for their warm endorsements which mean a great deal to me … We have a strong campaign building, and I would be remiss if I didn't introduce to you someone who deserves most of the credit for what you see today. That's my campaign manager, and the son of our late beloved county judge. Take a bow, Kirk Holland!"

Kirk waved to the crowd, which bestowed warm applause upon him. His introduction wasn't in the final speech draft they had reviewed that morning, Kirk mused, and he wondered what other changes Wedge might have in mind.

"Right there next to Kirk is my good friend and treasurer of the campaign. Mary Nell Stevens, take a bow!"

Nellie tipped her hat to light scattered applause. Most of the women in the crowd were either jealous of her wealth or her striking beauty, or didn't approve of her carefree lifestyle. Therefore, most of the men were cautious about expressing admiration for her.

"And over there, the fellow with the brightest shirt and the darkest sunglasses, my finance chairman, Brewster Blain."

Caught off guard, Brew quickly eased his can of beer under the table and waved to the crowd.

Standing next to Brew were Sidney Maylander and Nelson Parker, from the original group that had met at the Cadillac Bar to launch the campaign. Sidney had just given Brew three hundred dollars he collected from family members in Corpus Christi, and Nelson kicked in fifty dollars from his own pocket.

Wedge appeared to be relaxed and in command as he continued. "Well, if nothing else today, let's try to forget the drouth and have a good time!"

That line evoked applause, cheers, and a few whoops from the crowd that was warming to the young speaker whom very few knew personally.

"I have a stack of notes here about some of the important state issues that are going to come before the next Legislature. These notes have all the facts and figures involved." He set them aside. "I'm sorry, but you're not going to get to hear all that today!"

Again came favorable response.

"What I am going to tell you is that I'm ready, willing, and able to take on Frank Ganner's political machine!"

Sharp applause ensued with more whoops.

"But I need your help! Every one of you has to help! That's the only way we're going to whip Frank Ganner and his pack of coyotes!"

The crowd was hanging on his every word, shouting rejoinders, including, "Give 'em hell!"

Wedge paused and lowered his voice slightly. "The smart money in this race is on Wally Hooper, Frank Ganner's stand-in. They say he's got more credentials and money and political organization with him now than we could muster by election day. Well, they ought to know that things can change."

Pointing his right forefinger into the air above the crowd, he raised his voice again. "Let me start my campaign officially by issuing a challenge: I'll meet this Frank Ganner puppet anyplace, anytime in a real debate about the issues of this campaign!"

As another round of applause engulfed the park, Nellie gripped Kirk's hand. "What's wrong with him? We never discussed anything so drastic?"

"He's finally decided," Kirk said with a smile, "he wants to win this race."

"But Hooper would embarrass Wedge in a debate now. He knows so little about state government."

"Sure, but there's not going to be a debate anytime soon. Ganner doesn't want to give us that kind of recognition."

"Are you sure?"

"Sure as you can be in this crazy business."

"The most important issue," Wedge continued, "is independence! Which candidate can go to Austin and represent the people of this district. I submit to you that Wally Hooper could not serve on a fair, reasonable, and equitable basis because he would always be looking over his shoulder for orders from Frank Ganner.

"Our forefathers didn't win independence from a tyrant so we could have another one telling us what to do a hundred and eighteen years later. Give me your all-out support and I'll keep that tyrant from moving into our territory!"

As Wedge enjoyed another round of hearty applause, he prepared to make his final comments. But all attention was suddenly diverted by a strange noise from behind the courthouse, a heavy whirring-flapping sound unfamiliar to almost all those in attendance.

Soon in view came a large helicopter with "JDL For Senator" painted in bright red letters on each side. Only Wade Keene knew that Layman would make an appearance. Most of the crowd had only seen a helicopter in a newsreel, and as Congressman Jordan D. Layman's chopper descended upon the courthouse lawn, they scrambled for a closer view.

As the blades eased to a halt, Layman sprang from the chopper, unwinding his six-foot-three-inch frame while already waving his short-brim hat.

He wore a crumpled dark blue suit with thin dark tie hanging loosely upon his starched white shirt. He scanned the crowd with intense brown eyes locked into place under his crinkled forehead that melded into a receding black hairline.

"Excuse me!" Wedge shouted over the crowd's reaction to the first helicopter ever seen in Retama County. "Let me welcome our guest!"

He bounded from the podium and reached Layman near the chopper where Layman was shaking hands, while his pilot-travelling aide was handing out campaign brochures. Wedge escorted Layman to the podium where he prepared to introduce him. Layman shook the hands of the surprised dignitaries, including Gordon Hempstead, who was far from pleased.

"It's a signal honor for me," Wedge called out to the crowd, "to introduce to you one of the finest public servants Texas has ever produced! We're honored to have him with us today, Congressman Jordan D. Layman!"

About half of the crowd cheered heartily while the other half, mostly Witherspoon supporters, responded with brief, polite applause.

Layman stepped forth with a flourish, waving his hands several times until he sensed the crowd was ready for him to speak. "I'm going to address you as I did a few years ago when I was teaching school here in Justinville… My fellow South Texans…"

That brought an instant positive response from many in the crowd who had always felt neglected in their isolated part of the state, so distant from the economic and political power centers of Dallas and Houston.

A slight buzzing noise came from the sound system, causing Layman's twangy voice to come across as raspy and harsh, but he was nonetheless compelling by virtue of his reputation and daring entrance upon the scene.

"Folks, I'm real sorry that Dove Anne couldn't be with us. She sends her love. And I'm sorry I'm a little late. I winged out of San Antonio on time, but we ran into what's called a 'head wind' that slows you down a bit."

Layman glanced over to his rented helicopter where a mother was dragging her young son away. "Now, ma'am," Layman called, "let him climb in there! That's okay! I wish I could take everybody ridin', but it's against regulations. But let those boys take a look inside… "

Layman knew he had most of the crowd with him, but he understood he could lose them upstaging the local candidate with a long speech. "I came here today to pay respects to this young candidate and to all of you who are showing your commitment to participate in the process of electing qualified people to public office.

"This is what keeps the Democratic Party alive and growing as the party of the people. And let me tell you, I'm proud to be a Democrat! Whether or not Jordan Layman is your next United States Senator, you won't ever see me jumping ship to support some Republican candidate for President, or any other office!"

While those remarks drew moderate applause, Kirk whispered to Nellie, "If he goes on to hit Witherspoon by name, we're in real trouble."

But Layman proceeded quickly to his closing remarks. "Let me just say that I appreciate very much coming home, as it were, to spend a little time with you good people. And I'm sure looking forward to some of that great-smelling barbecue. Thank you all! God bless you!"

A strong wave of applause, spliced with a few cheers, followed Layman's final words.

"He's not at all handsome," Nellie murmured, "nor does he have a good speaking voice. But he sure as the devil knows what he's doing around here."

Wedge motioned for Layman to take Brother Denson's place on the podium as the Methodist minister stepped forward to give a benediction. When it was concluded, Wedge offered to escort Layman around the park, "pressing the flesh," and invited him to join them for barbecue at the table designated for dignitaries.

"It's a great honor to have you here," Wedge told him as they crossed the street. "It will be a big boost for my campaign."

"Yeah, well, don't take it as an endorsement, but I'm glad to help out a little… You know," Layman said with a chuckle, "old Holt went to San Angelo for some damned sheepherders' meeting. Hell, they're all for him anyhow. He shoulda come here, too."

"How's your race shaping up?"

"Holt has the lead now, there's no question about that. But he's running like Tom Dewey, sitting on his lead, not campaigning hard. I'm running like old Harry Truman, barnstorming, taking chances, giving 'em hell… There's three other candidates in the race, one of whom will draw a fair amount of votes, so I'm mostly aiming to get in a runoff with Holt, then go from there. How's yours looking?"

"I guess it's similar in that Frank Ganner's candidate is the odds-on favorite, but I feel good about my campaign, and we anticipate a Mexican-American candidate coming in soon. That would divide things up, maybe put me in a runoff."

"The only advice I can give you is to stay alert. There's no tellin' when something will crop up that you can jump on and make some hay out of."

Wedge smiled, motioning Nellie to meet Layman. Later they joined an impatient line of hungry people eager to enjoy the savory barbecue which had been sending tantalizing smoke drifting about the park. They soon were rewarded as each received a big plate heaped with generous servings of barbecued brisket, potato salad, and pinto beans, plus slices of bread, onion, and dill pickle. Beer, iced tea, and soft drinks were available, with cake and cookies for dessert.

As the band worked its way through "The Yellow Rose of Texas," Wade Keene approached Kirk, who was running through one of his checklists from the clipboard.

"Well," Keene said, lighting a cigarette, "he descended from the heavens on the wings of a great whirling bird to bestow his blessings upon your humble campaign."

"Did you have any idea he was coming?" asked Kirk.

"Sure."

"Why didn't you tell me?"

"Why should I?"

"That showboat act has hurt us with the Witherspoon supporters. Some warning would have helped."

"Look, Holland, let's get something straight. I hate Frank Ganner's guts, if he has any, but I'm not in the business of assisting anybody's campaign. Let the chips fall where they may."

Kirk tossed his clipboard onto a nearby table, then he retrieved a can of beer. "Okay, Wade, but what did you think of our candidate?"

"He did all right until he started gushing over Layman." Keene turned to amble away and mingle with the crowd, where he would learn firsthand their impression of Wedge Crayton as a candidate for the Legislature.

Among several other out-of-town media people to attend was Edgar Howard, editor-publisher of The Harmon County Herald, who brought his nineteen-year-old son, Bobby. Located between Retama County and Frank Ganner's base of Bantrell County, Harmon County was strategic and pivotal, insofar as Kirk's plans were laid to pull off an upset victory.

Howard was taking notes while his son took pictures. As Bobby Howard pursued some subjects beyond earshot, his father said to Kirk, "In a few years, it'll be the other way around. He's got a knack for writing as well. And he's learning the business end of the paper…"

"You know," he continued, surveying the vast crowd on the park lawn, "a good smell is in the air, a sense of resolve. It's damned encouraging."

"You ought to know." Kirk nodded. "You're the only editor in this district who has been taking on Ganner."

"I'll do what I can. Bring your candidate by for an interview, Kirk, at my office in the next week or so."

"Thanks, I surely will."

As Howard walked away to rejoin his son, Kirk waved to the bandleader for the livelier music he had promised. Webster responded with a boot-stomping rendition of "Under the Double Eagle," a rousing western song that prompted the men to lead their ladies with long steps and fast-paced movements.

Kirk hoped the festive atmosphere would help calm the nerves of Witherspoon's devout supporters who must understand that Layman's appearance was unforeseen and that Wedge had no choice but to be hospitable.

Gordon Hempstead shattered that illusion when he confronted Kirk. "Are you telling me that Jordan Layman came down here without telling you or anyone connected with our campaign?"

"Yes, sir." Kirk sighed. "He operates that way sometimes."

"Why?"

"I guess because he knows he can get away with it."

"He's a crude politician, that's all he is, and I didn't appreciate the way Wedge made a big fuss over him."

"Wedge was just surprised and overplayed the role of a good host."

"You're sure he's not for Layman?"

"All I can tell you is he's promised me he'll stay out of the Senate race."

"All right, I trust you, Kirk. But make sure he stays in line. Holt Witherspoon is an old friend."

"Mr. Hempstead, I know it put you in an awkward position, and I certainly regret it. But now that it's over, I hope we can continue working together because, all things considered, I believe we're having a successful event."

"You've done a lot of good work, Kirk. I appreciate that... You know, I just never liked Jordan Layman when he was here teaching, years ago. Always showing off, bragging, and telling jokes in mixed company that should've been confined to beer joints. One of my daughters took a liking to him, but I made sure that didn't go anywhere."

Kirk ran through his mind the forthcoming event at the plaza in

"Mexican town" at which Layman would undoubtedly want to speak, perhaps coming down even harder on Witherspoon's breach of party loyalty.

"Mr. Hempstead, I know this has been a trying experience, and I want to spare you any more difficult situations. Why don't you get some rest and let me worry about the next event?"

"That's a good idea. I've had enough for a day."

Kirk's mother and sister sat nearby, finishing their plates of barbecue, and he approached them. "Could I interest one of you lovely ladies in a dance?"

Estelle laughed. "You're not getting me onto that street. I paid too much for these shoes."

"Nor I," his mother said. "I'm afraid I'm a little too old for that."

"I'll bet," he said, "you never were really crazy about this kind of dance."

"That's true, but I never let your father know. The judge loved any kind of dance, and we, well, we made them all."

"If I could talk them into playing a waltz," Kirk said, "then—"

"No, Kirk, I simply couldn't, but thank you for your thoughtfulness."

After finishing the plates of barbecue, Wedge and Layman resumed working the crowd, including dancing with several women who seemed to be flattered. Street dancing wasn't easy on the ladies' shoes, but the band was playing slower, less demanding songs, including "San Antonio Rose," and "You Are My Sunshine."

Layman, who had sipped a couple of shots of Scotch from a flask in his coat pocket, approached the bandleader with a request for "somethin' appropriate for my return to Justinville."

Webster responded with the old Gene Autry favorite, "I'm Back in the Saddle Again."

With sundown approaching, Wedge took Nellie for the final dance of the function.

"You've done well," she said. "Of all things, you seemed to enjoy all the politicking."

"You know, I really did. Once I decided it was just one big party, it was fun."

After the final number, Wedge and Nellie prepared to leave for the function at the Plaza Gloria on the other side of the tracks in "Mexican town."

Wedge insisted upon driving Jordan Layman, who sat in the front seat while Nellie and Layman's pilot rode in the back. Brew drove the second car with Kirk, the mayor and the county judge as passengers. Wade Keene declined Kirk's offer to ride, opting to drive alone in his car.

They soon arrived at the plaza. Crayton posters were tacked to the trunks of trees ringing the park, which took up an entire city block. The plaza was almost two-thirds full and was drawing more each minute with the promise of free music, tamales, beer, and soft drinks. Many people had gathered near the covered bandstand in the center while others mingled on the large uncovered dance pavilion, awaiting the arrival of Wedge, which would signal the mariachi band's initial song.

Still others sat chatting on the concrete benches, enjoying food and refreshments. Men and women donned their Sunday best for this occasion, men in their finest suits or western wear, and their wives and their girlfriends wearing their colorful dresses and skirts with shawls or sweaters for the cool, crisp weather of the evening. The Mexican-Americans knew little of Wedge Crayton or the nature of the political contest, but their community's leadership had invited them, and in a drouth-stricken economy, this was an opportunity they didn't want to miss.

As Wedge pulled up to the curb, Jordan Layman was in an upbeat mood, enhanced somewhat by another shot of Scotch and soda taken on the way from the courthouse. He pointed to the modest one-story building of dark brick on a barren schoolyard across from the southern side of the plaza.

"There she is," Layman said. "Where I once taught school. Just this side of nowhere."

Wedge smiled. "Congressman, this is a homecoming for you, and I want you to be the featured speaker tonight."

"That's kind of you. I appreciate it very much."

On the sidewalk, the official greeting party met them, led by Father Antonio Rodriguez, a courtly middle-aged priest whose congregation at nearby St. Joseph's, the only Catholic church in Justinville, was ninety percent Mexican-American.

Of near equal importance was Arturo Martinez, a longtime political ally of Kirk's father and a counterpart to Gordon Hempstead as a father figure in the Hispanic community. As its most prominent businessman, his presence at a political function was influential since there were no Mexican-American elected officials in Justinville or Retama County.

The third member of the greeting party was Rudy Medrano, Crayton campaign chairman for the Mexicano community. He was an old friend of Kirk's from high school days who owned two barbecue stands and a tortilla factory that provided him with an income equal to that earned by a middle-class Anglo, plus spare time for political activity. Medrano had urged Kirk early on to hold a Mexicano rally for Wedge in Justinville before PAMAT might place a candidate in the race.

The preemptive nature of the move was now successful, but rumors persisted that the maverick Mexican-American organization would soon field one of its own. As Father Rodriguez extended his hand to Wedge, the mariachi band, Los Vaqueros de Laredo, struck up its opening number, "Rancho Grande," a traditional Mexicano favorite and one of the few known well in the Anglo ranching community.

The two trumpet players and five guitarists were all dressed in form-fitting black outfits with low-heel boots and huge sombreros, each trimmed with silver braid. All seven sang together at times, while some numbers called for a solo, and a few were rousing instrumentals. On that opening number, the trumpets provided a penetrating break in the relative quiet of the plaza, signaling the crowd that the festivities were under way.

Father Rodriguez, who had been in Justinville only three years, felt somewhat awed by his first meeting with the prominent congressman running for the United States Senate. But he was soon at ease as Layman slung his arm around his shoulder and led him across the street to "this beloved school where I taught the kids around here some discipline and how to think and learn."

Kirk detained Wedge on the sidewalk to inform him that Hempstead would not be there to emcee and suggested the county judge take his place.

"That won't be necessary," Wedge said. "I'm going to emcee this one, and Jordan Layman will be the featured speaker."

"What?"

"Layman can wow this crowd. I can't. This is in the best interests of the campaign."

"The hell it is. You're just kissing Layman's ass."

"You know, Kirk, the thing I dislike most about this campaign is that I don't have the authority to fire you. Otherwise, it's going great."

Kirk clenched his right fist, but as he squared his body to throw a punch, Nellie sliced between them.

"All right, you two," she said firmly, "it's been a long day, but we still have a way to go. Wedge, you'd better catch up with Jordan Layman before he works the crowd without you, and Kirk ..." she smiled, taking him by the arm, "...I'd like to try the tamales and listen to the mariachi band."

She and Kirk viewed a fiesta atmosphere at the plaza. The covered bandstand was decorated with streamers of red, white, and blue crepe paper. Small multicolored lights adorned that area and were attached to metal strands about four feet above the ground all around the large dance pavilion adjoining the bandstand. A bright moon shown from almost directly above, casting its soft pale light onto the trees and shrubs, blending with the artificial lights of various colors.

As they strolled to a bench near the bandstand, the mariachis began playing a lively Mexican folk song.

"Well," Kirk said, "as if ordered for the occasion."

"I'm not familiar with it."

"It's 'Gavilan.' They're singing about a man who envisions himself as a chicken hawk swooping down suddenly to capture his prey. Don't you think that helicopter looks like a hawk?"

"That's not a damn bit funny," she said. "You'd better unwind a little. You've been too tight, right up to this moment."

"I don't believe in changing the game plan unless you've fallen behind by two touchdowns late in the third quarter. We've just started."

"But you've been lecturing us on how far we start behind."

"Sure, but we can't possibly close the ground if we've got Holt Witherspoon's supporters against us."

"Nobody endorsed anybody today. Don't you think this will just slide on by?"

"Maybe, but your hero has got to understand he can't push this too far, no matter what he thinks about the Senate candidates. You know, it hasn't been so long ago since we were sitting around a table at the C.O.D. where Wedge was telling us that Jordan Layman is a crude politician. Why the big change of heart?"

"Crude perhaps, but so much more progressive than that old mossback, Witherspoon. Deep down, Wedge wants to win and take on the entrenched power brokers in Austin. And you have to give him credit. This is the first day we've seen him really think and act like a candidate."

Kirk excused himself to get beer and tamales. When he returned, they sat on a bench near the bandstand, enjoying the food and drink.

When Wade Keene parked near the plaza, he had seen Kirk and Wedge jaw-to-jaw on the sidewalk, but by the time he reached that spot, Nellie had separated them. He approached Kirk and Nellie, aiming a question at Kirk. "Any problem with Sir Lancelot and his tutor?"

"Nothing you'd be interested in," Kirk said.

"Well, your candidate patronizing Jordan Layman interests me. How far does that go?"

Nellie tensed, expecting an outburst or cutting remark from Kirk. Instead, she was relieved to see him reassert the "game face" of the cool campaign manager, unperturbed by a biting question that hit at the heart of his concerns.

"The official posture of this campaign," Kirk said, "is neutrality in the U.S. Senate race. As far as I know, it hasn't been changed. Layman is a guest. He's being treated with the same warm hospitality Holt Witherspoon would have received, had he chosen to make an appearance here today."

Keene smiled, tossing his spent cigarette to the ground. "I'll have a beer on that one."

For a change of pace, the band played a lilting love ballad, "Estamos En Las Mismas Condiciónes."

Kirk laid aside his can of beer and bowed. "My dear Countess, may I have the honor of this dance beneath the stars?"

They danced slowly on the crowded pavilion, enjoying the smooth guitar music and relaxed nature of the gathering.

"You know," she whispered, "we're the only white faces out here, but it doesn't seem to matter."

"A lot of nice people are over here. You've just never taken the opportunity to get to know them."

She glanced beyond the dance pavilion to observe Layman and Wedge working the crowd together. "I know what's keeping you so uptight, beside the campaign... It's the sweetheart of Sigma Chi."

Kirk didn't respond. He hadn't mentioned the precarious nature of his relationship with Carrie to anyone and wasn't in the mood to get into it with Nellie.

"All right." She sighed. "Anyway, I hope things go well for you in Austin next week. She's not the one I would have picked out for you, but it's none of my business, now, is it?"

"Nellie, I appreciate your concern, but this is something I've got to work through myself."

Jordan Layman, who could read the moods of Mexican-Americans better than most Anglo politicians, detained Wedge twice heading to the podium to start the program. "Not quite time," he said.

As more beer and tamales were served, the mariachis played vibrant old favorites, including "Adelita," "Guadalajara," and "Jalisco," in which the trumpet players pierced the evening air with strong clear notes and the others belted out the lyrics while strumming vigorously on their guitars. Those songs prompted repeated whoops, or "gritos," from many spirited Mexicanos who were in a loose, festive mood.

Kirk made a request he knew would please Father Rodriguez. The padre's parents had migrated to Texas from a tiny village in the Northern Mexican state of Chihuahua. The request was for "Jesusita en Chihuahua," a bouncy, intricate instrumental that required especially careful timing by the guitar players.

As that number ended, Layman and Wedge strode to the podium on the bandstand where the other dignitaries joined them.

Father Rodriguez knew well the potential downsides of involving himself, and therefore his church, in an uncertain political campaign. He had originally declined Kirk's invitation to be present on the podium since a Mexicano candidacy was rumored to be imminent.

But on that sparkling night, with a prominent member of the United States Congress present, he reconsidered. His remarks, however, were measured, favorable to Wedge but far from an endorsement. His comments regarding Layman were much more favorable, just short of an open endorsement.

The mayor and county judge made their same endorsement speeches for Wedge as before, but they were cautious in their remarks toward Layman, acutely aware of the position of their community's number one citizen, Gordon Hempstead, who was firmly for Witherspoon.

Kirk was particularly proud of Arturo Martinez and Rudy Medrano. They were already feeling the early heat from militant Mexicanos who anticipated a PAMAT candidate against Wedge and Wally Hooper. Martinez and Medrano took the position that if a qualified Mexicano from Retama County entered the race before Wedge Crayton, they would support him. But it had become obvious the Mexicano candidate would come from elsewhere, probably Coronado County.

Therefore, Martinez and Medrano contended they must support Wedge, the local candidate whose manager was the son of the most responsive officeholder the Mexicanos ever had in Retama County.

Martinez and Medrano made glowing endorsements of Wedge, and to no one's surprise, also endorsed Layman, who had been a friend of "Old Arturo" when he lived in Justinville and taught Medrano in school. Further, Holt Witherspoon, though not an enemy who aroused emotions, had never been viewed as simpático in Mexican-American political circles throughout South Texas when he was governor.

Wedge perceived it was a moment cut-to-order for Jordan Layman. But when he glanced over to the bench where Nellie and Kirk sat, Nellie stared at him with a quizzical expression and Kirk frowned with his arms crossed on his chest.

He drew a long breath, surveying the crowd, many of whom couldn't understand English. He hoped they would respond to gestures and voice inflection.

"I'm proud to be here tonight, and I'm proud to have received the endorsements from these outstanding men up here with me. I, too, ask for your support and I won't let you down if you send me to Austin… Now, let me make certain there's no mistake about something. We invited both candidates for the United States Senate and we would have extended the same hospitality to the other candidate, had he joined us. He did not, and I want you to know how honored I am now to introduce to you our guest, the former teacher whom so many of you knew and loved in that schoolhouse, en la escuela," he said pointing across the street to polite applause.

"This is a man who will, if elected, serve all the people of our great state, toda la gente del gran estado de Tejas. It's my pleasure and privilege to introduce to you tonight, one of our state's most respected members of Congress, a true servant of the people, y nuestro gran compadre, Congressman Jordan D. Layman!"

Amid hearty applause and numerous "gritos," Wedge ambled over to the bench where Nellie sat. She said, "I never heard you speak any Spanish other than to order food and drinks."

"Jordan gave me those lines. He said that would be just enough to let 'em know I've been thinking about 'em."

"Just enough," Kirk snapped, "to heap the highest praise upon one Jordan Layman."

Wedge started to respond, but Layman was waving for silence in order to launch his speech.

"Mis amigos," he called, "¡Buenas noches!" Then he summoned Arturo Martinez for an "abrazo," or hug, and raised their hands together in a gesture of camaraderie, which brought another round of warm applause and more "gritos".

Layman spoke in somewhat uncertain Spanish, "Porque no puedo hablar mas de un poquito de Español, tengo Señor Martinez para interpretar."

Kirk, though troubled by Layman's intrusion into their carefully planned events, couldn't help but marvel at the ease and effectiveness with which Layman presented himself before the Anglo gathering and now before the Mexican-Americans.

Rather than stumble through a speech in broken Spanish, or deliver an all-English speech half the crowd would miss, he let them know he could speak a little Spanish, but would depend upon their father figure to deliver a precise translation.

Each sentence Layman spoke was delivered with a driving sense of urgency as his rasping, twangy voice reached for the heart of his audience. He proceeded to extol the virtues of the Democratic Party to which he claimed lifetime loyalty.

He condemned "those heretics and turncoats," including his opponent, Holt Witherspoon, who had "jumped ship" to support Republican Eisenhower for President in the previous election.

"The Democratic Party has always been the party of the people, while the Republicans care only about big business and special interests. Now, my opponent will be coming to the people, hat in hand, as a candidate in the Democratic Primary because he knows he couldn't possibly win as a Republican in the general election. Let those who support Republicans show their true colors and run as Republicans!"

Holt Witherspoon branded such speeches as "pure old JDL demagoguery," but it was vintage Jordan D. Layman, priming his crowd's emotions with hard-hitting rhetoric against his opponent before addressing their true concerns and needs.

After thrashing Witherspoon, he changed gears, portraying himself as the champion of minorities, the poor and disadvantaged, promising relief through various federal programs, including his own set of new proposals he termed, "The Layman Program for Progress."

At last, he lowered his voice. "I venture to say that almost every one of you has felt the pain of discrimination because of your heritage and the color of your skin. I pledge to work against discrimination every step of the way until it no longer exists!"

As another hearty response subsided, he pointed to the schoolhouse. "Education is the key to the future. Every young child must go to school and go as far as his talent and dedication will carry him.

"That's the path out of the barrio. That's the path to opportunity and success, and you can count on me to make sure our government provides all the help that it possibly can!"

The crowd, emotionally spent, cheered again for Jordan Layman.

In English, it would have been only about a ten-minute speech, but with the translation time and numerous breaks for applause, Layman was before the crowd almost twenty-five minutes.

Kirk squirmed in his seat. Any more, he thought, and he's going to start losing them.

But Layman, with his sensitive political antennae, brought his speech to a close with a few kind words about Wedge, short of an endorsement, and his last call for votes for his candidacy.

With Martinez' final words of translation, Layman gave a vigorous wave to the crowd, about a third of whom converged upon him to shake hands. With another hearty ranchero number, the mariachis maintained the keen emotional pitch that pervaded the crowd.

Nellie grabbed Kirk's hand and turned him toward Wedge, who was still applauding Layman. "We've accomplished a lot today," she said. "I don't expect you two to ever become close friends, but we've got to pull together. How about shaking hands and moving on to the next round?"

Both paused like prize bulls pawing sand, awaiting some move from the adversary. She glanced at each again as their reluctant hands joined.

Layman declined Wedge's offer of lodging at the Crayton Ranch that night, explaining that he needed to stay at the Stockmen's Hotel, the only place in Justinville where commercial lodging was available. It was just past 10:00 P.M. when they arrived at the old two-story frame structure, with long porch, on the main street. Layman's pilot took the luggage inside while the Senate candidate bid farewell to Wedge, Nellie, and Kirk.

"I gotta be on the phone till midnight," he said, "then off early in the morning, riding the chopper."

When Layman walked inside, the ubiquitous Wade Keene appeared on the porch.

"Another interview?" Wedge said. "I'm worn out."

"Nah, we're off the record now. I just wanted to ask you if you know where Layman is going tomorrow?"

"Why no, I didn't ask him."

"He's going to a noon barbecue in Piedra Blanca for Frank Ganner's man, Wally Hooper, your distinguished opponent."

Wedge gasped. "I, uh… well, I guess it's just part of his duty to touch bases in Democratic Primary contests in South Texas. He's with me. Deep down, I know he's with me and will help me all the way, as best he can."

"Sure," Keene said, tossing his cigarette past the steps to the ground, "and you're probably expecting Santa Claus to arrive on the Fourth of July."

Chapter 6

On the following day, after seven solid hours of sleep, Kirk was ready to enjoy another of those fine family Sundays with grilled sirloin steak and homemade ice cream. Above all, he was exhausted, badly in need of a respite from the pressure of directing the campaign.

He was pleased that his mother and sister sensed his mood. They didn't mention politics, other than to commend him for a successful kickoff day.

While they attended church, Kirk read Wade Keene's coverage of the kickoff events in The Banner-Press. It was a comprehensive account and generally favorable with the desired anti-Ganner quotes from Wedge. He chuckled upon reading Keene's description of Wedge as "fairly articulate and sincere, but still wet behind the ears. Obviously, he was awed by the unscheduled appearance of the mercurial Jordan Layman, whose helicopter was more impressive than his folksy little speech."

Though Wedge would be upset, Kirk knew it was far better than what Keene could have written about Wedge fawning over Layman. That would have offended readers in the district who favored Holt Witherspoon.

"Dodged another bullet." Kirk sighed over his second cup of coffee. Then he tossed the newspaper aside and took their old border collie on a long, relaxing walk.

In the afternoon, he played canasta with his mother and sister before taking Estelle for a ride while his mother caught up on magazine reading. When they returned soon after dark, he found his mother asleep on the couch, "Reader's Digest" in hand, with a record playing the soft but precise sounds of Chopin's "Etude in E."

He kissed her on the forehead and retired to his apartment. He tried to reach Carrie in Austin, but discovered she had gone to dinner with friends.

Though tired, he was more content than he had been in weeks. The kickoff events had been successful and it was only two days before his trip to Austin and a return to Carrie's arms. He curled into bed for a long night's sleep.

The post-event meeting with Gordon Hempstead at the headquarters was long and tedious, but productive, since he required Wedge, Kirk,

Nellie, and Brew to explain exactly how each went about executing his or her role in the campaign. As they talked it through, answering numerous questions, they understood better how each needed to interact.

Feedback from the Saturday kickoff had been generally favorable, which Hempstead acknowledged, but he was mildly critical about the events costing more than $100 over budget, and he glanced at Wedge when Kirk reiterated the campaign's position of neutrality in the U.S. Senate race.

As the meeting stretched into the lunch hour, Mrs. Fogel brought hamburgers and soft drinks. At last, near midafternoon, Hempstead indicated he was satisfied. "I won't need any such meetings again, nor will I be involved in day-to-day operations, entrusted to Kirk. I'll defer strategy decisions to Kirk and Wedge, cost control to Nellie.

"Brewster," he said, turning to Brew, who anticipated being admonished. "I know you can't raise your goal, but it's not your fault. I'm going to commit to raise fifteen hundred dollars, five hundred of it coming from me today. That should ease your burden." He reached for a check.

After Hempstead departed, Wedge smiled as he poured a fresh cup of coffee. "Wasn't that great? We're going to have more money. We've got a powerhouse developing."

"It won't be that easy," Kirk said. "I suspect raising money outside this county is going to be even tougher because Ganner will now feel pressure and respond with intimidation wherever he can get away with it."

"Ever the pessimist," Wedge said with a smirk. "Except for you and that cynical sonofabitch who writes for the Banner-Press, I'm viewed as having come out of the chute with a full head of steam."

Nellie expected a biting response from Kirk, but he let that comment slide. He knew Wade Keene's observation had hit home with Wedge, which was all Kirk could ask for under the circumstances.

"Well," Brew broke the silence with a smile. "I believe you're both right. We're going to raise more money in Retama County than I had anticipated, but probably less elsewhere in the district. It's going to take a little slug of outside cash, from Austin or elsewhere, if we're going to meet the budget."

"It's good we've had this meeting," Nellie said. "We know better where we stand as a campaign, and we'll have to redouble efforts to bring in the money we'll need in time for the advertising commitments. Thank goodness that's not right around the corner."

Wedge excused himself to make a speech at a high school history class while Nellie went up front to her store and Brew left to make a few late afternoon calls on businessmen for contributions. Kirk sat down at his desk to review mail and newspaper clippings brought to him by Mrs. Fogel, who remained in the headquarters typing envelopes.

About an hour later, Nellie returned to ask Kirk some questions about Wedge's weekend schedule. She found only Mrs. Fogel, who said Kirk had departed abruptly without speaking to her, "which he's never done before. He just got up from his desk, tossed some paper in the wastebasket, and walked out."

Nellie retrieved the crushed letter which she smoothed out to read:

> Dear Kirk, I held this letter until Saturday to mail to make sure you wouldn't receive it until after the kickoff. I know how much that campaign means to you. I also wanted to hold it a couple of days to make sure it is what I should do.
>
> That's what it comes down to, what I should do, not what I want to do. I know I will love you as long as I live, but I have come to believe that things will never work out for us. The conflicts are too basic to be resolved in any manner other than a course in which one of us would be hurt for a long, long period of time.
>
> It's better to end it now and take the pain while we're apart, rather than face each other again. We would only try to rationalize our way through after another wonderful moment of passion and intimacy. I just can't do that again.
>
> Please know that you will forever be a part of me, a precious part, and I will always respect you very much.
>
> Carrie

Nellie noticed the key to the Laredo apartment was gone. She dashed to her car and wheeled the big green Buick from the parking lot toward the drive south to Laredo on Highway 81, accelerating right away to eighty miles per hour.

She hoped he might have stopped for a beer along the way, but saw no evidence of him during fifty fast minutes on the highway. She eased her car past the city sign.

If he runs to form, she thought as she entered Laredo, he will have gone across the river to our old starting place, the Cadillac Bar.

She cursed the delay crossing the crowded international bridge, but when she arrived inside the Cadillac parking area, she heaved a long sigh of relief when she spotted his car.

She gave the guard five dollars, pointed to Kirk's car, and explained it would probably be there overnight. She strode inside, intent upon letting him pour out his heart over however many drinks he might want, then taking him home in her car.

It was early evening, before the dinner crowd had assembled, but the bar was almost full. She glanced about the place and her eyebrows shot up when she could find no sign of him. She asked a bartender with a familiar face if he had seen Kirk, whom she described as best she could with her pidgin Spanish before he politely informed her he spoke a little English.

"He was here for only a short time. Drank three shots of tequila, derecho. Straight. Then he said, 'I'm going out there and get a new girl friend.' I said maybe he should take a cab, and he said that was a good idea."

Far south of the Cadillac, near the Monterrey Highway, Kirk had chosen his "new girl friend." She was a beautiful, well-endowed young prostitute with enough experience to know how to please a challenging customer, but not so much as to have become jaded.

In her dimly lit room, Kirk finished a beer with a flourish before undressing. In bed she clutched him against her firm, naked body, but he didn't respond.

"Too mucha drink?" she said in broken English but with a sympathetic tone.

"Nah, tired. Tired of... Ah, what the hell?"

Slowly, she rubbed his neck and shoulders. As his nostrils filled with the pervasive scent of cheap perfume, his mind moved gradually from poignant memories of Carrie to the soft body coaxing him her way. Her lips were on his neck, then his ears, biting gently. She kissed his lips, sliding her tongue inside until he felt his body tingling all over.

As he began making love to her, his anger and anxiety were transformed into powerful sexual energy, so powerful that he almost overwhelmed her with deep and rapid thrusting. But she adjusted and soon reached a shuddering climax shortly before he achieved his final seconds of intense pleasure.

Completely spent, he lay quietly beside her for several moments before the madam rapped on the door, contending their time was up.

"¡Espérate!" shouted the young prostitute, asking for a little more time.

The madam cursed but decided to drift away without a hassle, the young prostitute being one of her most productive employees.

Kirk appreciated her call for more time. He wanted to lie next to her just a few more minutes, savoring the temporary distraction.

Nellie departed quickly through the back door of the Cadillac to return to her car. She inched her way anxiously south on Guerrero Street, frustrated by the difficulty in maneuvering on the crowded thoroughfare that was always jammed in the market-downtown area that time of evening.

At last, she was able to make better time as traffic thinned on the far south side of Nuevo Laredo, where Guerrero Street became known as the Monterrey Highway.

She was looking for Papagayo's, the largest and best known of the brothels in that area, a considerable distance from the lower-priced prostitution zone in the deep east side known as "Boys' Town."

She dreaded the embarrassment of entering such a place, but she was also tantalized by the notion of seeing what she'd heard men of South Texas snicker about all her life. She soon spotted it, only about one hundred yards from the highway.

Its large bright neon sign shone in the crisp evening air as though flaunting the brothel's longtime presence in an uncluttered prestigious area containing a few large, expensive homes not far away.

As she drove up to park, she noticed the top of the ten-foot wall around the compound was filled with broken glass embedded in the adobe, a stark deterrent to anyone contemplating an unauthorized entry or exit. In the parking area, a security guard motioned her car to a spot with his flashlight, which he almost dropped when she came into view.

She marched past him, up the narrow sidewalk, and into the one-story building. It was a low stone and wooden structure, decorated in better taste than she had imagined, somewhat smaller and more intimate.

Though air-conditioned with window units, ventilation was inadequate and small clouds of smoke hovered about. A long bar, with dark red upholstery and matching stools, took up most of the far side. Tables with sturdy but comfortable chairs were placed all around the room, leaving only a small area for dancing.

She guessed about thirty people were there, half of them attractive, well-dressed Mexican prostitutes, catering to their Anglo clients in their twenties and thirties with the exception of two "old-timers" who appeared to be in their late forties or early fifties. Three couples were dancing slowly to "C'est Si Bon," a sultry song by Eartha Kitt that vibrated throughout the place.

The dancers were young men in casual attire with partners wearing bright form-fitting dresses and high heels. Their undulating bodies responded to music emanating from a flashy, multicolored jukebox at the far end, with its volume turned up a notch above normal.

Judging from the number of cars outside, she assumed several more men were in the compound enjoying themselves somewhere within the three little wooden buildings beyond the patio that contained the rooms for transacting business.

No madam was in sight, but a security guard was stationed unobtrusively near the glass back door where he could observe the front area and the patio.

A middle-aged bartender stood beneath a large painting of a voluptuous naked woman reclining on an elaborate couch. He rubbed his forehead in disbelief as most eyes turned upon Nellie, men intrigued by her very presence and the deep concern expressed on her beautiful face; women unable to hide their utter contempt for this "gringa chingada" making an unprecedented intrusion upon their turf.

Nellie had never experienced anything like this surrealistic atmosphere. She found it at once stimulating, yet frightening with the hostility toward her, the intruder.

Though anxious and nervous, she was determined to maintain her composure. She paused, scanning the people, refusing to engage the eyes glaring at her.

At last, in the far corner just past the bar, she spotted Kirk, huddled at a small table with a provocative young Mexican woman clad in a low-cut red dress slit halfway up her thigh. Nellie took a deep breath, eased past two gawking men at the bar, and tapped Kirk on the shoulder.

He turned around to face her, reeking of cheap perfume and with his lips and cheeks smeared with bright red lipstick. "Countess, you must be lost. The Cadillac and C.O.D. are a ways north of here."

"May I sit down?"

"But of course," he said, rising to arrange a chair for her. "This is my friend, Conchita. Conchita, meet my indomitable companion, the Countess of Justinville. Unfortunately, Conchita doesn't speak English, but that sounded good, didn't it?"

"I prefer," she snapped, "speaking to you alone."

He paused, with eyebrows arched. "All right," he said, gesturing to Conchita to leave.

"¡Cabrona!" she said with utter contempt, smashing her cigarette into the ashtray as she wheeled away from the table.

"What does that mean?" Nellie said.

"You don't want to know."

She handed him some facial tissue to wipe off the lipstick, which he did with some reluctance.

"Did you go to bed with that saucy little—"

"Whore? It's none of your business."

"I made it my business to find you because I thought you might want to talk about the situation with Carrie. I read the letter, and I thought it would be better to get it off your chest, rather than get wasted and maybe get in trouble."

"That's admirable of you," he said as he smiled, "but I was doing just fine before you arrived. And if it'll make you feel any better, I'm not drunk and haven't been in any trouble. Furthermore, I've only been to bed once with that little spitfire, but I must confess I'm thinking about another round. And you shouldn't be disrespectful to my new girl friend. This place was once named 'Conchita's.' Maybe after a relative of hers. You also need to know why some of us old gringos like to dally here now and then. These gals are much more into the preliminaries—drinking and talking and dancing—than their counterparts north of the border. They're also better in bed. More expressive, passionate, and—"

"That's quite enough! I understand."

He reached for his bottle, then poured a drink, downed it in one gulp, and chased it with a hearty swig of beer.

"What in the world are you drinking?" She glanced at the bottle of yellowish-colored liquor he had purchased on the way to Papagayo's from downtown.

"Mescal. It's a potent cactus juice that came along before tequila."

"What's that in the bottle?"

"Why, it's only a worm. There's a worm in every bottle of this brand of mescal."

"That's horrible." She grimaced. "How can you possibly drink from that bottle?"

"Well, I suspect that worm was pickled the moment he hit this stuff. In any event, I won't disturb him, and he won't disturb me."

"Why are you doing this?"

"Mescal is sort of a blue collar drink in Mexico. I may wear a white collar, but I'm just a blue collar guy, at heart. And let me recite for you something I just composed: Whiskey on beer, never fear. Beer on whiskey, kinda risky. Mescal and beer togetha, never hurt a fella… Not bad, is it?"

"If you stay here much longer, you're not only going to get drunk, you're going to get sick. Let's go downtown and get something to eat."

"No thanks. I like it here. Won't you have a drink?"

She wanted to leave, but she was more convinced than ever that he needed her to ride out the evening. But in this place? she said to herself, still uneasy from the effects of the animosity displayed around her.

"All right," she shrugged. "Just a Coke."

Kirk waved to the bartender.

"You know," he said, "I had to have a special dispensation from that bartender, old Paco, to bring this bottle in here. Ordinarily, it isn't permitted. You have to buy their whiskey in mixed drinks. Same old story about 'It isn't what you know, it's who you know.'

"I've known him since ten years ago when I first came in this place. I was a young virgin, a junior at dear old Justinville High School. I was plenty scared, but I made out like I knew what I was doing. I was drinking beer with some friends at the bar when I asked him who was the right gal for me.

"You know, I think he understood what a greenass I was 'cause he did me a great favor. Instead of sending me after one of the young hotpants I couldn't have performed with, and been terribly embarrassed, he steered me to the oldest gal in the place. And she broke me in the right way. Then, another—"

"Why are you telling me all this?"

He paused, toying with his empty glass. "I don't know. Maybe I just want to talk about anything other than her. I'm sick of her and I'm sick of politics."

"I know this a difficult time for you, but we really ought to leave. I'm afraid there might be trouble. The campaign would suffer if—"

"The campaign would suffer if I got thrown in jail. Always the campaign with you. Well, Countess, I really don't give a shit."

"You don't mean that."

"I don't? Well, I wouldn't be so sure." From his coat pocket, he produced a letter of resignation he had scribbled for Gordon Hempstead and handed it to her.

"All I needed to do was type it up tomorrow with carbon copies to you and Wedge, and it was all over. But now I'm glad you're here. It's more fitting that I resign to you since you're the one who badgered me into that goddamn campaign in the first place."

Nellie's emotions were swirling from a clashing mixture of contempt and compassion. She glanced over the letter and then crushed it in her hand. "What would your father think of this?"

Kirk glared at her. "When it comes down to whatever it is that needs to be done, it's my father's name that's brought to bear, or his old friends who come to the rescue. And when you want to singe my soul, you invoke my father. Dammit, that's Wedge Crayton's campaign. Not mine. Not yours. And not my father's."

He poured a double shot of mescal and downed it with one gulp, then shuddered from the biting aftertaste. He cooled his mouth by drinking the final third of his beer and promptly ordered another.

"And let me tell you something about our beloved candidate. He doesn't really yearn to nail Frank Ganner's scalp to the wall, nor Wally Hooper's, nor to serve with distinction the people of our district in the Legislature of the great State of Texas. He's on a macho ego trip. He's out to prove that his charm, wit, and pretty face will carry the vote so he can go to Austin and have a good time."

She took a puff from her cigarette, studying his face. "Isn't it true that deep down you're somewhat jealous of Wedge?"

He paused, lowering his head slightly while avoiding her eyes. "I guess I've never owned up to it until now. But most of all, today, Nellie, I just felt helpless… I can't compete in the league Carrie wants to play in the rest of her life. I sure as hell envy Wedge his money and standing. He's a player in that league."

"I don't see it that way. You're one of us, a player in our league, because you have the ability to understand power, how to attain it. You see things in the campaign that no one else sees. That ability can be carried forth in any career path you might choose. Carrie gave up on you. She didn't have much faith or patience. We appreciate your talent."

"Talent or curse? And your 'we' is only you. Wedge doesn't appreciate me. He dislikes me personally, and he resents the hell out of whatever political acumen I possess."

"Perhaps, but he respects you, and that's what counts for the campaign. Oh, I know you'll never like Wedge, but can't you at least admit some respect for him by the way he's warmed up to his role as the candidate?"

"Warmed up? The only time I've really seen him warm up was when he was playing water boy for Jordan Layman. Now, there's a real politician for Wedge to look up to, a true man of the people. He drops into our shindig in an expensive helicopter which is nothing but showbiz; drinks the best Scotch money can buy; hands out five-dollar bills to kids of our town to distribute his campaign material. That man of the people reeks of money, provided by his special interest friends in the oil and construction industries. Guess who he'll be looking out for in the United States Senate?"

"But he relates to more South Texans than does his opponent. That's what matters, and Wedge senses it."

"Fine, let him sense it but not go around gushing it in public."

"All right, have it your way tonight. But I do want to suggest you go on to Austin this week and seek more funding for the campaign. Wedge's father is balking, and Uncle Adrian has been scolding me about propping up the operation far beyond what I expected to do."

"You're not a very convincing liar, Countess. Hempstead has come up with enough to keep it going for a while and Brew will milk a few more bucks around Justinville in the afterglow of the kickoff. What you really mean is that in a few days, it might be time for me to approach Carrie."

"Take it any way you want. I just wanted you to know I still think a trip to Austin is a good idea."

A sardonic smile crossed Kirk's face. "You'd do or say damn near anything to keep me in that campaign… My dear, if the eyes are indeed windows to the soul, then political campaigns are searchlights, probing the soul, revealing much that we never reveal otherwise. Much we don't even want to admit exists in us at all… It's the quest for power, and it will devour your soul…"

Nellie shook her head. "Sometimes I can't believe you say those things. Why not get some sleep, go to Austin, and clear out the cobwebs?"

"No thanks… I'm thinking about going to California and starting all over… Excuse me, for the moment, I need to go south."

When he arose from the table, the mescal hit him. He paused, shook his head, and ambled into the restroom. He washed his face thoroughly after relieving himself. When he returned to sit down at the table, he found it more difficult to focus on Nellie, who wasn't making it easier by puffing on a cigarette. Through his diffused vision, she appeared somewhat distant, but sensuous and sensitive, and above all, beautiful as always.

"You know," he said, toying with a bottle of beer, "you're more beautiful than ever. You're more beautiful than Carrie."

"Now, Kirk, don't start—"

"No, it's true. You're more beautiful than Carrie, and you have more money. Why in the hell didn't I fall in love with you, instead of her?"

She wasn't quite sure whether he was teasing in a playful manner or turning to his bitter side, guided by the effects of the mescal. She reached for another cigarette, avoiding his eyes.

"Ah," he continued, "but that would also have been fruitless, because you are betrothed, at least emotionally betrothed, to the distinguished Wedge Crayton. But you know what? The hell of it is, he'll never marry you."

Rising from her chair, she tried to slap his face, but he caught her wrist.

"Goddamn you, Kirk! You had no right to say that."

"Sit down! If I didn't care about you, I wouldn't have said it."

She slid back slowly into her chair, her hands trembling so much she was unable to retrieve her cigarette.

"You need to understand. No matter how much you love him or how well you've rationalized that out over the duration, it's time to face up. You're much too beautiful and dynamic a creature to wait out all your good years for him. He's always taken you for granted. He's too goddamn stuck on himself to ever love anyone else ... And even if he did marry you, you'd eventually be miserable."

"I didn't come here," she snapped, "to discuss my personal life. It's yours that I'm concerned about."

"My problem, dear Countess, is history. Carrie said just look up at the scoreboard, game's over. I accept it. It's all over, and I don't intend to ruin this evening by crying over spilt milk. I came here to have a good time and listen to music. Doesn't that sound great?"

A Mexican number with a mambo beat came blaring from the jukebox. It was "Mi Corazon," later to be converted for the American market by Perez Prado as "Cherry Pink and Apple Blossom White." That vibrant music prompted more couples onto the dance floor, but Nellie declined Kirk's request to join them.

As Kirk watched the dancing, Nellie cooled down, driving from her mind what he had said about her long relationship with Wedge. She felt isolated, fearful that her efforts to keep Kirk in the campaign had failed.

What if he walks out of here, she asked herself, and we never see him again?

She lit another cigarette, sipped on her Coke, and watched the lively dancers a few feet away.

"Why so pensive?" he said.

"Kirk, you may be stumbling through a dark little corner of hell tonight, but your heart is still in the campaign. Don't leave us now, on a bad impulse."

"You can manage it, Nellie."

"I may have been a fool about some things now and then, but I'm not fool enough to delude myself into believing that."

He was experiencing the need to do double takes every few seconds to keep her face in focus. The thought of more mescal was repugnant, but somehow he continued drinking beer.

If I should express what I'd really like to do, Kirk mused, she's going to slap the hell out of me or just get up and walk out. Or both. Ah, why not try?

"Nellie, you've forced me to rethink my position, but it would require more than money and power and glory to get me back into that damned campaign."

"What do you mean?"

"Just this." He smiled. "I'll make a deal with you. You sleep with me tonight at the Laredo apartment, and I'll go back and manage that campaign for you lock, stock, and barrel."

Instead of reacting swiftly, as he anticipated, she paused, studying him at length. "You're serious?"

"I may be just a bit tipsy," he said with a shrug, "but I'm sure as hell serious."

She took a last puff from her cigarette before smashing it out. "All right, hotshot, let's go."

For a moment, he was exhilarated by her surprise answer, anticipating an easy conquest of this fascinating woman a hundred men in South Texas had fantasized about seducing for years. This was a way to get even with Carrie. Sure enough.

But as he rose from the table, the mescal hit again, and harder, with his head throbbing. The low clouds of smoke around him seemed to edge back and forth, as if trying to keep time to the pounding mambo music.

When they walked outside, the fresh air was uplifting for a moment, but a strong breeze from the south stirred dust into his nostrils. He coughed and sneezed. He staggered toward her car with his arm over her shoulder.

With help from the security guard, she eased him onto the front seat. Halfway to the international bridge, he passed out. Lucky for them, the

American customs officer on duty recognized Nellie and waved them through without questions or inspection.

At the one-bedroom apartment, she used a wet towel to coax him into a state of consciousness sufficient to walk the few steps inside. She steered him to the bedroom where she had almost no time to remove his coat before he fell into the bed, sound asleep. She removed his shoes, then slacks, and tucked him in. She gave him a soft kiss on the forehead, retrieved a blanket from the closet, and curled up on the couch in the front room.

In the morning, Kirk awoke to the unsettling smell of breakfast cooking. When he sat up in bed, he was hit with the effects of a searing hangover.

Nellie soon walked into the bedroom and offered him a glass of orange juice. He shook his head. "All I want," he groaned, "is aspirin."

She brought him two, and he reclined again. "Lord, Nellie, I haven't been out of control since Korean days. What the hell happened?"

"I believe it's fair to say you had a little too much to drink."

"Sure, but what happened? I remember us talking a lot at Papagayo's, arguing at times. About Carrie, Wedge, and the campaign. But I don't remember if anything was resolved. I know I offered to check out of the campaign, which you weren't too happy about."

"We reached an agreement about that. You pledged to manage the campaign, 'lock, stock, and barrel' were your exact words as I recall, if I would sleep in this apartment with you last night. Now, I've kept my share of the bargain, and knowing what an honorable man you are, I fully expect you to keep your share."

Kirk shook his head again, still awaiting relief from the aspirin. He took a sip of ice water, closing his eyes for a moment, trying to jog his memory. "Nellie, I... well, I just can't remember much. Did we, uh... well, you know what I'm trying to ask."

"The bottom line is that I stood by my commitment." She tilted her head to one side. "You must now honor yours."

"For Christ's sake, I can't go back and face Wedge without knowing what the score is, or was, between you and me. Now, that's just not fair."

"What was fair about my having to bail you out from that... that place last night? Don't try to weasel out. The question is, are you going to honor your commitment to manage the campaign?"

Kirk sighed. "Aw, hell, you could outmaneuver General Patton. All right. Now, tell me what happened last night."

"You got drunk and I was your babysitter. That's about it... Now, it's time for you to try some coffee. We're going to get your car in a few minutes, then return to Justinville. There's work to be done."

"What would have happened last night," he said, rubbing his forehead, "if I hadn't been so damn drunk?"

"Well," she said with a twinkle in her soft brown eyes, "I guess we'll never know."

Chapter 7

For two weeks, Kirk immersed himself in the tedium of the campaign, taking each day at a time, trying to keep Carrie from dominating his thoughts. After a long day's work, he relaxed at Barney's with a few games of shuffleboard or visited his mother and sister to play cards and listen to records and radio programs.

Most of the time he worked at the headquarters in Justinville, while Wedge roamed the district, speaking wherever a small gathering could be found that would listen. Often, Wedge spent a day walking sidewalks of the various communities, handing out campaign cards, talking to only one or two people at a time.

Kirk and Nellie were encouraged to see Wedge steadily improve as a candidate, surer in what he was doing, somewhat more perceptive and sensitive. He always carried plenty of cash to pick up tabs for food or beer, but he had learned to be sensitive toward those people who might resent being patronized by a relative stranger. On occasion, he would lapse into an aloof mood, failing to respond to jokes about life in drouth-stricken South Texas, since his points of experience and understanding were so limited.

But that was better, Kirk reminded Nellie, than responding with a naive or insensitive remark that would be repeated, creating lasting ill will toward their candidate.

For a change, Kirk had charted a two-day schedule in which he would accompany Wedge to enhance their understanding of grass roots people and to assess whether any changes in strategy or tactics might be warranted.

As they prepared to leave the headquarters, Mrs. Fogel brought the early edition of The San Antonio-Banner Press. It displayed front page news they had hoped to see ever since the Wedge decided to enter the race.

Under a headline of "South Texas Race Heats Up," Wade Keene described the development:

"Ernesto Garcia of Lantana, a young schoolteacher, made it official Tuesday when he announced for the open state representative seat, joining the field that includes Wally Hooper of Piedra Blanca and Wedge Crayton of Justinville.

"Speaking to a group of supporters on the lawn of the Coronado County Courthouse, Garcia outlined a vigorous reform campaign.

"Calling for 'competition, independence, and new directions,' he pledged to 'expose the fallacy of the patrón system in South Texas. It really should be termed a 'patronizing system' because they patronize us so they can exploit us… I'm going to campaign for more jobs, for better pay, working conditions, and health care. I'm going to call for improving education in order to provide more opportunity for our people. Above all, I'm going to lead the fight to free our people from the stifling effects of the corrupt and stagnant political system that dominates South Texas. At the core of that system is the poll tax which keeps so many of our people in political bondage. It must be abolished.

"Garcia enters the race with the solid backing of the Political Association of Mexican-Americans of Texas (PAMAT), a new maverick outfit that is openly critical of the patróns and jéfes of South Texas. Garcia is a founding member of that organization, becoming politically active after his return from military duty in Korea. He's a graduate of Texas A&I in Kingsville, another credential for a political candidate in South Texas.

"In the land where elections are usually decided at the outset by the dictates of a political boss, this race now has all the ingredients for creating suspense right down to the wire.

"Garcia will undoubtedly strike at the heart of the economic and political power structure created by the late Ernie Ganner and nurtured to greater heights of control by his son, Frank, 'The Baron of Bantrell.' For Garcia to win or to run a campaign with lasting impact, he'll need to secure his home base of Coronado County and chip away at Mexicano votes throughout the district, including the Ganner bailiwick of Bantrell and Will Dodd counties. That's no easy task, but this campaign could signal a new era in South Texas politics.

"Hooper is the handpicked candidate of Ganner, conceded to be the most powerful political boss in South Texas. Hooper entered the race as a heavy favorite, but with the vote now due to be split three ways, his vote potential has been seriously altered. There might well be a runoff in which anything could happen.

"Lonnie Hardner, editor of The Texas Progressive, the state's leading liberal journal, has already indicated he will support the PAMAT candidate. That means the few Anglo liberals living in the district might be disposed to support Garcia, rather than Crayton, who is running a narrow anti-Ganner campaign with little attention to legislative issues."

Wedge, who stood reading the newspaper article over Kirk's shoulder, slammed his fist on the desk. "Goddamn that Wade Keene! Every time I get what looks like a break, he has to bring out some negative opinion of his."

"Just be glad Garcia got into the race. I suspect Ganner exerted all the pressure he could to keep him out."

"What does this really mean for our campaign?"

"You just went from a fifty-to-one shot to a ten-to-one shot. Get in a runoff with Hooper, and you'll be about three-to-one. Odds where even I might think you could pull it off."

Nellie, who had read the article earlier, came into the headquarters smiling. "We're a step closer to victory."

"I wouldn't ice down the champagne just yet," Kirk said, "but it's a building block."

As they donned their coats to leave, Nellie complimented them. Wedge had a candidate's glint in his eye as he completed his "crumpled suit uniform" by tightening his tie into place just below his collar. Kirk wore a freshly pressed brown corduroy coat with open collar. He never designated that attire as a "uniform," but it was his obvious favorite.

And today, she mused, his eyes appear a little more determined.

With Kirk driving, they headed for Owen Kesterman's ranch. It was a cool, crisp April morning in which the South Texas sunshine was pleasant, an innocent precursor to the steaming heat that usually began in May. They observed the parched pastureland whose chief occupant was mesquite—not cattle— augmented by brush, prickly pear, and dead range grass. Near the road were a few patches of wildflowers, including bluebonnets and yellow buttercups.

"And so, what's the purpose of this rural schedule today?" Wedge said.

"I wanted us to get a closer look at how much impact the drouth is having on less fortunate ranchers and farmers."

"You mean the ones without any oil or gas production?"

"Yeah, or even leases."

"Sounds good… You know, Old Podnah, I've been damned cooperative lately, haven't I?"

"I suppose so."

"Haven't been complaining about scheduling or anything else."

"It's been going okay."

"Well, I'd like to ask a little favor."

Kirk had never experienced such a casual, polite approach from Wedge and he turned his head to one side and winced. "What is it?"

Wedge paused, glancing at Kirk. "All these years, Nellie and I, well, we've had sort of an unspoken rule about not delving into one another's private lives. We've never had a formal engagement, as you know, but we're much more than just friends."

"What is it you want from me?"

"It's just… I never could track down you or Nellie that night a couple of weeks ago, and Mrs. Fogel claims she doesn't know where either of you were."

Kirk adjusted his sunglasses without speaking or changing expression.

Wedge sighed. "I just want to know if you two were together."

At first, Kirk was inclined to simply tell Wedge the whole story, but upon reflection, he realized Nellie hadn't told him anything. Kirk savored the idea of Wedge being left in the dark, wondering if his lover had jumped fence.

Maintaining his stoic expression, he kept his eyes trained upon the dusty road. "All right, I'll tell you we were together. That's all you asked, and don't ask about it again."

Upon arriving at the ranch headquarters, Kirk observed that little had changed since his last time there, a hunting trip with his father years ago. The old one-story ranch house of stone and wood needed painting but appeared to be in good condition, resting under the shade of a lone, sprawling live oak tree that dominated the front yard.

Out back a retama tree and a few mesquite were evident, along with a tight row of oleanders. About fifty yards beyond, the corral, stable, and small barn appeared to be functional, and the windmill, which provided vital water for people and horses, was whirring away, thanks to a brisk southerly breeze.

Owen Kesterman met them near the old bunkhouse in which four cowboys once lived to help Owen and his late father work the spread of twelve thousand acres that had been in the family for three generations.

Observing it for the first time, Wedge noted everything about this ranch seemed to have been done with an eye toward saving money. No frills anywhere, not even around the house, where Owen, at age fifty-eight, lived alone since the death of his wife five years ago. His two daughters had departed already, one to teach school, the other to get married.

Owen's face was heavily lined from working outdoors most of his life. He wore faded denims that day, as he always did while working at his ranch. He was lean and tall, his height accentuated by weathered boots and sweat-stained old straw hat, blocked in traditional western style.

Though the place hadn't changed, Kirk detected a trace of weariness in Owen's resolute blue eyes, reflecting effects of the intractable burdens of drouth and loneliness pressing hard against a stubborn spirit.

"I have a couple of cowhands out there working today," Owen said, leading them toward his home, "but they live in town and drive out in their pickup. I wonder," he said as he smiled, "what my grandfather would think of that. His cowhands only left the ranch one day a week."

On the long back porch, they sat down with tin cups of fresh coffee the Mexican-American cook had prepared. His wife served it along with a platter of pan dulce, brightly colored sweet pastry they cooked twice a week.

"Kirk, I remember your dad bringing you out here to hunt javelinas when you had just turned ten. Remember?"

"Sure." Kirk nodded. "I remember hunting, and all the fine-looking cattle you had."

"Until the drouth. Now I can't afford to keep a large herd anymore, but every cow I sell, I lose money on. I may have to let those cowhands go if we don't get some rain soon."

"What kind of cattle are you running?" Wedge said.

"Still have the Zebu. Great cattle. My neighbor to the south has Charolais; to the north, Angus. They're all good cattle, but the odds of any of us surviving this drouth aren't good. We've got nothing to fall back on."

"I seem to recall," Kirk said, "you had some fields in cultivation. I guess that's over during the drouth."

"Yeah," Owen said with a nod, "and that's really hurting. If I only had some means to irrigate those fields and grow feed, I know I could stick it out."

Wedge stood up, surveying the countryside. "Suppose it were to rain three inches tomorrow. What would that do?"

"If it rained hard and fast," Owen said, stirring his coffee, "it would bring some fresh surface water for the stock tanks. That's sure important, and we'd have a little revival of the grass, but we'd need more than one heavy rain to break the drouth. We'd need some soaking rains too in order to bring this country back."

"But even then," Kirk said, "you've got the mesquite problem."

"Sure as hell do," Owen said. "Mesquite saps a lot of moisture that should go to the grass... You know, my grandfather used to sit me on his knee and talk about the days when he first settled here not long after the Civil War. He said this country was gentle plains with tall grass and not many trees. When it became real cattle country, the mesquite spread from cow dung, and it spread all over. I've tried everything I could to rid this ranch of mesquite. It's been cabled, chopped, and root plowed. Nothing works for long; it always comes back."

"You know, Owen," Kirk said, "with the problems you've got, ones you can't control, maybe you ought to open your ranch to deer hunting next season. You could charge enough to pay some feed bills."

"No, I'm not going to do that. This is a ranch, not a shooting gallery. If I can't operate it the way my grandfather and father did, then I'll just have to sell it and move to town."

In his old pickup truck, Owen drove them around part of his ranch to observe firsthand the ravages of the drouth. Near a dry, dusty creek bed, he stopped.

"See how scrawny they are," he said, pointing to several cattle searching for food in the pasture. "I've been burning pear and bringing in a little hay, when I can find somebody to sell me some at a price I can afford. Keeps 'em going, but it's not worth it, the way the market's stayed down."

Owen drove up to his largest stock tank, representing five acres of excavation done years ago that had provided, until the drouth, a dependable watering place for cattle on the vast pastureland around it. Now, its dry banks sloped down to only a few feet of muddy water remaining where three deer, a buck and two does, stood drinking.

All at once, Owen spotted a mountain lion perched on the far bank, slowly wagging his long grey tail as he observed the deer and planned his attack. Owen reached for his 30-30 rifle mounted behind the heads of Kirk and Wedge and eased out of the pickup. At the instant he took aim, the lion spotted his adversary and reeled from the edge of the tank.

Owen's shot sent dirt spraying just behind the lion, which disappeared unscathed into a nearby thicket of brush and mesquite. The deer scrambled up the bank behind them and fled to safety far from the thicket.

In disgust, Owen spat tobacco juice on the ground. "That sneaky sonofabitch has been killing some of my calves and goats. He's another one of the curses brought on by this goddamn drouth. They come over from Mexico looking for food, and they can take anything smaller than they are, plus anything they figure is weaker, large or small."

"You never hear much about them," Kirk said.

"That's because they're so damned smart and fast. You hardly ever see 'em. Best way to get 'em is by trapping, but that's a lot of time and effort, and I got too much else to do."

When they returned to the house, the cook had "dinner," as the noon meal was usually termed, waiting to be served on the long table in the old bunkhouse. Owen introduced his cowhands only as "Bud and Jake" when they sat down with their boss and his guests.

The centerpiece of this workingman's meal was a big platter of barbecued beef. Rounding out the meal were fried potatoes, pinto beans, and camp bread, a heavy mixture cooked that morning in the oven nearby. Barbecue sauce and ketchup were on the table, plus butter and molasses were provided for the bread. Iced tea with lots of sugar was the favored beverage during the warm days of spring and summer.

Kirk ate, enjoying every bite of this hearty food he had learned to love as a boy on hunting trips with his father and later with friends. Wedge found the tough stringy beef none to his liking, and the bread too thick for his taste, but he knew Owen's approval of him politically would rest upon his ability to relate there on the ranch. He ate some of everything at the table, as Kirk had admonished him to do before they arrived.

When they finished, the cowhands returned to their work while Owen, Kirk, and Wedge lingered at the table with coffee and pastry. Owen told more tales about life on the ranch while Wedge yearned to make his pitch and move on. But every time he glanced at Kirk, he caught a "leave him alone" signal.

At last, Kirk announced it was time for them to depart.

"Well," Owen said, glancing at Wedge as they walked to the car, "we never did get around to talking politics."

"I just assumed you'll vote for me," Wedge said, lighting a cigarette.

"Yeah, 'cause Kirk had told me you're going up against the handpicked candidate of Frank Ganner. I don't want that bastard in our country."

"I see. Is there anything I could do for you when I'm in the Legislature?"

Owen tipped his hat and smiled. "Pass a law that says it has to rain thirty inches a year in South Texas."

When they drove away, Wedge sighed, "I never realized how much better we have it at our ranch."

"Sure, and revenue from oil is the difference. Your dad can keep a large herd of fine cattle and feed them what they want, the high-priced feed Owen can't afford to buy. Your dad may wind up making more money on his cattle than if there weren't a drouth. Doesn't seem quite fair, does it?"

Wedge didn't respond. He continued viewing the bleak terrain as they moved onto a bumpy dirt road with a high center. Kirk veered about now and then to avoid having his car scraped underneath.

"What's this crazy road like when it rains?" Wedge said.

"We wouldn't be on it in a car. You'd need a pickup or jeep."

From Owen's ranch they drove to a crossroads "filling station" where they greeted several rural people when they stopped for gasoline. In the late afternoon they arrived at the Wortham farm home which stood on a gentle rise about one hundred yards from the Nueces River. It was a modest, one-story frame house with three bedrooms and screened porches, front and back. Its sloped tin roof glistened in the midafternoon sunshine.

Kirk squinted as he surveyed the area. A tall line of salt cedar trees provided a windbreak north of the house, and various trees—notably live oak, willow, and mesquite—abounded near the house and throughout the area toward the river. Beyond the backyard stood a windmill in need of repair, plus a chicken coop, a goat pen, and a barn where two milk cows waited in the shade. Farther, beyond a flat of thick dark green sachahuista reeds near the river, was the hog pen, barely visible to Kirk. He waved and whistled at two old hound dogs making a halfhearted challenge to their arrival.

"This is the Wortham place," Kirk said, "the pride of Garth Matthew Wortham and his wife, Sarah Beth. They lost two children at childbirth, right there in that house, but they've raised three others while scratching out a living on this farm the past thirty years or so. They're resourceful, God-fearing people who don't drink or smoke or take kindly to those who do."

Wedge removed the pack of cigarettes and matches from his shirt pocket and tucked them into the glove box amid Kirk's maps and envelopes.

"Also…" Kirk pulled to a stop near the house. "…this meal won't exactly be—"

"I know, Old Podnah. They're poor, but they're proud, sensitive people, and I'm to eat whatever they put on the table."

They encountered Sarah Beth in the side yard, hanging out clothes. A sturdy woman of medium height, she wore a simple blue cotton dress. Upon seeing them, she removed her matching bonnet. Her greying brown hair was swept back into a severe bun, the way she always wore it. Having known Kirk for many years, she greeted him with a brief, but sincere, smile and firm handshake.

Sensing Wedge was uneasy, she took him by the arm. "Garth's slopping the hogs. Be here soon. Let me show you my garden… The drouth has been terrible, but at least we have enough water, irrigated water from the river, to keep this garden and about a hundred acres."

"Your garden looks great," Wedge said, surveying the well defined rows of various vegetables. "I had no idea you could grow all this in early spring."

"Sure," she said with a nod. "We never even had a freeze this year. I can grow some things just about any time. That's Mother Nature's joke on us. We can grow good things year-round in our irrigated area, yet we can't grow anything on most of our land. More than five hundred acres is worthless at this time."

"Well," Kirk said, "couldn't Garth qualify for the Soil Bank Program?"

"Of course, he could," she said as she sighed, "but he won't. He's stubborn as an old mule. He says the government should never pay people not to grow crops, no matter what."

"So, it's been pretty rough," Kirk said.

"We can't afford the kind of well we need to irrigate more land. Our old pickup is about to give out, but we sure can't afford a new one… I haven't bought a new piece of clothing for Garth or me in almost two years. We haven't been out of the county in three years… Yes, it's been pretty rough, and I don't see much hope. We've had a few showers the past couple of years, but nothing like what's needed to break the drouth."

"Not the kind of situation to keep kids on the farm," Kirk said.

"I don't complain about that. Our two boys are in the Army, served in Korea, and didn't even get wounded. Thank God. Our daughter married a feed salesman from San Antonio. She's happy living there. Anyways, if the boys were here, there wouldn't be enough farm work to keep 'em busy. Garth spends half his time huntin' and fishin' 'stead of farmin' like he did 'fore the drouth came along. We don't have any money, but we eat real well."

Garth soon appeared, walking from a path through the sachahuista flat, carrying two empty buckets. He was an imposing figure at six-feet-four-inches and two hundred thirty pounds, all muscle. He wore overalls with multiple patches and a frayed cotton shirt, both bearing mud and other markings from the hog pen.

He waved to them before rolling up his sleeves to wash his hands from a hydrant near Sarah Beth's garden. With hands dripping, he wiped locks of graying but thick dark hair from his forehead, revealing his firm, friendly blue eyes. His handshake was the strongest Wedge had ever encountered, stinging his palm as Garth released it.

The stocky farmer slung his arm around Kirk. "You know, I used to tell your dad when he brought you all the way out here that he shouldn't do that unless he wanted me to take you fishing. Your father never had to ask for my vote; he always had it. He was a God-fearing Christian of the highest order. I loved him like a brother… Well, I suppose this young man I've just met is of like quality or you wouldn't have brought him here."

"Why, of course, Garth," Kirk said.

"How do you intend to ride out the drouth?" Wedge surveyed the barren, dusty fields beyond the distant south fence line. They were large fields that once grew cantaloupes, watermelons, onions, and peanuts, or whatever Garth might choose, including some types of grain.

"The drouth," Garth said in a resonant tone, "is an admonition from God. He wants people to stop ignoring Him while they try to make life so easy. You know, we've only had electricity and a telephone here on this farm for a few years. Now, I understand people want to air-condition their houses and automobiles. They want motion pictures called television in their homes, all the time. They drink and smoke and eat food from cans that I wouldn't feed my hogs. All people want to do is indulge themselves. It's destroying the moral fiber of all those who need to learn how to work hard to provide for their families and to develop what's really important, their relationship with God… No, I'm not worried about the drouth. I've come to grips with it."

"I guess mesquite isn't much of a problem for you," Wedge said.

"Once fields are in cultivation, mesquite is no problem for the farmer. It's in the pastures that it always comes back, sooner or later. But what those ranchers don't tell you is that most of their fence posts are mesquite or that they burn mesquite in their fireplaces and campfires. Any good hog farmer will tell you that mesquite beans are a good source of food, a cheap plentiful source with a sweet taste hogs really like. Now, I can't speak for everybody else, but I think there's no better eating than goat meat cooked over mesquite coals. Remember, Kirk, how much your dad liked to eat my barbecued goat?"

"Sure do, and he liked to eat fried fish here that he said only Sarah Beth could cook so well."

"Say, on that score," Garth said with a twinkle in his eye, "we just might have enough time to run my lines before supper."

They walked on another path through the sachahuista to the river where Garth kept a trot line baited at all times across the channel, plus several throw lines tied to oak limbs hovering over the water. He also fished there for hours with a bamboo pole. This was his favorite spot, a wide part of the river just below an unrepaired old dam that had been torn apart decades ago by a big rise.

"The Good Lord steered me to my land," Garth said, "with this hole close by. It's the deepest hole I know of in this old river; still holds better than twenty feet of water today. It's my life insurance." He smiled, patting the pipe extending from the ground to deep into the water. "We pump enough from here for Sarah Beth's garden and the hundred acres I still work."

"That hundred acres make you any profit?" Kirk said.

"I haven't had a money crop since the drouth started four years ago, but we live as the Lord provides. You walk in God's path, son, and you don't need a lot of money."

Kirk hadn't been there in years, but he experienced, as he had before, a sense of containment in this area. Large oak and willow trees grew close together, connected by dense vines forming thick curtains of foliage. It was a difficult area in which to maneuver except for the concrete remains of the dam from which Garth did his pole fishing.

Garth checked his trot line and found no catches, with most hooks devoid of bait. "These darn turtles are the problem," he said. "They just chew the bait off and don't get hooked."

"Do you catch any black bass around here?" Wedge said.

Garth chuckled. "There aren't many bass in the river, and now that this water is so muddy, they can't even see the bait. Mostly, I catch catfish, crappie, gaspers, and lots of sun perch. They're all good eating. And then, there's some weird creatures that hang around here. I saw an old alligator one time, and there's an alligator gar I'm after that's as big as that little canoe over there. I landed a six-foot eel three years ago that pulled harder'n any fish I ever caught. There's some feisty water moccasins as big around as your arm. I never fish here except in daylight ever since I stepped on one at night and he bit halfway through my work boot."

He lifted his right pants leg to display fang marks on his thick boot. "See?"

Without asking if they wanted to join him, Garth handed cane poles to Kirk and Wedge. They fished for almost two hours, using earthworms Garth had dug from nearby. Kirk was trying as best he could, but Wedge was bored by this mundane type of fishing, for him, slow and tedious compared to the constant casting for sporty bass in the big stock tanks on his father's ranch. They were able to catch only a few small perch, nothing worth keeping.

"I guess," Garth said at last, "we got no choice but to give up here. But maybe, just maybe, there'll be something on one of my throw lines."

Garth weaved his way through the vines and mud as he went about checking his lines tied to limbs without success until he led them to a sprawling oak tree with branches leaning into an area of stobs and brush in the water. As they approached, the oak limb with the line splashed furiously in the water.

Garth had fished all his life, but he always felt a special thrill when suddenly knowing a powerful fish was down there, its size and identity posing intriguing questions soon to be answered. The muddy bank made it difficult for them to move fast, but Garth led them steadily toward the line.

Consumed by anticipation, Kirk glanced over his shoulder and yelled at Wedge to keep pace, but Wedge had caught a cuff of his suit pants on a thorny vine and he waved to Kirk to go ahead without him.

"Dadgummit!" Garth yelled to Kirk as he neared the limb. "I forgot to bring the net. You lift him up, swing him over, and I'll grab him."

"Okay." Kirk eased into position by the splashing branches of the limb. "Ready?"

Garth planted his right foot in the muddy bank and placed his left into shallow water as far as he could step toward the line before reaching the drop-off point into deep water. "I'm ready! He's about three feet under the surface!"

Kirk took a deep breath. He steadied himself by holding onto a larger limb with his left hand while pulling hard with his right. But he couldn't bring the fish to the surface. Cursing under his breath, he suspected it might have run the line into some submerged brush. "Garth, I don't know what's down there, but we better get him up before he breaks the line!"

Wedge caught up to the action, offering to help.

"You're gonna muddy-up that fancy suit," Garth said, "but if you wanna help, hold Kirk around the waist so he can use both arms. Hurry!"

Pulling the line with all his might, Kirk felt the fish coming to the surface. As he brought its head into view, it suddenly thrashed about mightily, splashing muddy water onto all three of its excited captors.

"Heavens to Betsy!" Garth yelled, reaching for the line, but barely missing. "That's a big catfish! A darn big catfish!"

Kirk moved the heavy limb a few inches closer to Garth, who managed to grab the line above the head of the angry fish and bring it onto the bank. It squirmed in the mud, struggling to shake free.

With one hand firmly holding the line just above the fish's head, Garth used his other hand to pass his hunting knife to Kirk, who cut the line near where the knot was tied to the limb. Garth dragged the heavy fish several feet from the water, then lifted it up for them to see.

Wet, and still trembling from excitement, Kirk and Wedge marveled at the big catfish Garth estimated to weigh thirty pounds.

"You know, my friends," Garth beamed, "this is the biggest catfish ever taken out of that hole. We'll just have to hurry on up to the house and tell Sarah Beth that it's not fried chicken for supper, it's fried catfish."

As they trudged along the path to the house, Garth held forth about the value of such a fish. "I haven't had a bite of beef in almost two years. I sure miss it, but the Lord has been smiling upon us. We have all the chicken and pork we can eat, plus I kill a few rabbits now and then, and deer. Venison is good, almost as good as beef, at least the back strap.

"We like javelina, too, if it's about half-grown. Any larger and it tastes musky. But, now, you take this catfish. There just isn't any better tastin' meat, 'specially since he's so big. I'll just kinda cut chunks or steaks and then we won't have to worry about bones."

Sarah Beth took a picture of Garth with his prize, flanked by his assistants who promptly hung out their coats to dry. While Garth cleaned the big catfish, Sarah Beth went about preparing other items for the evening meal. She planned to offer field corn on the cob, fried okra, and yellow squash plus a large tray with sliced cucumbers, onions, and tomatoes, all fresh from her garden.

As they stood behind their chairs waiting for her, Kirk smelled a tantalizing aroma from a pan of thick buttermilk biscuits she had just removed from the oven. Homemade churned butter and honey taken that morning from the Worthams' own beehive were set out to enhance them.

When they sat down to eat, Garth said the blessing. "Bless us, Oh Lord, your humble servants as we follow the spirit and love and teachings of your son, Jesus Christ. Always remind us of Thy will and guide us upon the path of righteousness ... We thank Thee for the blessing of bountiful food, here upon our table. We thank Thee for this fine young man whose destiny it is to serve Thee and the people in the honorable and trustworthy manner of the late beloved Judge Holland, who is in Your hands in Heaven. In Jesus' name we pray. Amen."

Kirk nudged Wedge whose "amen" came a little after the others at the table.

Garth handed the steaming platter of fried catfish to Wedge, whom he had designated as honored guest. As plates were served, Sarah Beth placed a bottle of ketchup on the table, along with a saucer of sliced lemons.

"Well," Garth said, with a note of sarcasm in his voice, "you're welcome to put ketchup and lemon juice on your fish, but for me, there's nothing like the pure taste of good old catfish." He bit into his piece, chewing vigorously at first, then slackening up.

Wedge took a hearty bite of catfish he was barely able to keep in his mouth. My God, he thought, it tastes like mud.

Kirk glanced around the table before taking a bite. The other three had paused, seemingly at a loss as to what to say. He cut off what appeared to be a large bite, but slid it behind his biscuit, and sliced a smaller piece. That nibble convinced him of his suspicion.

Hell, he thought, old Garth is so proud of this damned catfish, but it was one of those bottom feeders, living in the mud.

"Well, now," Kirk said as he smiled, "I believe this fish is one of the kind I just read about. Some research outfit has found that bottomfeeding fish are the most nutritious. For fish to feed on, nothing in the river has more food value than crawfish and turtle eggs. The only way fish get to them is at the bottom, or in the banks... you know, where it's muddy."

"Where'd you learn about this?" Garth said, rubbing his chin.

"Some article in an outdoors magazine."

"You know," Garth said, studying the tray containing several thick pieces of catfish, "come to think of it, I had a big crawfish for bait on that line, instead of frogs like I'd been using with no luck."

"There you are. You'd never have caught that beauty unless you switched to the muddy-type bait. Now, the downside is that the fish tastes a little muddy, so probably the best thing is to use some ketchup or something to help the flavor."

"Kirk, I'm sure glad you brought this out," Sarah Beth said, "'cause I've had some tartar sauce stored in the ice box for a special occasion. This will be it."

With the catfish soaked in ketchup, tartar sauce, and lemon juice, it was tolerable. As they munched away, Sarah Beth said to Wedge, "We're honored you came all the way out here, where hardly anybody ever comes. We have only two votes. Are they that important to you?"

"Why, yes they are," Wedge said. "The vote of every single person is important."

"What made you decide to run?" Garth asked.

"I guess I want to improve things for people. Help make life better."

"Is that our duty?" Garth said. "Or, is that the duty of each person?"

"Government can help sometimes when help is needed." Wedge studied Garth's face.

"Well, just remember what I said about making things too much easier. Far as I'm concerned, air-conditioning, television, and all such as that, are making life worse, not better. People don't spend enough time outdoors anymore. And when they're inside, they're watching television or listening to the radio. They don't read the Bible. They don't read anything."

"I respect your views, Mister Wortham," Wedge said, "and I hope you will respect my integrity. That's really all I have to offer."

"Garth," Kirk said, "we may not agree on some issues and trends, but that integrity is what counts when you think of Frank Ganner moving in."

David and Goliath crossed Garth's mind as he studied the serious, slender young man who was challenging the powerful forces of Frank Ganner. The Lord does indeed move in strange and wondrous ways, he thought, glancing at his wife, who nodded. "You need all the help you can get, son, against the evil force you seek to defeat… We'll vote for you."

As they drove away from the farm, Wedge lit a cigarette he had been craving. After exhaling a long puff, he sighed. "Wow, what an experience!"

"They're part of a dying breed, but I wanted you to get a feel for all that."

"Sure, I understand… but don't ever accuse me of demagoguery. That bit about the muddy fish being more nutritious almost cracked me up."

"That wasn't demagoguery. That was a bald-faced lie."

"Do you really think he believed you?"

"I don't know. I just tried to think of what Dad would have said. He had a way of making people feel good, no matter what... I guess I felt just how proud old Garth was of that damned catfish and I didn't want to see all the wind let out of his sails."

On the following morning, they campaigned for two hours in the tiny community of Hallockville where the center of attention was the general store with its lone gasoline pump. The back room was the only gathering place for the men of the village who kept a domino game going constantly with the heavy odor of stale cigar smoke hanging in the air.

Kirk "shot the bull" with whomever was willing to talk in the store. Wedge, after overcoming a few coughs and sniffles, shook all the hands available and passed out cards there and at the little restaurant nearby where they would eat lunch. Kirk noticed Wedge was becoming more accustomed to such heavy noon meals as that placed before them that day, the sixty-five-cent special that included two big pieces of fried chicken, mashed potatoes with cream gravy, green beans, and cornbread, plus a large glass of iced tea and a small dish of chocolate pudding.

Halfway to their final destination of the day, Wedge retrieved a file folder from his briefcase. It contained clippings from The Harmon County Herald, the weekly newspaper published by Edgar Howard, who had scheduled Wedge for an interview that afternoon.

Howard's paper was published in Morgandale, population almost five thousand, about forty percent of which was Mexican-American. Some six thousand more people lived in small communities and on large ranches around the county of one million acres, roughly the size of Retama County. As was true in most sparsely populated South Texas counties, there was only the one newspaper, published in the seat of county government.

Skimming through the file, Wedge was surprised to find so many editorials critical of Frank Ganner, dating to three years ago when Howard first sensed Ganner was itching to expand his influence into Harmon County. Since the state representative race had officially started, the hard-hitting thrusts had been intensified, along with comments favorable to Wedge.

Early on, Howard had termed Ganner "an ambitious neighboring political figure who bears watching ..." Of late, he had branded Ganner with such as "the Baron of Bantrell County is a ruthless tyrant who must be stopped. Every law-abiding, freedom-loving citizen should be aware of what's really at stake in this election."

Wedge read aloud excerpts from the editorials, plus a highly favorable feature story about their campaign kickoff function in Justinville. "This is an editor after my own heart."

"Yeah, he knows how to write purple prose. If we had a newspaper like his going in every county of this district, we'd be in the driver's seat. Instead, we only have this one."

"It was nice to get an early endorsement from our hometown newspaper, but why doesn't that editor hit Ganner the way Howard does?"

"Who knows? Some people don't like controversy. Then, maybe Howard's a little unusual. He's more of an old-school, crusading newspaper editor. He moved down here from West Texas ten years ago. He just flat refuses to accept corruption in any form, and he's feeling the heat from the Ganner machine next door."

"And then," Wedge said dryly, "there's the old master himself, Wade Keene."

Kirk kept his eyes trained on the road, but his hands tightened on the steering wheel. "Don't knock him. He's not a charter member of your fan club, but I sure as hell hope he stays on top of this race."

They drove straight to Edgar Howard's newspaper office. The editor-publisher took Wedge around to meet his three-member news staff and the five people working in the "back shop." There, a job printing business was being conducted along with the production and distribution of the newspaper. Edgar directed a beehive of activity, and now in his early fifties, was grooming his only son, Bobby, to succeed him.

At nineteen, Bobby had become the "spitting image" of his father, according to the Herald's employees, not only in physical appearance, but in possessing boundless energy and dedication to the newspaper and the community.

Edgar informed them he was tied up for an hour or so. Bobby was assigned to take them around for brief get-acquainted sessions with key leaders, including the president of the bank, owners of the two car dealerships, a farm implement and feed store owner, and the superintendent of the high school.

"On that last stop," Edgar said to Wedge, "the superintendent will take you to a PTA meeting at which I want you to at least show an understanding of the Gilmer-Aiken legislation. I know you're running an essentially anti-Ganner campaign, which I support all the way, but you've got to show some of these people you'll know what to do in Austin, regarding their interests."

Wedge glanced at Kirk, who shrugged.

"I'm familiar with that legislation," Wedge said. "I'll be happy to discuss it with them."

As they made the rounds, it became obvious Edgar's spadework was effective. The community leaders appreciated their clean county government and were ready to support Wedge as the alternative to the possible intrusion of Frank Ganner's machine. They were uneasy about the upstart PAMAT candidacy, afraid it might be the vanguard of a developing radical movement that could eventually polarize their community along purely ethnic lines.

For Wedge, who had worked the streets of Morgandale handing out campaign cards on a previous visit, this was his first opportunity to persuade opinion molders that he was more than just an anti-Ganner alternative. He was a well-informed candidate who would represent them well in Austin.

In the uncertain political climate that hung over the community, Wedge was well-received and no difficult or embarrassing questions were raised.

Driving to the school, Bobby wiped tousled brown hair from his forehead, squinting into bright sunshine. "Mister Crayton—"

"First mistake, Bobby," Wedge said as he smiled at him. "Don't dignify politicians too much. It's plain old 'Wedge.'"

"Well, Wedge, I just wanted you to know I think you're doing real well, and whenever you need some help in this county, let me know. Dad is real strong for you, but he's awfully busy."

"How is it you're not in school?" Kirk said.

"I finished my first semester in college, but I convinced Dad I ought to work with him this semester. What better way to learn the newspaper business than with my dad? He's the best editor and publisher in South Texas."

"And you just happen to be his only son?" Wedge said.

"Only child. Mother and Dad lost my little sister to pneumonia when she had just turned five. She was three years younger than I. That nearly killed Mother 'cause she believed if we'd have lived in a big city, better medical treatment would have made the difference."

Wedge gave a thorough presentation about the landmark Gilmer-Aiken bill, enacted a few years previously, impressing teachers, administrators, and parents.

Upon leaving the school, Kirk said, "Where'd you get all that?"

"While you've been drinking beer and sliding pucks down a shuffleboard at Barney's, Old Podnah, I've been doing my homework."

In his cluttered office, Edgar Howard conducted a wide-ranging interview, leading Wedge into several of the desired anti-Ganner comments, and he allowed Bobby to weigh in with a couple of questions. Satisfied he'd covered all the ground needed for the newspaper, Edgar closed his notepad and lit his pipe. "Now, let's go off the record… How do you see this Garcia candidacy and the PAMAT movement?"

Wedge deferred to Kirk, who said, "It may portend some difficult times ahead for race relations in South Texas, but it's a Godsend for our campaign. Unless somebody produced a picture of Wally Hooper making love to a billy goat, I don't think there's any way we could defeat the Ganner machine without an ethnic division… And, of course, we have to have a hot Senate race to further stimulate voter turnout. How do you see that one shaping up?"

Edgar tapped his pipe in the ashtray. "Appears as though Jordan Layman will carry South Texas by a wide margin, but if I had to bet money, I'd put it on Holt Witherspoon. It's hard to overcome a candidate who will probably carry Dallas, Houston, and most of West Texas."

"But, Edgar," Wedge said, "what about my race, here in Harmon County?"

"In this county, I believe you will receive forty to forty-five percent; Garcia, thirty to thirty-five; balance to Hooper."

"If we go into a runoff with Hooper," Kirk said, "and he has run third in this county, it would be a real psychological boost for us."

"We'll do all we can," Edgar said. "My disdain for Frank Ganner is about as pervasive as the drouth."

"You've hit harder than anyone around," Kirk said. "It's bound to have had some effect."

Edgar stood up, indicating the meeting was adjourned. "All right, how about supper at our place? Meat loaf, mashed potatoes, and all the trimmings."

"Thanks, but we can't," Wedge said, shaking his head. "We need to grab a hamburger and hit the road. Heavy schedule tomorrow."

Darkness was falling as Kirk and Wedge drove from the newspaper office to a service station for gas and on to a small hamburger stand on the main street. There they encountered Harmon County Sheriff Arnold Donovan, a tall, wiry fifteen-year veteran of law enforcement whose aura of authority was enhanced by the prominent badge he displayed with pride, plus the imposing ivory-handled, .45-caliber revolver he wore in a brown leather holster on his right hip. While slowly stirring a mug of coffee, he tipped his grey Stetson, and they joined him at a small table under the arbor behind the hamburger stand.

A friend of his father's, Kirk had known the sheriff for several years and respected the reputation he had earned for even-handed enforcement of the law. They chatted about the drouth and politics, enjoying their hamburgers while the sheriff drank coffee.

As they prepared to leave, they jolted at the unmistakable sharp crack of a rifle shot nearby. Kirk and Wedge jumped into the car with the sheriff, who muttered, "Hope to hell they didn't get Edgar."

The sheriff drove the two blocks to the Howard house, without using his siren or special lights, hoping to surprise whomever fired the shot. He pulled up first to the only unlighted area nearby, a vacant lot with mesquite trees and cactus that could have served as concealment.

No one was in sight except a small boy with his bicycle, standing behind a large clump of prickly pear a few feet from the road.

"Stay there!" the sheriff called to him as he wheeled toward the Howard home.

A body lay on the ground in a shadowy area outside the back door, near the garage. They made out a second figure leaning over the fallen body.

Racing from the car, they came upon the driveway and recognized Bobby on the ground, in his father's arms. Mrs. Howard, apron flapping from her cotton dress, came out the back door, screaming with hysteria.

The bullet had torn a gaping hole in Bobby's chest, and it was bleeding profusely. Edgar held up Bobby's head, coaxing him to hold onto his body, but he didn't respond.

The sheriff knelt down, then eased back for a moment as Mrs. Howard took her son from Edgar, and held his head in her arms while tears streamed down her cheeks. Bobby lurched slightly, and his mother looked at Edgar with pleading eyes. "He's still alive, isn't he?"

Edgar bowed his head, closing his eyes. "No, Mama, he's gone."

Feeling faint, Wedge stepped back into the dark shadows near the garage. Instead of needing to vomit, his stomach had simply tightened up on him, a wrenching sensation that lasted several seconds. After he steadied himself against the garage, he was able to rejoin the group.

For a long moment, Mrs. Howard clutched Bobby to her bosom, sobbing and trembling. At last, she looked up to them and whispered, "Take him in the house, to his bed."

Kirk and Wedge carried Bobby's body to his room under her direction, while Edgar collapsed, head in hands, at the kitchen table.

After the sheriff had determined Bobby was dead, he wheeled around and strode to the vacant lot where the boy, though trembling with fear, was still standing next to his bicycle. He was the ten-year-old son of a neighbor, who said he had stopped after sundown to chase a cottontail rabbit in the vacant lot.

He told the sheriff he was crouched down, looking for the rabbit near some prickly pear when a car pulled up nearby, with a driver and another man in the front seat. They parked in the shadows, away from the street light down the block.

With the driver remaining in the car and the motor running, the other man stepped out. He aimed and fired the rifle. He stepped back into the car and they drove away.

The boy was unable to identify either person, nor tell the color of their skin, but after the car drove away near the street light, he told them, "It was pretty new and green with fancy white sidewall tires."

Satisfied that was all the boy knew, the sheriff relayed the description to the nearest station of the Texas Department of Public Safety which immediately alerted its units in the area, then notified the wire services, AP and UP. Radio coverage might assist in finding the killers, but the sheriff believed the murder wasn't the work of amateurs, and avenues of escape were indeed varied. Morgandale was something of a crossroads for that area of South Texas. In addition to the two state highways that ran through the town were three ranch roads, and those hooked up with others not far from town.

The sheriff trudged back to the Howard home where a few friends and neighbors had gathered. The Howards' pastor, Wesley Blanchard, soon arrived to console Mrs. Howard, giving Edgar a chance to get some fresh air outside. Kirk and Wedge stood by as the sheriff put his arm around Edgar, who broke into sobs.

"Oh God, Arnold, that bullet was meant for me… I always check back at the paper one last time each night just after sundown. It's a habit more than anything. Tonight… Tonight, my bad knee was acting up, so I asked Bobby to go… Oh, my God, look what I've brought about… "

Kirk and Wedge stood by, their blood-soaked coats in hand. Wedge wanted to console Edgar, but Kirk restrained him, sensing only the sheriff might help at the moment.

The sheriff knew full well that from the assassin's position in the darkened vacant lot, viewing the dimly lit area near the house, Bobby could easily have been mistaken for Edgar. But he wasn't thinking as the veteran sheriff of Harmon County, he was thinking as the old friend of a man whose heart and soul had just been ripped from his life.

"Now, Edgar, let's not jump to conclusions. We don't know what the motive for this was, and until we do, let's just try to remember how much Bobby meant to his family and community. That's what's important now. That's what Bobby would want."

As the news spread, more friends of the Howards came, filling the modest frame home and backyard. The sheriff departed to participate in the search, after assuring Kirk and Wedge there was nothing more they could do.

On the return trip to Justinville, Wedge sat in silence for several minutes as Kirk set a brisk pace. At last, with trembling hands, he lit a cigarette and looked at Kirk. "What was it like over there?"

"What do you mean?"

"In combat, when you saw somebody killed?"

"Hell, I was just thankful it wasn't me."

"Yes, but how did it feel when it was someone close to you, like a buddy?"

"Well…" Kirk shrugged. "It's hard to remember… I guess I asked some of those hard questions I knew no one could answer, like, 'Is what we're doing over here worth dying for?' Or, just, 'who really gives a shit?'"

"You didn't seem to react much to what happened a while ago."

"There wasn't anything I could do."

"But you didn't seem to, well—"

"Look, Wedge, every man is different. I've seen men die, more than I'd like to recall. Bobby was a helluva nice young man; but he's gone."

"I just don't know," Wedge said, his voice faltering, "how anyone could do something like that, and in cold blood."

Kirk sighed. "Look, you need a drink. Fish around in the glove box. A flask of whiskey is in there somewhere."

Wedge took a swig of bourbon, then another. When Kirk declined, he returned the flask to the glove box and smashed his cigarette out. "But you do believe the bullet was meant for Edgar?"

"Yeah."

"And the motivation was the anti-Ganner campaign?"

"Edgar has been a crusading editor for years. Against illegal drugs, which Ganner doesn't deal in, plus exploiting wetbacks, which all the honchos do. We don't know anything at this point. We may never know."

Wedge paused. "We're in a war with Frank Ganner."

"Sure, but that was true before what just happened. Now, you'd better be careful. You can't say anything publicly to imply Ganner had a hand in this unless there's some evidence to support it."

"Don't you think that was a professional job? Quick hit, hidden in darkness. The perfect crime if that kid hadn't been chasing a rabbit."

"It was well planned all right, but until there's some evidence, we can't allege, charge, or imply a damned thing."

"I'm convinced it was a professional job carried out by paid killers. That car is already stashed in some nearby hiding place, the murder weapon has been buried, and those two guys are driving around in another car, probably in Bantrell County."

"You're the lawyer. We need evidence."

Nellie greeted them at the headquarters. "I heard the news on the radio. I took the liberty of canceling campaign activity for two days, until after the funeral. I believe we should all attend."

"Sure," Kirk said, glancing through his stack of mail and newspaper clippings. "I'm going home and get some rest."

Alone in the headquarters, Wedge and Nellie seemed distant and uncertain to each other for a few moments since their lives had been touched by the same event, yet they hadn't been together to share the experience.

"I guess you're pretty worn down after a day like this," she said.

"I'd give anything for a cool shower."

"Let's go to my place. Remember, you're off until the funeral. Rest, relax; then we'll regroup."

On the drive to her ranch home, they chatted briefly about trivial items, neither caring to rehash the tragedy in Morgandale, nor even discuss important aspects of the campaign.

He took a shower and they went to bed. She lay on her side, viewing the star-filled sky. She waited to hear his gentle snoring, usual after he fell asleep, but his breathing remained constant.

"What is it, Wedge?"

"Nothing. Why don't you go to sleep? We can talk tomorrow."

"You need the sleep more than I do. What's troubling you?"

He sighed. "I guess it's just that I'd never seen anyone die before, much less murdered… He was just a kid, a damned nice kid."

She sat up in bed, reaching for a cigarette. "All we can do is fight harder to win this race."

"But is it worth it? Is it worth it to cause the death of innocent people?"

"I suppose that's something you have to confront again. I thought we'd crossed that bridge when we decided to launch this campaign."

"You two are the gut fighters. Relentless… I'd like to be in the Legislature, sure, but I'm not equipped to fight this kind of war. I want out."

She paused, exhaling a long puff. "Oh, hell, you can't mean that. Look what's been accomplished."

"I surely do mean it. I'd rather bow out now, before the filing deadline. Let Kirk run. He's up to this, and besides, he relates more to the people at the bottom of the ladder. I don't relate to them, and they don't like me. Only reason they'd vote for me is because I show up with Kirk, whose old man they adored… Or, father figures, like Edgar Howard and Gordon Hempstead, assure them that it's okay to vote for this rich stuffed shirt. He's the alternative to that no-good sonofabitch, Frank Ganner, and his puppet, Wally Hooper… I don't like it at all… I'm sick of it."

Again, she paused, choosing her words carefully lest she drive him even further in the direction he had just indicated. "Kirk wouldn't run. He made that clear at the Cadillac pow-wow before you agreed to make the race."

"That was before he lost his life's love in Austin. Now, his heart is back in South Texas."

"Wedge, he won't run. He lives week-to-week. As he stated, he couldn't afford to win, much less run."

"You know a lot about him, don't you?"

"Sure. We've worked together closely."

"You care for him as well."

"Of course, I've known him since he was a little boy."

"I mean 'care' in a stronger context."

She bristled. "I'm not sure what you're implying," she snapped, "but I'm not going along with it. If you still care for me, you'd better stop whining about quitting the race… Are you blowing all this smoke to cover your fear that there's another bullet out there, and it's meant for you?"

Trembling with anger, he sat up to confront her. "Goddammit, I'm not afraid!"

"Then, I suggest you knuckle down to the task at hand."

In the semidarkness, he stared at her in silence, unable to engage her eyes, but studying the contour of her lovely face and the soft hair, barely visible, resting upon her gently rounded shoulders. Bit by bit, his anger subsided. He pulled her to him and they soon fell asleep in each other's arms.

Bobby Howard's funeral drew an overflow crowd to the small First Methodist Church of Morgandale. Bobby had been senior class president in high school, an outstanding student who lettered in football and basketball. All his friends attended, along with friends of his father and mother, who had long been active in church and community activities. Bobby's appeal crossed ethnic lines. Three of the young pallbearers were Mexican-American, and their parents, plus friends, were in attendance.

In the back of the church, Sheriff Donovan stood by the door, maintaining a stoic expression, though his eyes reflected the fact he had slept little since the murder. Nearby, Kirk sat thinking of key forthcoming events in the campaign while Wedge and Nellie studied the people as they walked slowly to the open casket at the front to bid farewell to Bobby.

More than sorrow etched their grim faces; traces of anger, bitterness, and frustration over the tragic loss of this bright, young spirit who had provided so many sparks to enrich their lives in that lonely little town. The testy mood was intensified by the fact no trace of the killers had been found.

Shortly before the service was scheduled to begin, Ernesto Garcia of Lantana, the PAMAT candidate for the legislative seat sought by Wedge and Wally Hooper, arrived to stand near Kirk.

Smart move coming here, Kirk mused, but he surely doesn't look like any combat veteran or firebrand politician in that bland suit and glasses.

To Nellie, he appeared clean-cut and fairly attractive, his dark hair trimmed well and his tie in place almost perfectly. Though thin and of medium height, he had a presence derived from confidence and determination expressed in his large, brown eyes.

Upon seeing him, Wedge smiled and reached over to shake his hand.

"Do you think," Nellie whispered to Kirk, "Wally Hooper might show up?"

Kirk shook his head. "Not," he muttered, "if he's interested in living any longer."

Beyond a large display of flowers, clad in customary black suit, was Blanchard, the slender, sixty-two-year-old pastor of the church. He sat at attention, near the pulpit, Bible held tightly in his lap, as the choir worked its way through that most challenging Methodist hymn, "Are Ye Able?", which was a favorite of the Howard family.

Kirk sensed that Blanchard felt ill at ease, confined by the standard funeral format. The grey-haired pastor spoke in measured tones as he carried out his duty, and when the young pallbearers removed the casket for the brief ride to the cemetery, he consoled Edgar and Marjorie Howard. Edgar's bad knee had been buckling on him, forcing him to use a cane and to stoop over now and then. He appeared to be shorter than his wife; a man, Kirk thought, who had aged ten years in two days.

At the barren, dust-swept cemetery, a supporter who wanted to whisper a few words of advice detained Wedge near their car. Kirk escorted Nellie to the only tree near the gravesite, an old live oak that afforded some protection from the hot sun and the swirling wind blowing dust across the grounds. She held onto her hat as Kirk moved away to allow more women access to the shade. He almost bumped into Wade Keene, who had just arrived from San Antonio, and they stood silent as the last of the people assembled.

When Rev. Blanchard stepped forward, flaps from the temporary tent for the family were popping from the persistent wind and gusts. He recited the Twenty-Third Psalm, his voice slowly gaining in strength and resonance. As he finished, he looked down at the closed casket, covered with flowers. It was a long pause, during which only the flapping of the tent and a few coughs were heard clearly, though it was obvious many people, in addition to the Howards, were weeping quietly.

At last, Blanchard cleared his throat, surveying the crowd. "Today, I have preached and I have prayed, but I have something more to say... This young man was taken from us by the hands of vicious murderers! They had no cause to do this! I hear it said they were after Bobby's father. They had no cause to kill him!...

"My friends, no one on this earth has the right to kill another except in self-defense or in time of war. Let us all rededicate ourselves to the proposition that we shall re-create a safe community, and preserve honest government for the people. In this hour of great sorrow, extend the hand of friendship and the heart of love to Edgar and Marjorie Howard. They have suffered a loss far greater than any of us can imagine..."

Blanchard's face contorted as he continued, pointing his right forefinger above the crowd. "For those of us who have understood the danger incurred by Edgar Howard's unstinting opposition to corruption and his dedication to honesty and integrity, there is a conclusion that must be drawn."

Wade Keene whipped out his notepad.

"The political corruption in the adjoining county may very well have spawned the dastardly deed that occurred here recently. Their denials mean nothing! Let those who fuel the corrupt machine submit themselves to thorough examination by law enforcement officials we trust, such as our own sheriff and Texas Rangers. The denials mean nothing because they come from men without one ounce of integrity in them! They're corrupt overlords who prey upon their ignorant, innocent victims by manipulating the political process to their liking. They're cheats, four-flushers, men who take more than they ever should from taxpayers, large and small. They've been so corrupt, for so long, that they believe that's the way of the world! They can't tolerate a voice of freedom and responsibility, as expressed by Edgar Howard and his newspaper!"

Kirk observed the crowd was hanging on every word as the preacher worked himself into a near frenzy.

"Just this very morning, a law enforcement officer told me I shouldn't mention Frank Ganner and his political machine. 'This is a volatile situation,' he said. 'Let things simmer down. Let us nail down some evidence.' Well, I'm not concerned about simmering down or nailing down! If they want to shoot me, too, so be it!

"But I want to see justice served in this case, and I'm convinced Frank Ganner is behind the murder of Bobby Howard! If there's pressure in a volatile situation, let the pressure be upon his conscience if he has one! And let there be great pressure, culminating in bringing him to justice!… Above all, let the wrath of God be brought to bear against him! Oh Lord, we beseech Thee, don't let Bobby Howard die in vain!"

As the crowd slowly dispersed, Keene turned to Kirk. "You want to back up the preacher with a strong quote or two about Ganner?"

"No, thanks."

"This is one hell of a big opportunity. Feelings are running high."

"I know, but I think we'd better pass."

"Mind telling me why?"

"Not for publication."

"Oh hell, then go off the record." Keene sighed as he returned the notepad to his coat and reached for a cigarette. "I'm sure you know an extensive manhunt has been going on since the murder, but nothin's turned up yet. The only roads they couldn't block rapidly the other night were next door, in Bantrell County. That's a pretty strong indicator the killers went through there."

"Maybe they did." Kirk shrugged. "But no obstruction has been alleged against Bantrell County officials. The proximate escape routes were through Bantrell County, regardless of who pulled the trigger."

"I don't understand your problem. You're not in a court of law. You're in the political arena."

"Yeah, sure, but if we jump on this bandwagon and along comes some startling revelation pointing elsewhere, our credibility is gone."

"I think you're missing a bet."

"Look, Wade, most of the people in this town already believe Ganner's behind it. Those who are disposed to be against him around the district believe he's behind it. Why take the risk?"

"Don't you believe Ganner had it done?"

Kirk paused, catching sight of Nellie's signal for him to join them. "I'm not sure, but it was a professional job, so I'm not holding my breath expecting any arrests soon."

"You're a calculating rascal," Keene said, tossing his cigarette to the ground.

"So are you." Kirk turned to work his way through lingering mourners.

Before he could reach Nellie and Wedge, Edgar Howard detained him. "She cried all night," he said in a low, strained voice. "She'd like to sell out and leave."

Oh God, Kirk thought, I'm not one to give advice in this situation.

"I... I guess you'll take some time to think it over."

"No more time. I just told her we're staying. Bobby loved that newspaper and he'd never have left it if it had been me out of the picture."

Kirk slung his arm around Edgar's shoulder as they walked toward their cars. Nellie thought she detected a tear in Kirk's eye, but he was quick to adjust his sunglasses, complaining about the dust.

Two days later, at the request of a Texas Ranger, Sheriff Donovan drove to the Lower Rio Grande Valley to assist in checking out rumors and tips of possible escape routes and hideouts used by the killers. After a long, fruitless day's work he ate dinner with the Ranger and retired to his motel at McAllen. He placed a call to his office.

His excited young deputy, J.E. "Red" Barnes all but shouted into the receiver. "Sheriff, I... I've been tryin' to reach you for an hour! You... you won't believe what's happened! You won't believe it!"

"Slow down, Red, take a deep breath."

"Okay, Sheriff, I... I was sittin' here in the jail, reading the paper when this guy, about thirty, walks in and says he drove the car for the killing. He broke down crying, said he had to confess. Said he never, ever thought a youngster might be killed."

"What's his name?"

"Fisher Hawkins. Said he was a deputy over in Coronado County a few years ago."

"Yeah, I remember him. Wasn't much of a deputy. Who pulled the trigger and who hired them?"

"Says he won't talk no more until he gets a lawyer. I booked him and locked him up."

"Have you told anybody about this?"

"No, I was waitin' to talk to you."

"Good, don't tell anybody and for sure, not Edgar Howard. He might kill him."

"Okay, Sheriff. You know, I don't feel so good here alone. When can you get back?"

Donovan's first impulse was to hit the road, but he was bone weary and a Gulf breeze was blowing dust to limit his night vision which wasn't all that good any more. "I've gotta sleep five or six hours, then I'll leave around four. Be there by breakfast time."

It was quiet at the jail with only two drunks there sleeping it off, in addition to Hawkins, who remained quiet after being incarcerated. Red tried to stay awake all night but fell asleep before dawn and was sound asleep when the sheriff arrived.

Donovan shook him awake and they walked around the corner, down the corridor between cells where they gasped when they found Hawkins dead. He was hanging by the neck from a sheet tied in knots, secured to a pipe running below the ceiling.

The sheriff cursed under his breath as he and his deputy lowered the body and searched it, then the cell, for a suicide note. There was none.

Red's hands trembled as he sat down and lit a cigarette. "God, I'm sorry, Sheriff. I never should have put him way down here where nobody could see or hear him. I thought I was making it easier for him to sleep."

"No sense second guessing," Donovan said. "He may have been determined to do it, one way or another."

"Why would he come here to do it?"

"Maybe he wanted that confession on the record."

"But why not identify the killer?"

The sheriff sighed. "Who knows? Maybe he planned to, then thought of some problem, like danger to his family. When he got that confession off his chest and really thought things through, he knew he was in for a long term in the pen if he lived to get there. Then, he probably decided he'd rather die now by his own hand. Get it over with."

"Where does that leave us in catching the killer?"

"Nowhere… Don't repeat this, Red, but I'd bet the killer has disappeared in Mexico and we'll probably never get him."

Chapter 8

News of the driver's confession and apparent suicide rekindled the Bobby Howard murder story onto the front pages of Texas newspapers, but no more tangible threads developed in the following weeks. A story surfaced about a suspected assassin from Houston, but it was quickly dispelled when he put forth an airtight alibi. Rumors about a hit man from Mexico were never substantiated.

The candidate filing deadline in early May passed without fanfare, leaving no change in the three-candidate field of Wedge Crayton of Justinville, Ernesto Garcia of Lantana, and Wally Hooper of Piedra Blanca.

Kirk ran unofficial polls every day by calling people around the district whose political judgment he trusted. The murder of Bobby Howard had hurt Frank Ganner's standing, but did not rub off that much on Wally Hooper, who had proclaimed all along he knew nothing about it. Ganner had also denied any involvement, but Wade Keene's articles, though stopping short of spelling out any implication, quoted many anti-Ganner sources and always pointed out the Howard newspaper was staunchly against Ganner.

Kirk was encouraged that Wedge had nailed down his home base of Retama County, but progress elsewhere was difficult to measure. Hooper's strength was obvious in Ganner's home county of Bantrell and almost as evident in Will Dodd, an adjoining county. Hooper's only real challenge in those counties came from Garcia, who campaigned for the Mexican-American vote.

Garcia had solidified Mexican-American support in his home county of Coronado, but Wedge and Hooper were contesting for Anglo votes there and in the other counties of the district.

Often after reviewing election history, poll tax sales, and other factors, Kirk commented that in a three-candidate field, with one of those a Mexican-American, any analysis was "nothing more than a sophisticated crap shoot." In addition to the unusual field of candidates, too many people were in what he termed the 'Big U Column,' voters who were undetermined or undecided.

Throughout rural communities, some people had made up their

minds but didn't want to disclose or discuss their preferences. Others, less concerned about politics, took the trouble to vote, but never made up their minds until right before they entered the voting booth.

Wedge was running hard, traveling the vast distances to work every rodeo, parade, cattle auction, dance, or other activity he could possibly attend. Yet, by Kirk's best estimate in mid-June, Hooper still held the lead, remaining the odds-on favorite to make a runoff.

Kirk pegged Hooper at thirty-seven percent of the vote, while Wedge and Garcia had approximately twenty percent each, with the balance of twenty-three percent unknown. Kirk had always conceded that Frank Ganner had the most effective political organization to turn out his voters on election day, a factor that might add another two or three percentage points to Hooper's projected vote.

As the last days of June sped by, Kirk gave more thought to the importance of the double-barrel schedule of conventions looming in early July, the Southwest Texas Chamber of Commerce in San Antonio and the Political Association of Mexican-Americans of Texas (PAMAT) in Corpus Christi. With the first primary to be held on July 24, those conventions might indeed be pivotal to Wedge's political fortunes.

Kirk backed off his opposition to Wedge and Nellie traveling alone together after learning how much better Wedge performed when she was with him. With Nellie driving, Wedge had begun carrying a briefcase, studying articles and reports dealing with the drouth and other economic matters relating to South Texas. He tested ideas on her and asked her to critique his delivery when practicing a speech.

Kirk studied developments in the U.S. Senate race on which he continued to count for help in turning out votes for Wedge. The main contenders remained Jordan D. Layman and Holt Witherspoon. Several unknown aspirants had filed right before the deadline. They didn't have a chance of winning, but their "nickel and dime" votes added up would make it more difficult for either contender to achieve a majority.

Witherspoon, the steadfast former governor, was still favored to lead the pack, perhaps winning without a runoff, but Layman, the aggressive young congressman, was campaigning vigorously, often by helicopter, with the goal of forcing a runoff.

With preachers in South Texas literally praying for rain, the devastating drouth continued. Relief appeared possible when a hurricane meandered into the Gulf of Mexico, raising hopes for spinoff rains throughout South Texas. However, the hurricane hit the Mexican coast and was blowing itself out inland, bringing showers to Northern Mexico, but apparently nothing for Texas.

Without warning, the erratic dissipating hurricane sent a sudden final thrust into West Texas. On a balmy night in late June, Wedge and Nellie returned to the campaign headquarters after dinner to finish a long day's work. Brew Blain joined Nellie to review their contributor list in order to decide whom to court again for much needed funds.

Wedge was working on his convention speeches as Kirk revised the schedule for the following week while listening to one of San Antonio's popular music stations. "On Top Of Old Smokey," by The Weavers, was playing when an announcer broke in.

"We interrupt this program to bring you a special news bulletin. Cloudbursts of up to six inches have been reported in West Texas, in a region bounded by Ozona and Sonora on the north, to Langtry on the south near the Rio Grande. The Department of Public Safety urges all motorists in and near the area to use extreme caution. Stay tuned to this station for further developments."

They all gathered near the radio.

"Hell," Wedge said, "isn't that the irony of fate? That sheep and goatherder country is getting enough rain to fill all their tanks tonight, while we're still parched out."

"I don't know that I'd want that much that fast," Kirk said.

"How close is that area to the headwaters of the Nueces?" Nellie said.

"We're safe," Brew said. "Those rains are a long way west of the Nueces headwaters."

"What about the Rio Grande?"

"Calm down, Nellie," Wedge snapped. "The Rio Grande doesn't flood from that area to the Gulf. The bed is too wide and deep."

"What made the bed wide and deep?" Kirk said.

His question went unanswered as they returned to their work and the music resumed. About thirty minutes later, the announcer again broke in, reviewing rapidly the previous bulletin, then adding, "There are confirmed reports of flooding along the Devil's River and the Pecos. There is an unofficial report by a rancher who claims that more than twenty inches of rain have fallen on his ranch. All highways and roads leading into Ozona, Sonora, and Langtry have been closed."

Kirk pulled a large map from his desk drawer, surveying the described area, which he estimated to be about two hundred and twenty miles up the Rio Grande from Laredo. "Wedge, does your father still ranch that spread below Eagle Pass?"

"Yeah."

"Well, if I were you, I'd call him right now and find out if he's been listening to the radio. May need to get his cowhands out there at sunup and round up the cattle. Get 'em away from the Rio Grande and any big creeks nearby."

"You're an alarmist," Wedge said. "Some rancher makes a wild statement. A couple of little rivers are flooding two hundred miles away... We're not looking at a wall of water crashing down a narrow canyon. The Rio Grande bed is wide at Del Rio, just below where that water will be coming in. It's wide most of the way past Laredo, to the new dam."

Kirk studied the map. "We're talking about a cloudburst on the Rio Grande at Langtry and, if that rancher is halfway accurate, two incredible spillways from the Pecos and Devil's River gushing water into the Rio Grande. We're looking at one helluva flood on the Rio Grande."

For a moment, Wedge's latent animosity toward Kirk flared in his mind but he didn't respond. Brew wrapped up his work and left shortly before Kirk called it a night, leaving Wedge alone with Nellie.

"My father..." he said uneasy as he lit a cigarette, "will take me for a fool if I call him now. He's never relied upon my advice for anything."

"You save a thousand head of his best cattle," Nellie said, "and he'll start respecting you a great deal more."

"So, as usual, you agree with Kirk."

"Don't start that."

"You... You really think he's right?"

"Probably. Even if he's not, all your dad's out is the time and effort of his cowhands."

Wedge placed the call to his father, whose concern had already been raised by radio reports. He accepted the warning.

In the impact area, the flood that developed was the worst on the Rio Grande in recorded history. It crested ten feet higher than the previous record at Eagle Pass and Laredo, far beyond its banks. Fed by the two overflowing rivers and several cascading creeks, the Rio Grande's churning waters, laced heavily with debris, generated prodigious momentum, destroying the protective levee at Eagle Pass and rendering useless the international bridges at Del Rio and Laredo.

Hundreds died and thousands were left homeless as the rampaging water tore into communities on both sides. Devastation on the Mexican side was particularly severe because of dense populations near the river whose community leaders had never contemplated the vast rescue operations that were needed.

Spared from the fury of the vicious flood was the lush, densely populated Lower Rio Grande Valley of South Texas, near the Gulf Coast. Only the previous October, the Falcon Dam and Reservoir had been completed below Laredo and that vast project absorbed the momentum of the flood before it could reach the Valley.

When the flood waters subsided, Kirk, Wedge, and Nellie drove to Laredo. The area around the international bridge resembled a war zone, cluttered by debris and with sandbags still in place on the Texas side. Army engineers were already at work, laying plans for a pontoon bridge just east of the bridge, which had lost three strands to the flood and would have to be replaced.

Their favorite gathering places on the Mexican side, the Cadillac and the C.O.D., had sustained severe damage and would be closed for an undetermined time.

For a long silent moment, they peered up and down the river.

"It just all seems so incredible," Nellie said, shaking her head.

"The old lady is subject to bad moods," Kirk said. "This was her worst."

The river that had stormed through Laredo cresting above sixty feet had calmed down to a normal nine feet, resuming her steady role of providing water for irrigation and many other uses; above all, serving as the longest continuous international river boundary in the world.

Across the river, a priest consoled a homeless family, the father and mother each carrying a child, with three more in tow. The melancholy sounds of church bells summoned beleaguered survivors to their spiritual home, a sturdy structure that had withstood the furious waves of churning water.

Turning away, Kirk pointed to a relief shelter nearby where a group of people had gathered around a coffee urn. "Three or four reporters are in that crowd," he said, pulling a news release from a folder. "Let's give 'em this."

Wedge glanced at the release. "I'm not about to give this to them. It's nothing but a self-serving statement, making political points out of a disaster."

"Hell, Wedge," Kirk countered, "this is just an expression of sympathy with a pledge to work in the Legislature for flood control research… This is a helluva opportunity, biggest story in the state. Get some coverage in the district and in Austin where it'll help raise money."

"No way I'll do that." Wedge turned to view the destruction again. "That's too far beyond the pale."

Kirk shook his head. "All right, Professor, and while you reflect upon the plight of humanity, I'm going over to that little cantina and get me a cold beer."

As he walked away, Nellie took Wedge's hand. "Darling, you're both right. It would be poor form to run up there release in hand, but there's nothing wrong with mixing and mingling with the reporters. Wally Hooper should be here. He's not, and you are. Let's just let them know."

"I've learned," Wedge said as he smiled, "I can never fight the both of you."

On the return ride to Justinville, they sat in silence for several moments, still somewhat awed by what they had seen. Kirk broke the ice with a few suggestions for Wedge's crucial speech at the forthcoming convention.

During the following days, between campaign activities, Wedge thought about and practiced his speech for the annual convention of the Southwest Texas Chamber of Commerce, to be held in San Antonio. When they arrived there, Kirk toured the stately Municipal Auditorium, near the narrow, winding San Antonio River. With five archways and ornate carvings on pillars dominating the front view, it appeared more like a large rustic mission than the city's premier gathering place for large organizations.

Big, colorful banners plugging the candidacies of Jordan Layman and Holt Witherspoon for the U.S. Senate were displayed at the auditorium and in the lobbies of the Gunter and Saint Anthony Hotels, where most delegates were lodged. Despite Kirk's argument for the Gunter, the convention headquarters hotel, Wedge insisted upon staying at the Saint Anthony, "where my family always stays."

Kirk contracted for a hospitality suite at the Gunter, where more than half the delegates, dominated by ranchers, gathered. Nellie served as hostess for the suite, a welcome sight for the mostly male delegates who also enjoyed beer, whiskey, soft drinks, and snacks that the Crayton campaign provided. Nellie was charming and persuasive in convincing many delegates to take campaign literature and bumper stickers, though some lived outside the legislative district.

"If you're driving in South Texas," she said over and over, "we surely would appreciate it if you'd put a sticker on your car or pickup."

Wally Hooper didn't have a formal hospitality suite, but he and two of his campaign operatives outspent the Crayton campaign by working restaurants and bars, picking up tabs, large and small.

Ernesto Garcia had no funds to expend at the convention, but his volunteers promoted his campaign by distributing brochures and bumper stickers.

Until the Chamber convention, Hooper had followed the script Frank Ganner had laid down, avoiding any joint appearances with Wedge, denying him the opportunity for any direct upstaging. But in the stretch run, Ganner and Hooper had decided they better accept the Chamber invitation.

The candidates drew for position and Kirk considered their draw to be ideal. Garcia would go first, soon after breakfast when the delegates would still be half asleep. Hooper was scheduled next, the spot to warm up the crowd for Wedge's midmorning speech, when all delegates would be alert, plus Wedge could pick up on Hooper's speech. Further, the bitter contestants for the Senate nomination, Layman and Witherspoon, were scheduled after Wedge, still before noon, guaranteeing high morning attendance among the six hundred delegates.

For their final tune-up, Kirk and Wedge moved away from the flow of delegates and reporters to the coffee shop of the Menger Hotel, adjacent to the Alamo. Kirk coached him like a boxing manager, knowing how important it was for him to be at his peak emotionally; to be confident but not cocky; informed but not boring; able to use humor, even scorn and ridicule, without being too self-deprecating or vindictive toward his opponent.

At last, over their second cup of coffee, Wedge set down his cup. "All right, Old Podnah, all right. Now, I want to get over there and hear every damned thing Wally has to say."

At the convention hall, Wedge reported backstage while Kirk found Wade Keene taking notes toward the end of Garcia's speech. "How's he doing?"

"He's a smart kid with guts." Keene looked up at Kirk. "But he needs a big dose of political acumen. You don't come before a Chamber of Commerce gathering and calmly call for a state minimum wage, repeal of the poll tax, and doubling state spending for schools in South Texas. But I sure as hell enjoyed the way he raked Frank Ganner and Wally Hooper over the coals."

Garcia soon departed to polite applause. Kirk monitored the crowd closely as Wally Hooper was introduced. He guessed that about forty percent of the audience applauded with some degree of enthusiasm.

Though he had worked hard in his campaign, Hooper remained

substantially overweight, unable to resist hearty portions of the heavy Anglo and Mexican food available around the district. Under the hot lights on stage, he wiped his brow with a handkerchief prior to starting his remarks. He stayed straight on his campaign themes and issues, pointing first to his "unique qualification as the only candidate in the race with experience as an elected officeholder, a proven servant of the people who won't need on-the-job training."

He pledged to hold the line on taxes, support economic development programs, and help provide good schools for "your children and mine." That line led into what he considered to be his dramatic close about being the only married man and father in the race, "the only one who truly understands the long-standing burden and grave responsibility of providing for a family. Yet, I know of no greater calling, nor do I ever expect to feel more gratification than I do by being with my family, sitting at the head of the table where I feel their love and respect upon me. With them in my heart, and you good people in my mind, I wage this campaign, confident of victory. Thank you and God bless you."

After finishing his speech, he made a courtly bow and walked from the stage.

As warm applause spread across the crowd, Kirk said to Keene, "How do you rate him?"

"Pompous here, patronizing there, but he said all the right things for this crowd. Unlucky for you, he went before your man."

By Kirk's estimate, only about one-third of the audience gave Wedge a warm welcome. At the podium, Wedge laid his prepared remarks to the side and adjusted the microphone upward a bit. He managed to make that gesture appear to be casual, though his heart was pounding rapidly as he took a deep breath.

He was buying a moment to rearrange his opening, having decided on the spot to take a swipe at Hooper with an unrehearsed thrust, picking up on a comment Hooper had made moments earlier.

With a clear, steady voice, he thanked the moderator for "that kind introduction ... You know, friends, Wally makes some darn convincing points. He convinced me that it is, as he termed it, 'a grave responsibility' to be there in Piedra Blanca, serving as husband and father, providing for his family. I'm so convinced, Wally, that I believe you'd better pursue that mission and withdraw from this race. You can't be in Piedra Blanca and way off in wicked Austin at the same time."

The crowd was caught off guard, but several delegates chuckled and a few laughed out loud.

"Now, permit me to move right into the real issue of this campaign, which is independence. If you're trying to decide between Wedge Crayton and Wally Hooper, that's the true issue upon which you should make your decision. If I'm elected, I'll be free to exercise independent judgment on every issue. I'm not beholden to any individual or special interest group. Now, on the other hand, Wally has a problem. Let me explain it this way…

"When I was growing up, my favorite radio program was Edgar Bergen and Charlie McCarthy. Bergen is a great ventriloquist and Charlie is a most engaging puppet. But I'm here to tell you that Frank Ganner and Wally Hooper can upstage that act any day. Remember how Bergen was always close to Charlie? Well, Frank can put words in Wally's mouth whether he's close by or a hundred miles away."

Wedge paused as hearty laughter reverberated around the hall. Hooper had passed muster a few moments ago, but the audience couldn't resist the derision involving Ganner.

"And so," Wedge continued with a straight face, "I'm going to excuse Wally for refusing to debate me. It would be too dull since Frank never changes a word."

Again, the crowd roared, with part of Keene's preconvention article in mind that referred to "Wally Hooper's chicken-hearted refusal to discuss the issues with either of his challengers."

The first joke had been ad-lib, the second practiced over and over and delivered with style. Wedge was now confident he was going to win the day and proceeded with his serious prepared remarks, some of which covered subjects already discussed by Hooper but nonetheless deemed "sacred cows" for this audience, such as economic development.

He then moved into what he and Kirk had considered to be the innovative points they guessed correctly Hooper would not make ahead of Wedge. With a clear field, Wedge reviewed problems involved with the drouth and mesquite eradication. He pledged that, if elected, he would urge the State Department of Agriculture to intensify research programs aimed at eradication while also seeking markets for mesquite for cooking.

"Just recently, I've eaten beef and goat barbecued over mesquite and steak broiled over mesquite. Believe me, it's better than charcoal. We need to seek means and markets whereby we can turn this old range enemy into a friend."

Wedge paused, hoping for applause. There wasn't much, but some heads were nodding over what sounded like a reasonable new idea.

For his final point, he talked about the recent flood on the Rio Grande, painting a poignant picture of the vast devastation and misery it had caused, describing how he was deeply moved upon viewing the situation in Laredo.

"Since I was a little boy, I've heard talk about the need for a dam and reservoir on the Nueces above Justinville. That's a challenge we can't afford to ignore. Are we going to just sit around and wait for that terrible day when a cloudburst hits below the headwaters of the Nueces? Are we as citizens of South Texas and the Great State of Texas, content to sit by idly, tempting fate, knowing it can happen any day? Are we?"

A few delegates called out, "No!"

Raising his voice, he encouraged them again. "Well, are we?"

Shouts of "No!" reverberated across the hall.

"All right! Now, if you want to do something about it... If you want someone who will go to Austin and fight for that dam and reservoir, fight for all the people living below the headwaters of the Nueces, then I need your vote in this election!"

It was one of those hard dramatic thrusts in a political speech that either works wonders or falls flat on its face. Wedge had pulled it off, leaving the stage amid applause, whoops, and cheers, having tapped deeply held emotions.

Nellie was on her feet, clapping and jumping. Next to her, Brew applauded and lit a cigarette, more confident that his late fundraising goal for the first primary would be met. Kirk glanced at Keene, making a final note.

"You know," Keene said from the side of his mouth, "I wish my paper allowed four-letter words. Your man just kicked the shit out of Ganner's man."

Behind stage, Wedge encountered a nervous Jordan Layman, puffing on a cigarette while waiting to be introduced. His dark calculating eyes suddenly sparkled as he saw Wedge and he slung his arm over Wedge's shoulder. "You're a helluva lot better speaker than I heard that day at Justinville. You're coming across real well. How's it looking?"

"A little boost here and there, and I should make a runoff."

"I'm in that same boat, 'cept old Holt has finally started kicking at me. I guess it's good the old bastard is feeling some heat, but he's sure bearing down hard, which I didn't expect until we got into a runoff."

"Well, my opponent keeps on ignoring me, but I won't stop kicking him as hard as I can."

When Layman was informed it was time for him to appear, Wedge walked from backstage to the foyer, searching for Kirk and Nellie. He encountered Ernesto Garcia, who shook hands in a perfunctory manner.

"Is that really your platform?" he said in a snide tone.

"The audience seemed to appreciate it," Wedge snapped.

"Yes, your demagoguery upstaged Hooper's. But no one's going to market mesquite for cooking outside South Texas in decades, if ever. And there's not going to be any dam built above Justinville on the Nueces. So, you and Hooper should compare clichés and platitudes about economic development. Neither of you even touched upon the many problems of the less fortunate, the people who are suffering. The people who aren't here."

"Apparently, that's your mission in life." Wedge turned away to seek Nellie.

She greeted him with a hug and kiss. "God, I'm proud of you. You never flinched. You were terrific."

"Believe me, I was nervous as hell, especially taking that dig at Wally off the top. But I couldn't resist poking that pompous ass."

"It was great. Here comes Kirk with your favorite reporter. Surely now he'll have something positive to say."

"What did you think, Old Podnah?"

"Went well." Kirk smiled, shaking Wedge's hand.

"And Mr. Keene?"

"Not bad, Crayton, but just remember, only about half of those folks cheering for you are eligible to vote in your election. And of them, thirty percent are serfs in Frank Ganner's kingdom who will change their tune when they wake up in reality at home tomorrow morning."

"You know something, Keene," Wedge said, "I could hand you the keys to paradise and you'd demand that I hold the door open for you."

Keene chuckled and returned to his position near the stage to cover the speeches of Jordan Layman and Holt Witherspoon, whom he had described in his preconvention article as "prize bulls in the Texas political arena who don't always perform up to their pedigrees."

Kirk, Nellie, and Wedge took seats near the back of the hall while Brew returned to the hospitality suite to meet with potential contributors.

Layman's campaign press secretary distributed to reporters two pages of excerpts from the forthcoming speech, reflecting Layman's attention to detail in trying to achieve maximum coverage at every appearance.

The congressman opened his formal remarks by assuring the audience he had been on top of federal relief efforts for the Rio Grande flood which he termed "a tragedy the likes of which I've never before seen, not even in the recent World War during which, as you may recall, I served our country with some distinction."

Layman reminded his audience he was a pioneer in promoting rural electrification and had become known as one of Congress' most effective members in passing various conservation and education measures. Repeating the most oft-used cliché in his lexicon, he declared that "education is the real key to the future."

To polite applause, Layman stroked the sacred cows of the Chamber audience, the most important being economic development. He added a point that his congressional experience would make him a more effective senator than Witherspoon in dealing with the "clear and present danger of Communism" and in "bringing home the bacon" of federal funding for various programs.

Foremost among those, he said, was spending for national defense, vital to the economies of several South Texas communities, most notably the host city of San Antonio with its long established air force and army bases. He also named benefits for veterans and the elderly. Since Layman estimated more than half of the audience had voted for Eisenhower two years previously, he steered clear of mentioning the more controversial programs of the New Deal and Fair Deal he had supported.

Though his political points were on target, Layman lacked the clear, steady, upbeat delivery Wedge had employed to help capture the audience. His raspy voice sounded almost hoarse and flat at times. Still, he kept boring in, raising his voice occasionally as his only means of demonstrating emphasis.

Working into the close, he wanted to hit his opponent hard since he anticipated another scalding from him. "You know, just yesterday, Governor Witherspoon was telling some folks he was running against me because I'm a so-called progressive. Now, let ME just tell YOU what I am before he comes to bat today… If it's progressive to look forward instead of backward, then I am a progressive.

"He looks back all the time, always talking about when he was governor, he did this and that. I'm not arguing with him about what he did. Far as I'm concerned, he was a good governor. But he's been out of office for a while, and he's lost touch."

Layman paused. "Sure, I am a progressive in the sense that I'm looking ahead, and I know in the United States Senate, we need more people looking forward, not backward. He likes to throw labels around... well, the truth is, he's a reactionary, a voice from the past.

"I'm the voice for the future. I've outlined a program, a program for progress that we can achieve without creating any undue tax burdens ... Having said that, I want to reassure you all that when it comes to our great Texas traditions, no one is more conservative than I.

"Over there," he shouted, pointing in the direction of Houston, "one of my forefathers fought at San Jacinto for Texas independence. Our traditions of freedom, independence, and greatness are deeply ingrained in me. You can count on me to uphold those sacred traditions of ours until the day I die!"

At the end, Layman elicited a fair smattering of more enthusiastic applause. He had fired his best shots, but it was still a pro-Witherspoon audience.

Holt Witherspoon had been standing behind the stage, listening carefully. He would never remove his Stetson until the actual time of speaking and his hat cast shadows across his clear blue eyes, the deep lines on his face, and his square jaw. He had frayed many a reporter's nerves with his penchant for "winging it," speaking without prepared text or even notes.

Unless a reporter had a tape recorder, he or she would have to try to take down every word.

"Anybody can hit an audience in the head," he once told an aide, "but you can't hit 'em in the heart until you know their mood. And you won't know their mood till you look 'em in the eye a time or two."

Witherspoon had launched his campaign expecting to win without a runoff, due to his recognition among Texans from two terms as governor. Of late, he had become concerned Layman's frenetic campaign was proving to be effective by the sheer number of communities Layman was contacting in person among some one thousand spread over the vast Texas landscape. Even more nettling was Layman's pervasive thrust that his congressional experience and relative youth made him more qualified for the Senate.

As he prepared for his turn, Witherspoon adjusted his suit coat and tie, removed his hat to smooth out thin patches of white hair above his ears. The West Texas warhorse was set to give his opponent a thrashing, but first, on stage, he told an old cowhand joke, then spun through a litany and chronology of his accomplishments as governor. He emphasized those measures that had helped the Texas economy, measures that had benefited businessmen, farmers, and ranchers, the people sitting before him. He brought the audience along, confident they were with him before he turned to his opponent.

"My friends, I wonder if my opponent actually believes we'll swallow that line about serving one congressional district makes him more qualified than I am to serve the entire State of Texas. That's nothing but hogwash! We have twenty-one congressional districts in Texas. He's served only one - that's all. I've served the entire State of Texas. I know what's involved, and I know what our needs are— the needs of all Texans—in the United States Senate."

From his coat pocket, Witherspoon retrieved a handful of newspaper clippings. "Now, let me point up a few things about the way this man has been campaigning. First, this clipping from Amarillo, surely one of the most conservative communities in Texas. It says, and I quote, 'Congressman Jordan Layman made it clear today in a speech before local business leaders that he supports all measures of the Taft-Hartley Act which benefit business and economic growth.' End quote. Here's one from Dallas, again a staunch conservative area. Quote, 'In answer to a question, Congressman Jordan Layman told the local Chamber of Commerce today he strongly favors the Texas right-to-work law enacted in 1947 under Section 14-b of the Taft-Hartley Act.' End quote."

Witherspoon paused, surveying the delegates who were following his every word. He summoned an aide with a tape recorder which was placed next to the microphone. "Now, yesterday, over on the West Side, here in San Antonio, old Jordan was speaking to a group of barrio leaders. He knew no reporters were present, but he didn't know I had a friend there with a tape recorder. Turn it on."

The tape contained the raspy voice of Jordan Layman addressing "Mis amigos" time and again about their needs, ending with a pledge "to get rid of all those anti-labor provisions in the Taft-Hartley Act. It may take some time, but we'll do it."

"So, there you have it, ladies and gentlemen. Jordan Layman the liberal and Jordan Layman the conservative. He wants to be all things to all people. But you can't have it both ways when it comes time for major decisions to be made; when it's time for major directions to be taken. Mark my words! You send Jordan Layman to the Senate and one of these days, he'll lay our right-to-work law upon the altar of political expediency. Because this man is consumed by ambition, boundless ambition, to seek the presidency. The Senate is but a rung on the ladder for him.

"On the other hand, I'm not trying to scramble up any ladder to the presidency, and I'm not willing to let expediency, or party loyalty for that matter, blind my judgment regarding the best interests of our state. Now, in South Texas, the Gulf Coast, and any other areas carried by Adlai Stevenson, Jordan Layman is castigating me for having supported President Eisenhower. Isn't it peculiar that you didn't hear him say anything today about my support for President Eisenhower?

"Sure, I supported Ike, along with Governor Shivers, and I'm proud of it because we are for our tidelands, offshore mineral rights guaranteed to Texas by the federal government when we joined the Union in 1846. Those tidelands provide vital funds for our schoolchildren and there is not a doubt in my mind this was the decisive issue for Eisenhower in carrying our state two years ago.

"Now, let no one misunderstand my position. The Democratic nominee was on the wrong side of this critical issue. I'm proud to stand for Texas–far more important than blind party loyalty."

Those words drew a hearty round of applause, providing Witherspoon with a break he used to take a sip of water.

"And further, my friends, I assure you no double-dealing, pussy-footing politician like Jordan Layman will ever badger me into out-promising him!"

That stinging statement prompted warm applause, including a few shouts of "Give 'em hell, Holt!"

"He gave you no price tag for his program, but I'll tell you the truth–it would cost a pretty penny. Such a pretty penny that you hard-working, tax-paying citizens will be digging into your pockets for years to cover the horrendous cost, not to mention the freedom our state would concede to the federal government. What he calls the 'path to progress' is nothing more than a shortcut to inflation, debt-ridden federal spending, and higher taxes!"

Again, the audience applauded with more rejoinders of "Give 'em hell, Holt!"

"Yes, to the highly partisan audiences, he's been promising the moon and calling me a Judas for supporting Ike. But you don't hear him saying that here, before this audience, or in Amarillo or Dallas. That's because he isn't really a party loyalist or a true progressive, and he sure as the devil isn't a conservative. He's nothing more than an opportunist, a chameleon. This election comes down to whether you want a conservative you can trust, or a chameleon who will change colors at the drop of a hat; who will say anything to get elected and vote Lord knows how in Washington. That's the choice, my friends, and I'm confident you'll walk another mile with me. Thank you and God bless you."

To a standing ovation, Witherspoon waved good-bye and ambled off the stage. He returned for a moment, Stetson in hand, to wave once more before retiring to his hotel room.

As the convention wound down, Kirk, Nellie, and Wedge joined Brew in the hospitality suite. Brew smiled, greeting them with the news he had gathered enough cash and pledges to cover the cost of advertising and general overhead through the remaining three weeks before the first primary.

"After that," he said with a sigh, "we'll have to start all over again."

"We'll worry about that when we make the runoff," Kirk said.

As Brew fixed drinks, Nellie kicked off her high heels, lit a cigarette, and relaxed on a couch. "It was our day, but I'm not at all enthused about those last two speakers. Senator McCarthy is tearing this nation apart with his redbaiting witch hunts, half the world is starving or in turmoil, and our contenders for the greatest deliberative body in the world are carping at each other like schoolboys. I hate to say it but our choice is between a conniving chameleon and a tired old fogey."

"I still feel strongly," Wedge said, "that Jordan is the better qualified candidate. He has a vision for the future of our state."

"He has," Brew said with a smile, "a vision for Jordan Layman."

"Just be thankful they're slugging it out," Kirk said. "We're still counting on getting our fair share of that voter turnout they generate beyond what would otherwise vote in our race. I'd sure as hell like to know whether Frank Ganner is going for Layman, Witherspoon, or just might sit it out."

"Well, regardless of what Ganner does in the Senate race," Wedge said, "it appears to me the die is cast in our race. All the building blocks are in place for the first primary. Aren't they, Kirk?"

"Yeah, for the first primary. I don't foresee any major developments or events that would change anything markedly... but, of course, we have to be on guard."

"With that in mind," Wedge said, "I'm going to beef up my final three weeks with on-the-street campaigning and let that PAMAT convention slide."

Kirk set his beer bottle on a table nearby and confronted Wedge. "Have you lost your mind? You have to appear before that group."

"So they can jeer and hoot me down? That's Garcia's organization. Wally Hooper isn't going to appear and neither, for that matter, is Holt Witherspoon."

"Of course. Neither has anything to gain by appearing there. You have—"

"I cannot see the merit," Wedge snapped, "in being subjected to a totally negative experience. It will hurt us more than help."

Kirk shook his head. He wanted to be derisive of Wedge, but he felt caught in a trap with Wedge having performed so well that day and with all of them knowing that prospects were slim indeed of chipping away any Mexican-American votes from Garcia. Wedge was carried away, he mused, with the adulation he had received and just wasn't prepared to take the hard licks that needed to be taken.

Running his hand through his hair, Kirk thought back to the very beginning of the campaign. "All I want you to remember is a potential winning coalition in a runoff with Wally Hooper requires you to pick up most of Garcia's vote from the first primary. You must establish some credibility with them before the first primary and that PAMAT convention is the only opportunity."

Wedge glanced at Nellie. "Need I ask how you feel about this?"

When she arched her eyebrows, he turned to Brew. "Et tu, Brew?"

"I'm afraid so, my friend," Brew said with a shrug. "Kirk's called 'em right so far."

"Very well," Wedge said, shaking his head. "I'll go get chewed up by Ernesto Garcia et al."

On the following day at the headquarters, Kirk chuckled upon reading Wade Keene's coverage of the convention, an article he knew would infuriate Frank Ganner. Keene described Wally Hooper as "a cartoon character who looks like Porky Pig but was portrayed by his opponent as more like a puppet to Frank Ganner, the Baron of Bantrell. Some South Texans who came here committed to Hooper seemed to have been more impressed by his young opponent, Wedge Crayton."

Keene had described the Senate race in detail with a biting close.

"Many people are wondering what the Baron of Bantrell, who might be recast as the Sphinx of the Brush Country, is going to do in this race with only three weeks remaining until the first primary. Of course, few people outside South Texas understand that Ganner doesn't have to make a public endorsement at all.

"He can turn his machine on quietly right before the end, thereby avoiding controversy for whomever he chooses to support. Or, he might not take sides. Only an overlord with the tightest-run political operation in Texas could afford that luxury, but such is the absolute nature of Ganner's domination in his domain."

Kirk was alone in the headquarters at midafternoon when he received an anonymous call.

"If you want," said a guarded male voice, "to find out what Frank Ganner is up to in these political races, meet me at sundown in the parking lot of the Brush Country Restaurant."

"Not unless you identify yourself."

"I can't do that, but if you want some inside information, be there, and be alone. No tricks."

"Why meet out there?"

"'Cause it's in the country. Nobody will know the difference. So long."

After ringing off, Kirk debated in his mind the risk involved. He had to admit the restaurant was a logical meeting place since it was isolated, about fifteen miles from Piedra Blanca, the nearest town. But the fact it was located inside the Bantrell County line concerned him. He'd been to the Brush Country Restaurant several times and knew the longtime owner, Sandy Jones, fairly well. He placed a call to her, asking her to keep a lookout in the parking lot, which she agreed to do.

He arrived shortly before sundown and surveyed the large old wooden structure and dusty parking lot. Three cars and two pickups were in the lot, which was partially lit from one large protected bulb on the side of the building. He nodded to Sandy before settling in to wait for the caller, sitting in his car listening to the radio.

Darkness fell as he sat there, glancing around occasionally, unable to detect any movement in the lot. Suddenly, the lone light fell dark and a figure approached, opening the door next to him. As Kirk stepped out, he could see the figure wore a bandana masking his face, and he felt the pressure of a pistol held to his stomach. He was hustled over to a car easing up to the lot, whereupon the driver, also masked, got out to blindfold him and tie his hands behind his back with a thin strip of leather.

What a damn fool I was, he thought, to fall for an old trick like this.

Kirk was forced into the back seat with the gun at his side. For a few moments, they rode without speaking until the driver chuckled and said, "Now, we're going to take you to meet a friend of ours."

Variables flashed through his mind. Is my life in danger? Are they taking me to Ganner? Have I fallen into a trap set by Ganner with unknown consequences?

His mind worked back to times in combat when he entered each challenge with one thought foremost, that of not becoming disoriented. Then he tried to keep his sense of direction, which wasn't easy with the blindfold and turns in the road.

Kirk smelled whiskey in the car and thought his captor nearby took a swig. Listening to them talk, he discerned the driver had a slight Mexican-American accent, the kind one hears from a South Texas native who speaks English most of the day, but Spanish at home. The voice of the nearby captor matched that of the anonymous caller, belonging to a middle-aged Anglo.

After what Kirk estimated were six or seven minutes since leaving the lot, the man in the back seat nudged him in the ribs. "Here we are. Get out."

Upon removing his blindfold, they led him by flashlight several steps to a point where he stood near a small tin shed. He estimated it was located about twenty yards from an old abandoned farmhouse with an open porch visible and little else discernible.

"Here's where you meet our friend." One of them laughed as he opened the door.

They forced Kirk inside the dusty, cobweb-strewn shed, only five feet by eight feet. Glancing about, he could see nothing else inside as he stooped to enter and sat down against the wall near the door. The hollow click of the latch outside made his stomach tighten while the closed door shut off most of the moonlight.

His first concern was of scorpions and tarantulas that might have taken refuge in his cell. A crack in one of the walls let in a sliver of moonlight and he determined to keep his eyes trained on that portion of the floor that he could see.

He took a deep breath, exhaling slowly. His captors stood nearby, laughing and joking, probably on the porch, as they popped open beer cans.

Perhaps, he wondered, somebody, surely not Ganner, is coming out here to interrogate me. And maybe they're going to hold me a while just to sweat me out. But why? And for how long? It's hot in here. No water.

He rubbed his hands together, feeling the tightness of his bonds, or was it looseness? I'm not tied very tightly, he mused. Maybe they want me to try to escape. Escape? I might be able to simply bang loose a portion of the shed and hit the ground running. But I don't know where I am. They have guns and flashlights and know where they are. I can't be more than three or four miles from the Brush Country Restaurant, but in what direction?

He was perspiring heavily from fear and uncertainty, combined with the lack of fresh air in his cramped quarters. For a few torturous minutes, he sat there until his captors approached.

"We brought our friend," one of them said as he chuckled. "He's coming to see you."

Toward the far end of the shed, only five feet from him, they opened a little door, and from a box, permitted a chilling figure to slither inside. Kirk could barely make out its lines, but there was no doubt in his mind. It was a diamondback rattlesnake about six feet long.

"Now, y'all can get to know each other," one of them said with a laugh, closing the little door and latching it.

Kirk froze. He knew any movement might agitate the snake and he prayed it hadn't yet recognized his presence. He had no means of defending himself except with his shoes and only then by kicking from a sitting position. He rubbed and stretched his bonds again, feeling a slight loosening.

Perhaps, he thought, the rattler will settle in, knowing I'm here, but remain passive so long as I don't threaten him.

Some old rancher had told him years ago that rattlers aren't natural enemies of man; they have to be agitated or threatened before they will coil and strike.

But how long, he asked himself, can I last in here? How long before I move and he feels threatened? What if these bastards plan to keep me in here all night? I can't stay awake forever. I fall asleep, move around, and he bites me until I quit moving. Holy shit, I'd rather be back under fire in Korea. I'd rather be in hell.

His captors made noise on the porch, laughing and drinking beer. He jumped at the sudden sound of thumping noises above, as beer cans and rocks hit the roof. For the first time in years, he detected the unique chilling sound nearby as the huge rattler let it be known it didn't like the disturbance. Trembling a bit, Kirk had to suppress an urge to tell the rattler he didn't do it, that he wasn't a threat.

Christ, he told himself, hold yourself together. If you've got a chance to ride this out, you've got to keep quiet and not move at all.

To bide the time, he counted to ten over and over. Little time passed before the next round of beer cans and rocks crashed onto the tin roof. The rattler coiled, sounding his stern warning.

Kirk could now make out the clearly defined structure of the viper head as it weaved slowly back and forth atop the massive coil. Moonlight shone through the cracks of the shed upon the snake's body, revealing it was almost as big around as his forearm.

Again, he worked his wrists back and forth. They were drenched in perspiration that was soaking the leather, acting to give him a little extra slack. The stifling heat and intense anxiety were draining him to the point he was becoming lightheaded, barely able to keep his head from moving.

He laughed to himself, what the hell am I going to do if I get my hands free?

Yet, that was the only goal he could entertain at the moment, and he worked the leather back and forth, easily and quietly.

He continued counting to ten as seconds elapsed without any noise close by, only the sounds of whoops and laughter from the porch. Then, another round of beer cans and rocks slammed onto the shed, again sending the snake into a tight coil as it rattled furiously. The hard, loud thumping prompted the angry rattler to strike in the direction of the sounds of those objects hitting the tin wall near its head.

At last his right wrist and hand eased out of his bonds, then the left came without effort. Watching the rattler's preoccupation with the barrage, he was able to move his hands into his lap without notice.

What the hell are those bastards up to?

From the sounds of their voices, he could tell they were well on their way to getting drunk.

I know what they're gonna do. Have their fun with me, get me bitten by this rattler, then pour me out of the shed and leave me to die. No evidence of foul play. Just a guy who wandered up to this abandoned farm and got himself killed by a rattlesnake. Clever goddamn plan.

Noises of the barrage ended, yielding to an ominous silence outside the shed. Inside, silence soon came after a few less agitated rattles from the big snake, leaving Kirk to contain the sound of his breathing as best he could. His back remained tight against the wall and his hands were folded in his lap as if in prayer. Through several seconds of agonizing silence, he wondered what the hell was next.

His question was soon answered when an abrupt kick from behind by a boot slammed against the outside wall made him jerk. He lurched forward, into the striking range of the angry, coiled rattler. As he sought to shield his face, the snake's fangs sank deeply into his left wrist. He hardly felt the bite as adrenalin shot through his veins. He had to kill the snake.

He tried to grab its head, but missed and the rattler bit him in the palm of his right hand, and blood spurted upon the snake. Though Kirk couldn't stand, he rose to a humped position and landed a kick to the snake's head. It was a glancing blow, but as the snake sought to recoil, he landed another hard kick to its head.

As fast as he could, he followed with repeated kicks until the rattler was no longer reacting, merely wrenching in its death throes.

His captors had opened the large door to observe the electrifying moment of close combat and they permitted him to stagger out the door. He lunged to the hood of the car, which he leaned against, panting while trying to work through the intense emotions churning inside him.

At last, he looked at his wrist and hand, bleeding from the rattler's fangs. "Get me to a doctor."

One of his captors hooted with laughter, heading for the porch. "I'll get you a beer. I believe you've earned one."

"I don't want a beer. Look, I don't know your game, but I may not live if I don't get to a doctor soon. How about it?"

The captor nearby chuckled, then laughed long and hard, placing his flashlight on an oil drum as he took a long swig of beer. "We just played a little joke on you, tenderfoot. You ain't gonna die. We milked the rattler when we got here. He didn't have enough venom to give you a headache."

Adrenalin again shot through his veins. He quickly closed the two steps between him and his unsuspecting captor. He kicked him in the crotch, and he doubled up in pain with his head exposed perfectly. Kirk hit him with a hard uppercut to the jaw. Reeling from that blow, the man tried to grab his flashlight, but Kirk followed with short, fast combinations of punches to the head and midsection. As the man crumpled to the ground, he yelled for his companion.

Kirk dashed away, vaulting over a low barbed wire fence.

The captor on the ground was slow to get up, complaining he thought his jaw was broken. His companion grabbed the flashlight and shone it in the direction Kirk had taken. Kirk dived into a thicket, grateful for the cover, but paying a painful price when his forearms encountered some curved thorns from "tasajuillo" cactus.

After working his way through the thicket, Kirk soon found a welcome "sendero," a long wide path cut through the brush by a bulldozer, which he followed in the pale moonlight. Upon finding a windmill, he doused his head in the water tank and took a few gulps of the cool liquid. He climbed the windmill ladder to survey the area and found he was on a fairly good course to the Brush Country Restaurant. He estimated he was three miles from the restaurant, whose lights were visible from his vantage point.

A car drove up on a nearby road, using a searchlight.

Could be some illegal hunting in progress, he thought, but more likely my captors.

He charted a route to avoid them. When he came upon the dirt road he wanted to take, he was exhausted. He sat down to rest a few moments, but jolted upright when headlights came over the hill behind him and a searchlight scanned the pasture.

Shit, he thought, they've doubled back.

He dived into a storm sewer beneath a little wooden bridge. Their car approached slowly and the search beam lit the pasture as though a single eerie strip of daylight were upon it. The car stopped just before it reached the bridge.

Oh my God. Kirk sighed. Maybe they've spotted me.

"I gotta take a leak," the driver said before he relieved himself on the side of the road. Urine splattered on the ground near the storm sewer, making the voices above barely audible to Kirk.

"Well, shit," one said, "what are we gonna do? The boss said not to hurt him. Now, what's gonna happen to us if we report back without knowing what happened to this guy? Suppose he dies out there somewhere?"

"I think the sonofabitch broke my jaw. I don't give a shit what happens to him."

"Now, you're talking like a crazy man. The boss is liable to cram prod poles down our throats and no telling what else… I told you that rattlesnake business was a bad idea."

"Aw hell, he'll turn up. Let's pack 'em in. I want the doctor to look at my jaw."

"Yeah, pack 'em in. Call it a night."

Kirk had caught only bits and pieces, but that final sentence came through clearly, and he heaved a long sigh of uncertain relief as they drove away. Though deeply grateful to be rid of them, he wasn't sure he could walk the remaining distance to the Brush Country Restaurant.

Bone-weary as he trudged along the dirt road, Kirk called time and again for that one more bit of strength until he passed a curve. The welcome lights of the restaurant appeared only about one hundred yards away. At once, he was able to pick up the gait, closing the final steps to his destination. When he arrived, he leaned against his car, catching his breath, yearning to drive home.

But he had to admit he couldn't make it. He was completely exhausted. He staggered through the back door and told Sandy what had happened.

A large buxom woman crowding sixty, she appeared crusty and cynical most of the time, but she had her soft side. After taking one look at his drawn face and tattered, blood-soaked clothes, she pulled him into her arms. From the closet of her late husband, she provided clean clothes, and he accepted her offer of the spare room and a pistol.

"That's the least I can do for you, honey," she said. "I should have thought about someone flipping that damned outside switch without me knowing it. They were gone before I could get out there to catch a license number."

"Probably a greeting committee sent by Frank Ganner, but I doubt I could ever prove it. They don't leave tracks."

Kirk took a bath, locked the door and slept uneasily with the pistol under his pillow.

At sunup he was awake and happy to find Sandy had already made coffee, anticipating early customers. She soon prepared for him a hearty breakfast of two fried eggs, bacon, and biscuits.

He was enjoying his second cup of coffee when a tall man walked in, clad in khaki shirt and trousers, boots, and wearing a neatly blocked Stetson, plus an imposing deputy sheriff badge.

"Frank wants to see you," the deputy said to Kirk.

Kirk eased back in his chair. "Oh, he does, does he?"

"Yeah, soon as you finish your coffee, we'll go."

"Look, I realize I'm inside the Bantrell County line, but isn't this still a free country? Do you have a warrant for my arrest?"

"No."

"Are you going to pull that gun on me?"

"No. If you don't want to see Frank, I'll tell him."

Kirk studied the deputy. "Did you have anything to do with what happened to me last night?"

"I don't know what you're talking about."

"Never mind," Kirk said, glancing at Sandy behind the counter.

She shrugged while pouring herself a cup of coffee.

"All right, but I'm driving my own car, and I won't meet with him anywhere but his office in the courthouse. In an hour."

The deputy, who hadn't changed expression during the exchange, turned to leave. "I'll tell him," he said, tipping his hat to Sandy.

When the deputy departed, Sandy sat down with her coffee next to Kirk. "Keep my pistol," she said with a sigh. "You may need it."

"No, thanks. If Ganner wants to get brazen in his lair, one pistol won't make any difference."

"You're crazy to keep pressing your luck. Why not get on back to Justinville where it's safe?"

"Now, why would I do that?" he said with a smile. "I've been wanting to meet Frank Ganner for a long, long time."

Kirk called the campaign headquarters, leaving a message with Mrs. Fogel that he would be in later that afternoon. He read the newspaper casually, purposely causing him to be fifteen minutes late for his appointment.

When he arrived, Ganner's longtime close associate, Al Hernandez, met him outside Ganner's office with a challenge. "You're late."

"And you're rude." Kirk glanced inside the anteroom where a bodyguard was stationed.

"Did you say 'rude'?"

"I did. I'm supposed to be a guest in this friendly land, and I haven't been afforded many courtesies."

"You're no guest. You're a meddler, an intruder, and you have no place here. You only want to stir up trouble."

"Well, if it'll make you feel any better, I'd much rather be in Austin or Houston or Timbuktu. I'll be damned glad when this election is over with."

"So will I, assuming we get favorable results."

Frank Ganner appeared, walking briskly toward them from the commissioners courtroom. He nodded to Hernandez, who departed, and he motioned to the bodyguard to remain at his station.

Ganner and Hernandez had quarreled over the advisability of this meeting, but Ganner was more determined than ever to size up Kirk firsthand after his men came in red-faced and empty-handed the previous night. Ganner shook Kirk's hand and led him into his office.

"Let's get one thing clear." Ganner closed the door. "Anything said in this office is not for public consumption in any form."

"All right," Kirk said, "but you're taking quite a chance with a guy who is plenty damned upset about what happened to him last night."

"I'm not concerned. I've checked you out thoroughly, and your word is good in a bargain, as is mine. Besides, you never were in any real danger last night. I told those boys to give you a little initiation, nothing more."

"Initiation with a rattlesnake."

"That wasn't my idea, but what the hell, you got your licks in. One of my boys came in with a broken jaw."

"He got a little careless."

"Yeah." Ganner chuckled, "But you were a little careless coming over here the way you did. A fat pigeon on a low wire."

"Can't argue with that." Kirk sighed.

"You're not prone to make mistakes. You were careless because you were too damn curious about what's going on here. You should have contacted me for a meeting instead of dealing with an anonymous caller. When you took that kind of sneaky bait, I figured you were up to no good... But I'm glad you're here.

"I'm not pleased with the way you're chewing on my candidate in the state rep race. On the other hand, I appreciate smart politics and you've pushed your hand about as hard as you can. Your candidate won't make it, but he'll do a helluva lot better than I first thought."

"So, what's the purpose of this meeting?"

"I want to talk politics, but first, business. I knew your dad fairly well and he knew how to run that county. Only he died with less than five hundred dollars in the bank and just a little land. Not much for the family."

"We made out all right."

"Maybe so, but you impress me as a guy who wants more out of life. A guy who is capable of achieving it."

"What's your point?"

Ganner leaned back in his chair with a confident expression. "I'll make you an offer you should accept. Come to work for me and I'll double what you're making and pay you a two thousand dollar bonus if the elections come out the way I want."

Kirk had no intention of accepting the offer, but he stared at Ganner as though he were considering it. If this were an avenue to determine Ganner's plans for the Senate race, he was willing to walk down the path a step or two.

"That's Wally Hooper, of course, but what about the race for U.S. Senate?"

"I'm going for Jordan Layman." Ganner's tone was casual.

"Why? I thought you and Holt Witherspoon were friends."

"That's what it is, 'we're friends.' I'm looking for some help in the future with federal matters. I believe I can count on Jordan. Witherspoon double-crossed me on a major appointment when he was governor. I haven't forgotten."

"With Layman, you get a say in who gets named to federal judgeships in South Texas soon as the Democrats retake the White House."

"That's correct, plus I want to be on the inside for the whole spectrum of federal patronage. There's a lot at stake."

"So, you're looking for a political operative to cover all of South Texas for Jordan Layman?"

"Yes, and keep tabs on all the contested races. The state rep race is part of the territory, as you know, but I want to make sure you understand I place a much higher premium on the Senate race.

"The one thing I don't want to happen in the rep race is for that smart aleck Garcia kid to slip in. I don't want him to even make a runoff. He's already stirring up trouble among gullible Mexicanos. I want him stopped."

Kirk winced. "Even if it means repeating what happened to Bobby Howard?"

Ganner's eyes grew cold as he trained them squarely on Kirk. "I've never ordered anyone killed."

Kirk returned the scowl. "Sure, and I suspect if Hitler were here today, he'd assure us he never flipped a switch that killed a Jew."

Scowling, Ganner rose from his chair, but Hernandez swung the door open, informing him he was needed for a few moments with the commissioners. Ganner departed without saying another word.

Even this conniving bastard, Kirk thought, might get careless now and then.

He shuffled rapidly through papers on Ganner's desk, finding one that intrigued him. It contained locations of voting precincts in Bantrell and Will Dodd counties, with routes and points where special vehicles were stationed, including trucks and pickups. This was the blueprint for Ganner's machine to turn out the vote. He made a mental picture of the map and returned it into the stack just before Ganner's footsteps sounded outside the door.

Ganner stomped to his desk, removed his glasses, and again looked straight at Kirk. "You're a little too big for your britches, Holland, but I need you. I'm willing to disregard your intemperate remarks. This Senate election is damned important to me and I want that rep seat.

I'll up the offer, double whatever you're making, plus a three thousand dollar bonus if Jordan Layman wins, one thousand for Wally Hooper. That's a helluva good deal."

"You said you checked me out. You've forgotten I've been a soldier and a reporter. I'm used to low pay. Forget it."

"You're a damned fool, just like your father," Ganner snapped. "Get out of my office!"

Chapter 9

The sky was clear and the air hot as Kirk drove from Piedra Blanca to Justinville. He weighed political developments while watching mirages form and disappear over the long stretch of steamy highway. Though he had hoped Ganner might sit out the Senate race, he wasn't surprised to learn of his support for Jordan Layman. It was the South Texas thing to do, plus Ganner had his own selfish reasons, about which he had been candid.

And probably more reasons hadn't been laid on the table. But now the picture was clearer, it was disturbing. Layman would carry South Texas by a substantial margin and, with Ganner's highly effective turn-out-the-vote machine, that margin would be maximized.

Unfortunate as it was for Wally Hooper, that factor meant his potential in the Ganner-impact counties of highest probable yield, Bantrell and Will Dodd, would be enhanced a great deal. Kirk knew he needed to adjust his voter projection for Hooper upward a bit. Goals for Wedge in the "free" counties would have to be upgraded, and the need to court Garcia supporters was more evident. But all considerations were subordinate to the foremost goal at hand, that of making the runoff.

That afternoon he arrived at the campaign headquarters, where Wedge and Nellie greeted him. They both asked about his bandaged wrist and palm.

"You might say," Kirk said with a grin, "I got a little careless with a critter."

He tasted a cup of thick coffee and set it aside. "I have some news. I've been to the friendly land of Frank Ganner and he tells me he's supporting Jordan Layman. My friends, our destiny has become intertwined with that of Holt Witherspoon."

"What?" Wedge's eyebrows shot up.

"Are you suggesting," Nellie said, "we move off our position of neutrality in the Senate race?"

"Not at all," Kirk said, "but you'd better grit your teeth. This isn't going to be a pleasant situation with Ganner pushing Layman, who already has the advantage in South Texas. And it means Wedge must stop bad-mouthing Witherspoon, period."

"That old mossback reactionary," Wedge barked. "I can't entertain the notion of his being elected our next United States Senator."

"Just don't criticize him. Leave him alone."

"Do you think," Nellie said, "Ganner will run Layman and Hooper in tandem?"

"My guess is, not in public," Kirk said, "but through his political organization, by word-of-mouth... yeah, sure he will, at the very end of the campaign."

"It would be to our advantage to create an issue of this," Wedge said. "I'll call Wade Keene and alert him to what's going on."

"No, you can't do that. I made an agreement with Ganner not to discuss this publicly at all."

"You what?" Wedge tossed a stack of papers aside.

"You heard me, I gave him my word."

"My campaign manager making deals with the most rotten political boss who ever lived? Come on, Kirk, this is absurd!"

"Take it easy," Nellie said. "I suspect things weren't all peaches and cream over there at Piedra Blanca."

"What about the murder of Bobby Howard?" Wedge was almost shouting.

"Of course, he wouldn't own up to it, and I didn't see or hear anything to point in his direction; but, he's still a logical suspect."

Wedge shook his head. "I just don't understand how you could sit down and talk to that sonofabitch."

"I wouldn't say it was easy." Kirk walked away.

Wedge paused, frowning at Nellie. "Once again, I question what he's doing and once again, you take his side. What kind of spell has he cast over you?"

"Don't taunt me!" she snarled. "You wanted to make this race very badly, and I went out on a limb to get him involved when he didn't want to come. We're poised to take a good crack at the first primary, and you're sitting around wasting time bitching about every move he makes or suggests. You'd better get your nose pointed in the right direction." She turned to leave.

"Okay, okay," he said, grabbing her hand. "I'll go over that damned PAMAT speech if you'll get me a hamburger."

She held her frown for a moment, then eased into a smile. "All right, Hotshot, I guess this is just a little pre-primary tension among the players."

She kissed him on the cheek and walked away.

Later that afternoon Kirk collapsed on his bed, exhausted, but slept only a couple of hours before a terror-filled dream—with the angry rattler's fangs again aimed at his head—shook him awake. He got up and drove away to get something to eat.

He wasn't in the mood for Barney's with the backslapping and game-playing, nor did he want to eat at the regular places where the Anglos gathered and he would have to talk about the drouth and politics. He wanted to be around people, yet alone, so he drove to a little Mexican restaurant, near the Nueces River bridge, named Casita Flores. He hadn't been there in years, but he decided to try it since he recalled its clientele was predominantly Mexican-American, yet Anglos were welcome.

He took a small table in a corner and ordered a beer. The restaurant was decorated with brightly trimmed black sombreros hung on the walls next to colorful bullfight posters. A soothing purr from a window unit air conditioner blended with soft guitar music drifting from a jukebox on the far wall. He relaxed and decided against eating just yet.

A few feet away, at the cash register, a young Mexican-American woman flashed a smile at him as she prepared to process a customer's tab. She was strikingly attractive, though unpretentious, dressed in a dark green flowing skirt and white blouse. Her large brown eyes were shifting, yet appeared to be sensitive, and she wore only a subtle coverage of lipstick. Her soft black hair was combed behind her shoulders. A small silver cross hung from her neck, the only jewelry she wore, and her fingernails were polished, neat but trimmed rather short in order not to impede her work.

Kirk watched as she maneuvered about the restaurant in sandals that seemed to facilitate her movements and accentuate her well-defined ankles.

She's businesslike and efficient, Kirk mused, yet what a stunning woman with a fine figure.

He was about to finish his beer and reorder from the other waitress when she stopped at his table. "Well, Kirk Holland, do you always forget your classmates so easily?"

"Oh, for Heaven's sake! Briana Flores. Sorry, haven't seen you in, what, eight years? Believe me, you've changed."

"For the better, I trust."

"For the better… and if you are allowed to sit with a customer, please join me."

"In a few minutes, perhaps. Would you like another beer?"

"You bet."

There had been, Kirk recalled, a bit of chemistry between them in high school, but in the ethnically divided town, it never went past a glance or two in the hallway between classes. That chemistry was percolating again. He watched her work the cash register, wait tables, and overall run the place. With only one table of customers remaining, she joined him.

"You're a waitress and general manager. Do this all the time?"

"No, thank heavens," she said. "My parents have gone to San Antonio for a few days. I work twice as hard when they're gone."

"Say, I know this is awful short notice, but how about having dinner with me tonight?"

She smiled, then laughed, shaking her head. "You know we shouldn't be seen in this town together other than here, with you as a customer."

"Of course, we shouldn't. So, let's get out of town."

"Oh no, I couldn't. I have to be here early in the morning. Besides, you and I… why should we go on a date?"

"Why not?"

"It's not something I think is wise."

"Sometimes, it might not be wise to think."

Her lips twitched as she again shook her head. "It just wouldn't be right for us to go out on a date."

"Well then, don't call it a 'date.' Let's ease down to Aguilar for a bite to eat. It's only thirty miles away, but relatively safe for the reputations. Scout's honor to have you back by midnight."

She shrugged. "Well… All right, but back before midnight."

On the way after closing the restaurant, they chatted a few minutes before she fell silent.

"What's wrong?" he said.

"I was just thinking, I have a little confession to make."

"I won't hear it. I'm not a priest."

She laughed. "When I saw you tonight, I recalled vividly when you ran for class president our senior year. Remember?"

"Of course, I won. Had I lost, I wouldn't remember."

"You won by four votes."

"That's correct. Not exactly a mandate, but I was damn glad to win. My opponent had higher grades and the teachers seemed to like him better."

"Yes, and I'll bet you don't recall how the Mexican-Americans voted."

"I recall I had most of the Mexican-Americans on my side."

"Do you know why?"

"Well, I assumed they liked me. I tried to treat them the same, as classmates and teammates."

"You were better liked, but a few were leaning the other way. I talked four of my girlfriends into voting for you."

"Based upon that startling revelation, I indeed owe you a big dinner with drinks for having provided the winning margin in that election that was crucial to the welfare of our beloved community."

She smiled. "Aren't you going to ask why?"

"And spoil your tender nostalgic moment of unrequited love?"

Again, she laughed. "Still fast with words, I see. Seriously, I want you to know I was for you because I felt you and your opponent saw the world beyond the county borders, but you alone understood the unmarked border between our side of town and yours."

He paused, glancing at her before returning his gaze to the highway. "That's a high compliment. I appreciate it."

For a moment they rode in silence until he said, "Now, I remember one I want explained. How did you beat me out in that essay contest?"

She laughed. "I suspect you beat yourself. It was during basketball season and you gave that more attention than your writing."

He grinned. "All this talk is making me hungry. Have you ever eaten at Cano's Place in Aguilar?"

"Believe it or not, I've never really been to Aguilar. Only driven through on the way to Laredo, with my parents."

"Let me guess. You've never been south of Laredo nor north of San Antonio?"

"You're close, but I have been to Dallas once, Austin twice, and worked in Corpus Christi."

"After high school, did you live in Justinville?"

"No, I spent two years in San Antonio in a convent. Then, my mother became seriously ill and my father summoned me home."

"Were you disappointed?"

"At first I was because I enjoyed my studies very much. Later I came to believe I wasn't destined to be a nun. I'll always love the church, but I am relieved to be where I am."

"And the remainder of the time you've been in Justinville?"

"Except for a year working at my uncle's restaurant in Corpus Christi. After my mother recovered, I grew bored at our place and welcomed the time in Corpus. I made some good friends there and I visit now and then. When my parents persuaded me to return, they gave me additional responsibility, so the past couple of years have been a little more fulfilling."

"Tell me, why hasn't some handsome young buck come along to sweep you off your feet?"

"Probably too independent for the macho tradition." She paused. "And just why hasn't a beautiful young woman caused you to walk down the aisle?"

He shrugged. "I'll never tell."

She laughed. "Well, you don't have to tell me where you've been. I've followed you through our newspaper. University of Texas, Korean War, working for the newspaper in Austin, then back to Justinville for this political campaign. Does that cover it?"

"That's about it."

"I suppose I shouldn't ask, but isn't this campaign... I mean the fact you're against Frank Ganner... rather dangerous?"

"Only if you wander into his territory."

On the outskirts of Aguilar, a dusty little town with a population of twelve hundred, Kirk pointed to a large store across the railroad tracks to his right. "Over there is the old mercantile building, the pride of this town, and these next two blocks are about it for the action. There's old Cano's, and you'd better like it. It's the night life for this area."

Cano's Place was located in a small one-story building with a modest patio out back. When they walked in, Cano, a short pudgy man in his mid-forties, was scurrying about the place and waved briefly to Kirk, whom he hadn't seen in two years.

A few regular customers in the front area paused over their food and beer to study them, not because of the ethnic mixture, but because they were unfamiliar. The bland building was in reasonably good condition, but Cano believed in working for profit with low overhead, spending little on decoration except outside, where some of his steady customers often gathered for an evening.

They walked to the patio and found two small tables, vacant among six filled with residents from in and around the tiny community. One large table seated ten people who were enjoying themselves from trays of food, buckets of ice, and bottles of beer and soft drinks. Cano's was the only place between Justinville and Laredo that catered to customers who liked to sit and drink and visit, or dance, in addition to eating generous portions from his limited menu.

Kirk had brought a bottle of bourbon in a brown paper sack which he placed in the middle of their table. For mixing, they soon had a bucket of ice, a pitcher of water, and a bottle of Coca-Cola, since bourbon and Coke was the only way Briana said she could tolerate whiskey. "When I can't taste it."

Glancing around, Kirk recognized none of the customers. "Only a few people from Justinville ever come here, so maybe your reputation won't be sullied so badly after all."

"Why is it different here?" She scanned the tables and focused on two other ethnically mixed couples.

"I don't know. Maybe because it's closer to Laredo."

Small lights of various colors were strung around the patio on a wire about four feet from the ground, and the weathered old jukebox near the patio entrance beckoned couples to dance on the scuffed red and green tile.

Briana toyed with her drink, taking in the scene, including the pale moon and stars dominating a clear summer sky. She was happy yet uneasy during her first public moments of an initial date with an Anglo.

"Penny?" he said.

"I feel as though we're somehow cheating fate. We're only two people here, so removed from where we live. It's pleasant here."

"Everything tonight will be pleasant. I trust you know I ordered this gentle breeze, just strong enough to cool things down, but not strong enough to stir up dust."

"You won't let me have a serious moment, will you?"

"You don't need those. You need to have a good time."

"And so do you, I would imagine."

He asked her to dance a soft number and they moved awkwardly at first, but soon adjusted to each other. When the song ended, they strolled to the jukebox to make their own selections.

As a well-traveled soldier during World War II, Cano had developed a taste for sentimental American popular music, such as that of Glenn Miller and others. That accounted for about one third of the scratchy selections he offered, along with some traditional Mexican music and the ubiquitous country western, popular throughout South Texas.

Kirk selected "My Happiness," "Prisoner of Love," "To Each His Own," and one of his all-time favorites, "I'll Be Seeing You."

She looked over the Mexican records, then sighed. "I'm just too tired to dance those polkas," she said, pressing her selections for "Maria Elena" by Beto Villa, "Viajera," and the bouncy favorite "Rancho Grande."

"Now don't be a chicken." He watched a record someone else had selected ease onto the turntable. "We need to loosen up a little."

It was the lively "Beer Barrel Polka" and they swirled around the dance floor to the bouncy old tune. When it ended, she collapsed into her chair, a bit winded but happy.

After a couple of drinks, the old seventy-eights didn't sound scratchy at all. They became smooth, blending with the pleasant breeze and sounds of laughter around them.

They danced and drank slowly, savoring every moment. Their moods had meshed well, as though they no longer needed to speak, only to enjoy each other and the music. On the dance floor the warmth of her firm body against him prompted Kirk to want to hold her closer and kiss her lovely lips. But a careful balance had to be maintained, with people looking on, plus her sense of restraint, which he perceived was fighting the affection her eyes could no longer conceal.

When she finally glanced at her watch, it was almost 10:30, and she insisted they eat. Kirk ordered Cano's specialty, a platter of fried cabrito, small chunks of goat meat, with a bowl of fresh guacamole salad made from avocados that weren't cut until the order was placed, plus large French fried potatoes and fried onion rings.

"I can't believe all this food," she said, confining portions on her plate to cabrito and guacamole.

"Every once in a long while," he said, "I'll indulge in this food. Eat it every day and I'd soon weigh five hundred pounds."

She couldn't talk him into having a cup of coffee, but he compromised by finishing his night's drinking with a beer, rather than more whiskey. On the way home, she fell asleep, resting her head on his shoulder. When they arrived at the restaurant in Justinville, she awoke and he inquired about the location of her house.

"It's only a block away, but I must walk. My brother and sister might wake up if you drive there."

"Come on, Briana, you don't need to walk in the dark at this hour."

"It's better this way. I'll be all right."

He tried to put his arm around her to kiss her lips, but she moved her left hand in his way. She kissed him, brief and soft, on the cheek before slipping across the seat to depart.

Later, Kirk lay awake in bed, recounting the evening with Briana. Was it, he forced himself to ask, anything like falling in love with Carrie?

Or was it the old rebound, of which he'd often heard?

Or maybe, he thought, falling asleep, I've just found a shoulder to lean on during this goddam crazy campaign.

On the following day, Kirk whizzed through his work and headed for Casita Flores in late afternoon, arriving before the dinner crowd. His heart sank as he scanned the two rooms and didn't see her. He took a small corner table and ordered a beer from the only waitress on duty. He started to inquire of Briana's whereabouts but realized that would be a dead giveaway.

Hell, he thought, I shouldn't have let her walk home alone… But this is Justinville. If anything had happened, I'd have heard about it by now. She ought to be here… She ought to be here…

Suddenly, she burst through the swinging doors from the kitchen, scanned the rooms, and came to his table. "I had a really good time last night, Kirk. Thank you."

"Well, it just so happens I've thought of another nice night."

"Oh, no, I couldn't."

"Oh, yes, you could and will. Now, I'll pick you up at closing time, and we'll have our own dinner, which I'll cook. You can't beat that."

"You must be crazy. I won't go to your apartment."

"I'm sure you wouldn't. But how about a barbecue, down the river?"

"And who else will be there?"

"Only the moon, a great chaperone."

"Kirk Holland…" she beamed at him, "…you're absolutely impossible."

After closing the restaurant, she walked gingerly in the shadows to his car. On a narrow farm road, they drove a few miles to the one piece of land still remaining in the Holland family, a tract adjacent to the tree-shrouded Nueces River.

Kirk stopped in a small open area near the old corral and bunkhouse, long abandoned. A huge, winding live oak tree dominated the area, casting its shadows on the twisting mesquite tree formations that hovered over sagebrush, prickly pear, and dry range grass. Bathed in soft moonlight, the scene brought a surrealistic beauty to those various forms that appeared so harsh and dusty, even grotesque, during the day.

She opened the door, stepped out, and viewed the surroundings. "It's lovely here, as though there's no drouth at all."

"Don't worry, it'll be back in the morning." He unloaded his purchases for the barbecue.

She helped him spread a quilt a few feet from a long shallow ditch he would use for a pit in which to build a fire from mesquite limbs. "Why ribs? They take so long."

"We've got the evening," he said, laying a grill across the far end of the pit where he planned to slow-cook the ribs. He then retrieved a portable radio from the car and tuned it to a popular music station in San Antonio he had always enjoyed. They sat by the fire, savoring a glass of wine, listening to the music.

He nudged her as the disc jockey intoned, "And now a special request for the folks down by the river."

When the first notes of "I'll Be Seeing You" came on, Kirk stood up, bowed, and asked for a dance. They moved slowly on the dusty ground, her soft sandals providing a little smoother footing than his tennis shoes.

"That bit about the chestnut trees," he said. "Just close your eyes and pretend these old mesquites will fill the bill."

She laughed. "I don't know what a chestnut tree looks like and probably never will."

"Doesn't matter. Just close your eyes and pretend this is a special place."

They danced without further talking, savoring the smooth music and soft moonlight. When the song ended, he paused, holding her body in a strong embrace. She resisted briefly before his lips pressed hard against hers for a long, arousing moment.

She tried to ease back, but he held her closer. "Oh, Kirk, I just can't… "

Breathing heavily, they collapsed upon the quilt where he enfolded her in his arms. A sharp sense of exhilaration consumed him, an imminent discovery in his life that would be total, both physical and emotional. Perhaps even stronger than he had ever felt with Carrie.

But at the final instant of intense anticipation before making love, he felt her body go limp. Then, she trembled; not, he sensed, from anticipation or passion, but from fear.

"Oh, G… God," he wailed, "I'm sorry… I… I had no idea."

Crying softly, Briana pulled herself to a sitting position. Her mood changed to anger. "You had no idea!" she sobbed. "What did you think? That all the little Mexican girls around town have many lovers, and you were next in line for this one?"

"No, believe me. I just didn't think—"

"That I could be a twenty-six-year-old virgin? Well, I am, and I shouldn't have allowed myself to get into this situation tonight."

He stood up, poured himself a shot of bourbon, and walked to the fire. He stood there silently, gazing at the coals burning down slowly. She sobbed again.

Without facing her, he spoke. "I'm sorry. God, I'm sorry. The last thing I'd ever want to do is to hurt you. You're one of the few people I truly respect."

Tears again welled in her eyes. "I don't believe you respect me. I hate you. I hate you for disrupting my life because you're only looking for a fling."

He paused for a long moment, studying the coals. "I guess," he murmured, "I'd better take you home."

After wiping away tears, she climbed into the car. For a few moments they rode in silence before she leaned her head on his shoulder. "Oh, Kirk, what's this all about? Today, I was miserable. One minute vowing I would never go out with you again, the next minute longing to see you walk through the door; knowing we have no future, but wanting to squeeze every second that might be available. I just don't know what to think."

"Neither do I. I know when we started dancing in Aguilar, everything else, people and noise, faded away. I only wanted to be close to you, and it's a strong feeling. I'm sorry it turned a little sour tonight."

When he let her off, she kissed him softly on the cheek. "Don't be a stranger," she said.

Kirk was working in his headquarters office the following day when Nellie walked in. "I'm sorry," she said, lighting a cigarette, "to have to bring up something unpleasant."

"I know, Wedge hasn't got the PAMAT speech cold, but he's coming around."

"No, it's about you."

"All right."

"Gordon Hempstead complained to me today that there's talk around town of you seeing a young Mexican woman."

"She was born in Justinville. That makes her just as American as you or me."

"Oh, you know what I mean."

"Yes, I know what you mean."

"It's just that Gordon wants things to run smoothly."

Kirk tossed his pencil at the wastebasket. "Don't you think our distinguished campaign chairman ought to spend his time raising money, rather than spreading gossip?"

"Well, is it true?"

Kirk sighed. "Yes, it's true, but I don't know why it's an issue. I'm not the candidate."

"Come on, Kirk, you know what's involved. Some of our supporters look to you for leadership. They don't want to be associated with anything like a gossip mill. And your mother wouldn't be too happy about this either."

Kirk trained his eyes squarely on Nellie. "Maybe you're right, but I'm not going to stop seeing her. She's a wonderful person and she respects me. If you and Wedge want another manager, that's your prerogative."

"Do you love her?"

He winced, looking down at the desk, chin in hand. "I'm not sure. I guess things have been happening a little too fast."

He rose to leave, but Nellie detained him, placing a firm hand on his shoulder. "My dear young soldier, you're just bouncing hard on the rebound. Don't do anything you'll regret for the rest of your life."

Yeah, he thought, pulling her hand aside, or don't pass up something you'll regret for the rest of your life.

Driving toward Casita Flores, sharp pangs of confusion and frustration, as though unseen powerful forces, tore at him. Inside the restaurant, he took the small table in the corner. He saw her, but she was preoccupied with customers and slow to return his glance.

He caught a look from her father, who was working the cash register. Kirk read nothing in that impassive face, but a foreboding mood fell upon him. Things might be different since her parents had returned.

At last, she came by his table. "I can't talk now. Meet me at the fork under the river bridge at ten."

Though it was only a few blocks from the restaurant, that location was isolated, with live oaks, willow, and salt cedar trees forming protective curtains. He got out of his car to greet her, but she held him at bay, refusing to embrace him. He could tell she had been crying.

"I'm very sorry, Kirk, but I must not see you again. My father has forbidden it."

"Because I'm a suspicious gringo out to exploit his beloved daughter?"

"Please, he respected your father and he respects you. But we can't—"

"Can't keep seeing each other. We're too goddamn happy to be going together around here!"

"He says it will only lead to heartbreak and loneliness for both of us."

"I want to speak to your father."

She shook her head, leaning into his arms. "No, my love. Please don't, you'll only make it more difficult."

He sighed, then kissed her gently on the forehead and hugged her again, holding her close for a long moment. "Let me take you home."

"Only to the restaurant."

They spent the final minutes together that night in silence. At the restaurant parking lot, she kissed him on the cheek, squeezed his hand, and departed as tears welled in her lovely brown eyes.

Each afternoon for several days, Kirk drove by the restaurant but was unable to bring himself to enter. The thought of seeing her without being able to speak beyond the moment was an even heavier burden he couldn't bear.

At a slow pace, he worked his mind back into the vortex of the campaign, which was swirling toward the first primary. Wedge's personal campaign schedule was heavier than ever, more bumper stickers, posters, and brochures were being distributed, and from throughout the district, word came that all three candidates were running strong.

It was another of those hot, dry summer days when Kirk joined Wedge and Nellie in her air-conditioned car for the drive to Corpus Christi for the showdown Wedge had been dreading. Upon arrival, they ate dinner and retired early in preparation for a long day of activity.

Kirk estimated two hundred delegates were attending the state convention of the Political Association of Mexican-Americans of Texas (PAMAT). They assembled that morning in the brand new Memorial Auditorium by the bay near downtown Corpus Christi. The convention was held two weeks prior to the first primary, timed to give Ernesto Garcia a late boost in his race for state representative.

PAMAT had earned just enough credibility to attract news media from sizeable Texas markets with large Mexican-American populations, including El Paso, Laredo, San Antonio, and the Lower Rio Grande Valley, in addition to host Corpus Christi. Also, media representatives were present to cover Jordan Layman. They were disappointed his major opponent and the perceived frontrunner, Holt Witherspoon, had chosen not to attend, but curious about what impact Layman might generate upon this potentially potent force in the Texas political arena.

True to what Wedge had heard, Wally Hooper had also chosen not to attend, claiming a schedule conflict. Kirk suspected Frank Ganner had forbidden Hooper from attending since Ganner and the other political bosses of South Texas, both Anglo and Mexican-American, considered PAMAT to be a threat.

As the chairman prepared to gavel the convention to order, Kirk mingled around the coffee urn in the press section with several he knew well, including Wade Keene, who was still searching vainly, along with law enforcement officials, for clues relating to the murder of Bobby Howard. Kirk chatted with him a brief while about their campaign before turning to Lonnie Hardner, editor of The Texas Progressive, who had recently given Garcia a strong endorsement in his magazine, the liberal voice of the state.

"Don't we get some pledge points for just showing up here?" Kirk said to Hardner.

Hardner always wore an intense expression, even when speaking in impassive tones, as he did in now. "I'm still looking for some substance to your campaign."

"You mean agreeing with Garcia?"

"Yes, if you want to put it that way. He's developing some important issues that affect most of the people in his district, people who need help."

"But they don't all vote, and some of 'em will vote for Ganner's man, come hell or high water... We've got to hold onto some businessmen, teachers, and the landed gentry or we're nowhere."

Hardner shrugged. "Garcia has stoked a smoldering fire. He'll make the runoff against Ganner's man. He's a credit to this movement and I'm supporting him, period."

"Ever," Kirk muttered under his breath, "the magnificent egghead."

The PAMAT state chairman, Bexar County Commissioner Celso Portillo of San Antonio, soon called the convention to order. He was a shrewd veteran of political combat in his home territory who had earned respect throughout South Texas among those who appreciated independence from machine politics.

After exemplary service in World War II, he had returned to San Antonio to land a good job in a brewery, worked hard, and paid his dues in church and civic organizations. He took some night courses toward a college degree but found politics more inviting. He won his commissioner seat by campaigning door-to-door during long, hot evenings of a spring and summer, with little money for campaign materials and none for media advertising.

He participated in LULAC and the American G.I. Forum, but he found himself longing for more aggressive thrusts. He had founded PAMAT with the help of Garcia and other independent-thinking Mexican-Americans who wanted a totally political vehicle with which to advance their cause.

Portillo, a short, wiry man with a resonant voice, recognized the meager handful of Mexican-American officeholders in attendance. Aware of the reporters present, he decided to pitch some of his remarks their way.

"It's apparent," Portillo said, scanning the hall, "many South Texas Mexican-American leaders are absent. This is unfortunate because within these walls is a spirit of resolve and unity that can accomplish more in a few years than has been accomplished in past decades. Where are they? Why are they absent?

"I must tell you, most are safely on the sidelines, content with whatever transpires. Many are shackled by the bonds of political machines they either run or serve.

"By whatever name, they are not serving the interests of the people. They exploit native Mexican-Americans, and they exploit "mojados" or "wetbacks," as the Anglos call them. All those people are merely serfs, working for their feudal landlords, the political and economic bosses of South Texas. Always remember, my friends, their power is maintained through political machines that reach deep into the root system of the lives of those struggling to make their way.

"And so, the question becomes, 'Where can the oppressed people of South Texas turn for political action and reform?' Let this convention's record clearly reflect the fact we are united to provide effective, responsive political leadership for the Mexican-Americans of Texas!"

That statement generated a rousing round of applause, spliced with hearty "gritos".

"Now, it's my understanding," Portillo continued, "Frank Ganner will soon set up shop nearby in the beautiful Driscoll Hotel where he'll serve his friends, along with his prospective friends, big steaks and expensive whiskey. At noon we'll break instead for a barbecue on a dusty high school football field. We'll eat tough, stringy meat and drink the cheapest beer we could buy. But let me remind you of something, my friends. We're free, and they aren't!"

A sharp burst of applause engulfed the hall.

"Also, let me assure you Frank Ganner won't be there out of the goodness of his heart. He'll be there to intimidate us; to remind us of his oppressive power and constant desire to expand it. But we are not going to sell out to him or any of the other patróns and jéfes of South Texas!"

Again, the delegates responded with enthusiasm.

"We have a mission and a vision for our people. It's our mission to provide leadership to reform the stagnant, degrading economic and political system that pervades most of South Texas. We have endured injustices because of the color of our skin. We have endured injustices because of our Spanish surnames.

"Prejudice among the Anglos will subside very slowly unless we claim our rights and fulfill our responsibilities. We will continue..." Portillo raised his voice, "...to endure injustices until we meet the challenge head-on, in the political arena!"

A sharp round of applause followed that statement.

"And with success there, our vision of freedom, justice, and opportunity will be realized... Now, my friends, mis compadres, it gives me great pleasure to present today one of our own, one who is carrying forth our banner against the most corrupt and powerful political machine in Texas. He's a man who displayed great courage on foreign battlefields and upon the battlefield of that state representative district which Frank Ganner seeks to control. I present to you one who will serve us—and all the people of his district—in an honorable, responsive manner in the Texas Legislature. A fine individual, a tribute to Mexican-Americans everywhere, our convention keynote speaker, Ernesto Garcia!"

All delegates jumped to their feet, waving banners and cheering Garcia, who strode into the arms of Portillo for a hearty "abrazo," as trumpets in a mariachi band blared away with piercing bursts. At the podium, Garcia waved to the crowd, preparing to speak.

While the commotion continued to engulf the hall, such a rousing welcome appeared to surprise him. He'd never spoken to such a large crowd with so many reporters in attendance, and his hands trembled from anticipation. Calling for the applause to end, he adjusted his glasses and glanced at a page of notes before him.

"I come before you today in a spirit of gratitude, thankful for your support, encouraged by my reception around the district, yet acutely aware of the awesome challenge we face."

"Still sounds like a professor," Keene said to Kirk. "You ought to give him some lessons."

"As long as they listen and believe. That's what counts."

"We've made great progress in this campaign," Garcia continued, gaining some confidence in his voice. "I can report to you that in five of the seven counties in the district, we have a chance to lead or finish second with a good percentage. But in those two machine counties, under the direct control of Frank Ganner, the majority of the Mexican-

American vote will go to an Anglo candidate. A candidate who cares absolutely nothing about the aspirations and needs of our people today, not to mention the heritage and traditions of the Spanish-Mexican culture. Now, that to me is disgusting! That, we must change!" He raised his voice to a spirited round of applause and cheers.

"My friends, loyalty is a sharp, two-edged sword. I'm proud of my deep sense of loyalty to my country which I have served in battle, yet I find that blind loyalty to our political party—the Democratic Party—means we are too often taken for granted. The party takes care of the machines; the machines take care of the party. Most of our people know no other way, and they survive with whatever the machine chooses to provide. There is a better way. There is a way of freedom and opportunity. Military service carried me to California, where I saw more and better jobs available for Mexicanos. Now, I didn't want to stay in California, but I don't want South Texas to stay as it is. So, I submit to you that we've been taken for granted too long! ¡Ya basta!"

About half of the delegates responded with applause and "gritos."

"If reform is not forthcoming; if the Democratic Party doesn't respond to our record of loyalty, to our aspirations and needs and hopes and dreams, then I say we should form our own political party!"

Half of the delegates were on their feet applauding and shouting "gritos" while the other half was divided between those responding with polite applause and those choosing to remain silent in their seats.

"He just needed to warm up," Keene said, scribbling rapid notes.

Portillo, Ramirez, and the few other Democratic officeholders in the hall were silent while the young activists applauded with vigor. The incumbents didn't want this volatile issue within the organization debated openly during the election year. Though they were disappointed in Garcia for raising it, they took note of the emotional pitch it generated among the young firebrands.

"Quite a challenge, wouldn't you say?" Kirk said to Hardner.

"More of a threat," Hardner snapped. "I'd much prefer he stay with the issues. I've never been in favor of an ethnic splinter party. All that would do in the long run is help the damned Republicans in statewide races."

Behind the stage, Jordan Layman had been puffing cigarettes, listening with careful attention and observing crowd reaction. Following the splinter party threat, he withdrew the third page of his speech which had been used to castigate Holt Witherspoon for having supported Eisenhower and calling for party loyalty. He instructed his campaign press secretary to remove that page from all the hand-outs to the press.

"But Mr. Layman, my typewriter is at the hotel. I don't have time to change the numbers on the pages."

"Change 'em in ink."

"But the press will know something has been removed at the last minute. They'll ask questions."

"I don't give a shit! Change 'em, and just tell those people you made a mistake typing the speech."

Garcia proceeded to pound hard on his legislative platform, calling for "repeal of the insulting poll tax, a critical change that is basic and central to breaking the stranglehold of the political machines;" a state minimum wage of sixty-five cents an hour, which he termed "barely adequate to provide food and shelter, but certainly better than the paltry forty cents an hour some of the workers now receive;" an education program "that recognizes the peculiar needs of our young people who must receive some instruction in Spanish while learning English. The concept of bilingual education is valid and must be pursued.

"Remember, also, most of us in this hall are native South Texans, year-round residents, with something of value to fight for in our communities. As Mexican-Americans, as Christians, and as concerned citizens of this great nation of promise, we have the responsibility, and the opportunity, to fight for economic and educational reform; and, above all, my friends," he called out, raising his voice again, "to fight for political reform that will free us from the bondage of oppression and stagnation!"

All the delegates jumped to their feet, applauding. He waved to them to be seated and spoke of lesser issues, moving toward his closing remarks.

"Let me remind you this is a three-candidate race. Frank Ganner's candidate chose not to appear today; or Frank Ganner told him not to appear today. Take your pick - 'no le hace.'

"The other candidate will speak to you later and I ask you to treat him with courtesy and respect as he has treated me on the campaign trail. But just don't listen too closely, my friends, because he's part of the old Anglo South Texas establishment that isn't in the Frank Ganner patrón system, but is nonetheless patronizing. They have provided us with little economic or political opportunity and this man has made no positive statements to this time."

Wedge had joined Kirk and Hardner. He blushed at the biting remarks about him, slamming a newly lit cigarette into a coffee cup. "Why the hell is he carping about me like that?"

"Hell, you almost got off unscathed," Kirk said.

"I don't care," Wedge snapped. "Those were damn demeaning remarks."

"Perhaps," Hardner said, "but also quite true, in the opinion of this crowd."

Like a confident bullfighter completing an impressive series of passes, Garcia wound up his speech with a call for all-out support of his campaign, then waved and walked gracefully off the stage to a standing ovation.

In his raspy voice, Jordan Layman made a speech that was fairly well received by the delegates, mostly due to the fact that Holt Witherspoon had ignored them. Layman bore down on the importance of the local jobs that the Corpus Christi Naval Air Station provided, a facility he pledged "to keep open, come hell or high water."

He then reaffirmed his commitment to a few of the goals of PAMAT, though he spoke in general terms. Since he had worked out a quiet agreement with Frank Ganner for his support, he was in no position to attack the patrón-machine system of South Texas. But he was striving to be all things to all people and spoke with apparent dedication and understanding about the need of educating children, relying upon his experience as a teacher of Mexican-American youth in Justinville.

And he punished "the absentee candidate, Holt Witherspoon, who doesn't care a whit about the plight of the people. Right now, I bet he's at some fancy country club in Dallas, drinking fine whiskey and getting ready to eat a steak that's bigger around than this podium here."

In his closing remarks, Layman assured the delegates he would win if only they would support him as they were supporting Garcia. He departed to polite applause and conferred right away backstage with Portillo, who assured him PAMAT would endorse his candidacy.

Assuming Frank Ganner keeps quiet, as he knew he would, Layman mused, he would have the votes on election day from the haves and the have-nots in most of South Texas.

Wedge delivered his speech well, but he drew, as Kirk expected, only slight applause for his general statements of concern for Mexican-Americans. Even his strident attack upon Frank Ganner was greeted with modest applause. Their man Garcia had that issue, and they didn't want the press to get any mistaken notion that any support around the convention in that race was for other than Garcia.

When Wedge finished, he rejoined Nellie and they prepared to leave for lunch. "Well, there you have it," he said to Kirk. "Just as I anticipated.

A total waste of time."

When Kirk didn't respond, Nellie invited him to join them for lunch.

"No, thanks," he said. "I'm gonna stick around awhile. Meet you at the hotel before two."

"What could you possibly find of interest," Wedge said, "in staying here?"

"The only way I ever bagged any wild turkeys was to catch 'em roosting. Spook 'em up in the open instead, and they'd outsmart me every time."

Shaking his head, Wedge took Nellie's hand and they walked to her car.

Shortly after they departed, Kirk noticed Garcia leaving alone and followed him near the bay.

"I needed some fresh air," Garcia said to Kirk.

"So did I."

"I'm surprised you'd speak to me after what I said about your candidate."

"You didn't say it about me."

For the first time that day, Garcia smiled, unwinding from the intense anticipation of the convention, the total effort in delivering his speech, and the exhilaration of the unexpectedly powerful response from the delegates.

"You know," Kirk said, "you impress me as one who might be in this for the long haul, one who could make a real impact like Doctor Hector Garcia, from here in Corpus. Related to him?"

At Kirk's mention of the founder of the American G.I. Forum, Garcia paused long enough for a reflective expression to form. "Not related by blood, but by cause. He's one of my few heroes."

"To have that kind of impact, you're going to have to slow down a bit, aim a little more carefully."

"What do you mean?"

As they walked along a sidewalk, Kirk tossed a pebble at a seagull hovering near the beach. "Well, let me mention something an old state senator once impressed upon me. 'In a political campaign, never ever take on any more folks than you have to.'"

"Oh, you mean I shouldn't have threatened a splinter party movement? Shakes up the big boys in Austin? Well, they haven't paid us the time of day, and some fear in their hearts might help our situation. Besides, we need controversy to survive and grow. The press goes for it."

"I guess I can't argue with that," Kirk said, "but when you get down to the basics in this race, Frank Ganner, d/b/a Wally Hooper, has a lock on leading the field in the first primary. But since it appears Hooper won't crack fifty percent, the question is whether Wedge Crayton or Ernesto Garcia will make the runoff. You shouldn't be needling Wedge, because if you happen to make the runoff, his support will be pivotal to your chances of winning."

"I don't see it that way. I've got strong Mexican-American support throughout those five counties. I'll chip away enough support in the counties Ganner controls to outdistance your candidate. In the runoff, I'll count on anti-Ganner sentiment among Anglos to put together a winning coalition. That sentiment should be there, regardless of what your candidate might say. Had I seen it any other way, I wouldn't have run. I believe in our cause, but I'm not a kamikaze."

"It's a plausible plan since we've never seen this kind of race before, but I'm convinced Ganner's strength is such that it can't be eroded substantially in his counties. The only way to beat him in a runoff is to score sufficient majorities in the other counties."

"You're entitled to your opinion," Garcia said. "I just don't see it that way."

"You see a yacht, like that beautiful baby docked over there, and you see Wedge Crayton, don't you?"

"What the hell do you mean?"

"Well, I know Wedge is a charter member of the landed gentry of South Texas, one of your foremost adversaries behind Frank Ganner, but the fact of the matter is, he's your key to the kingdom. Believe me, in a runoff, you'll need him and all the other Anglo politicians you can muster in order to stand up to the kind of concerted pressure Ganner will bring to bear."

"You speak as though you're in awe of Ganner."

"Let me just say my grudging respect for the way Ganner operates has been reaffirmed recently."

Garcia paused, scanning the bay. "Why is your candidate's platform so devoid of meaningful issues?"

"It has to be that way. It's the only way to win."

"A political platform without conviction is worthless."

"Not if your number one objective is to stop Frank Ganner."

"What do you think of my platform?"

"I'm not in the business of trying to save the world."

"Those are the words of a junior grade Wade Keene, but I watched your eyes during Portillo's speech. You're sympathetic to our cause."

Kirk winced, fighting off the memory of Briana sobbing her farewell in his arms on the river road near Justinville. "You're reading too much into the script. My job is to elect Wedge Crayton. That's all I care about. Truth be known, Wedge is sympathetic to a few of your issues, but he's in no position to be crusading on those in this campaign. Might change a little if he makes the runoff and might surprise you in Austin if he's elected."

"I'm new at all this maneuvering, but I sense you're driving at something. What is it?"

"I'll lay my cards on the table. I want a simple deal between your campaign and ours. Whoever fails to make the runoff is pledged to give his all-out support, including public endorsement, to the one who does."

Garcia stopped near the Yacht Club, a private club and the city's long-standing and most prestigious gathering place. "I'd invite you in, but my membership has been pending for three decades."

Kirk chuckled. "Don't feel so bad. I couldn't afford to apply."

"I'll have to think it over," Garcia said, viewing a small boat easing out into the bay.

"What's to think over? No matter how dear your legislative program may be to you, it's highly ambitious. Won't pass for years, whether you win or not. But we could hit this one big lick this year, a lick that would have a lasting impact upon South Texas. Beating Frank Ganner out of extending his tentacles. Proving to people they can stand up to that rotten sonofabitch now and then. Showing the downtrodden, your people, that a handout from a tyrant isn't the only answer."

Garcia sighed, watching in silence for a long moment as sails were hoisted on the boat weaving in the sparkling water of the bay. After the boat sailed farther out, he turned to Kirk.

"All right," he said evenly, offering a firm handshake.

Chapter 10

In the constant, intense heat and dust of July, the final frantic days of the first Democratic Primary spun down in drouth-stricken South Texas.

Kirk couldn't argue with conclusions drawn by Wade Keene in his election eve article.

"It appears," Keene wrote, "that the bitter U.S. Senate race has tightened up recently with Jordan Layman, the aggressive 43-year-old Congressman from Central Texas, more likely to make a runoff with front-runner Holt Witherspoon. The former governor hasn't campaigned with a very heavy schedule until the past couple of weeks when he's been feeling the pressure.

"In the scorching race for the open state representative seat, Wally Hooper of Piedra Blanca, Frank Ganner's stand-in, apparently still holds a substantial lead, but a runoff is likely. It's a toss-up as to who will make it.

"Wedge Crayton of Justinville started out as an awkward young aristocrat but has developed into an acceptable campaigner. He's been selling his limited qualifications while knocking the Ganner-Hooper tandem along the way. He'll carry his home county of Retama, but his appeal elsewhere is questionable.

"Ernesto Garcia, the firebrand young Mexican-American candidate from Lantana, was the last candidate in the race, but he entered with a political organization, PAMAT, behind him. In addition to attacking Ganner constantly, he's put forth a progressive platform that his opponents keep at arm's length. Some leaders of PAMAT, including Garcia, threaten a separatist ethnic political party if the Democrats don't show them some respect at the polls tomorrow and beyond. Among Mexican-Americans, he appeals to a slowly awakening animosity toward political bossism in South Texas. That's significant, but Frank Ganner's machine will hold its own. Like Crayton, Garcia will carry his home county of Coronado, but elsewhere it will be tough."

Primary day dawned clear and was soon hot. Throughout most of the long, tedious afternoon, Kirk stayed on the phone, checking for indications of how heavy the voter turnout might be. The frantic push by

Jordan Layman had indeed stirred a fairly heavy vote throughout their seven-county district, with Frank Ganner's two counties reporting heaviest voting, as expected.

Late in the afternoon, with less than two hours remaining until the polls closed, Kirk suddenly realized there was nothing more for him to do but wait. In a vacuum, with his mind completely sealed off from distraction, he walked alone on the quiet main street of Justinville, then trudged two blocks to the park near the Retama County Courthouse.

For a few moments at sundown, he stood in the middle of the park, gazing at the stately courthouse. Long shadows from wilting trees almost covered its sparse lawn, ending another wretched day of heat and drouth.

Mesmerized, his ears perked up at the sounds of faint echoes of the campaign kickoff, of the country western band stirring the crowd before Wedge spoke; of Jordan Layman's dramatic helicopter landing and the heady presence of a Congressman running for the United States Senate upstaging a happy Wedge; of beautiful Nellie charming the men and drawing envious glances from the women; of dancing and merriment alongside uneven lines waiting for barbecue and beer; above all, of a community galvanizing behind a candidate.

But how much impact would Retama County provide tonight? It had to be the flagship among the "five free counties" in order to compete with the certain power of Frank Ganner's bloc-voting machine in Bantrell and Will Dodd counties.

For the first time since he'd taken command of the campaign, Kirk felt alone and lonely, longing for his father, with whom he could talk over strategic thrusts for winning the runoff, assuming they made it. He yearned to discuss plans sketched in his mind, but there was no one around whose political judgment he trusted. He looked up to the silent courthouse where his father had spent most of his waking hours during his long service as county judge.

"I think I know how you'd handle it, Dad," he murmured, before turning away for the return walk to the headquarters.

Right before the polls closed, Mrs. Fogel arrived with several members of her volunteer committee in charge of decorations and refreshments. Upon the long table covered with red, white, and blue crepe paper, the ladies provided a variety of sandwiches and cookies, plus coffee and iced tea.

The polls had only been closed a few minutes when Wedge's family and key supporters arrived, including the cast from the original campaign meeting at the Cadillac Bar - Brew Blain, Sidney Maylander, and Nelson Parker. Wedge and Nellie soon arrived, barely in time to welcome Gordon Hempstead, their prestigious campaign chairman who had raised about one-third of their budget for the first primary.

As usual, Nellie looked stunning on that night with a new green dress, snug but just on the side of good taste as opposed to flaunting her fine figure. Wedge wore a freshly pressed tan suit. He soon removed his coat and loosened his tie, but that didn't prevent his short-sleeved white shirt from getting soaked with perspiration as the cramped headquarters filled and tension built.

Kirk's mother and sister dropped by early to chat with him and to visit with the townspeople in attendance, but his mother couldn't long tolerate the heat and crowded quarters.

Two radios were set on a table near Kirk's desk, one turned to a San Antonio station that would follow the U.S. Senate race while giving periodic reports on their race, and the other tuned to the only station in the district. Ironically, it was located in Will Dodd County, of Frank Ganner's domain, but was independent of Ganner's control.

There is no greater cloud of uncertainty and raw tension, Kirk mused, than that in a political headquarters before those first returns finally break the ice.

People moved about acting nervous, and he listened to their aimless chatter, more of it town gossip than attempts to predict what the results might be. Traces of confidence and relief were etched upon the face of Wedge, who mingled amiably among his supporters.

I wonder what the hell, Kirk asked of himself, is going through his mind?

Kirk reflected upon their often testy relationship that had produced several conflicts only Nellie could settle. He concluded Wedge's mood at this point must be peculiar to a political candidate. Only he truly feels the emotional and physical demands he has endured, and why.

Kirk had large county-by-county sheets mounted on the walls, with Nellie and two volunteer ladies standing by to post and tabulate. The headquarters was completely packed with local supporters when the first precinct returns were reported from Retama County.

"Absentee and two other boxes from here," Kirk called to Nellie, "show Wedge with seventy percent."

Cheers and applause resounded through the building as the raw figures were posted for the absentee box and two precincts. Soon thereafter, spirits were tempered when Garcia's home county of Coronado reported almost complete with an eighty-percent majority for Garcia, which pushed him into the lead temporarily. But first reports from Ganner's counties soon placed Wally Hooper in a strong plurality lead, carrying the patrón's domain by almost ninety percent.

That didn't surprise Kirk, but it was a bad signal for Garcia, who had counted on chipping away substantial Mexican-American votes in those counties, despite Ganner's machine.

It wasn't long before the San Antonio station carried a decisive bulletin from Dallas:

"The Texas Election Bureau projects a runoff between former Governor Holt Witherspoon and Congressman Jordan Layman for the Democratic nomination for United States Senate. After about one million votes are finally counted, Witherspoon is expected to garner approximately forty-two percent while Layman will take about thirty-five percent. The balance will be divided between other candidates with Riley Fowler leading the group with fourteen percent."

Though Retama County would vote strongly for Layman, in the headquarters it was evident that sentiment was equally divided between Layman and Witherspoon. Since Hempstead had made it clear from the start that he strongly favored Witherspoon, Wedge and Nellie were careful not to display their preference for Layman.

With the temperature outside remaining above ninety at ten o'clock, Mrs. Fogel kept the window unit air conditioners running at full strength, but the cramped headquarters had become almost unbearably stuffy. Yet, most of Wedge's supporters remained, their spirits high with anticipation.

About eleven, Kirk summoned Wedge, Nellie, and Hempstead into his office.

"Home base is in strong. We're getting slight pluralities in the swing counties, not enough to overcome Hooper's staggering totals from the Ganner counties, but adequate to assure second place and force a runoff. There's not enough out to change this projection. It's going to be Hooper first with forty or forty-one percent, Wedge second right at about thirty-two percent, and Garcia out of the money with twenty-seven to twenty-eight percent, about three hundred votes behind Wedge."

Wedge smiled, but before he could respond, Hempstead led him before the tally sheets at the far end of the headquarters and called for the attention of the crowd.

With a loose salute and wide smile, Wedge stepped forward. "Thank you so much, Gordon, for your steadfast leadership and unstinting support. To my family, friends, and many supporters, who are fast becoming friends, this is the happiest, most fulfilling moment of my life. Thanks to Retama County and all of you, we're in the runoff!"

The crowd applauded and cheered.

"From the bottom of my heart, thanks for your volunteer work, your contributions, and most of all, for your faith. We finished second, and it's still uphill, but it's going to go our way because the people of our district want responsive, independent representation! They don't want to be dominated by a political boss! With your help, and with your continued support, we're going to whip the bloc-voting machine!"

Applause and cheers again reverberated through the little building.

"We're going to whip Wally Hooper!"

As the applause and cheering were rapidly rekindled, a photographer from The San Antonio Banner-Press worked his way toward him. Wedge raised his right arm, pointing his forefinger in the air, as the crouching photographer prepared to take his picture.

"And best of all!" Wedge shouted, "We're going to whip Frank Ganner!"

Applause, cheers, and sharp whoops resounded through the building.

Congratulations and backslapping were bestowed on Wedge, who smiled wearily and shook hands while supporters filed out into the still summer night. When the crowd dwindled to the core group from the Cadillac meeting, plus Hempstead, they cleared the table and sat down to relax and reflect. Brew served beer and drinks, the first time alcoholic beverages were evident in the headquarters that night.

"Anything unusual reported from the Ganner counties?" Hempstead said.

"All quiet on the eastern front," Kirk said. "I guess Ganner had both races figured to the point that there was no sense in his taking risks when they wouldn't affect the outcomes."

"What's it going to take to win the runoff?"

Kirk sighed. "I've been giving it some thought. We've got to spend at least four thousand to compete with Ganner."

"That's out of the question," Hempstead said. "With only thirty days to election, we'd be fortunate to raise half that much. Remember the drouth and the way Ganner can intimidate some of our best prospects."

"Yes, I know, but we've got to be able to promote Wedge right away among Garcia's supporters, and we've got to hit Ganner and Hooper with everything we can those last two weeks when voters will tune in again."

"We have the pressing problem," Nellie said, "of having to put almost all that advertising money down at the time we order. Very few extend credit to political campaigns."

Hempstead looked at Brew Blain, the finance director, and Wedge's two wealthy friends, Sidney Maylander and Nelson Parker. "Between the four of us, gentlemen, let's pledge to raise—kick in to make it if necessary—two thousand no later than ten days from now. That money will be guaranteed for advertising or whatever early commitments are necessary. As the runoff campaign heats up, we'll be able to raise some more."

"That's a good start," Kirk said, "but late money won't spend nearly as effectively. I'll go to Austin and see if I can scrape up some more there."

"In a weak moment tonight," Wedge said with a smile, "my father pledged another three hundred."

"Despite the admonition from my Uncle Adrian, who oversees my financial affairs," Nellie said, "I'll put up another three hundred to match that. I'm convinced we must be able to make our moves in this runoff period without always being worried if there's money in the bank."

Kirk wondered whether Wedge and Nellie had rehearsed that little act, but it didn't matter since it made Hempstead and the others more confident that the runoff funding could be raised.

Hempstead summoned his group to his office down the street to review contributor lists, leaving Kirk, Nellie, and Wedge at the table.

Kirk placed his new runoff projections next to Wedge. "Well, Professor, it doesn't take a genius to figure out a major part of our strategy. Hooper's lead is fairly substantial. We've got to somehow motivate most of that Garcia vote to vote for you in the runoff."

Wedge had relaxed. He took another soothing sip of Scotch and soda, glancing over the figures. "Raise money, Garcia vote, sure, but I haven't taken time to tell you, Old Podnah, you did a helluva job. We're in the running… and by God, we're gonna win."

"And what of the Senate race?" Nellie said.

"Looks like a two-edged sword," Kirk said. "On the one hand, a hot runoff there helps by inspiring turnout we couldn't stimulate, just as happened today. But on the other hand, Layman ran even stronger than I anticipated in South Texas. If Ganner should sell Layman and Hooper in tandem, even if just behind the scenes, I'm afraid we might not be able to overcome that."

"First things first," Wedge said. "I'm calling Garcia now to ask for his support."

"I wouldn't do that," Kirk said. "I imagine he's pretty damned upset with what happened and needs a day or two to lick his wounds."

"I don't buy that," Wedge snapped, growing edgy. "It's election night, and proper protocol for me to congratulate him on the race he ran. And under the circumstances, I see nothing wrong with asking for his support."

Kirk shrugged. "It isn't necessary. He's already committed to support you, including a public endorsement."

"What?" Wedge's eyebrows shot up. "How can that be?"

"I made a deal with him before the election."

"Deal?" Nellie said. "What kind of deal?"

"Just that whoever didn't make the runoff would support the one who did."

Her face flushed, Nellie almost choked on cigarette smoke as Wedge slammed a fist on the table. "Goddammit, Kirk, you had no right to commit to such a deal! Where would I be with my family if I had to endorse Garcia and that visionary platform of his?"

"Visionary?" Kirk smiled. "Seems to me that when we first started this campaign, you wanted to advocate the very same proposals as Garcia came out with. Can it be that you've bowed to ambition and pragmatism?"

"Let's not be cute!" Nellie snapped. "Wedge is right. How could you possibly justify making such a deal?"

Kirk shrugged, taking a short swig of beer. "All right, you want the unvarnished truth, here it is. Garcia and his people don't respect Wedge, nor do they trust him. They trust me. I figured we would have more bargaining power before the election than after. It well might have been thumbs down, had I waited. This way we've already got a strategic building block set into place for the runoff."

"Regardless of all that," Nellie said, "you had no right to commit him to such a deal without consulting us, or at least informing us as soon as you did it."

"Ah, 'us' it is, not just the candidate as Miss Nellie assumes equal billing with the candidate, or will it be even greater billing, as she seeks to satisfy the deepest desires hidden in that overly possessive heart."

Nellie bristled. "Don't bait me, Kirk! I could lose my temper very easily.

The least you can do is recognize you were wrong and apologize. Otherwise, you might just get the hell out of this campaign."

Kirk stood up, setting his bottle of beer on the table. "All right, Countess, I'll leave, but I'll not confess my guilt. As I retire to the north, I'll miss the heat and dust, but not you two."

He moved toward the door, but Wedge grabbed him by the arm. "Come on, Old Podnah, how about another look at this? Let's let things simmer down. We're just all worn out. Nobody works tomorrow; we meet for a late breakfast Monday. Nine o'clock at The Green Wagon. Okay?"

"And what about her?" Kirk glanced over at Nellie, who sat in angry silence at the table, taking another puff from a cigarette while glaring at the ashtray.

Wedge leaned over to put an arm on her shoulder. "A good day's rest and we'll all be back at it, right?"

Without facing him, she whispered, "It's your campaign."

"Okay," Kirk said, standing by the door, "but one other thing. We need an issue from Garcia's visionary platform, as you termed it. One that will help sell not only Garcia's people, but Lonnie Hardner and The Texas Progressive crowd. I suggest repeal of the poll tax. It's a big issue, but doesn't hit the landed gentry with the direct wallop of something like a state minimum wage."

"Fine with me," Wedge said.

After Kirk departed, Wedge poured another round of drinks. "You know, it's funny as hell you finally sided with me in an argument against him… But when I thought it through, I could see he was right about Garcia."

She smashed her cigarette in the ashtray. "I'm delighted you thought it was so damned amusing."

Kirk retired to Barney's where he unwound with back slapping, beer drinking, and several games of shuffleboard, including another stem-winder with Barney.

Barney won but insisted upon buying all the beer Kirk could drink for "having shown that bastard Frank Ganner a thing or two."

On the following morning, Kirk slept late at his apartment before retrieving the Sunday San Antonio Banner-Press. Over coffee and toast, he scanned the front page, which carried file pictures of Holt Witherspoon and Jordan Layman under a banner headline with the U.S. Senate story.

Below the fold, he was amused to see a story on their race with a picture of a pudgy, patronizing Wally Hooper next to "Wedge Crayton, the young reform candidate" as the cutline stated beneath the picture taken at the headquarters. Wedge had his forefinger pointed forward in a gesture of total commitment to the future.

"Give him a helicopter," Kirk murmured, "and he'd outshine Jordan Layman."

For lunch he joined his mother and sister at their home for another standard Sunday Holland family meal featuring grilled steak, baked potatoes, tossed salad, and homemade ice cream.

Kirk spent Sunday afternoon alone in the headquarters, stitching together a strategic plan for the runoff while calling around the district for more precise voting results and gathering general reaction from key supporters. He also called Ernesto Garcia, who was bitter over not making the runoff, blaming "the awesome power of Frank Ganner," but who was somewhat optimistic about Wedge's chances of pulling an upset.

For breakfast with Nellie and Wedge the following morning, Kirk met them at a quiet table in the back of The Green Wagon Restaurant on Highway 81, a block from the headquarters. Following his first swig of coffee, he laid out his plan in a confident, precise manner.

"First and foremost, here in our home base of Retama County, we must maximize our vote to an even greater extent than we did Saturday. The Senate runoff will help stimulate voter turnout here and throughout the district. All our people agree on that, and we'll need to be aware of major developments in that race anywhere in South Texas.

"Next, we're going to treat Coronado County as virtually an entity unto itself. Whichever runoff candidate carries Coronado County will probably win the election, except that we can't afford to win with a low, apathetic turnout there. That makes Ernesto Garcia the centerpiece. He must help us turn out the Mexican-American vote, and it must go sixty percent for Wedge."

Kirk said he had already nailed down a date for a major rally in Lantana, the county seat, at which Garcia would publicly endorse Wedge. It would be on the last Saturday night of the campaign, a week prior to the runoff.

"Is the time ripe for me to call Garcia?" Wedge asked.

"Yeah, and you can tell him you're going to endorse repeal of the poll tax. That'll lighten his burden. Now, as to the four other 'free counties' that are up for grabs. We did well in them during the first round, so you can bet Ganner and Hooper will spend bundles there in the runoff. Mostly, we campaign as before, heavy on personal appearances, handshaking, mixing and mingling. For advertising, we'll use the bolster point that Wedge was 'first choice of our county in the first primary.' 'First-first' has a ring to it. That language will be added to Wedge's billboards and newspaper ads in those counties. What has to be done in all four of those counties is to change Saturday's pluralities into runoff majorities … For the Ganner counties, the plan is simple, 'Stay out, grit your teeth, and hope they don't steal us blind.'

"With the election on a Saturday, I've planned heavy newspaper advertising in all but the Ganner counties in the final two weekly editions, most of which are published on Friday. I've scheduled six days of heavy radio advertising leading into the election, and a district-wide mailing to all known supporters to arrive three days prior to voting. In addition, we'll send a few smaller mailings to key groups off special lists."

Kirk laid out a chart with vote quotas and projections, county-by-county, showing if Wedge ran to his maximum potential, he would achieve fifty-one percent.

"Scary, but realistic," Wedge said over his second cup of coffee.

"It's an interesting plan, for sure," Nellie said. "I hope we can pay for it."

Other than her bland greeting when they first met that morning, it was the initial comment by Nellie during the conversation. Kirk detected a trace of scorn and skepticism in her voice, but nothing like the bite of Saturday night.

He trained his eyes upon her. "Keep pushing Gordon Hempstead and old Brew. Hound 'em every day. I'm leaving for Austin today to get whatever I can there. Really only have one good source, but he can spring pretty heavy if he wants to."

"And there's the matter of The Texas Progressive endorsement," Nellie said, lighting a cigarette while avoiding Kirk's eyes.

"Yeah, I want to start early on Lonnie Hardner in case he has a long gestation period over that decision."

"Anything else in Austin?" Wedge asked.

"Just a couple of routine calls. I'll be back tomorrow night. And, uh, Nellie, would you mind fine-tuning the scheduling plans for Wedge in those four free counties? You have a better feel for that than I do, having been out there on the trail so much."

"All right," she said in a casual tone as Kirk stood up to leave. "I'll see what I can do."

Ever since his first trip from South Texas to Austin as a boy, Kirk had always felt an invigorating sense of pride upon cresting that high hill from where the Capitol and University tower first came into view. Those were the classic symbols with which he identified so deeply as a Texan.

But on that steamy July afternoon, he experienced a hollow feeling instead. He couldn't quite come to admit that his down mood was caused by confronting Austin for the first time since he and Carrie had broken up. He merely tossed it aside as a product of having been away a few months.

He drove first to the Driskill Hotel, where he stopped in the coffee shop for a late lunch and to read The Austin Capital Times, his employer before the campaign. The coffee shop was buzzing with speculation about the Witherspoon-Layman runoff, and the newspaper's front page was covered with pictures and feature stories in the swirling aftermath of Saturday's election.

Kirk chuckled upon reading propaganda quotes from both candidates.

"I never took the young rascal seriously," Witherspoon was quoted as saying, "while he was clowning around in that helicopter. I won't make that mistake again."

Layman proclaimed that "Old Holt never thought I'd force a runoff. There's no question who's got the ball rolling! There's no question who's going to win!"

Kirk had placed calls from Justinville to Lonnie Hardner and Jarvis Harrison, speaker of the Texas House of Representatives. He proceeded to The Texas Progressive, where he met Hardner in the editor's cluttered office.

"I believe I can alleviate your concern," Hardner said. "After you called, I spoke with Ernesto Garcia and was impressed to learn he's going to endorse your candidate."

"Did he mention repeal of the poll tax?"

"Yes." Hardner smiled, training his eyes upon Kirk. "But tell me, was that your idea, or a genuine outpouring from the candidate?"

"Lonnie, I told you early on that Wedge is more on the progressive side than the campaign would reflect. That was just the one big issue we could settle on for the runoff."

"Well, it's an incentive for me. Nobody wants to fight the patrón system of South Texas more than I, but I want to feel we can elect a reform candidate with conviction and accomplish something beyond strapping a little setback on Frank Ganner."

"Your endorsement will have an impact on the reporters covering the race. Could you make it as soon as possible?"

"I'm not a campaign cohort," Hardner said in a stern tone, "but I will do it this week. I understand the crucial nature of timing, and I believe it's important for our endorsement to come early and for Garcia's campaigning to come late."

Relieved, Kirk was ready to wind down the conversation and leave, until he sensed Hardner had more on his mind.

"Holland, we've never been close friends, but I trust you, and I'd like to discuss another race, in complete confidence."

Kirk shifted in his chair. "I'm sure you mean the U.S. Senate race. Whatever's said stays in the room."

Hardner stood up, turned to the window behind him, and gazed outside at passing traffic while he spoke in reflective tones. "I've been around the Texas political arena for quite some time, covered a lot of campaigns and legislative sessions. Never faced a dilemma such as this."

"I don't understand. Jordan Layman is a Franklin Roosevelt-Harry Truman protégé. New Deal, Fair Deal, down the line. Surely, he's your candidate for the runoff?"

"I wish it were that simple. I'd bet almost all our subscribers voted for Layman. They believe he'll support most of the federal programs about which they feel strongly. And to them, Witherspoon is nothing but an old reactionary. Not a viable alternative."

Kirk paused. "Come to think of it, I don't recall you endorsed Layman in the first round."

Hardner turned to face Kirk. "That's right, but the pressure will mount quickly for my endorsement in the runoff. You can already feel the tension building in this town for that showdown."

"I recall Layman has undercut your faction from time to time at conventions, but he's still on the progressive side overall. What's your real concern?"

"I'm often accused of being an academic type, the eggheaded liberal who bogs down in too much research and analysis before hitting the typewriter. With Layman, it's what you campaign operatives would term a 'gut feeling.' No truly tangible evidence, but a deep concern about his own direction and the direction he might take this country. That's a big question."

"He's ambitious as hell, but what young politician isn't? He just goes after it with a little more zest."

"More like a frenzied tiger shark. But that's not what troubles me. It's the unhealthy feeling that he and many of his closest supporters look at the federal government first as a big rock candy mountain, the source of political power through control of various programs for the people, and the source of wealth, in addition to power, for themselves."

"I'll confess I don't know that much about Layman's personal dealings. Are you implying he'll use his power in office, beyond usual patronage, to line his pockets and those of his top supporters?"

"Not implying he'll do that. He already has, but only as a Congressman. Put him in the Senate and he'll be at it in a more heavy-handed manner, on a much larger scale. Further, that man's ambition will carry him toward a bid for the presidency, where his appetite for power and wealth would really be whetted."

"You're leaping to conclusions, moral judgments. Might be hard to explain to your readers as justification for not supporting a fairly progressive candidate against a staunch conservative."

"Yes, I know, but of even greater concern to me was covering the race these past few weeks. When that third-place candidate started the harsh right wing rhetoric, Witherspoon and Layman had to respond, which I understood. But I've never sensed anything more clearly in my life. Witherspoon went along as simply meeting a new dynamic of the campaign; Layman relished the changed climate. His strongest rhetoric, his most convincing voice inflection, came with his sharp thrusts against Communists wherever they might be found.

"I tell you, the man is obsessed with the desire for power. He wants to follow Roosevelt's domestic philosophy, which is what my readers view so favorably about him, but what scares me is I'm convinced he wants even more to preside as Roosevelt and Truman did in World War II. He'd love to be a wartime President, making glorious pronouncements with every American hanging on each word."

"Lonnie, you're reaching too far."

"Am I? Remember, we're talking about a man who sat in on one mission—sat in, didn't fly, bomb, navigate, or man a turret—in a combat zone during World War II and somehow came up with a Silver Star. That's one of our nation's highest honors, and nobody else on the mission was decorated at all. I'm telling you, something is there besides political ambition and zealous patriotism."

"You've got my confidence in this discussion, but that's a far-fetched theory. I wouldn't try to fly it in print."

Hardner sighed. "Oh, I know, but I haven't slept well in a couple of weeks, and I wanted to lay this out to someone who could understand it."

"I thought I'd been wrestling with some tough problems. I can see how dicey this becomes for you."

With a sardonic smile, Hardner chuckled and tapped his pencil on the desk. "And to top it all, Jordan Layman is in bed with Frank Ganner, which has an impact on your race."

"Enough to make a man want a cold beer. How about it?"

"Just one." Hardner stood up and grinned. "Or, maybe two."

After three beers under the shade trees at Scholz Garten, Kirk was barely on time for his late afternoon appointment with Jarvis Harrison at the Speaker's favorite hangout, the elegant Austin Club in the Commodore Perry Hotel. Before reporting to the bar, Kirk ducked into the bathroom to comb his hair and straighten his tie, which clung to his limp, sweat-soaked white shirt.

Harrison was waiting alone at his customary spot, "The Speaker's Table," at the far end of the bar, a position he jokingly compared to that of a gunfighter in the old west, "where nobody comes in unnoticed behind my back." The paunchy Speaker was usually in a jovial mood, but as Kirk shook hands and sat down, he detected a mood of deep concern.

Glancing about him, the Speaker pulled an envelope from his inside coat pocket and handed it to Kirk. "There's a mild endorsement letter in there for your candidate from Holt. He agreed to do it since he's written off that area. In fact, he wondered why you wanted it, because it could be a negative factor."

"Well, we're only planning to mail it to known Witherspoon supporters, late in the campaign when our opposition won't have time to respond. But then there might be some other use along the way."

Harrison shrugged. "There's also four hundred in cash, which Holt doesn't know about. Keep my tracks out... I'm sorry, but that's all I can get you now. We've woken up Holt to the fact he's in a helluva tough race, and suddenly, he's pinned down damn near every dollar we've raised since Saturday's results came in."

"Thanks, Mister Speaker, I appreciate your assistance very much. But we're running short of money and we're in the throes of that damned drouth. Can you help more in the next couple of weeks?"

"I'll try, but don't count on it. I'm telling you, Holt is finally on the warpath and, of course, he's got priority."

"Sure, I understand, but as you believed he would, Frank Ganner has come into play in South Texas strongly for Jordan Layman. In our seven-county district, we're going to try like hell for honest counts. The more pressure we bring to bear, the better for your candidate."

"I know, I know, and I appreciate what you're up against. But it's an indirect kind of politics, and Holt just figures he's going to get clobbered in South Texas, no matter what."

"If I were Witherspoon, I'd want to slow that Ganner-Layman juggernaut any way I could. Have you looked closely at those South Texas returns?"

"I sure as hell have, and I'm afraid they'll be even higher against us for the runoff. But once Holt found out Ganner was going against him, he just wrote off South Texas in his mind."

Kirk toyed with his glass of beer. "Deep down, how do you see the race? I won't quote you to anybody."

Harrison paused, rubbing his chin. "If we could vote tomorrow, I'd feel all right about it. But I've gotta admit that goddamn Layman had some momentum going that he'll rekindle with helicopter flights, country western bands, free beer and barbecue, and you name it. The scary thing is, Holt isn't up to that kind of campaigning. Oh, he's in good physical condition, but he still believes people will vote for him if he goes around puffing on that pipe, shaking hands and visiting, and then run a few newspaper ads. Hell, we're just now convincing him to plan a well-rounded campaign. Another dangerous thing about Layman is he has people with deep pockets. They'll spend whatever they think it takes to win."

"You just used the term 'dangerous.' How do you mean that?"

Harrison took a long drink of bourbon and water. "I didn't mean to use that term. Just a figure of speech about one of his big assets in the campaign."

"Mister Speaker, I've listened to you conduct the House's business many times and we've talked a few times, just the two of us. There's more on your mind."

"Holland, you're not a reporter now. Quit digging."

"It's just that I'm curious as to how you truly feel about Layman beyond his role as challenger to your old friend Witherspoon. I promise I won't quote you to anyone. You know you can trust me."

"Hell, I'm not even sure what I think of him personally… Maybe I'm a jealous old politician because I'm on the downside of a career and he's going up fast if he wins the runoff. Faster than anyone I've ever seen."

"How can you be sure he'll move up fast in the Senate? That's supposed to be a tightly knit club, with leadership determined largely by seniority."

"I'm just telling you that no one plays the game like he does. People see him as a tireless campaigner and think how wonderful it is that he's trying so hard for a promotion. What they don't know is how he operates behind the scenes. There's something peculiar about him, something different from all the politicians I've known the past thirty years. From his staff secretaries to reporters to colleagues in Congress to presidents of big corporations, he always knows what makes each of 'em tick. He gets what he wants."

"Well, you're one to know how best the game is played."

"Sure, and being mighty ambitious is okay, I guess. But I just wonder, in the back of my mind, what the hell will satisfy that man's ambitions? I've always thought it was foolhardy for a Texan to aspire to the Presidency, but I bet he fuels on that every single day of the world."

"We don't have any problem charting his ambitions in the next three weeks or so."

"No, but I'll tell you something else people don't see. The amount of money flowing into his campaign is obscene, and it's not going to be reported."

"I've always believed," Kirk said with a smile, "our campaign finance laws were written by clever, successful politicians to protect clever, successful politicians. Not to hold them accountable."

Harrison chuckled, finishing his drink. "Guess you have a point there. Well, I've got to go."

"If you can sidetrack a few more dollars, don't forget us."

"I won't." Harrison stood up to leave. "I want to cut our losses in South Texas."

Satisfied his meetings had gone well, Kirk decided to treat himself to a steak dinner at Hoffbrau's, a longtime favorite on West Sixth Street. The small place was full of customers, so he sat at a wooden table outside where overflow was served in warm weather.

Several friends and political acquaintances greeted him, two of whom joined him for the casual meal of steak grilled in lemon butter, tossed salad, and large, thick French fried potatoes, washed down by a couple of cold beers.

Great food, he thought, but miserable weather.

From there, he went alone to enjoy a Humphrey Bogart movie in a theater on "The Drag" near the University campus. In airconditioned comfort, he let himself slide into a smooth relaxed mood in which the variables and demands of the campaign were set aside.

Rather than take a motel room, he opted to pay a visit to the nearby Oak Room where he would ask the manager, B.B. Hencik, for the use of his apartment couch for the night. After he drove into the parking lot, three young women were leaving, waving to friends as they stepped outside.

In the soft light, he didn't recognize them, but as he neared the door, he was stunned to encounter Carrie. When her friends saw the sudden, intense reaction between them, they walked without speaking to their car, leaving her standing at the door with Kirk a couple of steps away.

"I… I did," she stammered, "…I didn't know you were in town."

"Just for a couple of days. And you?"

"The same. Checking on some items for rush, that's all."

"May you rush well," Kirk smiled evenly though his body trembled a bit.

"How's the campaign?"

"Shaping up."

"I…" she said as she shrugged. "I guess I'd better be getting along. It was nice seeing you."

"Yes, nice seeing you, too."

Kirk wanted to turn and watch her walk away as he had so many times, but he bit his lip, resisting that temptation. It would only remind him of how pert and lovely she was; of how much he had longed to hold her and to make love to her once more. Reaching for the door knob, his hand shook. He walked inside, greeted Hencik, and sat down at the bar.

"You look like you've seen a ghost," Hencik said.

"I have," Kirk said.

After Hencik served him a beer and gave him a spare key to his apartment, Kirk relaxed somewhat, but he couldn't drive Carrie from his mind. At last, he asked Hencik if he knew who she'd been dating.

"A high-powered fraternity guy named Collin Asherton. Nice new car, deep pockets, top drawer all the way."

"Well, maybe that's better for her."

"Not only her, my friend, but you. I never thought you and she were the best match in the world."

"Maybe not, but we were awfully close for a while."

"If you want my advice, you shouldn't get serious about any woman for a few years. You live too much for the hour."

A sardonic smile crossed Kirk's lips as he thought of Briana and their brief time in Justinville. So recent, but so remote.

"I didn't ask for your advice. I asked for another beer."

Hencik changed the subject to baseball, and they were soon engaged in a running conversation about which teams were likely to win the major league pennants. While working rapidly through two schooners of beer, Kirk was not sullen, but Hencik sensed his mood was on the verge of becoming gloomy and he regretted being too busy tending bar to maintain a steady conversation.

Hencik was delighted when two of their friends, Charley Burner and Joe Goff, came on the scene with their usual bit of fanfare. They were roommates, South Texans attending the UT law school, undergraduate classmates of Kirk and Hencik. They were the types who studied hard, but also partied hard, drinking for hours in a jovial mood.

They waved at Kirk to join them at a nearby table.

"Any man who takes on Frank Ganner," Burner said, raising his right hand in a salute, "is a genuine hero. Barkeep, a pitcher of your best beer for this great warrior from the south."

As he joined them, Kirk couldn't help paying special notice to how they were dressed. Goff was sporting an all-white outfit of slacks, shoes, and tee shirt which was trimmed in orange, including, on the front, a small orange longhorn steer, the UT mascot. Burner wore western attire, cotton shirt with blue denims, and fancy stitched boots.

"Burner," Kirk said with a chuckle, "you can't really be a serious student of the law of the great State of Texas, wearing those obnoxious green boots."

"What's wrong with green boots?" Burner grinned. "I may be German, but my heart's Irish."

"Don't say 'Irish' around me," Goff said. "We're playing Notre Dame this fall and I'm already getting fired up."

"You've got to be kidding." Kirk smiled. "It's too damned hot to even think about football."

"That's all he ever thinks about," Burner said. "In the dead of winter, during gentle springtime, or in the throes of a long drouth. You see, the problem with Goff is that he's an insufferable, chronic cheerleader. For two years, he was a real Longhorn cheerleader, but now, three years after the fact, he doesn't understand he's supposed to be an ordinary fan like the rest of us."

"That's grossly unfair." Goff stood up to make a grandiloquent gesture with both arms pleading to Kirk. "My friend, come to my aid with all dispatch. I'm being denigrated and persecuted because of my courageous convictions. You see, as an article of faith, I happen to believe that when the Longhorn Band strikes the drumroll prelude to 'The Eyes Of Texas,' Gabriel and the other archangels pause to listen, with a faint hint of jealousy in their otherwise pure and pious hearts."

"Blasphemy." Kirk chuckled. "But your orange blood overfloweth." He took a long swig of beer, enjoying the carefree banter.

Within an hour, talk of the forthcoming football season and campus gossip became tedious. He no longer related to that. His head and heart were in the South Texas political campaign about which they listened only a few minutes before he sensed their attention spans had been exceeded.

Excusing himself, Kirk drove to Hencik's apartment. He pulled a cotton quilt from the top shelf of a closet and curled up on the couch, window air conditioner whirring above his head.

After breakfast the following morning, he drove to the Capitol for his final appointment, a meeting with the secretary of state, the chief elections officer for Texas. Walking across the rotunda, Kirk's mind spun through the salient political facts about Warren Clarkson, a close friend of the incumbent governor who had appointed him.

Clarkson's own gubernatorial ambitions meant he kept a steady schedule of public speaking engagements before civic clubs, giving the same bland speech about citizen duty to exercise the right to vote with "an awareness of the issues," which he never defined. He was a cautious man who didn't want to make waves, but who also understood well the political value of news coverage of his speeches, plus having his picture and name on election law brochures and other material distributed around the state.

Kirk surmised Clarkson—prematurely gray at forty-seven, wealthy, and self-assured—was poised to make his run for governor, just as soon as the incumbent announced his retirement. That was foremost in Kirk's thoughts as he settled into a thick leather chair and looked over the spacious, well-adorned office, waiting while Clarkson read a telegram an assistant placed before him.

Kirk scanned a wall displaying signed photographs of several Texas politicians, including most prominently, the present governor. Photos of previous governors and secretaries of state, almost all of whom had used the appointed office as a springboard to seek elected office flanked that one.

Each, Kirk mused, had his Achilles heel.

Placing the telegram aside, Clarkson turned to meet Kirk's eyes. "It's good to see you. I'd heard you left the newspaper for a South Texas legislative race. What can I do for you?"

"In case you're unfamiliar with the district, it includes Frank Ganner's bailiwick."

"Ah yes, I remember. Into a runoff with Ganner's candidate favored to win."

"Favored, but our candidate, Wedge Crayton, has more than an outside chance, and I want to do all I can to see that it's a fair election."

"But why come here? As you know, I have very little legal authority regarding the conduct of elections."

"You carry the title of the state's chief elections officer. To a lot of people, that sounds authoritative."

"Now, Holland, you're stretching the point. You know I have no jurisdiction. To imply otherwise would be unethical."

"Unethical? When dealing with Frank Ganner, I somehow don't think first of ethics."

"It's simply not in my power."

"Isn't it important to you and to the state of Texas that our elections be clean and fair?"

"Of course, but my office can't interfere down there to assure the sanctity of the ballot. The party runs the elections."

"Yes, the party. Who do you think runs the party in Bantrell and Will Dodd counties?"

"Regardless of what you may think of Frank Ganner, essentially local parties run local and district elections. No more, no less."

"You would concede Holt Witherspoon and Jordan Layman are engaged in a bitter battle that could lead to all sorts of fireworks?"

"I'll concede it's a spirited contest. I have no indication any voting irregularities are in the offing. To my knowledge, there were none in the first primary."

"Sure, but the blue chips weren't on the table."

"I'm not going to anticipate trouble without indication."

"What's wrong with dropping a news release in the Capitol Press Room right before the runoff? You could call upon everyone involved in conducting the election all over the state to take special care in the contest for U.S. Senate nomination. That's a statewide election and, most importantly, a federal office is involved. Violations might be dealt with harshly by the federal government."

"I'm a state's rights conservative," Clarkson snapped. "The federal government has absolutely no business interfering in a Texas election."

"Not even if Frank Ganner is importing wetbacks to vote using poll taxes he bought himself?"

"That's far-fetched."

"Is it? I wouldn't put anything past him."

"I'm sorry," Clarkson said. "There's nothing I can do." He reached for a stack of papers, anticipating Kirk's departure, but Kirk remained in his seat, studying him quietly.

At last, with Kirk's eyes still trained upon him, Clarkson looked at Kirk, a quizzical expression forming as he set aside the papers.

"How badly, Mister Secretary, do you want to become the next governor of Texas?"

"It's no secret I'm available to run when the governor steps down."

"You're more than available, you're eager. You've been maneuvering for that chance for years. If your heart's not in it, you don't have a heart."

Clarkson glared at him. "Holland, I always thought you were a good political writer. You ought to stick to that and not go prying into personal lives."

"Maybe, but I sense your public-spirited attitude, expressed so eloquently on the mashed potato circuit, doesn't apply regarding Frank Ganner. When you run for governor, you'll want his support. So, you won't ruffle his feathers now."

Clarkson blanched. "I deeply resent those remarks! Frank Ganner has no call on me, but I have no call to stretch my authority beyond what's set forth by law."

"Nonetheless, we are where we are, and I need your help… This isn't the most pleasant thing in the world for me to say, but I believe you owe me a favor, and I'm asking for it because—"

"Look, I don't know what you're talking about as far as favors are concerned. I don't owe you a thing, and my skirts are clean."

"Your skirts were clean, but that son of yours changed things, ever since he grew strong enough to lift a whiskey bottle."

Clarkson winced, squeezing the pen in his hand. "What are you talking about?"

"Just that I know you and your friend, the DA for that little county where it occurred, managed to work a fast cover-up. The girl changed her story, said she wasn't raped after all, and the charges were dropped.

Well, the record shows the charges weren't even filed, were they?

"But I happen to have an affidavit signed by the arresting officer who agrees with the original version. Could have been a nasty little case, but was set aside nicely, and my cautious editor let it slide since, as far as he knew, no charges were filed. But I've kept the particulars in my own little file... If that were an isolated case, you might ride it out in a political campaign, begging forgiveness for your son's one transgression, for which he's repented.

"However, not long thereafter, he got drunk again and rammed that poor kid on a bike. Lucky the kid didn't die, but it still must have cost a pretty penny to get your boy off without even a day in jail. Those items might make for some headlines in a campaign. Might even bear repeating—"

Rising from his chair, Clarkson slammed a trembling hand on his desk. "You... you're talking blackmail!"

"Nothing of the kind. I don't want your money, just a little bargain. You issue the news release and I'll burn the file. Otherwise..."

Clarkson sat down, slowly rubbing his forehead, avoiding Kirk's eyes. "You'll get your damned press release," he murmured. "Now, get out of here."

Back in Justinville at the headquarters, Nellie and Wedge updated Kirk about minor developments in the campaign during his brief absence. Wade Keene called to inform him a new poll would be released in two days showing Holt Witherspoon with only a three-point lead over Jordan Layman statewide and Layman pulling farther ahead in South Texas.

Early fundraising for the runoff was slow, due in part to the pervasive drouth and due as well to the fact some wealthy potential contributors still believed Wedge's opponent, Wally Hooper, would win. All the money Kirk brought from Austin was applied to needs for the top priority event, the endorsement rally with Ernesto Garcia in Lantana. Enough was committed "in the pipeline" to cover almost half of the other critical items, including the advertising portion of the budget.

Despite the scorching heat, Wedge campaigned ten to twelve hours a day, shaking hands on the streets and in the businesses of the many small towns in the district. Stopping by beer joints was still awkward for him, but he understood the value of that type of campaigning and had learned to hoist longnecks for long swigs in the popular manner of South Texas.

While Wedge had improved his techniques and endurance during the long summer, his opponent was slowing down. Huffing and puffing in the heat, the rotund Hooper found himself worn out by midafternoon and often napped two or three hours before meeting a night schedule. Frank Ganner's sharp complaints kept Hooper on the alert with his sponsor who sensed Wedge had developed into a fairly effective campaigner. Yet some undecided voters still perceived him as nothing more than an ambitious, inexperienced young candidate.

The days of the runoff campaign moved by at a fast pace. Hooper remained the favorite, but he was not only uncomfortable in the heat, but also was squirming from Wedge's various charges. Hooper refused every one of Wedge's challenge to debate.

With a snort, Wedge said, "Wally Hooper is hiding behind Frank Ganner. Only trouble is, Ganner casts such a long shadow that you can't find Wally."

With seven days to go to the runoff, Wedge's campaign tried to maintain suspense about the purpose of the rally with Ernesto Garcia that night in Lantana, Garcia's hometown and the county seat of Coronado County with its predominantly Mexican-American population.

Ganner had guessed early on and his operatives confirmed it was for an all-out endorsement of Wedge that would spur interest in the Saturday night event and beyond among Garcia's supporters. It had also keyed considerable concern among Ganner forces around the district. They hadn't seriously entertained the notion of Wedge pulling an upset until faced with Garcia's likely endorsement and late campaigning for Wedge.

That would almost surely move Coronado County from leaning to Hooper into Wedge's column. It might engender Mexican-American support for Wedge elsewhere, though not in Ganner's bailiwick of Bantrell and Will Dodd counties, which proved to be secure against Garcia in the first primary.

The potentially pivotal nature of the event had prompted Wade Keene and several other members of the big city news media to make the long hot journey to the dustswept little community. Lonnie Hardner couldn't attend, but throughout the runoff period The Texas Progressive ran biting denunciations of patrón politics and warm words of praise about Wedge.

Those pieces had set the tone Kirk wanted for many of the media people who were avid readers of The Progressive.

Much as she wanted to go, Nellie decided she better stay in the headquarters since so many people were calling in for materials and instructions, even on the weekend. Kirk and Wedge arrived in Lantana an hour before the event was scheduled to start. They drove to a modest restaurant on the town square owned by Garcia's uncle, Anselmo. The local politicos hung out there.

From curiosity, Wedge glanced at the menu, reading aloud some items with which he was unfamiliar, "barbacoa, caldo, chorizo, 'fideo,' 'tripas.' Old Podnah, why haven't I heard of these dishes?"

Kirk smiled, shaking his head. "I guess you're just now getting to the grass roots. This is a down-home Mexican restaurant. And it's going to be a down-home 'pachanga' tonight, politicking to their liking."

"Remember, I did okay in that kickoff rally at the plaza in Justinville."

"Yeah, but we called most of the shots that night, and Jordan Layman squired you around. It's Garcia's show tonight. He's not crazy about you, but I just hope his sense of duty remains high."

"We're paying this bill tonight. Why not control the format?"

"Oh, no, this is his turf. I don't want us stepping on any toes or bruising any custom."

Garcia's two older brothers, Eddie and Rafael, soon joined them. They ordered a beer and informed them everything was on schedule for the rally, with a large crowd expected. At six-thirty, activities would commence. Garcia was to arrive at seven, after completing some business in Corpus Christi. Food would be served until eight at which time raffle winners would be announced and the political program would be held - the priest's invocation, five or ten minutes for Garcia's endorsement speech, same for Wedge's response. After that, more music, mixing and mingling. Close down about ten.

Wedge accepted their offer to introduce him around until their brother was on the scene.

When they arrived at the park, the Garcia family, fueled by campaign money supplied by Kirk, had pulled all the stops to provide a festive event. Throughout the park were banners and placards, more than half of which were Garcia's.

Wedge furrowed his brow but didn't comment. Red, white, and blue crepe paper streamers were draped from tree limbs leading to the dance pavilion, where a brightly decorated platform with microphone appeared to be in good order. Off to a side was another decorated platform where the mariachi band, purported to be the best in South Texas, was assembling.

One reason for choosing that particular date was that it was Garcia's birthday, and the band would be prepared to play "Las Mañanitas," the traditional Mexican birthday song, upon his arrival.

Food and beverages were in plentiful supply, including barbecue, tamales, beer, and soft drinks. For the children, special items included balloons, a fireworks display, and piñatas, colorful paper figures filled with candy that were hung from tree limbs for blindfolded youngsters to try to smash open with baseball bats.

A cloud cover had eased over Lantana, making the early evening heat less oppressive as first arrivals began enjoying food and drinks. By seven, the park was almost full with about three hundred people, as Wade Keene and other reporters duly noted. In the lengthening shadows, the mariachis strummed guitars, pierced the soft evening air with trumpets, and sang many traditional songs, inspiring an atmosphere of camaraderie and merriment.

After Wedge completed a round of working the crowd with the Garcia brothers, he stopped for a beer and pulled Kirk aside. "God, I wish Nellie could have made it tonight. This might put us over the top."

"Yeah." Kirk said as he glanced at his watch, "but I wish the star would arrive. He's more than thirty minutes late."

"Ah, probably one to make a dramatic entrance before the home folks."

"I don't think he's that kinda guy."

"You worry too much." Wedge smiled. "Have another beer and enjoy yourself—you've earned it."

The music continued, keeping the crowd in a festive mood, but Garcia's brother, Eddie, soon approached Kirk. "I'm worried," he whispered. "This isn't like him. It's time for the program to start."

"Could have been car trouble."

"Maybe, but I believe he would have called in by now."

"What do you want to do?"

Eddie shrugged. "We can only wait and hope he comes soon."

It was almost nine when Wade Keene approached Kirk. "You were scheduled to start an hour ago. I'm going to miss the first edition if you don't start right away. What's the problem?"

"Probably delayed in Corpus. He'll be here."

Keene took a short puff and tossed the cigarette to the ground. "Between you and me, I bet he's in a ditch somewhere in Bantrell County. Either dead or wishing he was dead."

"Why suspect foul play?" Kirk snapped.

"Why not?"

The mariachis had almost finished their evening's commitment when Eddie conferred with Kirk and Wedge. "It's about ten, and we can't keep the crowd any longer. I suggest you make a short speech."

"The speech I had prepared was a response to your brother's endorsement. What should I say now?"

"Express regrets that Ernesto was unable to attend. Thank them for coming, and ask for their support."

Kirk frowned. "Eddie, will you get up there and endorse Wedge, standing in for your brother, who had pledged to us that he would endorse Wedge?"

Eddie stroked his chin, glancing at the empty platform. "I… I'm afraid I can't do that. I don't know why Ernesto isn't here. He might have changed his mind."

Kirk shook his head. "Well, then, nothing to do but salvage what we can."

After a brief, bland introduction by Eddie, Wedge handed his coat to Kirk and took the microphone.

"My friends, I regret I don't speak Spanish, but what I have to say is from the heart… I appreciate your coming tonight and I'm sure Ernesto Garcia appreciates it, too. We all regret he was unable to be here, but I expect him to join me in campaigning soon. You see, he and I may appear to be different in many ways, but in some very important ways, we are together. We know the price of freedom is always high, whether won on battlefields across the sea, where he has served our nation so well, or in the political arena, where our enemy of freedom sits only a few miles away in Bantrell County. Ernesto and I are together in our desire to defeat Frank Ganner and keep his power confined to just where it is at this time!"

That statement, similar to those they had heard in Garcia's recent campaign, evoked scattered applause.

"My friends, one major step we need to take in our state is to rid ourselves of the poll tax. No citizen should be required to pay his or her hard-earned money for the right to vote!"

Another Garcia theme and another round of moderate applause.

"The poll tax is the rope that patróns like Frank Ganner use to keep their people in human bondage. They buy their poll taxes, tell them how to vote, and by and large control their lives. That's a far cry from freedom, and it's our challenge to change it!"

While Wedge was doing the best he could, only about half of the crowd understood English well enough to comprehend all he was saying. But he was also acutely aware of the reporters' presence and the downside of Garcia's absence. He kept speaking, raising issues he knew most of the reporters would agree upon, including "a decent living wage for all workers," stopping just short of advocating a state minimum wage. In closing, he asked for support, to which about half of the crowd responded favorably.

Half a loaf, Kirk mused.

As the crowd dispersed, Eddie Garcia apologized again to Kirk.

"You and your family did a damn good job tonight. I just hope your brother is okay."

At his car, Kirk slid into the driver's seat and tuned the radio to a Corpus Christi station. Nearby, Wedge was shaking hands with Eddie and Raphael when they were stunned by the second item on the newscast.

"A prominent South Texas political figure, Ernesto Garcia of Lantana, was arrested early this evening and held in the Bantrell County jail at Piedra Blanca on charges of drunken driving, possession of marijuana, speeding, and resisting arrest."

"Let's go!" Kirk called to Wedge.

Three friends of the Garcia brothers standing nearby joined them in the second car, following as Kirk's car sprayed gravel and dust peeling away from the park. Not a word was spoken between Kirk and Wedge as they sped on a state highway into Bantrell County. Then Kirk took a farm road he knew would lead them to Piedra Blanca with minimum risk of being stopped for speeding. Raphael Garcia drove the second car, keeping the furious pace while listening to sharp strings of curse words aimed at Frank Ganner.

At the courthouse where the jail was located, all seven marched in together, expecting to be challenged by the sheriff and his deputies. Instead, they were surprised to receive an amiable reception by a genial Frank Ganner. He invited them into the commissioners courtroom.

Once inside, he addressed them in a calm, direct manner. "I know why you're here, gentlemen, and I want to be as helpful as I can. However, these are serious charges. Crayton, are you the only attorney present?"

When Wedge nodded, Ganner said, "Well, then, why don't you join me in my office? I'm sure he'd appreciate the advice of counsel."

"I'd like for Mr. Holland to accompany me."

"Why, sure." Ganner smiled.

As they settled into Ganner's office, Wedge asked, "Is he all right?"

"Yeah," Ganner said. "Defiant little rascal refused to eat his supper, but he's all right."

"Mr. Ganner," Wedge said in a curt attitude, "let's get down to business. These are indeed serious charges brought against Ernesto. I'd like to discuss the situation with the district attorney."

"That won't be necessary," Ganner said. "I've already conferred with the district attorney and the district judge. I understand what's involved, and I speak for them in this matter."

"Has bail been set?"

"Yes." Ganner stared at him. "Twenty thousand dollars."

Kirk had been working his hands together, staring at the floor while trying to contain his temper. He looked up at Ganner. "That's outrageous! What the hell are you trying to do?"

"Your friend," Ganner said, no longer smiling, "is an agitator, a troublemaker. He's been spreading lies about me and the candidate I support for the Legislature. I'm not going to tolerate that any longer."

"What you're really concerned about now," Wedge said, "is that his support might tip the election to me. Isn't that true?"

"Back to the facts at hand," Ganner snapped. "Garcia faces serious charges and we have evidence and witnesses. Marijuana possession is a felony; add those others in, and we're looking at a considerable term in the state pen at Huntsville and—"

"You send him to Huntsville," Kirk shouted, "and we'll make him a martyr who'll haunt you to your goddamn deathbed!"

Kirk thought he had scored a strong point, but Ganner didn't flinch. He had a prize hostage and would press his advantage.

"Holland, keep out of this! I'm talking to a lawyer about the law. Now, I was about to say I don't have any desire to see that young man's future destroyed. But he's a troublemaker, and I don't trust him."

"Don't trust him to do what?" Wedge asked.

"To stop stirring up trouble. My people don't need outside agitators telling them what to do. They're happy and peaceful as things stand. That's the way it's going to be."

"And what would you suggest?" Wedge leaned forward.

"I suggest a plea bargain. He pleads guilty to the lessor charges, we drop the felony, and he walks out of here tonight, on probation for six months. In exchange, I want your word and his to the effect that he won't be involved in politics or public affairs in any manner until after his probation period. Also, no one discusses the terms with the press. Is that clearly understood?"

"You rotten sonofabitch!" Kirk snapped. "You rigged this whole—"

"Hold on." Wedge held up his hand, palm forward. "We've got to think this through. I want to talk to Ernesto."

Walking up the stairs to the jail ahead of Kirk, Wedge spun through the harsh variables confronting them.

How could, he asked himself, an elected official sit there and do this to us? He'll destroy my one big thrust for the runoff.

He paused before reaching the landing. If we refuse, he's prepared to send Ernesto to the state pen. Sure, Kirk has a good point about making a martyr of Ernesto, but he'd be discredited somewhat for the runoff anyway and then be stuck in prison for years.

He continued his climb. In which case I'd probably lose the election, and that poor guy would lose some of the prime years of his life. Damn, I wish I could believe Ganner might be bluffing… but I don't.

The sheriff escorted them to Ernesto's cell. A smile crossed Ernesto's gaunt face when he saw them approach his steamy quarters. "God, I'm glad to see you," he said, loosening his tie from the sweat-soaked collar.

"Your brothers and some friends are downstairs," Wedge said. "I'm here because I'm the only lawyer available at the moment. If you'd rather have someone else, it won't hurt my feelings."

"No, I'm sure you know the law, and you're here."

"What happened?" Wedge said.

Garcia shook his head. "I was a damn fool to leave Lantana today. All day today in Corpus I could have sworn an unmarked car alternating with another were trailing me around town. Then, when I crossed into Bantrell County on the way home, I was pulled over by a couple of deputies. They said I was speeding, which I certainly wasn't. When I protested, they said they would take me in for questioning. I protested again, and they tried to handcuff me, told me I was going to be booked for resisting arrest. I've got a knot on the back of my head to prove they used force."

"Whiskey and marijuana," Wedge said. "Any truth to it?"

"Absolutely not. The whiskey bottle and the bag of marijuana were planted. My friends will testify I never drink anything stronger than beer, and not much of that. I've never used marijuana."

Wedge explained the settlement proposed by Ganner.

"That's outrageous," Garcia said. "He can't do that, can he?"

"I'm afraid so." Wedge sighed. "I believe you'd be better off accepting his offer."

"But what about your campaign?"

"I guess," Wedge said as he smiled, "we'll have to wait till next time."

Garcia turned to Kirk. "I'm very sorry to let you down. I know what that rally meant to the campaign."

"It's not over," Kirk said.

After Garcia's release, Kirk and Wedge waved good-bye from the courthouse steps as the carload from Lantana headed home. They stood there in silence for a moment, as if stunned by the ease with which Ganner had destroyed their best hope for victory.

Wade Keene, who had just arrived minutes ago and learned of Garcia's release, joined them. "So, no one will discuss the terms for the release," he said in a cynical tone. "You know something, boys? This courthouse isn't the seat of government for a subdivision of the great state of Texas. It's a political cesspool."

On their way to Justinville, neither spoke for several minutes, until Wedge tossed a beer can at the sign designating the Bantrell County line. "That's my defiant gesture of the night. Otherwise, the night belonged to the Baron of Bantrell."

Kirk accepted another beer but continued driving without responding.

"He did us in, didn't he?" Wedge moaned. "He took the last trump card right out of our hands... Hell, Kirk, we gave up without a fight."

"We didn't have anything to fight with tonight."

"And tomorrow? How are we going to replace Ernesto Garcia? You've told us all along he would be the key to winning this race. What the hell are we going to do?"

"The word will spread that he was framed. Some benefit will come from what happened tonight."

"But nothing like his endorsement and campaigning on the stump. That would have an impact on Mexican-Americans through all five of the free counties. As it now stands, Ganner will go after that vote and encounter little resistance. More people are going to be intimidated."

"We'd better forget about Garcia and what might have been. There's simply nothing that can be done to compensate. You did the best you could tonight."

For a few moments, they sat in silence, sipping beer. In a relaxed tone, Wedge reopened the conversation. "Old Podnah, if you have a few left down in the bottom of your bag of tricks, you'd better pull 'em out."

"I've been thinking about such things since we heard the news bulletin. There are a few I might like to try, but I'm afraid Gordon Hempstead,

Nellie, and some other of our key people would find them to be... shall we say, questionable and unorthodox."

"Are you serious?"

"Sure, but they would require some off-the-line cash and total confidentiality between you and me."

"How much cash?"

"About five hundred dollars."

"You'll have it no later than Monday morning. I don't want to know what you're going to do with it, and I don't want Nellie or anyone else to know. Just do it."

"All right, and I may have another item or two for tomorrow's meeting with Gordon and Nellie. Again, questionable and unorthodox, but we're at that stage of the game."

"If it'll give Ganner a migraine, you'll have my support."

"He'll be reaching for more than aspirin."

Kirk tossed in his bed most of the night, trying to reconcile the sudden turn of events Frank Ganner had orchestrated. Though their trump card had been removed, he was more determined than ever to play out the game with every ounce of political acumen, skill, and guile he could muster.

At daybreak he drove to The Green Wagon Restaurant for breakfast. He took his time reading the Banner-Press front page story by Wade Keene, recounting what happened at Lantana and Piedra Blanca. Keene slammed Ganner hard for "his frame-up that muzzled Ernesto Garcia at a crucial point in the runoff campaign." He described Wedge as a "strong-willed candidate, fighting for reform against the Baron of Bantrell, whose code of unethical conduct is unparalleled in Texas political history."

Other news media took similar tacks, virtually ignoring Wedge's opponent, Wally Hooper. Yet Keene, good reporter that he was, had to conclude Hooper still held the advantage because of "the large lockstep bloc vote Ganner is sure to deliver, come election day."

Kirk also studied the various news stories and features regarding the U.S. Senate race, taking note of the schedules of the two candidates during their closing days. Polls and spot observations around the state continued to indicate a tight race.

At the headquarters, he worked alone for more than two hours before Brew Blain dropped by with an envelope filled with cash and checks. Not long thereafter, Wedge arrived and handed Kirk an envelope containing five one-hundred dollar bills. "Caught Dad in a generous mood on a Sunday morning. He went to the safe and counted 'em out. But he also told me he's tapped out. No more."

"Yeah, Brew turned in a little over eight hundred bucks this morning, and he's chasing another hundred this afternoon. He says the good ones are all about tapped out."

"Can we make the advertising budget?"

"I think so…" Kirk smiled "… by kiting a check or two."

"Now, wait. You know Nellie doesn't believe in issuing checks unless the money to cover is in the bank."

"Sure, I know, but we're at the point where we either kite a few or cut where it will seriously dilute the impact. She'll be out campaigning with you this week, not hanging around here monitoring the books. Don't sweat it."

"You have that much confidence in Brew?"

"Yeah, he's worked his heart out in this campaign. If he can't bring it in off his contributor lists, he'll put the bite on your pals, Sidney and Nelson. They'll cover, if need be."

When Nellie arrived with little makeup, dressed in blue jeans with shirt hanging out, Kirk observed that neither her dress nor demeanor were in her usual precise, upbeat mold.

With coffee and cigarette, she scanned the financial report and tossed it aside. "I have things to attend to today. Any idea when Gordon will be here?"

"He called in early," Kirk said. "Told me a close friend died in Houston and he'll be out of pocket for a couple of days."

"That's just great." Nellie sighed. "What about his financial commitment?"

"He left a check with Brew and made a couple of calls. He's pretty well done all he can."

"Well," she said, tapping out her cigarette, "I'm not going to listen to any more lectures from Uncle Adrian. I've put all I can into this campaign… Since Gordon can't make it, let's move on with the meeting."

Nellie seemed distant when Kirk and Wedge briefly discussed events of the previous night. She offered no comment.

Nettled, Wedge looked at Kirk, who stood up and walked to the nearby blackboard. He sensed he had done such a convincing job in selling Nellie on the importance of Ernesto Garcia's support that she had now written off any chance of winning. What he had to say first could have been delivered sitting down, but he felt the need to stand

and be more forceful than ever.

"What I'm going to propose is based on how I believe Frank Ganner views the race at this time. If I were in his shoes, I'd be telling Wally Hooper something like this: 'I cut the heart out of their campaign last night. They're dead. Coast this week, don't take any chances. Make the rounds again, shaking hands, buying beer and meals, but by all means, stay away from your opponent. You've got it won!'

"If that's a valid assumption, then it follows that Ganner will devote most of his energy and resources to the U.S. Senate race, maximizing the vote for Jordan Layman. I'll admit that Layman is running even better than I expected in South Texas, and Holt Witherspoon has written it off. But Ganner hasn't tied Hooper to Layman in a public sense. Ganner never thought it was necessary, since he would promote the two throughout his organization, and his official neutrality left the door open for Hooper to pick up votes from people who support Witherspoon.

"Everything looks good for them, doesn't it? On the surface it surely does, but their strategy leaves them open to a late thrust by our side, and here's the first step."

Kirk unrolled a large piece of lined paper that served as a layout dummy for a full-page newspaper ad. Purely for dramatic effect, he paused, looking it over while holding it in such a way that neither could read the contents. He tacked it onto the wooden rim at the top of the blackboard. The bold double-decked headline read:

WEDGE CRAYTON EARNS THE RESPECT
OF BOTH U.S. SENATE CANDIDATES!

Below to the left was a large picture of Holt Witherspoon with his endorsement of Wedge appearing underneath. To the right were two pictures, together equaling the size of their counterpart, one of Wedge shaking hands with Jordan Layman, the other of Layman with his arm around Wedge's shoulder. The copy read, "Jordan Layman was a special guest at the campaign kickoff for the young reform candidate he respects so much. Layman took time from his busy campaign schedule to draw attention to Wedge Crayton and his solid platform for our district."

Centered toward the bottom of the page was a standard copy tract reaffirming key points of the campaign, including the anti-Ganner thrust and Wedge's qualifications.

Wedge was intrigued, following each descriptive comment by Kirk about items in the ad.

But Nellie frowned. "We're scraping to meet our minimum advertising commitments and you propose another full-page ad. It's out of the question."

"I propose," Kirk said, "we substitute this ad for the one we had scheduled."

"But that's an ad portraying the true Wedge Crayton, the total person. Pictures with people from all over the district, in all walks of life. This ad you've concocted is only about politicians."

"That's right," Kirk said, recalling Nellie had spent a considerable amount of time scheduling Wedge for those pictures and had made sure he appeared in varied changes of clothing. "But the Senate race holds center stage and Jordan Layman is going to clobber Holt Witherspoon all over South Texas. We've got to tie to Layman. We need to confuse people. Make 'em think that deep down, Layman really favors Wedge. And the great thing about this ad is timing. We hang this one on 'em in Friday's weekly editions, election eve, and they won't have time to respond."

Nellie shook her head. "The ad is inherently deceptive. Jordan Layman never even implied he'd endorse Wedge."

"We're not saying he endorsed," Kirk said, "and as far as I'm concerned, when that high-octane gap-shooter crashed our kickoff function, he left himself open to such as this. He cashed in on our deal. Let's cash in on his."

"Did you discuss this with Gordon?" she asked.

"No, I figured he had enough on his mind."

"Or did you avoid an explosion because you know he hates Jordan Layman?"

"I don't recall," Kirk said, "Gordon Hempstead's political judgment has ever been exalted around here."

"Perhaps not, but he's the most prominent citizen of this community. I see your high-risk stunt as great fun right before the election. But then after the election, you return to Austin and leave us with the burned bridge."

She shifted in her seat and turned to Wedge. "Has it crossed your mind what making an enemy of Gordon Hempstead will do for your political future?"

Wedge squirmed in his chair. Like a tennis fan watching a long, spirited volley, his attention had moved from one to the other as the exchange had unfolded. He paused and took a sip of coffee. But he chose not to respond, expecting Kirk to pursue.

"Nellie," Kirk said, "you sound like a defeatist. Sure, we took a hard lick last night, but did you read Wade Keene's piece this morning taking Ganner to task?"

"No, I didn't have time."

"Did you hear the news reports on the San Antonio stations?"

"I must have missed them. I don't recall."

Kirk shrugged. "If you two are ready to throw in the towel, then I want to know right now." He stared at Wedge, who continued avoiding the eyes of Kirk and Nellie.

She lit another cigarette, exhaling smoke in Wedge's direction. "Don't let him badger you into doing something outlandish, something that will hang over your head long after the election. Can't you see this is Moby Dick all over again? Our Captain Ahab is out to get his great white whale, Frank Ganner. But it's getting out of control when he wants to deceive people. We've never even contemplated campaigning like this."

Kirk knew she was baiting him with personal attacks, trying to ignite his temper. But he believed strongly the ad was essential, and he held his temper in check.

"Nellie," he said in a crisp tone, "I just wish you could have been with us in Lantana last night. Despite all the adversity, Wedge built a base in Coronado County. All things considered, it was the most effective speech he's made during the campaign. He's at his peak now while the opposition is coasting with a mediocre candidate. But we simply must respond to the lick Ganner hit us with last night. Create some sparks this week, and we might yet close the gap."

She sighed, again shaking her head. But she didn't continue at the moment, content to let the silence create more pressure on Wedge.

At last, Wedge spoke up. "Kirk, I'm going to put you on the spot. If we run this new ad, how would you rate our chances of winning?"

Kirk shrugged. "I'm not a bookie, but you'd have a helluva lot better chance. The puff ad would reinforce your base, people already inclined to vote for you. This new one will chip some voters away from Wally, and won't hurt you with your base."

Nellie drank more coffee, keeping her eyes fixed on Wedge.

He sighed, tapping a pencil on the table. "Those are good points, Kirk, but what makes you think Gordon Hempstead wouldn't hold a grudge against me?"

"Well, maybe he would, but I imagine if you win, it wouldn't last long. Like the rest of us, he hates Ganner, and, I suspect, more than he does Layman. In any event, I'd be gone, and you could blame the decision to run that ad on your overzealous campaign manager who was guilty of insubordination."

Nellie frowned at Wedge. "In addition to politics, Gordon Hempstead can affect your law practice. You'd be taking an awful risk."

The instant Nellie shifted her attention to the coffee urn for a refill, Kirk pursued his thrust. "I hate to push you, Wedge, but we just don't have time for deliberation. If this ad is acceptable, I move on to the next step. If not, I'm of no more use here. I may as well head for Austin and a renewal of my sanity, far from the great white whale of the Brush Country."

Despite his proximity to one of the air-conditioning units, beads of sweat built on Wedge's forehead.

Hell, what kind of decision is this? he thought. My law practice isn't worth much, but I want to run again if I don't make it on election day.

Wedge stared at the ceiling. But then, give Wally Hooper two years in Austin and he might do a decent job. Then, he'd be there forever and I'd have nothing available worth running for. If there's any hope of pulling it off, I better roll the dice…

Damn, but Nellie sure is drawing a hard line against Kirk, and she appears to be adamant. What'll she do if I choose to run the new ad? What'll Kirk do if I turn him down? He sounds adamant, too. No question Kirk's had the right instincts all along, but he may be getting desperate. Desperate? Sure, he is. It's a desperate situation…

"I've decided…" Wedge dragged his words out. "… I want to run the new ad."

Nellie stood up, preparing to leave. "If that concludes the business, I'll—"

"Nellie." Wedge raised his palm toward her. "Please don't take this personally. It's strictly a campaign decision."

"Don't worry, Wedge, I won't embarrass you by dropping out of the campaign. I'll keep the schedule and smile real pretty. Just don't expect me to help pick up the pieces after the election."

As she turned to leave, Kirk stretched out both hands. "Please stay. I have another proposal that involves you directly."

When she sat down, Wedge relaxed in his chair. He was confident he had made the correct decision on the ad and was relieved Nellie would stand by him through the final days of total effort.

Kirk refilled his coffee cup and took a deep breath. "I'd like for you two to announce your engagement tomorrow."

Stunned, Nellie stared at him, but was speechless.

After an audible gasp, Wedge sat still for an instant with flushed face before rising from his chair and throwing his pencil at the air conditioning unit. "That's beyond the pale!" he snapped. "What the hell gives you the right to suggest such a thing?"

"I haven't complained," Kirk said, "but over the course of the campaign, I've picked up a fair amount of gossip about your relationship. And for every one of 'em who gossips, two or three silent ones are wondering whether you'd tend to business in Austin or spend most of your time chasing skirts."

Regaining her composure, Nellie laughed. "I've wondered the same thing now and then."

"That's not a damn bit funny," Wedge snapped. "And even if some old biddies are snickering about the situation, it won't change with a sudden engagement announcement right before the election."

"It would help," Kirk said, "and beyond that, we could get pictures of you two in the dailies that circulate in the district. And in the weeklies, again we'd hit on election eve when they'd have maximum impact."

Wedge shook his head. "I've never heard of such a hokey scheme."

"Hell," Kirk said as he chuckled, "calm down. I'm not promoting a marriage. Far as I'm concerned, you can forget about it the day after the election."

Wedge stared at the table, refusing to look at Kirk or Nellie.

"What do you think, Nellie?" Kirk said.

"In all candor, I think it's a good idea. Some people might see it as a political stunt, but the story should be that we fell in love while working on this long reform campaign. An impending marriage would add a note of stability to Wedge's public image."

"You know, Wedge," Kirk said, "Nellie was a darn good sport to stay hitched despite her objection to the new ad. Now, on this plan, you need to be a good sport."

"Goddamn you, Kirk, you're trying to sandbag me into doing something I'm not prepared to do."

"You told me to pull out all the stops. That's what I'm trying to do."

"I'll relieve your anxiety," Nellie snapped. "I don't want you to do something you're not prepared to do… I don't want a ring! I don't want a commitment for marriage! And I damn sure don't want to hear you moan and whine about all this either. But I do want to win the election, and I thought that was foremost in your mind. If it is, then let's announce our engagement tomorrow and disengage quietly the day after the election."

Wedge sighed, staring at the table. "All right," he murmured. "What else?"

"That'll do it for now." Kirk rolled up his newspaper ad dummy.

After a long nap, Kirk drove across town early that evening to meet with Gus Batey, his summer boss on a seismograph crew, an oil exploration outfit, when he was nineteen.

Gus hung out at Paco's Place, a remote beer joint located behind a stand of salt cedar trees near a dirt road beyond the eastern edge of "Mexican town." It was the only cantina Kirk had put off limits for the campaign. He recalled his father having once told him never to enter that place after dark, but he knew that to deal with Gus, it had to be on his turf, with a few beers in his belly.

Paco's Place was a big weathered shack with a tin roof. Inside, Kirk scanned the crowded front room with long stand-up bar and tables for drinking. All the customers were men, mostly middle-aged Mexican-Americans. Walls were decorated with a few mounted deer heads and numerous old signs promoting Texas beers: Grand Prize, Pearl, Lone Star, and Southern Select. Behind the bar hung a framed American flag, with pictures of uniformed Mexican-American friends of Paco flanking it.

In the rear of the building was a cramped, smaller room in which was action on the two pool tables. It offered little space except for the players, who placed their longnecks on thin wooden shelves while shooting. To shoot in that room, players had to squint through layers of smoke hanging in the poorly ventilated shack with no air conditioning.

From the bar where he was talking with friends, Gus spotted Kirk looking around and motioned for him to join him at a table in a far corner. It had been almost two years since Kirk had seen the grizzled hunk of a man, whom he estimated had gained a few pounds to near two hundred thirty on his stout six-foot-two-inch frame. A proud Marine veteran of World War II, he displayed elaborate tattoos on his arms, including a waving American flag and an angry American eagle in a descending posture with claws poised for action.

"Welcome to Paco's, amigo," Gus said, removing a chewed-up cigar from his mouth that was almost obscured by three days' growth of heavy dark beard. "For an old 'gringo' like me, this is a nice, sleazy beer joint. For all these Mexicanos, it's a damned good hideaway cantina."

He placed his hand on Kirk's shoulder. "I'd asked about you at Barney's, and they told me you didn't go there much anymore."

"Nah, you know I just finally figured I didn't fit in over there. I don't give a shit for shuffleboard or dominoes. No women there, for another thing. Here, you can grab one now and then for three or four bucks. Beats the hell out of driving all the way to Nuevo Laredo."

"Yeah, I guess so."

Gus insisted upon buying a round of beer that Paco served. The owner took a long look at the clean-cut young gringo, indeed an unusual customer. But if he's a friend of Gus, he's okay.

For a few minutes, they talked about when they worked together, of Gus teaching Kirk and other young college students how to "doodlebug," the nickname for seismograph work.

The nickname derived from the process of the crew digging a narrow hole a hundred feet or more with a drill, then lowering dynamite into the bottom where it was detonated. Shock waves from the explosion were recorded by small geophones strung out on cables. The process was designed to provide clues as to whether oil might be in range below.

The crew member in charge of dynamite work was designated the "shooter," Gus' job, and those lining up geophones for shots and retrieving them afterward were known as "jug hustlers," of which Kirk was one. It had been long-hour work in sweltering heat, but Kirk enjoyed it since it wasn't as physically demanding as "roughnecking," working on an oil rig, or working on a construction outfit, which he had done the summer previous to "doodlebugging."

Kirk bought the second round. As it was served, he mentioned the jukebox was a curious blend of Mexican corridas and polkas, plus a few patriotic American songs from World War II.

"That's what I like," Gus said. "I bought some of those records for Paco, and he likes 'em. He was in the war, too."

The war, Kirk thought. The war. Hell, I served in goddamn heavy combat for months in Korea and nobody even calls it a war. But World War II, that was the war.

Ah, hell, what difference does it make? Play to him, yet don't overdo it - he hates to be patronized. He may not have a formal education, but he's still a shrewd sonofabitch.

From the jukebox came sounds of one of Gus' favorite selections, "There's A Star Spangled Banner Waving Somewhere."

"You know," Gus said, sounding wistful, "one time I heard Kenneth Threadgill sing that at the Split Rail in Austin. Man, there wasn't a dry eye in the place."

"I don't know how you do it, Gus. I just don't much like to think about my time in war."

"Hell, you just happened to be in the wrong war. Say, have you heard about the World War II vet who got called before his draft board? He told 'em, 'Look, I've already served my time. I've been shot at and shot up. I've had diarrhea, pyorrhea, and gonorrhea. But I don't want no part of that Korea.'" Gus howled with laughter, while Kirk stretched his facial muscles to force a smile.

A pensive expression crossed Gus' face as he looked at the American flag mounted behind the bar. "Well, I guess things were damned different for me. Sure, combat was hell. Losin' buddies, gettin' hit, wonderin' if the next hit would be the last. But comin' home was somethin' else. Somethin' real special. People loved those uniforms then. I never had it so good."

"Why didn't you stay in?"

"Truth is, I'd have stayed if there was more fightin' to be done, 'specially against the goddamn Russians. But I got bored and got out."

"If you'd have stayed in," Kirk said as he smiled, "you might even have become an officer."

"What for?" Gus snickered. "Shit, we hit beaches under fire so heavy there wasn't enough trees to go around for the officers."

Kirk laughed, ordering another round. "Tell me, have you been keeping up with politics this year?"

"Yeah, 'bout as much as usual. I always vote."

"How do you see the Senate race?"

"Voted for old Holt before. Guess I will again. He doesn't do much, or say much, but that's sorta the way I like it. I'd just as soon the government spend more money on defense and less screwin' around in our lives."

"You're not impressed with Jordan Layman?"

"I'll tell you one thing… I wouldn't get in a high stakes poker game with that guy. He's got the eyes of a hungry hawk. He's liable to get whatever the hell he's after."

"What about the Legislature?"

"That's a lousy situation. I got no use for that bastard Frank Ganner or the fat little dummy he's running. But I got no use for your candidate either. Nothin' but a spoiled rich kid who should have stayed in the country club. Hell, he couldn't bed a whore even if she was trying to give him a free ride."

Kirk laughed and took another long swig of beer. The smoke aggravated his sinuses, but he dared not suggest they change locations. He blew his nose and continued drinking from the cold longneck. "Well, Gus, you know why I came back to run the campaign?"

"Nah. I doubt it was a brilliant move."

"It wasn't, and I want you to know I've never been a personal friend of the candidate."

A curious expression came upon Gus' face. "Why are you telling me this?"

"Because I need to talk about it. I need your help."

Gus shifted around in his chair, his curiosity bordering on skepticism. "I knew that guy wasn't your type, or your friend. Didn't make sense to me for you to give up what I figured was a damn good job in Austin. Hell man, if I could make what I'm making here and live in Austin, I sure as hell wouldn't be sweating every day in this dust and heat."

"I came back to stop Frank Ganner! I know my dad would have fought against that sorry bastard trying to move into our county. When you get down to the nut-cutting, that's what this election's all about."

Gus stopped chewing on his cigar. "You know, I don't owe you a damned thing, but I owe one to your old man. Years ago, he got me out of that goddamn jail in Nuevo Laredo. Jesus, I thought I was goin' to rot in there."

"If you owe him one, I'm here to collect. And I'll pay for the service."

"What is it?"

Kirk placed a map of the district on the table. "I want Wally Hooper signs destroyed in these five counties on election eve. Roads marked in red are priority, leading to polling places. The last impression I want those voters to have will come from signs for our candidate, not theirs."

"No sweat," Gus said, "but why not work over those two counties where Ganner has his machine vote?"

"Because tearing down signs there wouldn't affect the vote. I have a little more daring task in mind."

From a pocket, Kirk retrieved a crude map he had drawn, based upon his glances at Ganner's voter turnout plan when he was in Ganner's office after the rattlesnake episode.

"I want you to organize a mission, a commando-type mission. On election eve, or in the predawn hours of election day, I want sand poured into the gas tanks of these twelve vehicles Ganner uses to transport most of his voters to the polls."

Gus blinked. "Darin'? Shit, man, that's dangerous as hell! Those pickups and trucks are sittin' near the courthouse and his men don't mind usin' their pistols and rifles and shotguns… What the hell makes you think a crazy idea like this would work?"

"Because Ganner won't expect getting hit right there at his base."

"Jesus," Gus said, rubbing his chin, looking over the map again. "I've done doodlebuggin' in that area, but I never spent a night in Piedra Blanca. Somebody who knows that town needs to be in on this."

"Know anybody you can trust?"

Gus summoned the owner, Paco Martinez, who designated his brother to tend bar while he sat with Gus and Kirk. Kirk guessed Paco to be about forty, a tall, deliberate man who rarely smiled. He, too, had patriotic tattoos on his dark brown arms that bore a few scars from breaking up scrapes during the years since 1946 when he opened the cantina. Around his neck he wore a cross, a close companion for a thick scar from a Japanese bayonet.

Gus explained the political situation to justify a raid on Piedra Blanca and included compensation for the participants.

Paco sat stoically for a moment, studying the crude map. "I was born and raised in Piedra Blanca, I left to join the Army. I learned how much I like freedom, living away from there. Frank Ganner has most of the people, even members of my family, thinking his way is the only way. If you don't go live somewhere else, you believe it… I don't want Frank Ganner or any of his people around here. I'll go with Gus, and we only need one more guy on this. Needs to be kept real quiet."

"That's right," Gus said. "Best thing would be for me to hire some kids to take care of the signs, and no one but the three of us will go on the little trip to Piedra Blanca."

Eyes widened, Kirk shook his head. "I can't risk going. We get caught and the campaign is caught."

"Nah," Gus said. "You drive the getaway vehicle. Paco and I take the big risk. If we get caught, you take off and come home."

Kirk rubbed his chin, still concerned about taking an additional risk he hadn't considered. "Isn't there anybody else around you guys trust?"

They shook their heads.

Kirk rose to leave, handing to Gus an envelope containing five hundred dollars in cash. "Let's hope for good luck, gentlemen."

"Shit!" Gus smiled. "Call us anything but that, and don't be talking about 'hope.' We'll draw up a good plan and execute it. You said one thing right. Ganner ain't expecting to get hit at his home base. Long as we have the element of surprise, we'll be all right."

At midweek, Nellie reported to Kirk widespread favorable response to the engagement announcement in the daily newspapers that circulated in the district. Since the campaign was in progress, she convinced those papers to treat the story as spot news rather than placement in the Sunday society sections after the election.

She anticipated another round of favorable publicity when the story would be carried in the weeklies on election eve.

Wedge called from Harmon County to report that Wally Hooper had canceled a joint appearance at a civic club luncheon where Wedge was allowed to speak as scheduled.

"It's like running in a vacuum," Wedge said. "Wally's nowhere around."

"That's fine," Kirk said. "You can run faster in a vacuum. Keep movin' round. Also, there's a schedule change for Friday afternoon. You and Nellie have been named to the official greeting committee for Jordan Layman at his airport rally in San Antonio."

"How in the hell did you swing that? We've been turned down twice."

"I found out the distinguished chairman is an avid deer hunter. I arranged a choice lease for him this winter at the Westerfield Ranch, first time that big spread has ever leased for hunting. That act of raw courage and patriotism on my part landed you on the greeting committee."

"Good work, but now I guess Gordon Hempstead will run both of us out of town."

"Just be there, and get in front of cameras."

Early Friday afternoon, Wally Hooper all but tiptoed into Frank Ganner's courthouse office, carrying a stack of newspapers. "Frank, I don't like what's going on. Crayton's all over the papers with pictures of him and his girlfriend, claiming they've just become engaged. Hell, they've been going together for years. This is outrageous."

Ganner chuckled, looking over one of the pictures. "Sounds like sour grapes, Wally. I gotta admit young Crayton has better taste in women than in politics."

Hooper shook his head. "I don't know how you can kid around. Have you heard Crayton is on the San Antonio greeting committee for

Jordan Layman at the rally this afternoon?"

"Yeah, I heard. Some dumb bastard let him talk his way into that, but what the hell, how many of our voters will travel out of this district to attend that rally? None. They've all seen and heard Layman before."

"I tell you, Frank, I have a bad feeling. Look at this ad."

Ganner glanced over the newspaper tear sheet Hooper handed him, folded it quickly, and dropped it into the wastebasket. "Trying to tie their guy to Jordan Layman is the kind of stunt that goddamn Holland would dream up. But it won't fool our people. They know they're to vote for you and Layman."

"I just hope enough of 'our people' will stay hitched."

"Quit worrying."

"How can I? Did you know The Texas Progressive ran another endorsement of Crayton? They're pounding us."

"You ought to get an award for handwringer of the year. Nobody reads that goddamn magazine but a few eggheads who wouldn't vote for you anyway. Besides, their editor is a two-faced bastard whose own people are going to question him. Claims to be a loyal Democrat, yet he wouldn't endorse Layman, the loyal Democrat candidate in that race."

Ganner took a phone call from his associate, Al Hernandez, who informed him of a news item on the radio quoting the secretary of state calling for an honest election the following day.

Ganner's eyes grew cold. "Who does that sonofabitch think he is? He doesn't have one goddamn bit of authority over conducting elections."

"Sure, we know that," Hernandez said, "but some of our people are nervous. They think that guy speaks for the governor, and then they think of Texas Rangers swooping down here with pistols on their hips."

"Al," Ganner snapped, "get all the precinct election judges in here now!"

When they assembled in the commissioners court room, Ganner stood on the dais with the determined expression of a veteran general preparing troops for combat. "Now, quit paying any attention to that crap on the radio! There won't be any Rangers coming down here! And if there are any investigations, I'll handle 'em! If any sonofabitch comes snooping around your precinct, send 'em to me!

"Remember, each of you is to make sure every voter eligible on your list votes. We'll make an all-out effort to get 'em all to the polls, but if some don't make it by seven tomorrow night, vote 'em and vote 'em right - Jordan Layman and Wally Hooper."

Ganner knew well how to manipulate election law to his liking. Key elements were how to use paper ballots and negative, or "scratch" voting, which required the voter to scratch out the name of the candidate not wanted in a given race.

"Now, remember, if you see a ballot for Holt Witherspoon and Wedge Crayton in which either or both opponents' names are not totally—and I mean totally—scratched out, then set the ballot aside and don't count it. If that happens on a ballot marked for our candidates, take a pencil, complete the scratching out carefully, and count it.

"If you work your precinct right, you should bring in about a ninety percent majority for our candidates. I don't want any reporters or anybody else looking at your voters lists or ballots. When you get through, bring 'em here, and I'll lock 'em up.

"When we break up, report to Matson Pace's office for your money. The allocation is adequate for whatever you need. Do a good job and there will be a bonus, as usual. Any questions?"

A middle-aged Mexican-American raised his hand. "Frank," he said with a wide smile, "do we get a double bonus if both candidates win?"

Ganner chuckled, "I'll run you off if they don't."

Matson Pace was prepared to dispense nine thousand dollars to the precinct election judges who functioned in the dual role of jéfes, political operatives in charge of delivering the vote. They paid workers to round up voters and get them to the polls, a secondary network to Ganner's major vehicle transportation program. In addition to cash, those operatives offered barbecue and beer as incentives to vote.

To an outsider, the system might appear to be somewhat loose, but if Frank Ganner wanted a ninety percent vote for Jordan Layman in Bantrell County, he would get it.

When the meeting broke up, Al Hernandez marveled again at Ganner's unique ability to convince all that whatever he desired would work. If it might occur to a precinct judge, one with a twinge of conscience, it would be easy to expose Ganner, on second thought he would realize no written evidence existed of Ganner's dictates, no paper trails of funding, and whoever might tell on him would find living in Bantrell County unbearable.

They all stayed in line, dependent upon him for their every need. Hernandez was of a more cautious nature and he reminded himself that Ganner's arrogance landed him in hot water from time to time. The stakes in the Senate race didn't appear to be nearly as high to Hernandez as they were to Ganner, who took Layman's election as a personal goal beyond the political significance to their county.

Next door, in Will Dodd County, Ganner's influence was strong, but his control was not total. Though he owned the only bank in the county seat of Marlene, his political dominance of the courthouse might vary from election to election, or when that county's Democratic Party chairmanship changed hands.

A candid meeting such as he had just held in Bantrell County was out of the question in Will Dodd County, but he maintained close association with several precinct election judges. Jordan Layman and Wally Hooper would carry that county by substantial margins, though ninety percent wasn't feasible.

Chapter 11

Jordan Layman winged into San Antonio by helicopter for the most important airport rally during his final frantic day of barnstorming the state. Thousands of supporters, well-wishers, and curious onlookers were crowded against the chain link fence near the runway, many of them waving signs proclaiming, "Give 'Em Hell, JDL!" and "JDL-The Real Democrat!"

A western swing band was playing spirited tunes, prompting many in the festive crowd to clap their hands and stomp their feet.

Despite the sweltering late August heat, people were in an upbeat mood, keyed by the rousing music and anticipation of hearing the candidate who had been stirring up more publicity in recent weeks than Holt Witherspoon, his reflective, pipe-puffing opponent.

Nellie expected Layman to appear haggard from the heat and grueling schedule, but as the helicopter blades ceased whirling, he sprang out and started working members of the twenty-member greeting committee. Somehow, on the steaming runway, Nellie withstood the heat and was stunning in a bright red dress with yellow straw hat.

As Layman shook hands with Wedge, he caught sight of her out of the corner of his eye. "Now Crayton, nailing down this young lady was the best damn move you could make. I'd never have gotten anywhere without Dove Anne."

Wedge gave him a sheepish smile, then a broader one as Layman kissed Nellie on the cheek. A Banner-Press photographer popped away, catching the three of them plus the mayor of San Antonio, who had greeted Layman a moment earlier.

Other newspaper photographers and a television crew worked by them as Layman moved through the loose configuration of official greeters.

"Well," Wedge whispered to Nellie, "we'll look good on television, but ninety percent of the people in our district don't have sets."

"I'll settle for appearing in tomorrow's Banner-Press."

Smiling and waving, Layman ambled to the fence to shake a few hands while photographers recorded his every move.

Wade Keene paused next to Wedge. "You can learn lessons from that guy. Nobody works a crowd like Jordan Layman."

Wedge smiled, offering Keene a cigarette.

"By the way," Keene said, "what are you doing here? This is out of your district and Frank Ganner is supporting Layman."

"It's my civic duty."

Keene shook his head. "You guys ought to rewrite that old line about 'politics and strange bedfellows.' It's too mild for this year."

"Remind me," Wedge said as he chuckled, "to join gap-shooters anonymous."

"The only anonymous gap-shooter I know is that campaign manager of yours. Though he's not here today, his presence is felt. You've run a damn good campaign, but I suspect Ganner defanged it when he sidelined Garcia."

"We've never given up. We still feel we're going to pull it out."

"Well, you'll know tomorrow night."

Layman soon ascended the banner-draped platform for the mayor to introduce him, prompting a long, loud response from the crowd, accompanied by a short, snappy routine from the band. With rapid hand gestures and a voice strained from endless speechmaking, Layman retraced his record in Congress, stressing his role in bringing electricity to rural areas, and his general support for the domestic policies of Roosevelt and Truman. Then he made a fervent call for a "strong national defense to meet the enormous challenge put forth by the treacherous Communists all over the world."

With a good voice, he'd be unbeatable, Wedge mused amid the cheering, but he seems to be stretching in these orations. His voice sounds harsh, rather than measured as it should be.

Layman was almost shouting as he denounced his opponent as "a Republican in Democrat clothing, one who doesn't believe in loyalty to the party that carried him all the way to the governor's chair."

With his familiar thrusts having all been recounted, Layman paused, as though he'd unloaded old baggage and was ready for a new course. Lowering his voice, his words were slow and deliberate. "Now, my friends, tomorrow is election day, our judgment day, if you will. Tomorrow, you and a million other Texans will make the judgment of your voting lives because this is indeed a campaign at the crossroads."

Raising voice and hands, he challenged his audience. "Are we going to give up and retreat to the past?"

"No!" shouted the crowd.

"Are we going to elect a senator who never looks ahead?"

"No!" again, longer and louder.

"Are we going to send a tired old man to Washington who can't even work with the leaders of his own party?"

A long "No!" spliced with shouts of "Give 'em hell, Jordan!"

"My friends, I need your support because I am the man for the future, a man with the vision to see it and the energy to reach for it. I know how to work with my party to get the most things done for Texas. For Texans… that's what this contest is all about, and you know I will do the job in Washington!"

The crowd responded with a round of cheers and applause.

"We stand here today in San Antonio, the gateway to South Texas. This is the region that backed me strongly in the first election. Without that support, I wouldn't be in this runoff."

At once, his hand gestures and harsh tones were at play again. "But I'm here to tell you the election tomorrow is going to be close, and it's up to you, every one of you, to pitch in and help! Tell your friends, family members, and neighbors to vote for Jordan Layman! Every vote counts! Remember, work hard tomorrow for me, and I'll work hard for you for six years! Thank you all, my friends, and God bless you!"

To a long round of cheering and applause, Layman shook hands with the mayor and a few greeting committee members nearby, then he strode to the helicopter to resume his hectic schedule.

Nellie and Wedge walked past Keene who stood near the fence, making notes.

"If you were a betting man," Wedge said, "who'd you take?"

Keene squinted into the late afternoon sunshine, watching Layman's helicopter disappear toward the Hill Country. "Layman's run the more aggressive campaign, no doubt about that. But old Holt's been movin' around, too, finally, and he has an awful lot of loyal supporters from times past… If I were a betting man, I wouldn't bet. Too close to call."

Nellie had scheduled a business meeting in downtown San Antonio relating to her dress shop. After rejoining Wedge in the lobby of the Saint Anthony Hotel, they ate a light dinner and started home. She was tired and curled up in the front seat next to him, leaning her head against his shoulder as he drove south toward Justinville.

After sleeping almost an hour, she awoke and lit a cigarette. "God," she said as she sighed, "it's hard to believe it's almost over."

"Yeah, I've been thinking about all the little things we might have done better."

"If they're just little things, don't worry. If we did the big ones right, maybe we'll be surprised tomorrow night."

"There's just one big thing I did wrong. One great big thing."

"What," she said in a puzzled tone, "are you talking about?"

"I should have married you before the campaign started."

"Don't kid about that! It hasn't been easy at all for me to carry out that ploy this week."

"Maybe I'm serious. You heard what that sage politician, Jordan Layman, said today about his marriage."

She smashed her cigarette. "You're really not being one damn bit funny."

He slid his hand into a coat pocket and retrieved a small box which he handed to her. "While you were tending to your business, I was tending to mine."

She opened it to find a beautiful, large diamond ring. She gasped, unable to respond.

"Thank goodness they know me there and let me charge on the family account. Otherwise, you'd have had to settle for a cigar wrapper."

She shook her head. "It's gorgeous, Wedge, but I wonder why you suddenly came to this. And don't tell me again about Jordan Layman's little pronouncement."

"Well, whatever... the result is, you're going to be stuck with me for the long haul."

"Is that so? I haven't accepted. I may want a few days to think it over."

In the early twilight, he glanced at the well-defined contour of her lovely face. "You've had a few years to think it over. If you need any longer, the offer will be rescinded."

She laughed. "Faced with such a sudden pivotal decision, I have no recourse but to succumb to your gallant gesture."

He pulled the car over into a little picnic area on a gentle hill where they could see the lights of Justinville about three miles distant. For a long moment, they kissed with warmth.

"Now," she whispered, "I want to know the truth."

Wedge sighed, straightening up in the seat to light a cigarette. "I guess the truth is, I've been miserable this week, carrying on the engagement charade. It made me think a lot about you, and about us. How long we've been going together. How much we enjoy each other, depend on each other. How damned hard we've worked together in this long ordeal we call a political campaign. Of all the pressure, the twists and turns. I woke up this morning thinking about it again. I realized we hadn't made love this week. You and I together going four nights without making love? First, I chalked it off to the heavy schedule. Then, I brought it home to the fact that our relationship had grown off-key, distant… It occurred to me that no matter what happens at the polls, it was going to be very awkward for us. It just seemed to me that we'd better clear the air before the election."

She paused, viewing the twinkling lights. "I've hated it all week. Here I had jumped on Kirk for what I thought was a deceptive idea, then turned right around and eagerly endorsed a deceptive act. I had about decided that instead of being good for one another, we'd become willing partners in corruption, chasing a little slice of political power as though it were the central thread of our lives … I had about decided we should call it quits after the election, win or lose."

He kissed her again, conveying relief and a spark of passion.

She eased him away. "We've still got the final reception at the headquarters in fifteen minutes. But if you insist on accompanying me home tonight, I won't object."

The election eve reception at the headquarters was a low key affair, simply a gesture of thanks to the volunteers who had worked so hard during the past few weeks. But Gordon Hempstead cornered Kirk before Nellie and Wedge arrived, complaining about the newspaper ad implying Layman was favorable to Wedge.

Kirk had his explanation rehearsed and was pleased Hempstead seemed to calm down. He was also thankful Hempstead had missed the evening news on his television set, one of the few in Justinville.

When he learns about Wedge at the Layman rally in San Antonio, Kirk mused, his blood pressure will rise again, even higher. But that will be tomorrow, on election day.

When Nellie and Wedge arrived at the headquarters, Nellie made the rounds, displaying her engagement ring, which elicited comments of admiration along with pangs of jealousy among the women.

As she approached Kirk, he bowed and kissed her hand. "My countess, wearing a ring fit for a queen."

"Kirk Holland, were you playing Cupid with your little plan this week?"

"On occasion, the gods may question the nature of my endeavors, but they must always keep faith that my heart is pure."

She laughed and turned to visit with a few late-arriving volunteers.

Wedge soon made a short, crisp speech, thanking the volunteers and predicting victory. It had been a long day, winding down an arduous campaign, and his speech was hardly elevating. But his role had been played out and he was weary. He wanted nothing more that night than to retire with Nellie.

After everyone departed, Kirk walked outside to view a dark evening, a favorable sign for his final plans of the campaign. While he relaxed with a beer at Barney's, two crews of youngsters gathered in the vacant lot adjoining Gus Batey's mobile home.

"Remember," Gus said in a stern tone, "tear down only Wally Hooper signs. Leave all others alone. Three guys to each pickup, ridin' in the cab. Driver stays inside with the motor runnin' at all times, the other two do the work.

"Now, if you spot a vehicle approachin' while you're workin', don't try to hide. Just jump in the pickup and move on down the road. You should have memorized your maps by now, so give 'em to me. They'd be evidence if you got caught.

"When you're ridin', keep the axe and hatchet in the bed of the truck, and don't carry any guns. That way, if a deputy stops you, there's nothin' suspicious. If he asks about the tools, tell 'em you're out gettin' some mesquite for barbecue and—"

"We always carry a rifle in our pickup," said one of the teenagers.

"Not tonight! Give it here! You can get it back tomorrow, when you collect your final payment, and a bonus if you can look me in the eye and tell me you got every goddamn sign on the roads we targeted. Whatever you do, don't wander into Bantrell or Will Dodd counties. They're strictly off limits.

"If you guys are careful, you won't get caught. But if you do, don't call me, 'cause I won't know ya. If everything goes okay, have fun with your money, but I wouldn't go braggin' about it tomorrow. If Crayton wins, you're heroes, but if Hooper wins, you're bums and he's liable to come after ya."

After the crews departed, Gus slept a few hours before Paco arrived to awaken him. Kirk parked his car at the headquarters and walked five blocks to find Gus poring over a map of Bantrell County, coffee cup in hand.

Kirk recoiled as he glanced into the box sitting alongside two bags of sand near the door. "Sticks, caps, fuses. What's this all about, Gus?"

"Look here on this map," Gus said. "We put the skids on the twelve vehicles, but what if Ganner replaces 'em fairly fast? He'll still get his goddamn vote out. But if we destroy the Three Points Bridge, over that creek with high banks, he'll play hell gettin' to a large chunk of western Bantrell County. Only a bulldozer could cross that creek and that ain't no way to transport many people."

Paco frowned. "Deputies patrol that area all night. It will be risky."

"Shit, not as risky as messin' round that goddamn courthouse. Have you nailed down the final route?"

"Yes." On the table, Paco placed a crude map of Bantrell County he had drawn. "We wind up on this unmarked little dirt road that comes to within three blocks of the courthouse. We walk from there."

"Okay, then I guess we'd better place the firecracker on the way in, and light it on the way out."

Kirk had stood in silence, listening, envisioning the destruction of the bridge. Pouring sand in gas tanks was a glorified prank compared with destroying a bridge. The challenge and the danger spun through his mind.

I could wind up in jail over this one, he thought.

He rubbed his chin, glancing at the maps time and again. Am I sinking all the way down to the level where Frank Ganner plays the game? Is there any other way to fight him?

Kirk's mind was drifting into the past with his father's stern face dimly appearing when Gus suddenly forced the issue.

"You're too damned quiet, Kirk. Not turning chicken, are you?"

Kirk avoided Gus' eyes, still concentrating on the maps. "No," he said, "I'm okay."

Paco checked his watch. "Almost 2:00 A.M. Time to get started."

They rode without speaking in Gus' pickup for several miles. Kirk knew both of his cohorts needed the money, but they would have attempted the raid for nothing. It was a unique, unexpected opportunity to relive those daring wartime moments when they pitted their courage and skill against an entrenched enemy. Moments of high challenge when intense preparation meshes with the exhilaration of facing imminent danger, a strange blend causing adrenalin to flow while they appeared to be calm.

Their preparations had been meticulous, each dressing in dark clothing with nothing bright or reflective visible. All wore cheap blue tennis shoes they had purchased for the mission. Gus' deep summer tan had made his skin almost as brown as Paco's, enhancing the camouflage for a dark night.

When they crossed the Bantrell County line, they encountered no vehicles en route to the Three Points Bridge. Gus wasted no time as he rigged dynamite underneath the old wooden structure while Paco scanned the area and Kirk kept the motor running.

Driving toward Piedra Blanca, they met two cars, but neither was manned by deputies. Paco soon pointed the way to the unmarked dirt road on which Kirk drove with his lights on dim for several miles. When he was within five blocks of the courthouse, Paco told him to drive without lights the final two blocks.

He parked the pickup next to a vacant lot on a quiet road with no street light. It was almost 3:00 A.M. when they looked over the area. Only one dim porch light was between their location and the courthouse where lights were visible around the building and in the parking lot. They taped strips of grocery bag paper over Gus' license plates.

Each carried a three-pound bag of sand, clutching it as though it were a weapon. In the shadows, they eased through the vacant lot and tiptoed the final two blocks to arrive near the back entrance of the courthouse. A small annex building was between the courthouse and parking lot where the twelve vehicles were stationed.

They observed two deputies in the annex, playing cards. Their patrol car was parked next to the annex, a tempting target for sanding, but far too risky under the bright lights.

With no other apparent danger evident, they crept up behind a large mesquite tree to survey the scene and realized it would be necessary to crawl the final yards in order to avoid detection. Without a sound, they crawled in the dust for several yards to reach the vehicles.

They took caps from gas tanks and poured a serving of sand in each. Paco had completed his designated six and joined Gus on his last, when they jumped at the sound of a dog barking.

Glancing to his right, Gus muttered, "Holy shit!"

A Great Dane charged at them at a fast clip. Gus looked on the ground for a rock or stick, but found none. The dog was within three feet of them when Paco tossed a handful of sand into his face. The dog stopped, shaking his head, yelping in confusion and temporary blindness.

"Let's get the hell out of here!" Gus called, breaking into a run.

As they dashed past the annex, the deputies shouted curses while strapping on their holsters. Gus and Paco covered the three blocks to the pickup in a hurry. They piled in as Kirk spun the pickup around and headed back down the dirt road. A siren blared as the deputies wheeled out to give chase.

"Jesus!" Gus sighed. "Another block and I'd of been outta wind."

The pickup was a Godsend on the old dirt road, more stable and maneuverable than the sedan chasing them.

"Better put some distance between 'em on this road," Paco said, "or they'll catch us on the paved road."

"We've gained a little," Kirk said, "but those bastards are movin' out."

"How long," Paco said in a matter-of-fact tone, "is the fuse under the bridge?"

"It ain't long, but I'll cut it shorter if we got time to do it."

Paco noticed both he and Gus had kept their nearly empty sacks of sand. He tossed them out the window. "No sense carrying evidence."

Tearing along at fifty-five mph, Kirk almost lost control when a coyote wandered into view. As he veered back onto the road, he again glanced into the rear view mirror. "At least that damn coyote caused us to kick up a camouflaging dust cloud."

When they reached the paved road, Kirk accelerated to eighty, which was the absolute maximum speed at which he believed he could maintain control of the pickup. Having just traveled that route, he remembered the curves and bends, but he could see he was losing ground to the deputies who knew the route well and had the advantage on pavement.

When the Three Points Bridge came into view, Paco pointed to a small mound of caliche near the road, a half-mile on their side of the bridge. Kirk tore into it, spraying the chalky dust all over the road, obliterating the center stripe, and blurring the vision of the driver in pursuit. He swerved off the road several feet, losing valuable seconds to clean his windshield before he could see well enough to resume the chase.

On the other side of the bridge, Kirk slammed to a halt and Gus scrambled down the slope. While he cut the fuse and lit it, Paco stood on the road, calculating the distance of the approaching car. "We got thirty seconds to clear out!"

Gus climbed up from the bridge and slid next to Paco as Kirk accelerated again. Paco said in a flat tone that the car in pursuit was less than a mile behind them.

"If an old shooter can't pull this one off," Gus said, slapping Paco on the shoulder, "something's wrong."

Seconds later the explosion tore apart the bridge before the deputies arrived. Bewildered and cursing, they dashed out of their car to view the impasse. In anger and frustration, they pulled their pistols and fired a few impossible shots at the speeding pickup as it disappeared in the darkness.

The three comrades arrived back in Justinville shortly before sunup. Gus was pleased to find a note on his screened door to the effect that the youngsters had returned safely, without incident.

He handed the note to Kirk, who had been rubbing his hands, trying to relax them after the long period of gripping the wheel. Weary, but cautious again, Kirk turned down an offer of a ride to his car, though it was dark and quiet in Justinville. Each step was an effort as he trudged the few blocks to the headquarters.

Almost exhausted, he drove to his apartment and fell in bed. For a few moments, he couldn't sleep, wrestling with second thoughts about what they had done.

Well, it's over, he thought, and we got away with it.

But the pulsating events kept spinning by, including sounds of the shots fired by the deputies as they sped into the safety provided by distance and darkness.

What if one of those wild shots had hit a tire? Or one of us?

But the questions trailed off as he finally fell asleep.

At daybreak in Bantrell County, the deputies decided they could no longer postpone facing the fury of their boss and informed Ganner about the bridge.

In a waspish mood, he conducted a survey of the damage, accompanied by the deputies and Al Hernandez, his close associate and county commissioner for the area. "Do you mean to tell me," Ganner snapped at the deputies, "you couldn't make out the license plate, model, or even color of their goddamn pickup?"

"No sir," one said. "We never got close enough."

"They damn sure got close enough to you guys. Moved right by you at the courthouse. If one of my dogs hadn't scared 'em, they'd have carried out their mission there. You guys are lucky they didn't steal your patrol car from right under your goddamn noses, and—"

"Still no idea," Al said, "what they were doing around the courthouse?"

"No, sir, we couldn't find any damage to buildings or vehicles."

Ganner dismissed the deputies to return to the courthouse. He paced around the bridge area time and again, studying the deep creek bed with steep banks. "If I ever catch the bastards who did this, I'll cut their goddamn balls off."

On the return ride to Piedra Blanca, Al asked if Ganner really believed Witherspoon might have ordered the raid.

"Well, he'd have the most to gain if we don't deliver those voters from out there."

"What about Wally's opponent?"

"Nah, they're amateurs. This was a professional job. Probably cooked up in Houston or San Antonio."

"What are you going to do?" Al said, fully aware from long years of experience that Ganner was rapidly thinking the situation through.

"I could get our judge to issue an order, giving us more time to vote those boxes out there, but I don't like that. If we don't conduct the election on time, the press will start meddling."

Soon after he arrived at his courthouse office, a wire service correspondent called to inquire about the bridge. Ganner gave him a few terse comments. Moments later, three of his voter roundup drivers reported to him that their vehicles had conked out within a few blocks from where they started. They suspected sand had been put in the gas tanks.

"Those goddamn bastards!" Ganner yelled, shattering a coffee cup against the wall. "So that's what they were doing around here!"

With his eyes glazed over from anger, Ganner cleared the room. For several minutes, he sat alone as his temper subsided, and he began functioning again as a political boss whose home base had been challenged and shaken for the first time.

He summoned Al and Matson Pace, his two most trusted associates. In a crisp, confident manner, he barked orders. "We need to move rapidly! Al, you're in charge of operations; Matson will provide whatever funding is needed promptly in order to carry out my instructions. First, I'll call that San Antonio contractor, Pick Hallerton. He's made so damn much money on our road and bridge contracts, he can't turn us down. I'm going to tell him to supply us with the necessary vehicles to replace those out of commission. If he doesn't have 'em all on hand, I'll tell him to get 'em somewhere in San Antonio and get 'em on down here immediately, and—"

"We can get vehicles closer to home," Al said.

"You didn't let me finish," Ganner snapped. "Sure, I know that, but I want those vehicles from San Antonio to arrive at the Three Points Bridge loaded with bags of cement. After they're unloaded, keep what vehicles you need out there in that area for voter turnout and bring the others here.

"Now, I'm going to call that guy who runs the Coastal Flood Control

District. He's got a nice loan at my bank in Marlene, so he's not going to say anything but 'yes' when I tell him I want to requisition his warehouse full of sandbags. I'll arrange for trucks to transport those to the bridge. Should arrive about the time the vehicles come from San Antonio.

"Al, muster all the county road workers. Have them out there at the bridge ready to go when all this stuff arrives. We're going to fill that creek bed with sandbags up to near bridge level, then stack cement bags to cover like frosting on a cake. It'll serve our needs till we rebuild the bridge."

Jesus, Matson Pace mused, that's a helluva plan, but how long will it take?

As though Ganner anticipated that question, he continued. "If everyone hustles, we'll have this done in five or six hours. That'll leave us the balance of the afternoon to get the voter transportation carried out. That's all. Get moving!"

Nellie and Wedge had enjoyed a sensuous night of love-making and deep, fulfilling sleep. She didn't awaken until after nine. When she nudged him, she smiled. "It's election day, hero. Up and at 'em."

After a leisurely breakfast, they left on their drive to Justinville. With Wedge at the wheel, she tuned a San Antonio radio station while casually scanning the terrain. "I seem to recall a Hooper sign on a tree near that bridge, and one on the other side. They're both gone."

"Might have been a whirlwind that took 'em down."

A newscast soon came on with a spicy bulletin, "The bitter U.S. Senate contest between former Governor Holt Witherspoon and Congressman Jordan Layman took a bizarre last-minute twist today when Bantrell County Judge Frank Ganner, a strong supporter of Layman, accused Witherspoon of destroying a bridge in his county.

"Ganner, the longtime political boss known as the Baron of Bantrell, said a strategic bridge in the western part of his county was destroyed early this morning. He charged it was the work of, and I quote, 'demolition experts hired to disrupt the election process. I suspect this was done by Witherspoon because he knows this county supports his opponent, our friend, Jordan Layman.' End quote.

"Witherspoon has just released a strong response, in which he branded Ganner's charge as absurd. Witherspoon countercharged, and I quote, 'Frank Ganner is laying out a thick smokescreen. If I were a betting man, I'd lay odds he blew up that bridge himself. He's trying to prop up his pal, Jordan Layman, the biggest two-faced politician in the history of Texas. He's been flying around the state, talking about the future while he's in cahoots with the worst old corrupt political bosses of South Texas. Frank Ganner is the kingpin of those bosses and he's waving the banner highest for Layman.' End quote."

"Wow!" Nellie said. "That ought to fire up supporters for both sides. I wonder who really did it?"

"Yeah." Wedge sighed, keeping his eyes trained on the road. "I wonder."

At the headquarters, Kirk handed Wedge telegrams from Ernesto Garcia and Edgar Howard.

From Garcia, "As you know, I am out of commission, but members of my family are not. They have been spreading the word. You will carry Coronado County by a substantial margin. Best wishes for victory."

From Howard, "Though the murder of my son remains unsolved, I now believe he will not have died in vain. Win or lose, your campaign has been meaningful, bringing real hope for reform."

Wedge was moved. "Well, Old Podnah, I guess we stirred the pot about as hard as we could."

Another account of the bridge destruction flap came over the radio, prompting Brew Blain to say, "Man, blowing up that bridge was pretty heavy stuff, felony-type stuff. Hard to believe old Holt Witherspoon would be involved."

Kirk pulled Wedge aside to whisper, "I think I better tell you what I did—"

"Hold it. I don't want to know."

The afternoon hours dragged by ever so slowly with little tangible information drifting in, other than reports that voter turnout was fairly heavy throughout the five free counties. Reports from Ganner's domain indicated the bridge had been made operational, and full-scale voter turnout efforts were in progress.

With little to do, Kirk felt edgy and took a long walk, winding up, as he had the day of the first election, in the park below the Retama County Courthouse. He envisioned his father looking down upon him from that imposing building, and he could almost hear his voice, admonishing him for recent activities.

"Maybe you're not proud of me," Kirk murmured, "but I gave it all I had… I bet Ganner never thought we'd fight him the way we have… Well, it's over. I'm tired, Dad. I'm glad it's over, and—"

Nellie's voice calling from the street made him turn around. When he reached her car, he could tell she was excited.

"One of my friends doing absentee counting sneaked out and gave me a call. We're running right on target around here."

"That's a nice piece of the puzzle in place. Cross your fingers."

As they had for the first election, the best friends of Nellie and Wedge, plus relatives, gathered at the headquarters soon after the polls closed, along with Gordon Hempstead, Mrs. Fogel, and many volunteers. Early returns trickling in were encouraging, particularly from Coronado County where Wedge was taking sixty percent. But tension mounted since no returns had been reported from the Ganner domain more than two hours after the polls closed.

On the Senate race, from the first Texas Election Bureau report at seven-thirty through the nine o'clock update, Holt Witherspoon held a slight lead over Jordan Layman.

At ten o'clock, Nellie had posted returns from all five free counties, covering more than half of their vote. "Our home base of Retama County," she called to the crowd, "is almost complete! We've taken seventy-four percent of the vote!"

A big round of cheers ensued.

"And for the district, we're running almost sixty percent!"

More cheers, as enthusiasm continued to build.

Kirk didn't share it. He felt desperate to learn what the Ganner counties were doing. At last, he received a call from Wade Keene, who was in the Bantrell County Courthouse.

"Grit your teeth," Keene said. "The master here is cranking 'em out. Looks like about a ninety percent vote for Jordan Layman and your opponent with voter turnout a little higher than in the first round."

Keene then read off figures per precinct, or "box" as the designation was often used.

"What about Will Dodd County?"

"Make it eighty percent there, also a little higher turnout."

Again, he read off figures.

"How many boxes out?"

"Just a few. Give me what returns you have, and I'll call you back when I get final numbers here."

Nellie and Wedge were watching over his shoulder as Kirk worked through the figures. When he finished, he sighed. "Hell, it's going right down to the wire."

Keene and the few other reporters in Piedra Blanca had no means of checking the validity of Ganner's figures, but their mere presence had a negative effect upon him. Instead of having created sympathy for himself over losing the bridge, he had undermined his own credibility by accusing Witherspoon.

Most of the reporters voted for Layman, but they believed Witherspoon to be an honorable person. They nettled Ganner that night by making jokes within earshot such as, "Holt stole Layman's helicopter and swooped down on the bridge. Lit the dynamite fuse with his old pipe."

But some grudging veterans of the political arena, including Wade Keene, gave Ganner high marks for having restored that bridge with incredible haste.

Keene received the final numbers from Will Dodd County about eleven-thirty. He kept badgering Ganner until the patrón brought forth at midnight his complete results for Bantrell County. They were staggering totals, as Keene had predicted to Kirk.

While waiting for more returns on their race, the crowd at the Crayton headquarters listened intently as the Texas Election Bureau reported that, with three-fourths of the statewide vote counted, there was still no winning trend for Witherspoon, only a small lead of a few hundred votes.

Since the bureau had no governmental authority, it had to wait until local parties reported, and many of those parties in rural areas had isolated precincts which might not report for a day or two. A casual attitude toward the process, rather than manipulation of results, often caused tardy reporting.

When he received the call from Keene, Kirk had already tallied all the other counties complete. With Nellie and Wedge hovering over him, he reviewed all the figures for almost twenty thousand votes cast throughout the district, handing figures to Mrs. Fogel to be rechecked on her adding machine.

At last, he released a long sigh of relief and told Keene, "Looks like we've won by one hundred and eleven votes."

"We've won!" Wedge shouted, pulling Nellie to him for a hug and kiss.

"Hot holy hell!" Brew Blain yelled, dragging out a case of chilled champagne he'd hidden in a storage closet.

Wedge's parents hugged him, and his mother wept.

Kirk's mother congratulated her son with a brief kiss on the cheek. "Your father would be proud."

His sister hugged him, brushing aside tears of joy.

Toasting, yelling, and backslapping engulfed the crowded headquarters. Amid the merriment, tears streamed down the usually stolid face of Mrs. Fogel, who had come to love and respect Kirk as a son.

It was his victory, she thought, as much as it was for Wedge.

Nellie soon waved for quiet as a San Antonio radio station followed its U.S. Senate update with a bulletin, "According to figures just provided to us, Wedge Crayton of Justinville has scored a big upset by edging Wally Hooper of Piedra Blanca, the handpicked candidate of Frank Ganner, the Baron of Bantrell. We tried to reach Hooper for a concession statement, but were unable to reach him or Ganner. Crayton, running a reform campaign, has apparently defeated Hooper by a margin of only one hundred and eleven votes."

Kirk stayed at his desk, making calls, also trying to locate Hooper.

Ganner wouldn't concede the sun will rise in the morning, but Hooper's not a bad guy. With all the votes counted, he ought to concede.

Wedge brought a bottle of champagne into Kirk's office, but Kirk declined. "Oh, come on, Old Podnah, relax. It's over, and worth a pop of bubbly."

"Yeah, well, I'd like to hear a concession statement from Wally."

"Don't sweat it. He's licking his wounds; probably won't concede until tomorrow."

The celebration continued for an hour, until the champagne was exhausted, and the crowd drifted home.

With only close friends remaining, Sidney Maylander raised the final toast. "To victory and to Acapulco! I've got a plane chartered in the morning. A week in paradise."

"Count me out," Kirk said. "I've got things to nail down around here."

Nellie pulled him aside. "Please, I want you to go."

"No, thanks. Have a good time, but keep in touch."

On the following morning about ten, Nellie called Kirk to inform him they were preparing to leave and to inquire about a concession statement from Wally Hooper.

"Not a word from him or Ganner," Kirk said. "They must be hiding out under a bridge somewhere."

It wasn't difficult for Kirk to be convincing by jesting in the aftermath of all the tension and exhilaration of the previous night, but he did it to cover his deep concern. He knew Frank Ganner might be playing by his own rules.

Wade Keene soon called, informing Kirk he'd been told Ganner,

Hooper, and some close friends had gone on a fishing trip in northern Mexico.

"What about a concession statement?"

"Hell, I didn't get to talk to either of 'em today. For all I know, the fishing story is true, but I doubt it. You may have to sweat this out until the votes are canvassed."

"What about the Senate race?"

"The election bureau people don't like to count on Sunday. We may not know anything definite until at least tomorrow. Close as hell, with about two percent of the vote still out.

For the next four days, Kirk kept busy with details related to closing down the headquarters, including compilation of various records. He wrote a post-election analysis. "So they won't have to reinvent the wheel next time," he said, handing it to Mrs. Fogel for retyping.

Each day was tedious, with no word from Wally Hooper. Tension mounted in Justinville and throughout the state over the Senate race, which was still unresolved. With only a handful of scattered rural precincts out, Witherspoon had a lead of two hundred seventy-three out of almost one million cast.

Surely those final precincts will be reported soon, Kirk thought, and the most knowledgeable people project it as a tight victory for Witherspoon.

However, the diligent Texas Election Bureau, trying to nail down a final total, hedged on declaring a winner until it could account for every possible vote cast in the state.

On election night, Ganner had been crestfallen by Layman's failure to win the Senate contest and infuriated by the setback in Wally Hooper's race. He had given Hooper two hundred dollars to spend a week in the Lower Rio Grande Valley, incommunicado.

In a sullen mood, Ganner retired to a remote hunting lodge on his immense ranch where he brooded in solitude, except during meals when he conversed in Spanish with the "vaqueros," whose ranch talk didn't include politics. He listened to radio reports about the incredibly close Senate race, but maintained no personal contact with his political operation for four days.

When he decided to return to his courthouse office, he thumbed through a stack of phone messages and returned one immediately.

In a voice made hoarse by the long campaign, Jordan Layman came straight to the point. "It's down to where we can count the final tally. I need your help, Frank. I need two hundred more votes."

"It's five days after the election."

"We can ride it through, if you hurry."

"Hell, Jordan, I've been in a federal pen, and Harry Truman isn't around to grant another pardon."

"Don't worry about that. You get me the two hundred votes, and I assure you nobody's going to any pen." Layman spun through a scenario to handle the legal ramifications regarding a correction being made to previously reported results.

"But I've already voted maximum strength in my county."

"What about the other one?"

Ganner paused. "I might be able to work something out. Goddamn, this is late! You paint a nice picture, but it would cause a helluva stink."

"I'm telling you, we can ride it out. Now, you want to strengthen your hand in South Texas? You know I'll help you any way I can."

"You better mean that twice over."

"Have you ever heard any of my friends complain I didn't take care of 'em?"

Ganner paused again. "Still, it's—"

"Sure, it's late, but that's what it's come down to, and you better look at real potential trouble in this situation. You think Holt isn't pissed off at you for deserting him this year? He's a vindictive old codger who'll hound you with threats and investigations if he wins. He'll have that courthouse of yours in turmoil night and day."

Ganner winced. "Give me a little more time to think about this."

"There isn't any time. I need those votes immediately."

Ganner paused again, glancing over precinct returns from Will Dodd County. "All right, but those lawyers of yours better goddamn well know what they're doing."

"You'll never regret this, Frank. And remember, this conversation never occurred."

"You're damn right it never occurred."

Ganner summoned Al Hernandez and Matson Pace. "This is the closest statewide election in the history of Texas. It's down to the lick log, and Jordan needs two hundred more votes."

"We've voted all our strength," Pace said. "Everything on the poll tax lists, and all of it reported and recorded."

"Reported and recorded." Ganner smiled. "But there could have been a mistake in tabulation, requiring a correction."

Hernandez shook his head. "We can't just manufacture two hundred votes. We've already voted our maximum, according to the poll lists. Report any more and we'd get caught hands down."

"That's true in Bantrell County," Ganner said, "but what about next door? That big Mexicano precinct, Box 13. Voted considerably less than on the poll list. We'll vote the others, and call it a correction."

"Hell," Pace said, "I've been loyal all these years, but you're really reaching too far this time. Five goddamn days after the election. How can you justify it?"

"You'll create a lot of problems," Hernandez said.

"I'll create our own United States Senator," Ganner replied.

Hernandez shook his head, and Pace chewed on a cigar, both refusing to engage the piercing eyes of their mercurial boss.

"You guys take me for a first-year law student? I've walked this through here and Jordan has high-powered lawyers who know how to handle it beyond. There's not going to be a big hassle, except briefly in party channels and some handwringing in the press.

"What's important is the party will decide whether to accept the correction. We'll wing through the local party, then it'll go to the state committee. From there to the state convention. When it's approved, the secretary of state will have no choice but to certify Jordan for the November ballot. Witherspoon won't be able to derail it through court action. Keep it a party matter and it'll sail right through."

"What if Witherspoon goes to federal court?" Hernandez said.

"He might," Ganner said, "but time's on our side and becomes a stronger ally closer it gets to the general election. The Supreme Court is not in session again till October. It would be too late for certification, printing, and distribution of the November ballot for the full court to decide on the issue when it reconvenes. If it goes to the Supreme Court, only one justice will rule, and Jordan's lawyers know where to steer it. It'll be a fast ruling up-or-down on jurisdiction, and we'll win."

Hernandez again shook his head. "Sounds too easy. The whole nation is watching this election, and Holt Witherspoon is nobody's fool. Are you sure you want to take the risk?"

"Hell yes!" Ganner snapped. "I'll have Jordan Layman in my hip pocket, and that's damn sure worth a high roll of the dice."

Ganner summoned Gilbert Ramos, election judge for Box 13 in Will Dodd County. Ramos was a middle-aged man who came hat-in-hand to Ganner, indebted to him for his having paid big hospital bills resulting from a bad car accident three years before.

Ganner assured him he could speak candidly in the presence of Hernandez and Pace. "Draw up a 'correction' of your tabulation in the Senate race," Ganner said in a crisp tone, "resulting in two hundred more votes for Jordan Layman. Make a notation that the same vote correction applies to Wally Hooper and Crayton. Report it to the county party, and I'll take it from there."

"I'm sorry, Frank," Ramos said, "but I don't think there were that many who didn't vote in my precinct."

Ganner spun alternatives through his mind. Involving another box election judge would be time-consuming and increase the risk of detection or something going wrong. "Well, find a few more names somewhere. Just don't take 'em from anybody else's box. But hurry! Get this done in three hours."

"What about ballots?" Ramos said.

"Don't worry about ballots. Just draw up a revised poll list to cover the additional voters, and bring it to me. I'll lock it up in my bank at Marlene. Nobody needs to be looking at that, unless absolutely necessary. I'll make the decision about that."

Matson Pace shook his head. He returned to his office, muttering to himself about the risk involved.

Juan Velasquez, his young assistant, inquired about his concern.

"Doin' it is one thing," Pace said. "Doin' it five days after the election isn't too goddamn smart."

"Will this change the outcome for the Senate or the Legislature?"

"Believe it or not, it'll change both."

After he left the office, Velasquez remained. When he had graduated from high school two years ago, he was grateful to land a job in his hometown with a decent salary.

Through family connections, he was chosen to assist Matson Pace, the unofficial treasurer of Ganner's vast political funding activity, which was constantly expanding. Ganner put money on statewide races, plus races all over South Texas. Some of that funding was made through third parties or dummy committees if Ganner didn't want his tracks to appear publicly.

The more the idealistic young Velasquez learned of Ganner's activities, the less he enjoyed his job. He was also a second cousin of Ernesto Garcia and was appalled when Ganner framed Garcia. He'd never met Wedge Crayton or anyone connected with his campaign, but he had grown sick of participating in shady and illegal activities in behalf of

Ganner.

He rummaged through Matson's locked files, taking some originals and carbons. He withdrew all his money in checking and savings accounts, totaling one hundred and fifty-two dollars. He went home, packed a bag, told his mother he was going on vacation, then began hitchhiking toward Justinville.

His destination was the Brush Country Restaurant in western Bantrell Country where Ernesto had told him to go if there was ever a reason to leave. He was to discuss the problem with the owner, Sandy Jones, who would direct him.

After he arrived and told Sandy what had happened, she right away called Kirk. "There's a frightened, but brave young man here who says he knows about some high-handed cheating Frank Ganner is gonna pull on the election."

"Sandy, I'm not in the mood to tangle with Ganner's rattlesnakes again. Besides, any cheating they'd have planned would already have been done. It's almost time for the official canvass."

Sandy was adamant. "Kirk, this kid is on to something! You better talk to him right away!"

Kirk paused, pondering her remarks. *She's no political wizard, but she has a sixth sense about people.*

At once, he detected a slight crackling noise, perhaps caused by a bugging device. "All right, now listen carefully. I want you to ring off, get that kid in your car, and get the hell out of Bantrell County as fast as you can. Go to Harmon County to Sheriff Donovan's office in Morgandale. I'll meet you there."

Kirk tore out of the parking lot, spraying gravel against the headquarters building. He soon reached the state highway to Morgandale where he accelerated to eighty, pushing the outer limit of safety.

When he met them, Kirk hugged Sandy. "You old battle axe, you ought to stay out of this sort of stuff. Might land you in trouble."

"Every now and then I like to do somethin' besides hustlin' hamburgers and chicken fried steaks."

On the ride to Justinville, Velasquez told Kirk what he knew about the vote fraud and gave him evidence as to how Matson Pace laundered Ganner's money into various races, including judicial races which were handled most discreetly.

"You're taking quite a chance," Kirk said. "Family in danger?"

"I don't think so. I have too many relatives in Bantrell County for

Ganner to persecute, and Matson knows I haven't talked before. They'll all be uptight, but they'll know I acted on my own."

Velasquez explained he was related to Ernesto Garcia and admired his campaign. "I could never forgive Ganner for what he did to Ernesto. I believe it is against God's will to covet and use power like that. I never realized where all this could lead until that happened. I just couldn't sit back and remain a part of it any longer."

When they arrived in Justinville, Kirk drove to the bus station. "Here's fifty bucks to help tide things over. Go to San Antonio, get a motel room, and call me collect at this number, from a pay phone. You'll be safe, and we'll figure out the future soon as the election situation is resolved."

Velasquez lingered a moment after shaking hands.

Kirk smiled. "You're in a tough spot, and you're wondering if you did the right thing. Who knows? But I'll bet you're gonna sleep a little better tonight."

At his office, Kirk reviewed the material. "This ought to be worth half a loaf," he murmured, placing a call to Piedra Blanca.

"Ganner?"

"Yeah, who is this?"

"Kirk Holland."

"What do you want?" Ganner snapped.

"I understand you're about to pull something real cute, like stuffing a ballot box?"

Ganner winced. "You're bluffing."

"Am I? One of your former employees has informed me of what's going on. He's also provided me with some interesting evidence of your campaign financing techniques, of which a master magician would be proud."

Ganner paused, unable to recall being notified of a recent defection, but sensitive to the incisive nature of Kirk's comments. "I don't know what you're talking about."

"Down to basics. If I were you, with all your vast power and lusting for more, I'd provide Jordan Layman with his precious Senate seat. You can do so by merely instructing one of your most trusted box election judges to report a little 'correction,' updating the results without even providing the ballots as evidence. Convince the courts this is a party matter; they have no jurisdiction. Sounds too tempting to resist, doesn't it?"

"Nobody is going to prove vote fraud against me."

"Perhaps not, but I know a state district judge in South Texas who you don't own and who doesn't know you recently slipped big bucks through your channels into his opponent's campaign. You bet on the loser and this judge is awful damn feisty. He's the kind who'd love to see some evidence of chicanery by Frank Ganner against him."

Ganner bit his lip, struggling to control his temper. Nothing could unsettle him more than the threat of coming under fire in an unfriendly court. "What is it you want?"

"Simply this. When you have your so-called correction reported, make sure the error you're correcting applies only to the tabulation of the Senate race. Leave the state rep result alone."

"And the Senate race?"

"What you do in the Senate race is none of my business. Leave the state rep race alone and you won't get any more flak from me."

Again, Ganner paused, his thoughts turning to his stand-in, Wally Hooper, who would win the Texas House seat with a two hundred vote favorable adjustment. Giving up on that seat was an unsavory consideration, but the Senate race was foremost in his mind.

"Holland, I don't know you as well as I knew your father. He wouldn't pull some heavy-handed deal like this; but regardless, I have to believe your word is bond."

"Maybe I don't operate like he did, but you'll have to assume my word is bond, like his always was."

News of the "correction" in favor of Jordan Layman hit the Texas political arena like a thunderbolt. The state was stunned. Veteran correspondents and operatives in the capital city had expected Holt Witherspoon to be declared the winner, but suddenly Layman was ahead by eighty-seven votes, with apparently no more results to be reported.

In San Antonio, when Wade Keene tried to inquire about the Texas House race, he couldn't find any party official who knew if the status had changed.

Witherspoon lost no time in organizing an investigation team which he led to Marlene, county seat of Will Dodd County. It consisted of two former FBI agents, Hollis Tindell and Arthur Garrison, plus Webb Brockman, an imposing former Texas Ranger captain who had worked South Texas for many years.

When they arrived at Marlene, they proceeded to the bank Ganner owned where they had been informed the election results were locked. Near the sidewalk by the bank, they observed several surly men milling around, as if they were unofficial watchdogs.

Still in the car, Brockman surveyed the scene and spoke to his colleagues in a calm, even manner. "Gentlemen, remove your coats and leave them in the car. I want them to see you're not carrying guns. I'm the only one they'll see carrying a gun."

See him, they did. Wearing boots and Stetson that augmented his solid, six-foot-three-inch frame, Brockman was indeed an impressive figure as he led the group toward the bank entrance. When they walked up the steps, they encountered five men who had formed a line to block their way.

Brockman paused, looking them over carefully with his stern blue eyes. He trained those eyes upon the man in the middle, the only one wearing a gun. "You people better make way for Governor Witherspoon," he said, his right hand resting upon his holster.

They paused briefly, then parted, allowing them to enter.

Inside, Witherspoon spotted Bill Werden, a bank officer who had been a strong ally in previous campaigns but was forced by Ganner to support Layman. "Bill, I want to see those new results from Box 13."

"Governor, I'm sorry, but I have instructions from Frank Ganner not to show those results unless he grants permission."

"Are you telling me, the immediate past governor of Texas, that I'm not entitled to see election results affecting a public office, the office I seek?"

Werden avoided Witherspoon's eyes. "Well, Frank takes the position that unless there's a court order, this is not public business. This is a party matter."

Hollis Tindell, a feisty young attorney with six years of FBI experience in South Texas, pointed a finger at Werden. "I don't give a damn what anybody says, you're obstructing justice! You know good and well Box 13 has been stuffed!"

"All right, all right," Werden said. "As a special favor to you, Governor, but just for a few minutes. I'll tell Frank you threatened me with a court order."

Werden escorted them to the vault where he unlocked a file cabinet to retrieve a folder containing results from Box 13. In addition to the list of those who had previously been recorded as voting, in the order they had voted, was the so-called correction list with names of about two hundred voters who had not actually voted.

Tindell glanced over the lists, noting first the list of original voters reported was all in black ink, while the corrected list was all in green ink. Further, the first several names listed in green were in alphabetical order.

That's a sure sign, Tindell mused, those came from the original poll list compiled before the election, but represented people who didn't vote.

Fast as they could, Tindell and Garrison began memorizing names on the corrected list, but a sharp command from Frank Ganner interrupted them, as he marched through the door, flanked by two deputies. "Stop it! Werden, what the hell is wrong with you! Do these people have a court order?"

"Well, no, but—"

"Then they have no goddamn right to be here!"

"Ganner," Witherspoon said, "what right do you have to deny the people of Texas an honest election?"

Ganner tossed the folder into the file cabinet and locked it. "The validity of these results will be determined by the party. None of you holds party office, or even public office for that matter. No court order. You have no business whatsoever in my bank, so I suggest you leave now."

Witherspoon bristled. "You're the county judge of Bantrell County. You have no authority in this county, public or party, nor do those gunslingers you're parading around. I've never seen such arrogance in all my life."

"By what authority," Tindell said, "do you control these election results?"

"By the authority," Ganner snapped, "acquired by my father. He worked this county, along with the late Will Dodd, long before any of you people wandered into this territory."

Witherspoon shook his head. "Let's get out of here. This may be a bank vault, but it's beginning to smell like a garbage dump."

After Witherspoon stopped for a few moments in the street to confer with reporters, he and his team followed leads picked up from the cursory review of the lists. They stopped by the cemetery to match several of the names in green ink on the so-called corrected list with names on gravestones.

Some frightened people they wanted to interview refused, but they obtained affidavits from three men whose names appeared on the corrected list but who swore they hadn't voted. Further, they obtained an affidavit from a woman whose name appeared as the last voter on the list of original voters. She swore she voted only minutes before the 7:00 P.M. deadline and there were no other voters in sight.

"The possibility," Tindell said, shaking his head, "of about two hundred voters having followed her to vote before the deadline is absolutely ludicrous. Governor, we have some very compelling evidence that

Box 13 was indeed stuffed to provide the winning margin."

On their return trip to Austin, Witherspoon sat in silence for several minutes, reviewing the list of the sixty-two-member State Democratic Executive Committee (SDEC) composed of two people from each of Texas' thirty-one state senatorial districts.

"As far as the party is concerned, we make our stand before the SDEC. Layman will promise 'em the moon, but half of 'em are my friends, and they'll stay hitched. Whoever wins there takes a big leg up for the state convention the next day. I want you two lawyers to prepare a request for a restraining order prohibiting the secretary of state from certifying Layman's name for the November ballot. If we lose before the SDEC, we'll need to go into federal court, alleging civil rights violations due to a dishonest election. We might get some quick action since we're already in September. We'd be wasting our time seeking relief in state court."

Wade Keene had arrived in Marlene in time to interview key people on both sides. He called Kirk to inform him that the state representative race was not included in the so-called correction, leaving Wedge's narrow victory intact.

Kirk breathed a long sigh of relief.

"But," Keene continued, "I'd better warn you that I've checked with reliable legal sources on the Senate race. If this mess winds up in federal court, the whole damned election may be nullified. Have to run your race all over again."

"Oh, hell," Kirk said, "we're tapped out of money. Ganner would whip us."

"I wouldn't worry till it happens. He sure as hell has his sights trained on the Senate race now."

"Any idea how Wally Hooper is taking this?"

"Rumor has it he won't concede because he's walked through that variable I mentioned about another election. I say 'rumor has it' because he's still under wraps somewhere, not returning phone calls. Also hear Ganner told him that since he tried hard but lost the race, he'd be first in line for the next judgeship opening around here."

"That clod a judge? Takes another sweet scent of victory from my nostrils."

"Well, if you guys ride it out, Ganner won't have a free rein on races in your area. Any idea why he didn't include your race in this vote fraud scheme?"

Kirk paused. "Under the circumstances, with the Senate contest the high priority, I suspect he just decided to relegate our little race to nothing more than nuisance status."

After the phone conversation, Kirk sat alone at his desk. He took a beer from the refrigerator and stood by a window, gazing at the sunset.

I should have gambled, he thought, and gun-decked that bastard on the Senate race, too. I wonder what he'd have done? Now, it looks like our victory may be secure only if he rides through his vote fraud… Damn, I wonder what the hell he would have done if I'd hit him across the board.

Further, he questioned his involvement in the vote fraud, something his father would never have done.

Kirk had intended to leave Wedge and Nellie out of the picture until time for a perfunctory vote canvass to confirm the winning margin. The canvass for their race had indeed become perfunctory, but now he was deeply concerned about the possibility of a Senate contest nullification forcing them to run another campaign. He called Wedge and they flew back from Acapulco to meet him in Austin.

From around the state, members of the SDEC gathered for the midafternoon meeting in the Driskill Hotel's Crystal Ballroom, dominated by a huge chandelier. Reporters, politicians, and political operatives huddled to compare notes and rumors as they filled most of the open areas around the seating section for the sixty-two members.

Stimulated by the sudden intense publicity, a few reporters from large out-of-state newspapers had recently arrived and were seeking update material. Tension was building as the Justinville contingent arrived and stood in a corner at the rear of the room.

Jordan Layman spotted them and came over. He shook hands with Kirk, kissed Nellie on the cheek, and slung his arm around Wedge's shoulder. "You ran a damn good campaign," Layman grinned. "You know, Frank Ganner's candidate told me I ought to sue you for that support ad you ran. Hell, I told him he should think about doing stuff like that instead of bellyaching all the time."

"How's it going to go?" Wedge asked.

"It's going to be mighty close, but I'll prevail."

Across the room, Speaker Jarvis Harrison conferred with Holt Witherspoon, who sat in the other corner, puffing on his pipe. Kirk dropped by to pay his respects.

The Speaker hugged him. "Son, that was a helluva campaign you pulled off. Congratulations!"

"Sure was," Witherspoon said, between puffs on his pipe. "I didn't think you could take Ganner's man down there."

"Your endorsement was helpful, Governor," Kirk said. "How do you see your chances?"

"Two of my people are sick, doubtful they'll get here. Without 'em, it's going to be awful close."

Wade Keene watched Frank Ganner enter the room, flanked by Al Hernandez and Matson Pace. He promptly challenged Ganner. "Might I inquire of you, Señor Patrón, if you plan to steal this one right under our noses?"

Ganner pointed a forefinger at Keene. "I've already answered the last question I ever will from you! You're nothing but a hatchet man, out to get me! Your goddamn article in today's paper was full of malicious lies and half-truths!"

"Half-truths? Well, I guess you might say Box 13 was only half stuffed. The other half actually voted."

Ganner strode past Keene, seeking Layman, who greeted him for a brief moment but made their relationship appear to be casual. In fact, when they shook hands, Layman positioned himself so that a group of people shielded them from photographers.

A uniformed security guard, one of four in the ballroom, had paid close attention when Keene confronted Ganner. A few moments earlier, he had broken up a fist fight in the lobby between partisans of the opposing candidates.

When the presiding officer, Hammond Eskell, called the meeting to order, six members were absent. A special rule was invoked whereby a late arriving member could vote, but no proxy would be allowed. In the interest of trying to achieve full attendance, Eskell decided to transact all other business before taking up the Senate controversy.

Petty arguments and skirmishes ensued over a number of minor issues, expending the balance of the afternoon. A two-hour dinner recess was agreed upon as welcome relief, but it was an open invitation for indulgent members to linger too long at a bar.

During the break, Layman and his cadre of lawyers and political associates continued wining and dining committee members in the favored watering holes of the capital city. Witherspoon relied on old allies and friends from gubernatorial days to contact and recontact favorable members of the SDEC.

When they reconvened at eight o'clock, nine members were absent, but within ten minutes, three of those had wandered back to their places.

Eskell, trying to maintain a posture of neutrality, made a short, cliché-ridden speech, reminding each member "to fulfill his or her responsibility, according to the dictates of conscience and fair play, weighing all the facts and factors at hand."

Since he was neutral, Eskell, a middle-aged lawyer from Fort Worth, wanted to see the controversy settled with a minimum amount of political bloodshed. He had worked with opposing sides to agree on ground rules; each would have thirty minutes to use as he chose with a coin flip to determine order. Witherspoon had won the toss and chose to go second. The opposing sides knew only a few members were uncommitted, open to weighing the arguments. All others were firmly committed, but they had been courted nonetheless because of their possible influence on the uncommitted.

Layman didn't consider going first as necessarily a disadvantage. From college days, he'd contended that a good debater going first can set the tone, preempt issues, stake out ground. The second debater must then adjust.

Layman strode with confidence to the podium with those thoughts in mind, along with the need to tailor his remarks for the press as much as for the committee members.

"Ladies and gentlemen," he began in a measured, patronizing tone, "I'm not here to tell you all the legal arguments concerning this election. Others are much better at that than I. The only one that really counts, and the one we must always uphold, is the right and jurisdiction of our party, the Democratic Party, to conduct our elections in the State of Texas. I've always believed in that, and I've practiced it even when it hurt the most. It was only a few years ago when I ran for this high office and was not defeated, but counted out in East Texas. However, I accepted that decision and returned to my duties."

Layman took a sip of water, adjusted his glasses, and continued in a slightly higher tone. "Over the years, I've heard complaints about problems with voting in East Texas and South Texas. But we've never succumbed to the temptation of overriding a local decision in order to change the outcome of a statewide race. My friends, that would set a terrible precedent, laying the foundation for political decisions by cliques of power brokers who would undermine the will of the voters."

Wade Keene nudged Kirk. "That's an old Layman tactic. Takes his greatest vulnerability and pawns it off on others."

Pointing his forefinger into the air, Layman raised his voice. "My

Republican-leaning opponent is a poor loser! And don't let him and a few handwringers in the press convince you otherwise!"

That stinging statement prompted hearty cheers from his partisans and a wave of boos and catcalls from Witherspoon's supporters.

"You can count on me to always serve as a loyal Democrat! You can count on me to serve as a Democrat in the tradition of Franklin Roosevelt and Harry Truman! You'll never see Jordan Layman scrambling around, trying to grab onto the coattails of a popular Republican presidential candidate."

Another biting statement drawing sharp reaction, stimulating feelings of strident Democratic partisanship in the wake of the 1952 crossover to Eisenhower by many Texas Democratic leaders.

Layman proceeded to speak to committee members as though he were their teacher. "Now, I want you also to consider what this election means to you, and to the people of Texas. If there's a question in your mind as to how to vote, ask yourself, 'Which candidate will be more valuable to our state? And for the longer period of time?'

"We're talking about a seat in the United State Senate where, day-in, day-out, one must work with his colleagues to be effective. You can't sit back, puffing on a pipe, and expect to get anything done. And let me remind you that seniority is very important in the Senate. At my age, I'll be able to accrue seniority for the benefit of all Texans. To make sure each citizen of this state receives his or her fair share of return for the taxes paid to the federal government. For the rural folks to know they'll have a friend, fighting for them in good times as well as in times of bad markets and drouth, as plague us these long hot days and nights. To make sure the hungry and the needy, who can't pay taxes, receive adequate care, compassionate care beyond material needs. To help make sure our nation remains free and strong, capable of meeting the challenge of Communism throughout the world.

"So, my friends, please bear all those things in mind when you vote tonight. Thank you, and I relinquish the balance of my time to Gabe Feldmann, my chief legal advisor who will answer any questions you might have."

To applause from roughly half the committee members and onlookers, Layman strode to the rear of the room, where his operatives gathered around him. Kirk surmised Layman had employed a clever tactic by structuring his presentation with speech only, taking no questions. That protected him from embarrassing questions regarding morality of the vote fraud and confined difficult legal questions to his top lawyer.

Layman listened intently as his most trusted operatives reported another careful nose count had been completed. With all fifty-six members now expressing a preference, Layman led by a margin of twenty-nine to twenty-seven.

Witherspoon's team had concluded the same count. Witherspoon glanced over the list again, returning to the name of Jacob Preston, a middle-aged farmer whom he described as "a populist sod-buster from Northwest Texas who owns only one good suit of clothes he wears to church every week, and to weddings and funerals."

Jacob Preston may be more comfortable with Layman's politics, Witherspoon mused, but he's a mighty religious man who loves this state from the bottom of his heart. If I can change one vote, it's his.

Witherspoon puffed on his pipe as Layman's lawyer worked through the balance of the time, often reminding members of the strong legal precedent for the party resolving its problems, honoring layers of authority from the precinct up the line.

Witherspoon decided to reverse the order Layman used. He sent Hollis Tindell to speak first, reviewing the vote fraud evidence in order to clearly establish in committee members' minds the flagrant nature of what had happened in Box 13 of Will Dodd County.

Tindell made a convincing case, but Ganner and Layman never flinched. They were certain the vote would go to Layman on pragmatic political considerations. Layman had twisted arms while promising favors and future patronage plums to all who were interested. Ganner had solidified South Texas members behind Layman and encouraged them to persuade members from elsewhere in the state.

Outwardly, Witherspoon had maintained his composure, but he was boiling inside, intent upon scorching the hide of his opponent. He was introduced to a solid round of applause from his supporters on the SDEC and sympathetic onlookers.

"My friends and fellow Texans, the piety expressed by my opponent makes him sound as though he ought to be a candidate for sainthood instead of the Senate. One thing he failed to mention to you is that when he ran for the Senate before, it was a special election and he did not have to give up his seat in Congress. His political career is dead if he loses this one, which he did. But he's trying to stay alive by stealing it through the vote fraud you've just heard described thoroughly and beyond a shadow of a doubt."

Though Witherspoon's remarks were indeed provocative, they didn't elicit emotional responses because he had delivered them in calm, measured tones.

"He also failed to mention that when he ran for reelection two years ago, he had only token opposition in the primary and no Republican opponent. So, his political hide wasn't threatened by sentiment for President Eisenhower at the top of the Republican ticket. It was easy for him to maintain his stand of party loyalty then and to demagogue about it now!

"It wasn't easy for many Democratic leaders in Texas to support Eisenhower, but we did so because it was clearly in the best interests of our state, on the tidelands issue alone as I've pointed out many times during the course of the campaign. And, ladies and gentlemen, we need to reexamine our concept of party in the light of this vote fraud. I've always believed that a political party should serve the people as a vehicle for screening and presenting qualified candidates for public office. It should not be an entity unto itself, with unbridled power to conduct elections.

"Ladies and gentlemen, have you stopped to think about what my opponent proposes? No accountability, no discipline, no responsibility, other than that vested in the foxes in the henhouse. Foxes such as Frank Ganner, who has nothing but contempt for the election process. Remember my friends, when you turn your backs on honest elections, crooked politicians like Frank Ganner will take over the party!"

Anti-Ganner sentiment rang from throughout the room with rejoinders from Layman's supporters.

Witherspoon paused, training his eyes upon Jacob Preston.

"Jordan Layman would have you believe the issue before us is simply a party matter. My friends, this is much more than a party matter, or a state matter. This is a moral issue, a clear question of right or wrong. Any God-fearing, law-abiding Texan worth his salt should see it as such!"

Noisy partisans from both sides responded to that statement. As Witherspoon scanned the audience, Preston stared at the former governor as if spellbound.

"My friends, one hundred and eighteen years ago, William Barret Travis unsheathed his sword at the Alamo to declare that he would rather die a free man than survive under the heels of a tyrant! That's a Texas tradition I'll always fight to preserve!"

Warm applause ensued, with no detrimental jeering from Layman's partisans.

"I'd rather walk away from the political arena, never to return, than to assume high office beholden to a tyrant whose flagrant vote fraud provided the winning margin. My friends, no public office is worth the sacrifice of honor and integrity. Thank you, and God bless you."

Witherspoon's supporters gave him a standing ovation while Layman's partisans grew anxious to get on with the vote.

Eskell banged for quiet. "The question is whether to certify the results reported from Will Dodd County, including the correction to Box 13. If you want to certify, vote 'aye.' If you want to vote against certification, vote 'no.' The clerk will call the roll."

Voting through the first half of the committee went as Layman had expected, but when the clerk called Preston's name, the farmer hesitated. Then, he blurted a loud, "No!"

"Ah, shit!" Layman said to his top operative. "Go find Wesley Hinton! We need the vote of that drunken bastard!"

When the clerk completed her roll call, she handed the tally to Eskell.

"The vote," he said into the microphone, "is tied at twenty-eight apiece."

Layman sought to stall. He eased up to a friendly committee member in the back of the seating area. "Ask for a verification," he whispered.

While the recounting was in progress, one of his operatives, out of breath, told Layman they'd located Hinton and were pouring coffee down him.

"If the sonofabitch can stagger on his feet, get him here, now!"

As the second roll call continued, Layman kept a watchful eye on the entrance. If his supporter didn't arrive soon, the tie-breaking vote would be cast by Eskell, a prospect Layman didn't like any more than did Eskell. To Layman, Eskell was "a goddamn blank page. I don't have any idea how he'd vote."

With the second roll call near completion, an anxious Layman stepped outside the ballroom. Wesley Hinton stood at the top of the stairs, a few steps from the entrance, leaning on his top operatives.

Layman grabbed the weaving Hinton, shoved him against the wall, and pointed a forefinger in his face. "Now, I promised you what you wanted! Get your goddamn ass in there and vote to certify!"

Eskell looked over the second tally as Hinton eased into the ballroom. "The verification has been completed. The vote remains twenty-eight to twenty-eight."

"Mister Chairman!" Hinton called in an unsteady voice. "I cast my vote to certify!"

Eskell instructed the clerk to "record Mister Hinton as voting 'aye.' The ayes have it, twenty-nine to twenty-eight."

Whoops and cheers from Layman's partisans rang out through the ballroom as signs and balloons suddenly appeared. Eskell banged his gavel for order, but the Layman demonstration was in full swing.

Kirk stepped outside, into the hallway where he encountered Lonnie Hardner, notepad in hand.

"Congratulations on your victory," Hardner said. "I never thought you'd make it."

"Your support was invaluable. Much appreciated."

"There was no other choice. Do you think you could turn right around and defeat Ganner again?"

"For the record, 'Of course.' Off the record, I doubt it. We're out of money."

"I understand."

Sounds from the Layman demonstration inside reverberated down the hall where they stood.

"You know, Lonnie, for all the hell we've been through, I guess you've had your share, riding out the entire Senate race without endorsing Layman."

"The pressure was intense during that period, but the vote fraud has brought many liberals to their senses. They voted for Layman, but they'll be watching him much more closely, assuming he wins, which appears likely."

"I won't ask how you voted."

"I don't mind telling you. For the first time since I started voting, I skipped a race on the ballot."

Inside, Layman waved to the demonstrators repeatedly and shook hands with prominent supporters. Then he marched to his suite nearby for a strategy session.

"We've got 'em on the run," he said to his political operatives and lawyers. "For all intents and purposes, I've taken over the party, and I have no intention of giving it back till the day I die. Now, spend whatever you need tonight to put the joy juice into the delegates for the convention tomorrow. I want a big margin approving the SDEC decision. That'll take whatever wind Holt has left right out of his sails."

On another floor of the hotel, Witherspoon met quietly with his close associates. "No sense asking my friends to lie down in front of a freight train tomorrow. I'll concede at the convention. Now, it's time for federal court. Hollis, you did a damn fine job tonight on the evidence. You and

Garrison make a request for a restraining order to Judge Ridgeway in the Dallas federal court. He's a tough, independent old bird who'll call it the way he sees it. With this evidence, he ought to do something."

In a crowded Austin bar, Kirk, Nellie, and Wedge relaxed around a table. "Put all the rhetoric and theatrics aside," Wedge said, "and it still boils down to a choice between a fairly young, moderate liberal with a great future versus a political Neanderthal, a tired old reactionary who wouldn't last more than one term. I sure as hell hope Jordan makes it."

"Would you feel that way," Kirk said, "if your victory were secure, and you didn't have to sweat the outcome of this mess?"

"Sure."

"The vote fraud doesn't bother you?"

"I don't condone it, but like Jordan said, he'd been counted out before. He's being counted in on this one."

"And you, Countess?" Kirk asked.

"After all we'd been through, I was just so thankful we weren't burned by the vote fraud. I really haven't thought much about it, until this business came up about nullification of the entire election."

"I've got a hunch Jordan's going to sail on through," Wedge said, "and so are we. You aren't bent out of shape are you, Old Podnah?"

Kirk shrugged. "Ah, what the hell? I guess we'd better just worry about running another race, if it comes to that."

Wade Keene stopped by their table. "Just got word that Witherspoon's lawyers are taking their case to a federal judge."

"What are his chances in that route?" Wedge leaned forward.

"I don't know," Keene said. "A helluva lot better than before the convention tomorrow."

As expected, the state Democratic convention affirmed the action taken by the SDEC, but the federal judge in Dallas found Witherspoon's evidence to be compelling. He ordered a hearing, indicating he might toss out the election, requiring a rerun of the Senate race and any race affected by votes from Will Dodd County.

Gabe Feldmann, the brilliant attorney from New York, played the final card in behalf of Jordan Layman. He filed a motion with Associate Justice Fargo Brown of the U.S. Supreme Court to quash the federal proceeding in Texas. Feldmann contended the election was a party matter, and the party had spoken. Further, the general election would soon be held, and any disruption of the process by the court would be meddling in the affairs of a sovereign state.

Justice Brown granted the motion, clearing the way for Layman to be certified for the November ballot, assuring his election to the Senate.

Kirk, Nellie, and Wedge heard the news on the radio in their headquarters shortly before Wade Keene called, seeking a quote from Wedge.

"Of course, I don't condone the alleged vote fraud," Wedge said, "but I'm greatly relieved to have the uncertainty lifted from my race. We're proud to have our victory. We earned every vote."

Wedge could almost envision Keene's face on the other end of the line, highlighted by a cigarette and scowl.

"Yeah, well it came down to the fact that Frank Ganner got away with stealing those votes 'cause Jordan Layman had the skids greased with that so-called justice in Washington. Rigged here, rigged there."

After he rang off, Wedge picked up Nellie and spun her around the room. "Round up Brew, Nelson, and Sidney, and we'll celebrate the confirmed victory at my place."

Kirk declined the invitation to join them. After they departed, he conferred with Mrs. Fogel about final plans for closing down the headquarters and informed her the following day would be his last.

He was about to leave when he took a call from Wally Hooper. "I just wanted to concede and congratulate Wedge on winning."

"I'll pass it along. Much appreciated, and how are you doing? Get some rest?"

"Sure have, and I'm feeling pretty good. Frank has me on the top of his list for a state district judge slot. You people might have done me a favor 'cause I'm going to make lots more money at that."

Kirk chuckled. "Well, I guess your boss is gloating over Jordan Layman."

"Yeah, sure is, but you know, he's still hot about somebody blowing up that damn bridge. I believe he'd give his car title to find out who did it. It'll probably just go down as another of those crazy things that can happen in a campaign year."

"Probably will."

It was sundown when he left the headquarters and stopped by a drive-in to purchase a barbecue sandwich and six-pack of beer. He drove down the little dirt road by the Nueces River bridge and sat down for a quiet supper on the river bank.

In soft shadows, the concerns and pressures that had consumed him for months were easing into part of his past. At first, it was difficult to accept the notion he was no longer needed in Justinville. But it was indeed time to pick up the pieces in Austin, as best he could. Memories of Justinville would be reconciled with the time and place, except for Briana. His brief time with her had been an awakening, but her memory left him with a gnawing, empty feeling of something compelling having been started, but not explored.

Tossing a pebble into the water, he remembered the moment when they had said good-bye, near this very spot. He drifted into a sentimental mood, mesmerized by twilight on the river. A slight noise caused him to glance to his left, and chills consumed his body as he saw what he at first perceived to be an apparition, a silhouette of a woman barely visible beneath an oak tree.

"It's only me, Kirk."

"Briana! You startled me. How did you know I was here?"

"I saw you drive by the restaurant. I slipped away and walked down this road. Somehow, I knew you would be here."

He stood up and walked toward her. She was lovely in flowing green skirt and soft white blouse. He pulled her to him and kissed her tenderly.

She responded eagerly, her soft warm lips meeting his again and again. They collapsed upon the soft ground beneath the oak tree and made passionate love, capturing the closeness and fulfillment that had eluded them before.

Afterward, he gazed into her eyes, as if to say, 'Why?'

"I missed you terribly," she said. "I often thought about what happened, and what didn't happen. I knew you'd be leaving, and I didn't want you to go away without knowing how much I care for you."

"You're a lovely, wonderful creature."

For several moments, they sat huddled together in silence. Then they strolled along the river bank, while vehicles crossed the bridge, gratified none came down the road to invade their sanctuary. She laughed as he tossed pebbles at bullfrogs barely visible, causing them to scurry into the water, splashing away from imagined danger.

They soon sat down by his car, embraced, and made love again. The first time had been fueled by desire and passion; the second was of a more tender nature, as an affirmation of deep affection. They fell asleep on the ground in each other's arms.

When she awoke, she glanced at her watch and nudged him awake. "I must go." She sighed.

They stood and kissed long, letting their emotions turn vulnerable.

"We said good-bye here before," he said, "and we met again."

"God be with you, my love," she whispered, and disappeared into the darkness.

The following morning, Kirk picked up a Banner-Press to view the entire front page covered with news and pictures regarding the decision in Washington confirming Jordan Layman's victory by a razor-thin margin of eighty-seven votes out of almost a million cast. Feature stories abounded, including one containing bitter comments from Witherspoon supporters, who dubbed their adversary, "Landslide Layman."

"I've never seen such extensive coverage," he muttered to himself. "The nation has been stunned. This is a memorable moment."

Kirk's eyes moved to page two, where Wade Keene's scathing column appeared. It recounted the entire process, including a precise review of the vote fraud.

"Adding insult to injury is the fact that Jordan Layman campaigned as a progressive, urging more activism by the federal government, then turned around to rely upon a narrow old state's rights argument to preserve his political hide.

"To paraphrase Franklin Roosevelt on Pearl Harbor, this election will live in infamy. It will forever stain our state's integrity because it was a flagrant vote fraud for which no one was held responsible. Instead, it provided the margin of victory for a politician whose unquenchable ambition troubles me deeply. Where does he seek to take us? For what purpose?

"We may never know if Jordan Layman personally orchestrated the vote fraud, but there's no doubt in my mind that Frank Ganner carried it out with great zeal and satisfaction. How could it happen? To paraphrase H.L. Mencken, you'll never go broke underestimating the apathy of the Texas electorate. We've sat back and let the climate develop. Why hasn't the Legislature insisted upon honest elections and provided the laws to ensure them?

"A few years ago in Europe, I almost got my head shot off several times, fighting against a tyrant who sought to impose his will on the world. Now, I wonder why we tolerate a tyrant in South Texas imposing his will on our entire state.

"At least there's one encouraging footnote to this sorry mess. Wedge Crayton of Justinville denied Frank Ganner's bid for the open South Texas seat in the Legislature. Crayton is no crusading giant, but he'll hold the seat if he does a good job in Austin."

Kirk was clearing out his desk when Wedge and Nellie joined him.

"Old Podnah," Wedge said, "you missed a great celebration last night."

"Well," Kirk said, "I celebrated in my own way... Have you read Wade Keene's column?"

"Yeah, overblown as usual. I'm convinced Jordan's on his way to the top. All the fuss will blow over."

Nellie laughed. "You've just never quite won Keene over. That was another of his backhanded compliments he paid you in today's column."

"Keene's one of those hard-boiled cynics," Wedge said, "and he doesn't like me personally. But I don't care. He won't go out of his way to gut me."

"Not if you do a good job," Kirk said.

Wedge extended his hand to Kirk, "I've gotta hit the trail to San Antonio for a radio show. See you in Austin before too long, Old Podnah."

They shook hands, and then Wedge kissed Nellie on the cheek and departed.

Kirk finished packing his box and turned to say good-bye to Nellie. "Countess, if I were Al Jolson, I'd sing a few bars to you from, 'I'm Sitting on Top of the World.' You're getting a husband, you'll have him in the Legislature, and you two got the man you wanted in the Senate, the irrepressible 'Landslide Layman.' On the contrary, I'm not acquiring a spouse, I'm out of work, and I'm almost broke. Where's the equity in all this?"

She laughed, handing him an envelope. "A little bonus for providing so much for Wedge, and for me."

He retrieved five one-hundred dollar bills. "Well, thanks. Thanks indeed. This surely takes care of the cash problem."

"And all you owe me is one favor. Throughout those long months of tortuous political activity, all that slipping and sliding around the Senate race, you never once let on how you felt about those candidates. I'm just curious. Who'd you vote for?"

He smiled. "Well, if you must know, I voted for Holt Witherspoon."

"But why? Jordan Layman was the South Texas candidate all the way, and your idea of linking him to Wedge late in the campaign probably put us across the line."

"It doesn't matter." He shrugged. "It's all over."

They hugged, and she kissed him on the cheek.

Kirk drove to his former home where he bid farewell to his mother and sister.

From there, he headed toward Highway 81 for the trip to Austin. As a light mist was settling in, he decided to drive by the cemetery.

No one was there when he stopped near the entrance to speak to the monument of his father.

"Don't worry, Dad. Ganner won't be coming our way. I guess old Layman will, though, along with all of Texas for who knows how long."

He turned to leave, then went back to where he had stood. "I know Layman and Ganner ignored the harsh words that appeared in Wade Keene's column today. I will keep those words in mind."

His thoughts came to Ernesto Garcia to whom he placed a call.

"Fight Frank Ganner. Fight him every step of the way. He can't keep you and your people down forever."

"I may need your help," Garcia replied.

"You can call me anytime in Austin. Here's the number."

Then he drove down the narrow dusty road to the highway back to Austin and his future.

EPILOGUE

Lyndon Johnson (Jordan Layman) was indeed en route to the Presidency.

He served as an outstanding leader in the U.S. Senate, and ran for President in 1960, but lost to John F. Kennedy, who requested Johnson run as his Vice Presidential choice. He accepted.

Kennedy was assassinated on November 22, 1963. Johnson became President. He defeated GOP nominee U.S. Senator Barry Goldwater of Arizona in 1964, and Johnson served until 1969 when he retired. He passed away January 22, 1973.

Republican John Tower filled Johnson's Senate seat. He served from 1961 until he retired in 1984. He was killed in a plane crash April 5, 1991.

With his political career ended, Coke Stevenson (Holt Witherspoon) retired to his home in the Texas Hill Country. He passed away June 28, 1975.

George Parr (Frank Ganner) was able to fend off allegations regarding Box 13 and other matters until he was prosecuted the final time by U.S. Attorney John E. Clark. Facing a ten-year prison sentence, Parr drove out to his vast ranch, took a handgun, and committed suicide on April 1, 1975.

ABOUT THE AUTHOR

John R. Knaggs was born and raised in Cotulla, a South Texas town between San Antonio and Laredo.

Cotulla is the seat of LaSalle County where his father served over several years as county clerk. Upon his death in 1940 when John was only six, his mother served in his post for a time while raising John and his brother "Dutch," three years older.

His mother returned to teaching English at Cotulla High School, where John was elected president of his senior class, and also played football, basketball and was a two-time district winner in singles tennis.

John holds a journalism degree from The University of Texas at Austin where he was sports editor of the student newspaper, The Daily Texan. He is a veteran of the U.S. Army.

In 1977, he published The Bugles Are Silent. A historical novel of the Texas Revolution against Mexico, the only book that tells the story from both sides including the important role of Tejanos, mostly in the San Antonio area.

A best seller at The Alamo for decades, it has also been sold at the Texas Capitol, the San Jacinto Battleground, and other venues and historic sites.

He also wrote Two-Party Texas, the John Tower Era, 1961-1984 and Kingmakers now in second edition.

A one-time political consultant, he wrote for newspapers – including two hundred weekly feature columns for The Austin American-Statesman – and was a state capitol writer for United Press International (UPI).

By a previous marriage, John had four children – Lisa, Ryan, Bart, and David, who was lost to leukemia.

He has been married to Helen Soto Knaggs for forty-seven years as of this writing. They live in Austin, Texas.